Kay Brellend never imagined she would become a writer, certainly not a writer of novels inspired by her own family. Kay's Campbell Road series, set in the 'worst street in North London' follows the same Islington family covering the years between WW1 and WW2. The Campbell Road series of books has been an absorbing journey and she has learned much about the toughness and resilience of her ancestors.

Her new series, starting with *A Workhouse Christmas* follows a group of characters connected to the Whitechapel Union workhouse in East London and their journeys through WW1 between 1909 and 1918. It has all the heart, grit and history that distinguishes her as one of the most exciting voices in the saga genre.

Please visit her website www.kaybrellend.com for more information

By Kay Brellend

The Bittersweet Legacy series

A Sister's Bond
A Lonely Heart
The Way Home

A WORKHOUSE CHRISTMAS

Kay Brellend

PIATKUS

PIATKUS

First published in Great Britain in 2020 by Piatkus

1 3 5 7 9 10 8 6 4 2

A CIP catalogue record for this book
is available from the British Library.

ISBN 978-0-349-42513-9

Typeset in Palatino by M Rules
Printed and bound in Great Britain by Clays Ltd, Elcograf S.p.A.

Papers used by Piatkus are from well-managed forests
and other responsible sources.

Piatkus
An imprint of
Little, Brown Book Group
Carmelite House
50 Victoria Embankment
London EC4Y 0DZ

An Hachette UK Company
www.hachette.co.uk

www.littlebrown.co.uk

For Sandra, with love.

Prologue

Christmas Eve 1909
South Grove Workhouse, Mile End Road, East London

'You've come to the wrong place. You should apply to your own parish. Tell the relieving officer at St Pancras the right tale and perhaps you won't have to enter the house.'

'I've seen him . . . he said we're not an urgent case. How could he say that!' The woman's shivering fists clenched in despair. 'Look at us . . . we must come in, sir. We'll all work. Do whatever we're told to and cause no trouble. Me and me kids haven't eaten a morsel in days . . . nor slept on a bed.'

'Better hurry along then, now it's turned to snow. You don't want to be sitting on St Pancras's step on Christmas Eve, do you?'

Maude Larkin couldn't get a good look at the fellow. She had sleet in her eyes and he had a heavy timber door to shelter behind to keep the weather off himself. All this 'yes sir, no sir' was making her boil up inside. It wasn't just a fever putting fire in her blood. She didn't want to be polite. She wanted to scream at him to take them in. But she could barely find the energy to keep talking.

1

'I've applied for out-relief, sir, and been refused. They said I'm idle for not working. But I look every day for work.' The last part wasn't a lie: she'd begged to do a shift at the laundry on Commercial Road just that morning. If she'd managed to control her hacking cough while she did so, the miserable cow in charge might have taken her on. But Maude had headed straight here when finally accepting she was too ill and dog-tired to stay on the streets. Keeping up the pretence that something would turn up and soon they'd have somewhere to call home was sapping the life and soul out of her.

Over a fortnight ago she had been evicted for again having no rent money. Pleading had done her no good: the landlord could see that she was too sick to work and soon settle up a month's back rent. They had been sleeping rough, moving from place to place in the East End. But she had refused to give in and ring the bell outside one of these hellholes. Last night she'd promised the kids she'd never leave them as they'd slipped unseen into St Dunstan's Church. Until dawn light they'd huddled together on a pew, trying to rest as they had done the night before. They'd not managed that trick again this evening. The church had been locked early. Perhaps the vicar had been making it look festive for a carol service on Christmas morning. Or perhaps he had cottoned on to vagrants using the place as a squat and his Christian spirit hadn't stretched that far. But for that misfortune, she might have spent another few days with her darling twins. No fancy treats or Christmas food for them, but they would have had the precious gift of one another's company a little while longer.

Maude Larkin knew what she was letting herself in for even if her children didn't. Once inside a workhouse they'd be separated, and she was aware that if she couldn't pull herself round she might never see either of them again. So it had to be the right place for them ... the best of the beastly bunch. Or the lie she'd told about them being together would be worthless and gnaw her to death.

'Open up, you heartless brute.' Both sets of Maude's grimy fingernails were curled about the edge of the door to stop the porter denying her his meagre light and warmth. She used a foot to kick on the wood. Even though crying in frustration, the irony of what she was doing wasn't lost on her. Such godforsaken places had always filled her with horror, and she'd always cross the road to avoid passing too close. The silent shuffling ghosts that could be glimpsed through the railings had aroused her pity and disgust. She'd been so cocksure she'd never be a workhouse inmate herself.

'Let me in!' She clung on so that if he shut the door he'd have to injure her.

'Sorry, but rules apply.' He was getting narked. 'Get along with you. I've work to do.'

Gathering what little strength she had, Maude jammed her thin body between door and frame. The effort had set her lungs pumping and her chest undulated beneath her cloak as she started to cough.

'I've two children you can see and another you can't.' She yanked at her ragged cloak to give her flat belly a bump of pregnancy. Her husband had been dead for more than four months, so she was confident she wasn't carrying, but she'd been spared the curse since she'd been existing on scraps to eat. In a rotten way, starving at least helped prevent another mouth to feed. 'If you don't let us in we'll all perish on this step,' she panted. 'It'll be on your conscience if I lose me little 'un and you find us frozen to death here on Christmas morning.'

'It won't; I'm just doing my job. Paupers apply to their own parish.'

'Mum ... come on ... let's try further along. Another place might take us.' A small icy hand was tugging at Maude's elbow. She knew her daughter was embarrassed by her humbling herself like this. But she was doing it for them. She'd do anything to keep her twins safe. She'd nothing left but her kids. If she didn't truly believe it was possible for Lily and Davy to pull themselves out of this mess, she'd throttle them now to put them out of their misery.

'This is the best place for you 'n' Davy.' Maude turned to her daughter, miming at her to shush. 'You heard what old Ma Rollins said: kids at South Grove get sent to the Cuckoo School. It's not too far off and I can visit you. Other industrial schools are too far away, love. I won't make it there to get you. And I will get you, soon as I'm well. They'll look after you at the Cuckoo till I'm better, Lily, and can come for you 'n' Davy. You'll be learning and setting yourself up for a good job. You and Davy won't end up like me and your father.'

Lily nodded vigorously to soothe her distraught mother, though she knew it wasn't a lack of good learning that had brought them to this. Her father had received an education. He'd been a clerk in a solicitor's office before whisky, or any other alcohol he could lay his hands on, had stripped them of everything they had.

The boy with them was listening to what went on, standing silent and sullen, with his chin low, resting on the turned-up collar of his coat. It had been his dead father's donkey jacket. A remnant from the days when Charlie Larkin had laboured and the sight of that garment pegged on the back of the door had been comforting to his family. It meant he was home and fit to earn, not passed out in a

4

gutter somewhere. He hadn't liked labouring; had thought himself too good for it. The humiliation of going cap in hand to the railway yard or the building sites for casual work had enraged him. The sooty coat swamped Davy and the tattered hem rested on the top of the dead man's boots, stuffed with newspaper so they didn't fall off when he walked.

Lily Larkin had nothing on her feet; not that she could feel the cold or cuts on them any more. They were frozen numb. On her thin, ten-year-old frame hung a patched cotton dress that barely reached her knees because her good one had been swapped for two loaves of bread and a twist of tea. This floral affair had been pretty when new. She'd grown out of it six months ago; it was too short but also loose over her emaciated belly. A blanket from the bed she'd last slept on had been butchered to a size that fitted about her shoulders. The other piece was wrapped around Davy, under his father's coat. Lily refused to call the rag a shawl, although her mother had tried to cheer her up by saying it was. The blanket hadn't even been theirs. Luckily, the landlord had been too intent on ejecting them from their room to notice that the cover was missing from the stained mattress.

Maude swung back to the porter before he shut her out for good. If she hammered on the door again he wouldn't open up to her. 'Let me in and ... and we can have a conversation.' Maude used another trump card – her final one – and in a selfish way she hoped it wouldn't work. She'd never done anything like that before. She'd sooner abase herself begging for charity. But it seemed even charity cost.

And so did love. Charlie had left her to battle on alone at keeping their family together. She felt guilty for having stuck by a man who'd taken them from comfort to poverty in under a year. He'd drunk himself to death and left his

5

family destitute. He'd been a good-looking charmer and Maude had felt proud, not jealous, when female eyes followed him. He'd sworn he'd never strayed and had only ever loved her. He'd said all the rest was malice and lies. She'd believed him, even when he'd sunk lower and grown distant and more ashamed of his boozing. Yet he couldn't stop, and fool that she was, Maude couldn't stop loving Charlie Larkin. She'd raged at him for his faults, but now he was gone she missed the useless item so much she couldn't breathe for grief when she thought of him. She swallowed a sob and pushed back the hood of her cape, allowing the stranger in the lodge to stare at her.

He knew what that brazen gesture meant and he was pleasantly surprised. The last one who had turned up – offering herself in return for admission – had turned his stomach. Pockmarked and at least forty, she'd been. This one looked more than a decade younger, although it was hard to tell when they were gaunt. But he noticed her large black eyes set in a white-skinned face and he noticed her hair. Thick waves of dark brown reached past her shoulders and looked surprisingly clean and shiny in the dim light. She was vain then ... a wig-maker would have paid her for that and she could have stayed outside a while longer. Some even sold their teeth to delay an inevitable walk of shame to yank on the bell of the local spike.

Maude sensed his hesitation and gave the door a shove, getting inside. Before closing it she turned to her kids to whisper, 'Just hang on there while I talk to him. Won't be long ...' And she hoped she was right about that. Now close beside him, she could see he was younger than his gruff manner had led her to believe; perhaps early twenties. And she remembered her husband at that age ... randy as hell.

She knew he was fair-haired and quite handsome too, but she didn't look at him for more than a second. As soon as the door was closed she dropped to her knees, keen to get it over. Old Ma Rollins had told her the way to service a man without risking getting a bun in the oven. That's all the assistance her old neighbour would give. Asking for the loan of some coppers to buy bread had resulted in Maude getting the door shut in her face. But as her situation had worsened, Maude had listened intently to the older woman's workhouse tales. Ma Rollins had been in and out of them several times over the years. The Cuckoo School had been the making of her boys, she'd said, and they were doing all right now. Maude kept that precious thought at the forefront of her mind as her shaking fingers fumbled at the stranger's trouser buttons.

'Not like that.' The porter pulled her up. He seemed to be in the throes of some inner turmoil as he gazed at her. 'Don't think this is a good idea.' He gave her a push towards the door, about to open it.

'It is . . . please . . . and hurry up 'cos me kids are freezing to death out there.' Maude put her back against the door, holding it shut, and undid some buttons to tempt him with a glimpse of her breasts, hoisting her skirts to knee level. Her husband had said she had a lovely figure; Maude knew she was skinny now. But the stranger's eyes were on her again in the way she wanted; then he closed them as though to block out temptation.

With a mutter he pulled her closer, bending her face down over a heavy oak table with an oil lamp on it. Maude could smell the kerosene, feel the heat on her face from its flame as he pulled up her skirts. She started to tell him she didn't want to do it this way in case she got knocked up.

She bit her tongue in case he realised she'd lied about being pregnant and shoved her back outside.

'Quickly ... please ... the children are waiting for me ... it's so cold ...' She panted in pain as he knocked apart her knees and forced into her.

Lily could hear her twin brother whimpering, though he was trying to muffle the noise by burrowing his face further into his coat.

'Mum said she'd not be long,' he moaned.

Lily brushed the settled snow from his slumped shoulders then enclosed him in her arms, rubbing her hands up and down on his bony back to warm him. 'Mum'll be back soon. She'll not give up until she makes him give us somewhere to sleep. And we'll get something to eat 'n' all, Davy. Toast 'n' dripping ... nice 'n' warm 'n' runny ... how's that sound, Shrimp?' She teased him with the pet name she called him because he was an inch shorter than her, and trailed a finger on his cold chin, mimicking melting dripping.

Davy jerked his face aside. 'I hate him ... look what he's done to us, Lil. Some Christmas!'

Lily heard the tremor in her twin's voice and felt his fury turning his body rigid in her embrace. She knew he wasn't talking about the porter in that lodge who was arguing with their mother. Davy blamed their dead father for all of this, and Lily had to admit it was hard to forgive Charlie Larkin for what he had done to them. Last Christmas they'd tucked into roast chicken and a plum pudding. They'd think themselves lucky to be offered toast and dripping tomorrow.

In the distance, an unseen choir were singing 'Silent Night' and the haunting melody made tears start to her eyes. A year ago she had sung carols at school, but she and Davy hadn't attended school for months. Their mother was too ashamed to send them dressed in rags after she sold their uniforms for rent money. Lily felt the shame too, and the loss.

They had lived in a nice house once ... a whole house that had a small garden. She and Davy had never missed a lesson. Their mother had dressed prettily and smelled of rose perfume bought as a treat from Gamages once a year and eked out a drop at a time. Then a man had come to their home, shouting at her father and shaking his fist. After he'd left, slamming the front door, she'd eavesdropped on her parents' violent argument and learned that her father had embezzled money and got sacked from his job. She was terrified he might go to prison and so was her mother. But he didn't. Their home had been sold to pay back his boss.

Gossiping neighbours had watched them move out. They'd all heard what had gone on but nobody stepped up to lend a hand. Her mother had told her to ignore them and keep her chin up, and Lily had. She'd helped her dad push the handcart with their few remaining bits of furniture that hadn't been sold off. She'd tried to smile at him but he wouldn't look at her, or at anyone. Just marched along and stared straight ahead. They had taken their first lodging rooms near King's Cross ... and they'd kept moving from place to place for the next ten months with the rooms getting smaller and dirtier and her father disappearing from home more often. Then the next man who came to bang on the door about her father was a policeman. He'd looked stern as he told her mother that her husband had been found dead by the canal. Lily could remember feeling just a sense of relief that the waiting for it to happen was over.

9

Now, trembling in the bitter Yuletide air, she knew those horrible days were gone and a new existence awaited. Her guts were curdling with terror over where life as a workhouse girl was likely to take her.

August 1910

'Don't go, Lily! You mustn't! If they catch you, you won't 'arf get the strap. And they'll starve you, too.'

'Don't care about that. This'll be me only chance to see Davy and tell him how poorly Mum is.' Lily shook off her friend's fingers from her arms. Margie Blake was trying to prevent her bolting out of the workhouse gate. But Lily had made up her mind; the opportunity to sneak away to the other side of the building to find her brother would never again present itself. The harsh, unyielding workhouse regime forbade contact between families. Once inside, an inmate was supposed to forget about loved ones separated from them by brick walls. Lily knew about the punishments too. She'd been defiant from the start, creeping out of the dormitory at night to dash about the corridors in the hope of finding one that might lead to either of the two people who meant everything to her. She'd risk another beating because the ache to see her twin brother was harder to bear than a lash on her back. Soon he might be all she had left of her family.

Lily was shivering in trepidation as she stepped past Margie and placed a finger to her lips. Her friend looked about to blub, and Lily didn't want her causing a scene and bringing an officer down on them. Swinging furtive looks to and fro to make sure all the staff were occupied, she slipped

10

through the crowd towards the gate. Her pace faltered as she got closer to the exit. But luck was on her side: the elderly porter had abandoned his post to assist the other staff with stragglers who were being evacuated. Some ancient women were shuffling slowly from the northern wing of the workhouse with smoke shrouding them. The acrid air was making them cough, in between moaning prayers for God's salvation from the fire. Lily could have laughed. What about death frightened them, now they knew hell was a place behind high walls on the Mile End Road?

She'd love to see the place in ashes. But if the workhouse did burn down, she'd only be transferred somewhere similar, and she might never again share the same roof as her family. She'd thought constantly about absconding, but at eleven years old she was unlikely to find work and, without money for food and lodging, she'd not make more than a few miles. More importantly, she couldn't leave her mother and brother behind. They were all stuck in limbo. Their lives and futures had been passed into other hands from the moment they'd arrived. They were powerless and were expected to bow and scrape and say thank you for their miserable existences. Lily didn't blame her beloved mother for bringing them here. Maude had truly believed it to be for the best for her children. There was a small happiness for Lily in knowing that her mother would be clinging to that belief as she lay gravely ill in the infirmary.

Lily jumped in her skin as the clatter of a bell rent the air, heralding an approaching fire truck. It would give her the cover she needed to make a dash for it. Instead of bolting, she shrank back into the shadows. The female officer she hated the most was hurrying through the gate, just yards from her. She had her head down and was huddled into a voluminous cloak, as though trying to conceal herself. The coward was probably frightened of the fire and saving her own skin. Lily curled her lip in disgust; Miss Fox was always the first one to offer to fetch the cane and carry out the master's punishments.

As soon as the coast was clear, Lily picked up the hem of her skirt, preventing it tangling in her boots, then pelted around the corner keeping close to the perimeter wall. It was six o'clock on a September evening and the sky was prematurely blackened by clouds.

'What you up to then?'

Lily gasped, spinning about. It wasn't Miss Fox, ready to drag her back to the women's side of the building. A fellow swigging from a beer bottle was eyeing her as warily as she was him.

'You belong in there, do you?' he slurred, jerking a nod at the looming outline of the workhouse.

Lily nodded, wishing he'd go away, until she realised he might be of use. She needed a hand. She'd twice tried to scale the brickwork but had slithered back to the pavement. Her hands were badly scraped and she wiped blood on to her skirt. 'Me brother's just over that side of the wall. But the rotten devils won't ever let me see him.'

The fellow sniffed the air. 'One of yers got hold of some matches, did you, and managed to set a fire?' He chuckled to himself. 'Ain't surprised. Bleedin' place gives me the heebie-jeebies.' He crossed himself.

'Would you give me a bunk up?' Lily asked. She wasn't sure how the fire had started, she was just grateful that it had. But he could be right and a desperate inmate had decided to destroy the home of his torment.

The stranger pushed back the cap on his greasy hair, squinting at her over the bottle at his mouth. Then his stubbly cheeks creased in a grin. 'You're breaking yer little brother out 'n' all, are you?' His eyes held a spark of admiration. 'Good fer you ... clever lass you are.' He cupped his hands for her to step upon.

Lily modestly gathered her skirt tight about her legs then – in for a penny, in for a pound – stepped up and launched herself to the top of the wall, feeling it abrading her fleshless ribs and legs.

She glanced down at her Good Samaritan, hissing her thanks before swinging her legs over and jumping down.

'Good luck, gel, and God bless you both.' The fellow knew she hadn't heard him and soon he was hurrying away, crossing himself again.

The drop winded Lily and she remained on the ground, panting. When the lights zigzagging in front of her eyes faded, she looked up. A lad of about six had turned away from the rest of the crowd and spotted her crouching behind him. He nudged the boy beside him.

Lily scrambled up. 'D'you know Davy Larkin?' she whispered.

The child shrank back, blinking as though she were an apparition. Quickly she repeated her question to another boy, who looked to be a little older than she was. He was almost bald, as though he'd recently undergone the admission ritual of being shorn. He boldly sized her up in a way Lily didn't like. Glaring her disgust, she was about to move on when he hissed, 'Oi ... Larkin ... yer doxy's come to see yer.'

Lily's heart leapt in hope and she began scouring the faces that were turning her way. Then she saw him and felt momentarily stifled with joy and relief. Rather rudely she began elbowing her way to his side to hug him. That raised some titters and lewd murmurs from onlookers. She could feel his bones and no doubt he could feel hers. But Davy looked well enough, so she forwent questioning him about himself. It wouldn't be long before she drew even more attention and officers came to investigate. And there were so many important things to ask and to tell.

'You'll get it for this, Lily.' Davy burbled a hoarse warning. He was rigid with shock at suddenly being brought face to face with his sister after eight long months apart.

'Had to come. Did you know Mum's very sick in the infirmary? Bet they didn't tell you, did they? Only found out meself from pestering Mrs Windham; she's a bit nicer than the other officers. She told me Mum's not getting any better. I've begged to see her but Matron won't let me, the rotten old cow!' Lily swallowed a sob. She didn't want to upset her brother, but he deserved to know that their mother might die. She couldn't keep something like that to herself.

Davy hung his head, his eyes glistening with tears. 'Nobody's told me anything. Ain't surprised though about Mum; she was suffering bad bronchitis when we come in.' He balled his hands into fists. 'We should've stayed outside. Sooner be dead than in here.' He whipped up his face and growled, 'Bet that's what Dad thought when he knew where we was all heading. He drunk himself to death on purpose, the coward.' He swiped his wet eyes with a sleeve. 'I hate it, Lil. Can't wait to go to the Cuckoo School. It can't be worse than this.'

'You *got* a place after all?' Lily's eyes widened on him.

Davy nodded and put his thin arms around his sister to protect her. A few older boys, starved of seeing any females, started touching her, more in wonder than in lust. Men and boys were dealt with by male staff. Their only contact with a woman might be if they were nursed in the infirmary.

'Aren't *you* going to the Industrial School?' Davy asked urgently.

'Matron said I'll have to keep attending the school down the road, and that I'd get taught how to earn me keep washing and mangling here in the laundry. Seems that's all she thinks I'm good for. Yet she can't even spell "miscellaneous". I saw it on the list she was writing,' Lily scoffed. 'Don't care, anyway, what she thinks of me. And I'm glad I'm not getting sent away to school. I wouldn't leave Mum. Not now ...'

'I won't go then ...'

'You will! You must!' Lily gave him a fierce frown. 'You'll get good work ... have a future, Davy. It's what Mum wanted. You have to go, for her sake as well as yours.'

He nodded in defeat. 'I'll come back for you, Lil, I swear it,' Davy croaked. 'Soon as I've got me job and me freedom, I'll come and get you.'

'Know you will.' She gave him a final hug. The increased jostling heralded an officer having spotted her and he was pushing a path towards them. She quickly distanced herself from Davy, hoping to prevent him being punished for what she'd done. Lily felt her shoulder being grabbed, then she was spun around to find a man thrusting his bearded face close to hers.

'You little hussy!' He sounded disbelieving and looked her up and down, seeing from her uniform she *was* an inmate. 'What's your name?'

'Larkin,' Lily said.

'How d'you manage this then, Larkin?' He shook her by the shoulder.

She knew whatever she said it wouldn't save her from

what was coming to her. She tossed back her head, sending her chin-length dark locks swaying about her cheeks. It had been waist-length when she'd arrived but had been roughly cropped months ago. 'Wouldn't you like to know,' she said.

He grabbed a hank of her hair, twisting it in his fist so her head was pulled aside. 'Let's see how funny you think it is when the master hears of this. Losing your crowning glory should keep you away from pestering the boys.'

Lily gave her brother a fierce frown, warning him not to get involved and jeopardise his school place. The shaven-headed boy acted as her ally, putting an arm round Davy's shoulder and steering him out of sight.

Another officer was close by, gawping at her. 'Larkin, did she say?' He whispered something to his colleague.

'Like your mother, are you, Larkin? Can see you've picked up her bad ways. Well, you'd better learn to curb your urges, 'cos fallen women often end up in the mortuary.'

'What?' Lily wrenched her arm free and grabbed at his instead, shaking it. 'What do you mean by that? What are you saying about my mum?'

He ripped free of her grip, then slapped her hard across the face.

Lily gasped but kicked him, needing to provoke him into saying more. Her face was stinging and her chest heaving so rapidly she felt faint. She could guess what he meant, and she could feel her heart slowly breaking. In a rage of despair, she thumped him double-handed in the chest. 'You tell me what you mean about my mum,' she screamed.

'I mean your mum's dead and so's the bastard she was carrying.'

Chapter One

March 1914

'Disobedient wretch! Show off in the street, would you? I'll have you punished by the master, you brazen little madam. Do as I say and move on.'

Lily Larkin received another hefty slap on the shoulder that sent her stumbling forward. She steadied herself from the officer's second blow. She'd barely felt the woman's first, neither had she heard an initial barked command to get going that had accompanied it. Catching her breath, Lily hurried to catch up with her fellow pupils some yards in front. But her gaze continued to dart to and fro, seeking the wiry figure who had shocked her to a standstill and brought the girl behind crashing into her with a yelp. Nora Clarke had fallen over and Lily could hear her whimpering as the officer dragged her to her feet.

'What's up, Lil?'

The hissed question came from a fair-haired girl, wearing an identical shapeless dress, pinafore and ill-fitting boots to Lily's. The two girls were marching side by side in a troop of students who'd turned out of the local

17

schoolyard to head back to South Grove workhouse in Whitechapel.

'Nothing's up . . . just thought I saw a face I knew. But I was wrong.' Lily told Margie Blake a lie because the truth was too astonishing and too precious to share even with her best friend. She *had* seen somebody she knew, and he had seen her.

In fact her twin brother might have been lying in wait on the Mile End Road to catch a glimpse of her. How she had longed for a glimpse of him over the years. She'd thought of him constantly, dreading that his dear features, so like her own, would grow unfamiliar as he turned from boy to youth. She'd stare at her reflection in the spotted mirror in the stone-cold bathhouse while pulling a comb through her washed hair, and imagine Davy with a moustache. But then she'd been told he'd never grow old, never need to shave. She'd been told her brother had perished. But he was alive and she had recognised him straight away. As he had recognised her. He had been gone from Whitechapel for several years but would remember the routine that she – and once he – had followed at the workhouse. The moment their eyes had collided, she'd frozen to the spot before instinctively rushing in his direction. But he'd slipped away into the throng on the pavement, and she had been hauled back into line by the dragon she hated.

Her twin hadn't intended drawing anybody's attention, even hers, and Lily regretted having nearly betrayed him. If he was a runaway he'd be punished if caught, then returned to the industrial school for the headmaster to decide his future.

Yet how *could* it be him if he was supposed to be dead?

The workhouse master and his wife had believed she'd

bawl her eyes out and need comforting when they broke the news of the tragic accident that had deprived Lily of her last family member. Instead, she'd shouted at them, incoherent with distress, and had been called an insubordinate, ungrateful wretch in return. Who did she think she was speaking to? The mistress had roared at her, smacking her face and shaking her, making her teeth rattle. Lily had been in such profound shock on learning the ghastly news that she had smacked the woman's face right back, earning herself more punishment. But Lily hadn't felt the cane on her legs or the hunger in her belly when she was denied her usual meagre rations, sent to solitary confinement and given gruel.

She had sensed Davy beside her as she lay weeping, waiting for dawn to spill some light into the icy, dark punishment room, which was barely big enough to take a chair, table and the straw pallet on which she slept. She'd dreamt of him warming and comforting her during those interminable black hours. Her brother was no phantom. He was flesh and blood, and she'd just passed within yards of him. Her heart felt as though it might burst through her ribs, such was her joy at discovering the master and mistress had been wrong about Davy Larkin's fate. She believed they'd been misinformed rather than had deliberately lied. She had some family left, after all; they might be orphans but they had each other. As children they'd been constant companions. Lily had always preferred being with Davy to mixing with school friends. He had been the one more likely to seek out chums to play with. Lily hadn't begrudged him his freedom, knowing his friends had teased him when his sister acted as his shadow. Davy had also been the more mischievous twin, likely to receive a talking to from his father. Much as Lily had idolised her brother, she'd known Davy had deserved his reprimands too. Nevertheless, she would try to share the blame and the punishment with him, as they shared everything else. She'd do that now too, if need be. They were both of an age to be working. He might have been indentured to an employer and have illegally absconded. Whatever had gone on, she reckoned he had landed himself in some sort of trouble. And she must help him out of it, as she always did.

As she continued plodding along, Lily was aware of the officer watching her and at intervals growling at Nora to shut up snivelling because she'd scraped her knee. Lily felt guilty causing an accident; she'd say sorry later to Nora when they were in the dormitory. For now she must play her meek part and stop herself whooping in delight as exciting plans whizzed crazily in her head. She knew the officer would take a delight in trying to destroy her hopes and dreams of being reunited with Davy.

At her side, Margie was still frowning and giving her inquisitive looks; though bursting to tell her friend her wonderful news, Lily knew she mustn't until she'd properly thought things through. Her breath was coming so fast that she might have been skipping along rather than trudging in time with the others. Outwardly she appeared as they did: downcast eyes, sullen expression. But beneath her unreadable excitement was anxiety. Her brother relied on her to be the sensible one, and already she was fretting he'd founder without her. She'd a thousand questions to ask about his escape from the fire at the Cuckoo School and his journey back to her.

After years of separation they were again close enough to breathe the same damp City air. The March drizzle had descended suddenly while she'd been doing arithmetic in the classroom. Though cold and shivery in her thin shawl,

Lily was glad of the mist. It would give her brother cover if he needed it. An image of him on the last occasion they'd spoken flashed into her mind. She'd climbed the wall at their workhouse, determined to be the one to tell him their mother was dying. She could feel again his sharp bones digging into her palms, and see the tears glittering in his eyes as they'd embraced. She'd insisted he go to the industrial school when he'd spoken of remaining close to their mother until the end. She'd no longer have to bear the guilt of persuading him to go away, and that felt wonderful. Something bad had happened to him at the Cuckoo School, though, and she hoped he would forgive her for sending him to it. He'd returned to rescue her just as he'd promised. He'd have to bide his time before visiting the workhouse and applying to discharge her. The master would want proof that Davy Larkin had employment and the means to provide for his underage sister. The fact that the master believed her brother to be dead was another obstacle to her liberty. But Lily refused to let any pitfalls deject her; soon she and Davy would be building a little home together. And things would be all right again.

'You'll be sorry for making a spectacle of yourself, Larkin, I'll make sure of it.'

Lily jumped as she was rudely jerked out of her thoughts. The threat had been issued close to her ear as she passed through the open gates of the workhouse. Lily raised her chin but kept quiet. Over the long years she'd been an inmate of South Grove, she'd learned to despise her enemies in private. She hadn't liked Harriet Fox from the start, yet the woman seemed nastier than ever.

The line of girls began filing into the northern wing of the workhouse where female inmates were housed, away from the men on the southern side. Once within its walls, the group dispersed quickly and quietly through long, sour-smelling corridors. Some of the girls headed to the sewing room to join those mending and sorting rags. Anything at all that might be salvaged – buttons, hooks and braid – were cut off to be reused or sold. The money raised was put towards the cost of their keep, Lily imagined, as none of them ever saw a farthing for working their fingers to the bone. Other girls would be rostered to help their elders press and fold the vast amount of washing that had dried earlier in the week. Then, in an hour, it would be time to congregate in the dining hall, to sit silently at wooden trestle tables and be given a pint of milk porridge and five ounces of bread for supper. When first at the workhouse, Lily could barely stomach the food, even though she'd been starving hungry. The memory of her mother's fare, even simple snacks like toast and dripping, was a distant one now, though, and she ate every scrap of the meagre rations put before her at mealtimes.

She made to follow Margie in the direction of the sewing room, but a pinching grip on her arm brought her up short.

'You can stay right where you are, Larkin. You're coming with me to the master's office to explain yourself,' Harriet Fox snorted. 'Damned wretch, deliberately causing a rumpus and pretending to run off!'

'I didn't ... it wasn't deliberate!' Lily protested, attempting to free her elbow. 'I jumped out of line 'cos ... I didn't want to fall down meself. There were loose cobbles.' It was a silly lie and had just tumbled out because her mind was still on Davy. Lily reckoned she'd have to continue with it now; she'd nothing better to offer, after all. 'I didn't want to rick me ankle in a pothole and miss school tomorrow.

We've got a spelling test. Later I'll apologise to Nora for what happened.'

'What are you gawping at, Blake? Get to the sewing room and move that needle as fast as you can.' Harriet cast a sneering look at the lame hand that Margie was concealing in the folds of her skirt. The girl was conscious of her disability, but Harriet took every opportunity to bring it to everybody's attention.

Behind Miss Fox's back, Lily pulled a face, letting Margie know that the spiteful cow wasn't worth getting upset over. It seemed to brighten Margie up because she smiled at the flagged floor before hurrying off.

'You're a liar as well as a show-off, aren't you, Larkin?' Harriet turned back to Lily with a triumphant smirk. There'd been no pothole to jump over, and all it would take was a walk back down the Mile End Road to prove it. 'You don't need school spelling tests. You're a dunce and no amount of extra learning will change that. Hard graft to knock the defiance out of you is what you need. And it's long overdue.' Harriet resentfully knew that the girl *wasn't* a dunce. Lily Larkin was a gifted student and had been shown favouritism because of it. It was time to end that, in Harriet's view.

The medical room was situated on the same corridor as the master's office to which Lily was being rapidly propelled. Before Harriet could bang on her boss's door, a young man in a white coat appeared in the corridor. Adam Reeve had been employed as South Grove's medical officer for several years and had taken an interest in Lily's education. Unlike his boss, he saw the point in encouraging bright children to learn and better themselves rather than regarding them all as fodder for labour in factories and kitchens.

'What's going on here, Miss Fox?' Adam Reeve started towards them. Meeting Lily's large blue eyes he gave her a sympathetic look.

'Nothing that need concern you, sir,' Harriet snapped back. He'd poked his nose in before and got the girl undeserved leniency.

'I'll be the judge of that, thank you. Is Lily Larkin in trouble?'

'Oh, yes. She's started a commotion in the street trying to run away, and caused another inmate to suffer an injury.'

'I wasn't running away, honest . . . I just—'

'Hold your tongue!' Harriet gave her captive's arm a shake. She wasn't sure why a man like Reeve had such a soft spot for the girl. But she knew why some of the other male staff showed an interest in Lily Larkin. She was developing fast. Unlike some of the other scrawny scraps of her age, Lily had blossomed into a pretty adolescent. Her mother had been a good-looking woman, despite the careworn lines etched into her face and the premature grey in her dark hair. Whenever Harriet thought of the late Maude Larkin, she resented Lily even more.

On hearing a barked command to enter, Harriet pushed Lily into the master's office, then made to shut the door in Adam Reeve's face. He thwarted her by placing a heavy hand on it and determinedly following her in.

'Beg pardon, Mr Stone, but I've bad behaviour to report.' Harriet thrust Lily forward in emphasis.

A baggy-faced fellow sprang up from behind his desk, clearly annoyed that a crowd had descended upon him just as he was enjoying tea and buns with his family. His wife remained seated in her chair. Harriet was pleased to see the matron with her husband, knowing she had an ally.

Mrs Stone had no more liking for any Larkin than Harriet had herself. But there was another gentleman in the room, and he had recently been showing an interest in Lily as she grew more like her mother in looks. Harriet had been keeping a close eye on her boyfriend. She gave him a private smile but barely received a flicker of acknowledgement back. With a mutter for his parents, Ben Stone picked up his hat from the edge of the desk and quit the office.

'Explain yourself, Larkin.' Mrs Stone was wiping crumbs from her mouth with one hand and reaching for the punishment book on her husband's desk with the other.

'I've done nothing wrong, m'm. Nothing on purpose, anyway.' Lily was still bubbling with emotion after seeing Davy and her reply sounded unintentionally flippant.

Bertha Stone pursed her lips. 'Let's have your version of what's gone on, Miss Fox.' She jerked her head at Harriet.

Harriet immediately made a meal of describing the disturbance, and the attention it had drawn from bystanders. With a flourish of her own skirt, she added that Nora Clarke's clothing had got torn, knowing that the master would prick up his ears. Uniforms cost money, and Mr Stone liked to keep his accounts showing a good profit. Impressing the Board of Guardians with his efficiency kept them from poking their noses too far into his business. The master got furious if people in the neighbourhood witnessed inmates' troublemaking. Any report of it reaching *his* masters would bring inspectors to his door.

'The culprit can give the other girl her own skirt and patch the damaged one to wear herself.' The master thumped a palm on the desk making the tea tray rattle. He flapped the same hand to shoo them out.

Harriet flushed angrily. She'd expected more punishment

to be dispensed than a bit of sewing. Mrs Stone's expression hardened too. She knew her husband was always shifty when Lily Larkin was brought face to face with him. Well, today he could squirm and suffer her presence. If Bertha had had her way, every one of the Larkins would have been gone from here by now.

'Disorderly and refractory conduct cannot be tolerated or it will spread.' She glared at her husband. 'An example needs to be made of Larkin.'

Lily knew that speech meant she wasn't going to get away with a telling off and some needlework. Adam Reeve usually stuck up for her when she got into trouble. She hoped he would now, though he'd hardly spoken so far. He was the kindest fellow she had ever known, and she included her late father in that judgement. In the early days Charlie Larkin had been a lovely man, but those memories were all but buried beneath what came after.

A reluctance to lose touch with Adam was one of the reasons Lily hadn't fled from South Grove. Many times, when outside she'd been tempted to bolt into a crowd of normal people hurrying about their business. She was determined the workhouse's pitiless regime would not break her spirit as it had that of others. The building was filled with souls who'd given up hope of ever leaving. And how they expressed their despair! The howl that erupted from their throats still had the power to chill Lily, though she must have heard it a thousand times. That eerie noise would echo in her memory until she died.

'What caused you to step out of line, Lily?' Adam asked mildly.

Lily gathered her thoughts and quietly repeated what she'd said earlier about the potholes. She couldn't go back on it though she hated fibbing to him. She hadn't fooled him; she could see the disappointment in his eyes.

'She's a liar as well as a troublemaker,' Harriet crowed. 'Every girl close by witnessed what she did. Larkin needs discipline and to be found employment. She's wilful and spoilt from being allowed to idle at school for far too long.'

Harriet Fox claimed to be a trained nurse, yet had obviously received little education, and was jealous of those brighter than herself. Adam guessed she was probably the daughter of a handywoman who'd picked up the rudiments of nursing and midwifery from her mother. Workhouse employment was low paid and unpleasant. Masters asked applicants few questions and took who they could get in the way of staff. He was an example of such indifference himself. It was a mystery how Harriet Fox had risen to be a supervisor, though. It was common knowledge that she was Ben Stone's lover, but that wasn't the reason Harriet had been favoured by the master. Adam had overheard Mr and Mrs Stone talking about their dislike for the woman who considered herself to be their future daughter-in-law.

'If Nora Clarke is injured, why isn't she waiting outside my door for treatment?' Adam found a pertinent question to ask.

'Larkin's punishment should be dealt with first,' Harriet snapped at him for bringing that up. Nora just had a graze that needed a wash.

'Enough of this.' Mr Stone pushed himself to his feet as his two employees locked glares. The Larkin family had been a trial from the moment they had arrived. In the receiving ward they'd undergone a routine of being bathed and shorn and clothed in uniform, as were all new inmates. Thereafter families were separated. Men and women – even those who were married – boys and girls all taken in different directions.

Maude Larkin had been a force to be reckoned with, especially protective of her snivelling son. Her fierce daughter had been made of hardier stuff, and still was. William Stone knew she was watching him now with those deep blue eyes that seemed to dig into him. 'A day's reduced rations and solitary confinement for Larkin, and Reeve can look at the injured girl if he will.'

'Reduced rations?' Adam spat. 'The diet here is barely adequate as it is. Children need sufficient nourishment. A lack leads to disease. If consumption takes hold again, it'll go through the wards like wildfire.' He strode forward, planting his fists on his hips.

'She's not a child any more.' Bertha Stone continued writing her husband's orders in the punishment book. 'Larkin is not to be shown any further favouritism. I fear that our benevolence towards her has been abused. She will be disciplined then found employment.' Bertha replaced the book on the desk, then hoisted her girth from her chair, mirroring the medical officer's aggressive stance.

'When *are* you fourteen, Larkin?' The master avoided eye contact with the girl, thumping his pen repeatedly on the blotter.

Lily knew school for her was finished and that they were planning to send her to slave away in a scullery. Yesterday that would have felt like a death sentence. But not now. Davy was more important than school or Adam Reeve or her friend Margie. She felt guilty to be leaving Margie behind, but Davy was her flesh and blood ... all

28

she had left of her family. Though she'd not spoken to him in years, she ached with love for her twin brother and would always put him first. She didn't care what job she got. Once outside, she intended to immediately abscond from it anyway, and find Davy. Together they would muddle along somehow. They had to, now they knew what the alternative was; they were never again entering a workhouse. 'I'm fifteen, sir,' Lily answered when reminded to do so by Harriet's elbow in her ribs.

That admission made William Stone stare at her in shock. The girl didn't look fifteen, but it was hard to tell sometimes whether the emaciated humanity that infested the building was aged twelve or twenty – not that he paid any of them much attention. 'It *is* high time you were providing for yourself then. There are individuals far more deserving of shelter here than a healthy fifteen year old.'

'Lily Larkin is exceptionally bright and that's quite extraordinary considering who she is and where she is,' Adam argued. 'You know very well she helps out as a clerk and that has saved the Whitechapel Union the cost of a salary. Her continuing further education should be put before the Board for discussion. A shining example of a workhouse child achieving exemplary heights is just what is needed to promote South Grove and other such institutions. By the time she is sixteen she will be equipped with a handful of higher education certificates and ready for a clerical position in an office.'

Lily sent him a startled look. She didn't want to further her education now, or be a shining example with a handful of certificates. It was too late for any of that. She wanted to be with Davy. That was all that was important, and she was sure if her mother could speak to her, she'd agree.

29

William Stone knew that the medical officer was right: Larkin was bright as a button and of use. He'd love to continue to have her free labour and also his own free time. The mountain of paperwork he was expected to do was an unwelcome burden, yet he was too mean to pay for an assistant. And he would adore to be lauded by the Board of Guardians for having produced gold from dross. The majority of children within these walls were fit for nothing but menial work, as were their feckless parents. But Reeve had brought to his attention before that this girl showed promise. If it had been anybody else, William would have overruled his wife and gone along with Adam Reeve's thinking.

'If Larkin's got energy to spare to make mischief, she's strong enough to be punished and to immediately be sent to work.' Her husband's hesitation prompted Bertha Stone to take matters into her own hands. 'No matter her ability, employers will reject her because she's too wilful. Larkin needs domestic work to keep her on her toes and tire her out.'

'She's too fine a student for that . . .'

The more Reeve challenged him, the more determined the master was to impress on all present his authority. Besides, the girl's presence was a constant thorn in his side. He'd sooner forgo any benefit to be had from keeping her and use this opportunity to rid himself of the last of the Larkins. 'The matter is settled and there is nothing further to say.' He flapped a hand. 'Remove the girl for punishment, and steps will be taken to find her a suitable job.'

Harriet was above-average height for a woman and buxom with it. Her facial features were not unpleasant, but a look of triumph skewed them as she jutted her chin at Adam. Momentarily it seemed he had fight left in him, but he retreated from the office, shaking his head.

Harriet ushered Lily towards the door. 'You know where to wait for me, Larkin. Go straight there.' Harriet strode after Adam, catching up with him just as he was about to disappear into the medical room. 'Don't stick your nose into my business again, sir, or you'll regret it.'

'What do you mean by that?' Adam turned to her, frowning. He was short for a man and their faces were level. 'I've said nothing that wasn't relevant or true about Lily Larkin. And I stand by every word of it.'

'You just leave me to deal with her for the short time she remains here. If you don't, I might turn my attention to dealing with you instead.'

'Are you threatening me, Miss Fox?'

'Wouldn't you like to know.' Harriet gave him a sly look. 'Take the word of an inmate over mine, would you, and try to get me into trouble?' Harriet smirked. 'Dear me . . . I thought you'd been here long enough by now to know the rules, sir. Seems you don't. So, I'll oblige: don't cross me or I'll remember I know things about you that I shouldn't.'

Harriet marched off, a gloating light in her eyes.

Chapter Two

William Stone looked less cynical than his wife, but both had difficulty disguising their scepticism at what they had just heard. Having exchanged a hasty glance, the couple returned their attention to an uninvited visitor who had arrived a short while ago.

'You say that Lily Larkin is your cousin, sir, yet there is no record of this girl having any living kin.' William was seated behind his desk; he leant forward, planting his elbows on its edge. Over the steeple he'd made of his fingers, he squinted suspiciously at the fellow.

'Well she is me cousin and I've come to get her. I've my own business and there's work for her to do if she's in agreement, that is. If she's not ... ' Gregory Wilding shrugged, curled his top lip and glanced about the master's office. 'She can stay right here if that's what she chooses. I'll find somebody who is keen to join the crew.' He was standing, legs akimbo, one hand casually thrust in his pocket. The other was idly swaying a natty homburg by its brim.

William Stone ran an eye over the man's get-up. Such tailoring – even when it was as tastelessly gaudy as this – cost a pretty penny. His resentment wasn't confined to the fellow having found the audacity to dress in Savile Row when he spoke like a barrow boy. He didn't like Wilding's attitude either. Who did he think he was, swaggering in here and looking down his nose?

The master's office was cosy, with its soft armchairs set upon a large square rug and landscape paintings on the wall, all lit by the dancing flames of a coal fire. But this fellow didn't seem impressed by his environment. William had no intention of ejecting him though. He'd taken against Gregory Wilding straight away; nevertheless, the man was a godsend.

'Have you more information about this family connection you claim to have with the Larkins?' Bertha Stone piped up. 'Inmates can't be discharged willy-nilly, you know.'

'Can see yer predicament, sir ... ma'am.' The fellow gave an emphatic nod. 'Let me fill you in on some background then. My mum was Lily's mum's big sister and they didn't get on. Never spoke for years, so us kids hardly knew one another. I don't have a gripe with Lily though. Not seen her since she was toddling, but when I found out on the grapevine that she was stuck all alone in Whitechapel workhouse, me heart went out to the girl. I reckon I ought to step up and do my duty to family. She's had more'n her fair share of knocks. Orphaned, then the poor kid lost her brother 'n' all.' Wilding shook his head, expelling air through his teeth. 'The lad would've been better off taking his chances on the street than going to that school and ending up burned to a crisp.'

William Stone inserted two fingers between his tight collar and his florid throat. He didn't like reminders of that episode; he regretted what had happened to the innocent boy. He was thankful, though, that the wretch who had accompanied David Larkin to Hanwell had left when he did, or he might have set a fire here rather than the Cuckoo School. Most of all he was sorry that the dratted incident hadn't been kept out of the papers. It was too much that an East End wide boy knew about it and had just thrown it in his face.

'Be surprised what's picked up on the streets, sir.' Greg had interpreted Stone's brooding look. 'Once gossip starts it don't stop and gets hairier along the way. I've heard folk say they'd sooner strangle their kids than hand 'em over to the Whitechapel Union.'

'Unfortunate accidents happen,' William snapped while his wife fidgeted.

'Indeed they do, but still makes me fret for me last remaining cousin, as you can imagine. Doesn't seem right her still being here.' Greg Wilding strolled to the window and stared out into a bleak April afternoon. 'I need more workers and she's deserving of a change of luck. No harm in helping kin who've done yer no wrong, is there?'

Lily had been standing just inside the door, ignored as though she wasn't worthy to be a part of this discussion concerning her family and her future. But it had suited her very well to keep quiet and listen intently through the sound of blood pounding in her ears. Her lowered gaze was busy watching all of them ... especially the handsome stranger.

Ten minutes ago, Harriet Fox had come looking for her and beckoned her away from the mangles in the steam-filled laundry room. Lily's questions about why she'd been summoned by the master and mistress had been answered

34

only by a scowl and a shove on the shoulder, sending her on her way to the office. Feeling apprehensive, Lily had hurried through the corridors preparing a defence, though she'd not a clue what she might have done wrong this time.

But perhaps she was in trouble. What was this man really after? She was sure she didn't have a cousin and was as doubtful as the master and mistress appeared to be about his motives in coming here to take her away. But an instinct was telling her to keep quiet rather than deny every word he'd said about them being related. Her dearest wish *was* to escape this place and be reunited with Davy; if there was a risk involved in achieving that, she'd take it.

When she'd first entered the office, the fellow had bowled right over and introduced himself as her cousin while patting her rough red hand, still damp from handling washing. Lily had almost snatched her fingers from his and called him a liar to his face. But he'd given her a certain look from a pair of oddly coloured eyes that were fringed by thick black lashes. She had quickly pressed together her lips, saying nothing. Seemingly satisfied that he'd made his point, he'd turned his back on her and attended to winning over the master and mistress with his patter.

He knew a lot about her family. Her mother *had* had an older sister she couldn't abide . . . Lily recalled the spinster aunt being mentioned between her parents long ago. Lily had believed her aunt childless, but Mr and Mrs Stone wouldn't suspect any of that. What really held Lily spellbound, though, was that this man knew about her twin brother. When he'd mentioned Davy's fate at the school, his narrowed, tawny eyes had held a significant glint as they'd found hers.

'Losing little Shrimp must've been a blow to the poor gel.' Wilding gave a sorrowful sigh and skimmed a glance past Lily's wide blue stare, wondering if she'd clued up yet. If the silly mare didn't get the hint soon that he'd come to do her a favour, he'd give up and sling his hook. He'd more important things to do than reunite a couple of waifs. Yet now he'd seen her up close, he wanted to help her more than ever. She was pretty – far prettier than she'd a right to be, considering where she was and what she'd been through. And Lily Larkin did have a look of his cousin, his real one, especially when she had a spark of defiance brightening her blue eyes. Greg feared he must be turning sentimental, and that wouldn't do when he'd tough customers to deal with.

Using the pet name Davy had told him about had made it all finally sink in. Her mouth had parted in astonishment before she started gnawing on her bottom lip to stop herself smiling. He was hoping she wasn't the dunce he'd first taken her for, because he really did have work for her to do, if she wanted it. Her brother had promised him this kid was bright, and she'd better be. She and her brother owed him, and Gregory Wilding always collected debts.

'So you say you have an employment offer for Lily Larkin. And that would be what exactly, Mr Wilding?'

'Costermonger, amongst other things, sir. I have fingers in pies, so to speak. It don't do to put eggs all in one basket ... or on one market stall, fer that matter. I'll sell you fish or fruit and veg or a nice line in bed sheets if you prefer. Reckon you must go through some here, eh?' Greg Wilding tapped his nose. 'I'll beat any quote and get you anything yer like.'

Bertha Stone crossed her arms over her chest. She imagined he *could* supply most things. Including young

36

virgins to old men. Oh, they'd had pimps in here before, pretending they were respectable employers in need of female domestics, when what they were really after were fresh young women to vilely exploit. Gregory Wilding was a good-looking sort with his blond hair and striking hazel eyes. He reminded her a bit of her son, although Benjamin was late twenties not early twenties, the age this fellow looked to be. Wilding had a rather coarse charm too. She could see him worming his way into the affections of silly young girls with his smiles and spiel. Though she had no fondness for Lily Larkin, Bertha didn't want the girl abused. Despite the loss of all her family, she was still proud and resilient. If she were discharged to this Jack the Lad then ill-treated, she would complain to Adam Reeve about it. He'd report it to the Board of Guardians and a furore would ensue. The chairman would only need to hear a whisper about mismanagement to eject the Stones. Bertha couldn't risk that when their son was in line to run this place on their retirement; by the time that day came, Bertha hoped that Ben would have outgrown Harriet Fox. The idea of him marrying that creature and making her matron was too much to bear.

A silence, punctuated only by the hiss of hot coal, was suddenly brought to an end. William pulled his thoughts together to announce, 'At this early stage I can only ask you to return another time for an answer to your request, sir. Lily Larkin's discharge must be discussed and approved by the Board of Guardians. There is a meeting at the end of the week and I will bring it up then. After that, the girl will be given a chance to speak—'

'I would like to take my cousin's offer.' Lily wasn't waiting and seized her chance now. 'I do remember him, and my aunt and uncle too, though I was little at the time—'

'Me parents went early to meet their makers,' Greg cut across her. 'Hardly knew them myself, so I doubt that Lily would properly recollect them.'

Lily sensed he was warning her to keep her mouth shut in case they contradicted one another. Her heart was thumping in excitement, and she felt like recklessly running over to him. She must be patient, though, and get out of this place before rattling off her questions. And heaven only knew she had a hundred of them spinning in her head, making her feel giddy. But she was certain he'd just let her know he was a friend of Davy's.

'I'd sooner settle the matter today and take the girl with me now.' Wilding pulled a gold watch from his waistcoat and consulted it. 'Time's money and I've got work needs doing.' Cocking his head, he gave Lily a lengthy assessment that dampened her spirit and made her bristle. ''Course if she turns out to be a dud then, cousin or not, I'll be returning her to you.'

'You will not!' Bertha Stone snorted. 'Once discharged she stays out and would need to apply for readmission like anybody else.'

'Hear that Lily, did you?' Greg said. 'You'd better shape up quick, gel, or it's back to milk porridge for you.'

'I will, sir.' Lily meekly lowered her eyes, having seen a spark of amusement in his that had made her want to grin at him.

'Come back on Friday afternoon for your answer.' William also wanted the matter settled as soon as possible, but there were procedures to follow. He also suspected this spiv's morals and motives weren't pure where the girl was concerned. But whatever the truth of it, he wasn't as bothered about it as Bertha. He didn't want his wife's conscience creating stumbling blocks to the removal of the last of the Larkins. They'd been a cursed nuisance from the moment they were admitted.

'We cannot discharge the girl into your care without proof of your standing as a legitimate businessman, and that you've the means to provide appropriate accommodation for her. Failing that, she will stay here.' A housekeeper had recently enquired about employing a hardworking kitchen maid. To Bertha that seemed a more suitable solution for Larkin than what this Cockney rogue was offering.

'A bank book would verify that you are who you claim to be.' William knew it wasn't necessary to have bank references, but he was inquisitive about the upstart sporting a gold watch and chain that looked nicer than the one ticking in his own waistcoat. Now Wilding had come closer to his desk, he could see the man's polished shoe leather peeping from beneath his trouser turn-ups. He didn't push a barrow for a living in that outfit.

'This should do the trick then.' Gregory pulled a roll of cash from his breast pocket and tossed it carelessly on to the edge of the desk, followed by several folded papers. 'Me last consignment of fish from Billingsgate ... some sacks of spuds and carrots off Solly Smithson in Spitalfields ... ' He continued reeling off a list of transactions while flattening out invoices and pushing them across the desk with fingers that bore the ingrained dirt of recent toil. 'No banks for me, sir; that's the safest place for me stuff.' He patted the pocket on his broad chest from whence it had all come.

The couple weren't looking at the litter of bills. And neither was Lily. Her eyes were also on the thick cylinder of banknotes in danger of rolling on to the floor. She was mesmerised by the sight of so much cash. Even in the good old days, when she had lived in a happy family with her mum and dad, she'd not seen more than a few pound notes together at the same time. There looked to be twenty times as much as that secured within that tight bit of string. For some reason Lily felt overwhelmed – tearful – and quickly cuffed at her eyes in case anybody noticed she was crying. How on earth had Davy made such a friend as this man? She wanted to run at Gregory Wilding and hug him. And what if he had told the truth and was actually their cousin? How wonderful it would be to have more kin, especially somebody with a family business who was prepared to pay them wages!

'Well . . . it seems we can report having seen evidence of your standing, sir,' William said stiffly.

'Good . . . you let yer guv'nors know then that I'll be back Friday to take her home with me.'

Gregory Wilding didn't seem quite as genial as previously and it hadn't gone unnoticed by the others. The balance of power between the adults seemed to have slickly shifted. A man – even a vulgarian – with that amount of cash was in a position to strike his own deal with the Guardians if he chose to. The last thing the Stones wanted was somebody going over their heads to their masters.

'Go back to your work in the laundry room, Larkin, I will speak to you later.' Bertha jerked a nod at the door.

'Yes, m'm,' Lily murmured. She peeked sideways, hoping Mr Wilding would look her way before she quit the room. She wanted to receive another one of his quick, sly smiles. The moment she'd got one of those, Lily had trusted that this man was on her side, whoever he really was. She hadn't felt a bond with any adult since losing her mother. But Mr Wilding seemed to have forgotten about her. His face was lowered and he was busily returning all his stuff to his inside pocket, a hank of fair hair covering his eyes.

Once outside, Lily didn't head to the laundry room but darted straight underneath the stairs. There was a convenient nook that inmates would use to whisper to one another, out of sight of the prowling officers, who'd bawl at them to keep quiet if they were spotted talking. Inmates only really felt free to speak to one another for about an hour, during their daily exercise taken in the courtyard. Some of the sad old-timers seemed to have lost the art of conversation; they slumped against the wall or sat on a chair, vacant-eyed and silent even then.

In her hidey-hole, Lily fidgeted impatiently from foot to foot, brushing brunette curls off her sticky forehead. The unpleasantly humid atmosphere in the laundry room always left her flushed and sweaty. But she was fast cooling down now she'd left the master's coal fire behind. She cautiously peered out, intent on catching Mr Wilding and speaking to him before he left. Enduring the torment of waiting many days to find out how Davy was, when she could do so now, was unthinkable.

After a few restless minutes that passed like hours, he still hadn't emerged into the corridor. Lily knew time was getting on: the smell of rancid food being reheated wafted from the kitchens. Lily didn't care about the prospect of another suppertime. She was too excited to be bothered by her empty belly. She was aware that Miss Fox might try to waylay her before she joined the others to finish her laundry shift. The nosy cow would want to interrogate her in private about what had gone on. Lily ducked behind the sturdy oak newel post as Adam Reeve came out of his office. Usually Lily adored bumping into him, but not right now. They hadn't spoken to one another since the day she'd been punished for causing Nora to take a tumble, weeks ago now. As the sound of his footsteps faded away, Lily could hear Miss Fox talking to one of the other officers somewhere on the landing, their voices echoing about the high walls. Disheartened, Lily supposed she ought to end her vigil and go back to work. Yet still her desperation for news of her brother kept her right where she was.

If she was discovered shirking instead of working, she'd be punished again. As soon as a person was admitted to the workhouse, it was drummed into them that their predicament was their own fault because they were lazy and idle. Industry was next to godliness in the master and mistress's book ... which was odd, Lily thought, as they seemed to do little themselves other than sit drinking tea and toasting their toes by the hearth. The sulphurous smell of burning coal jerked her to attention; though some distance away, Lily felt a faint warm breeze from the master's fire on her chilly skin. Then she heard some muted conversation before the sound of a door being shut. A second later she was pelting after the man striding towards the exit, her old boots clanging on the stone floor.

Lily heard her name barked out, and an order to halt, as Miss Fox spotted her and marched down the stairs. But Lily kept going and almost flew straight into Gregory Wilding as he spun about on hearing the commotion. He put out his hands and gripped her arms to steady her.

'How's Davy doing, sir? I know you've seen him ... please tell me how he is.' Lily had gabbled that out in a whisper while whipping a glance over a shoulder. 'Quick!

Tell me ... is he safe?' The speed at which Harriet was bearing down on them made Lily abruptly change her mind and stop clutching his sleeve in an effort to hurry his reply. 'Hush ... don't say a word in front of Miss Fox. She's a horrible cow and will get us all into trouble.'

Lily felt her arm almost ripped from its socket as the officer yanked her to her side. 'Apologise to this gentleman for your disgraceful behaviour, Larkin. How dare you accost a visitor like that!'

'Reckon it should be you apologising, Miss.' Gregory Wilding took a step closer to Harriet and pointed to her stubby fingers. 'Take yer hands off me cousin.' He didn't sound angry or threatening but Harriet obeyed, attempting to smother her astonishment at what she'd heard.

She had imagined Larkin had been summoned to a job interview in the master's room. In common with everybody else, Harriet believed the girl quite alone in the world, and this news came as a shock. She gritted her teeth on noticing Lily's amused expression. 'Cousin or not, sir, Larkin will be treated no differently to other inmates. Those who break the rules are punished.' She gave Lily a menacing stare. 'And she will be.'

'What rules?' He crossed his arms over his chest, tapping his hat against his torso as he waited for her reply.

'Please, sir, I have misbehaved. Running isn't allowed, nor is speaking to the master's visitors without permission.' Lily was desperate not to upset either of them. He could provide what she had long dreamed of: a way out of this foul place. She ached to go with him right now, but couldn't. She was still a workhouse inmate, as Harriet Fox had enjoyed pointing out, and must toe every line rather than jeopardise the master's approval to her discharge.

'I'm not his visitor; I'm here to see you,' he said.

Lily gave him a startled look. It was good of him to continue to stick up for her, but she feared he was making things worse. She now wished she'd returned to the laundry straight away; she'd been recklessly greedy wanting another sight of her saviour and a chance to talk to him alone. She gave him a meaningful glance: plea and apology mingling in the vivid blue of her eyes. She prayed he knew she'd only contradicted him against her will. He looked rather stern and calculating, as though he might be withdrawing from her. She mustn't let him do that. 'I can't wait for us to get to know one another again,' she burst out. 'I recognised you as my cousin straight away.' She spontaneously went on tiptoe and kissed his lean, abrasive cheek.

'Stand over there!' Harriet Fox snarled, and inserted her ample figure between them, giving Lily a shove to send her back against the wall.

After this Lily knew she'd be severely punished again, but she didn't care: she'd gladly eat any amount of slop and huddle alone in a cold dark room, knowing that soon she'd be reunited with Davy. A pair of eyes that reminded her of the colour of the whisky her father used to drink were still on her, making her feel flustered and reminding her of the kiss she'd just given him. She could still feel his cool clean skin on her lips.

'Right then, Lily,' he said, as though he'd summed up the situation. 'It'll be nice to get to know you again too. Not long to wait. I'll be back to take you home on Friday. And no need to fret 'cos everything's just as it should be. So toodle-oo till then.' He turned his attention to Harriet. 'Afternoon to you too, Miss Fox.' Harriet simpered beneath his easy smile. She wasn't unaware of his good looks, and could see why the little hussy had thrown herself at him just now.

'Goodbye, sir ... thank you.' Lily watched Mr Wilding strolling away, whistling. He'd given her what she'd wanted, and in that moment she felt intensely grateful and fond of him for letting her know Davy was well. Her tense expression softened into smile. In all the years she'd been stuck in this prison, she had never heard anybody whistle or sing.

The chirpy sound brought cherished memories with it. When her family had lived in their lovely house, her father would whistle while polishing his shoes and her mother's humming would drift from the kitchen as she cooked pots of thick, savoury stew. Lily swallowed the emotion blocking her throat as memories of sunny days spent in the garden filled her head. Here it always seemed dreary, no matter the season. She glanced up at the woman beside her. 'Sorry for misbehaving, Miss Fox. I was overexcited, you see, knowing my cousin had found me and come to take me home.'

'It's odd ... I'll give you that,' Harriet muttered, head cocked as she watched Wilding's broad-shouldered figure disappear from sight. 'It'll be good to see the back of you, Larkin. But it's not Friday yet. And a peck on the cheek won't sway such as him. Maybe that fellow will find himself another little cousin and think better of coming back for you.'

Chapter Three

'What? Can't be true!' Margie gawped at Lily, eyes as round as saucers. 'You've really got a cousin who's turned up out of the blue?'

Lily gave an animated nod. 'He knew about my family and he's coming back on Friday to take me home.' She couldn't be certain he was a proper cousin, but she was happy to accept Gregory Wilding as kin. She'd had an Aunty Hilda who hadn't been a real aunt but her mother's friend. That woman's children had been like cousins and playmates to Lily and Davy, until their father's antics put paid to all the friends they'd ever had. Maude Larkin hadn't wanted people's pity any more than she'd wanted their gossip; she had distanced herself rather than see her family shunned.

'What's that? What's happening Friday?' Nora Clarke had overheard some of their conversation and butted in. She was a sullen girl and hadn't forgiven Lily for causing her to fall over. The incident had happened a while ago, and Lily had apologised more than once, but Nora seemed keen to drag it out.

'Lily's leaving, the lucky thing. Her cousin's applied to discharge her,' Margie rattled off.

'Maybe she is, but she'll still have to do her punishment for haring about and being impudent with a visitor,' Nora said, flushed with jealousy. 'Master won't let her off that, and serve her right.'

'Shut up, you nasty cow.' Margie made as though to push Nora away, but Lily caught her arm, holding her back.

'No point getting into trouble 'cos of her,' Lily whispered. She was protecting herself too. She'd been minding her Ps and Qs since Mr Wilding's visit. She'd even offered to stay behind in the laundry and make up the time she'd lost loitering under the stairs. Harriet Fox had laughed at her, as though she knew she was after points for good behaviour. Contrary as ever, the woman wouldn't allow her to get into the master's good books.

In order that Lily Larkin didn't get out of doing a full quota of work, her solitary confinement had been arranged to run from the end of shift tomorrow until after breakfast the following morning, and her rations would be reduced during those meals. Harriet had laid it on thick when listing Lily's misdemeanours in the visitor's presence, especially when recounting her brazenness in kissing him. Lily hadn't thought Mr Wilding had shown disapproval or embarrassment, but Harriet had said he had, and Lily hadn't dared argue back for fear of the consequences. The master and mistress had listened raptly, and by the end Mrs Stone appeared about to explode. But for some reason the punishment meted out hadn't been as severe as Lily had been expecting. She suspected that they weren't being kind, but minding Mr Wilding's reaction to ever finding out about it.

The girls were outside in the front garden taking an exercise break. They continued on their walk around the perimeter of the large rectangle. Set in the centre of the paving were some benches and tables lined up in regimental fashion. The elderly women used those to take a rest more than the younger, who tended to keep moving to avoid a patrolling officer's inquisitive eyes. Lily loved being in the fresh air, even when it was damp and chilly. She would gulp in great lungfuls of misty drizzle to clean her nostrils of the workhouse's fetid atmosphere.

'Wait until Fanny Miller finds out about your news; she won't 'arf be jealous,' Margie said, curling her deformed fingers about Lily's hand and receiving a squeeze. Touching wasn't encouraged, so after a few seconds the girls reluctantly moved apart before they drew unwanted attention. 'Fanny'll be as jealous as Nora ... more, even.'

'I know, and I don't blame her,' Lily said on a sigh. Their older friend talked constantly about discharging herself. Fanny was on a different work rota and they hadn't seen much of her for days.

'Thing is ... I'm jealous too,' Margie admitted, giving up being brave. 'I don't want you to go away and leave me, Lil.' Her pretty features crumpled. 'I know I'm being selfish but, without you to talk to, I'll end up as barmy as the old howlers in here.'

'No, you won't!' Lily gave her friend a little livening shake. 'You'll get work and then we can meet up outside and have tea in a caff and go to the flicks and do all those things we planned.' It was fraudulent reassurance and Margie would know it. She was only a little bit younger than Lily but was overlooked for jobs. Few employers hired from an institution housing people who were considered the dregs. Those who did relied on the youngsters all being so downtrodden and desperate that they'd work till they dropped for a pittance. There were plenty of takers for slave labour, too. It was a freedom of sorts, and bosses could pick and choose from able-bodied kids desperate to show willing. One-handed Margie stood little chance of getting an interview.

'I'll come back and visit you. Promise . . . ' Lily hugged her friend, ashamed for talking rot. The only visitors welcomed here were those offering charitable donations or jobs. Lily knew she would feel jealous too if Margie were the fortunate one. Over the years, Lily had watched girls go out to family or employment from upstairs on the landing. She had felt bitter disappointment that she wasn't the one walking the cold, musty corridor for the final time, to emerge into the sunshine of a better life. Soon it would be her turn and yet she felt guilty, almost embarrassed, that finally fate was smiling on her.

*

'Here . . . saved you a spud,' Margie hissed, revealing a greyish lump concealed in the folds of her skirt. 'I'll give it to you as soon as she's gone.' Margie jerked a nod at the warden. 'Bet yer hungry, ain't yer, Lil, with just skilly to eat yesterday?' Margie's grimace displayed her disgust for the porridge-like gruel that was a workhouse staple. Made of oatmeal and water, an inmate would think it their lucky day were they to encounter a single sliver of meat within its insipid depths. Skilly was served at breakfast and supper with an accompanying chunk of bread. Once or twice a week, cheese or bacon with a dollop of potato might make an appearance at midday dinnertime. But nobody received a fraction of an ounce more than they should. Every meal was scrupulously doled out.

Margie delivered a light kick, signalling the coast was clear. The dormitory officer had disappeared into her private cubby hole. Her bed was comfortable, unlike the inmates' bunks covered in a flat mattress and a single blanket. Those box-like contraptions were pushed close together and ranged facing one another along the dormitory. Pale light peeped in from a bank of windows set high in the walls, but the staff were all eagle-eyed, even this woman who tended to be nicer than the others.

Lily took the boiled potato being thrust at her, fingers impatiently nipping off the bits of fluff it had gathered in her friend's pocket, before gratefully wolfing it down. It felt hard and tasted bitter and did little to ease the gripes in her famished belly, but she gave Margie a quick hug. She'd risked being disciplined, donating food after Lily's punishment.

'You two! Why are you idling? You'll be late for the master's speech. Get along now before I report you both for shirking. Matron will have you both scrubbing floors until suppertime instead of taking it easy in the boardroom.'

'Yes, Mrs Windham,' Lily and Margie chorused meekly, heading obediently for the door. They appreciated her leniency; Miss Fox would have immediately acted on her threats to report them.

For a few hours a rare treat was in store for the lucky chosen inmates. Considering her recent bad behaviour, Lily was glad and rather surprised to have been picked again to help serve refreshments to visitors.

When the heavy toil of washing and cleaning was beyond aged and infirm inmates, they contributed towards their workhouse keep by making crafts. Periodically a sale of articles was held in the boardroom. Local dignitaries and neighbours were invited to attend, and fawned over by Mr and Mrs Stone, in the hope they'd support the Whitechapel Union by making purchases. Lily looked forward to sale day as it broke up their monotonous routine. She also liked viewing the work the old women produced. Nothing much that was lovely originated here, but she would marvel at the delicate lacework and embroidery. Crocheted shawls and knitted dolls were favourites with posh ladies, who liked to be seen to be benevolent. They would pick over the handiworks and 'ooh' and 'aah', but edge away if an inmate came too close.

'What's he like, this cousin of yours? He must be a smasher to come and rescue you from this dump. Is he strong and handsome?' Margie sighed wistfully as they hurried towards the head of the stairs. The girls had been fantasising about just such happenings for years. If Lily's dreams had come true, Margie reckoned it wasn't baloney after all about heroes on white horses saving maidens.

'He seems nice, but it's too early to say for sure. If he turns out to be a rotter, I'll soon scarper and find another job and so will ... ' Lily bit her lip. She had decided not to mention Davy. An irritating voice in her head kept taunting her with looming calamities. What if it hadn't been Davy she'd seen, but a boy who looked like him? What if Gregory Wilding wasn't all he seemed? He could have spun a yarn from the report of the Cuckoo School fire. He had no reason to do so, and he had *seemed* nice and friendly ... but over the years, Lily had had the trust knocked out of her. She'd grown to expect bad things to happen; she must take nothing for granted. When brought face to face with her beloved brother, *then* she would know he was real, and her happiness true.

Margie hadn't noticed her friend's hesitation in answering. She was peering over the banister, frowning at a group of people by the boardroom door. 'Who's that, with the Strattons?' she whispered.

Lily stared in the same direction. A stylishly dressed middle-aged woman was talking to a younger version of herself. Mrs Stratton and her daughter were regular visitors. The Stones would entertain in their private quarters, sometimes as many as a dozen benefactors at a time. On those occasions a savoury aroma would waft about the building and the tormenting hint of gravy would start the old howlers off.

But Lily didn't recognise the young man. She guessed he was family, though, as he had the same auburn hair. Phoebe hadn't yet acquired her mother's grace and tact and tended to be condescending, speaking to inmates as though they were dim rather than poor. Perhaps the family weren't as high and mighty as they liked to make out, though. Lily muffled a spontaneous laugh with her fingers. They were arguing and, more than that, a male voice had just snarled some swearwords. Her reaction to hearing them had reached *his* ears; the fellow looked up and saw the girls watching him.

Lily dodged back, pulling Margie out of sight. 'He's got a right face on him. Hope he didn't see us.' Lily knew he *had* seen them and she hoped he wasn't about to snitch on them. 'Come on, we'd better get cracking before Miss Fox comes looking for us.'

*

'It's time those fools were put out to grass, and let us take over,' Harriet said. 'What the hell do your parents think

52

they're doing, giving *her* privileges after the way she's behaved? Larkin should be mangling in the laundry, not handing out bloody teacups.' Harriet had been aware of her boyfriend staring at Lily; it was hard to swallow that *she* turned his head. Presently the girl was pouring tea for people from a table that was set with crockery and an urn.

'My father's thinking of his bank balance, as he always does,' Ben Stone answered sourly, watching Lily arranging spoons on saucers. Beside her, Margie Blake was concealing her deformity in the folds of her skirt while using her good hand to offer a plate of cupcakes. 'He's picked the two prettiest faces in this place to brighten things up.' Ben jerked a nod at the neatly displayed handiworks. Seated around that table were half a dozen of the wizened old women who'd produced the crafts, needles weaving in evidence of their skill. 'It'd seem a bit grim if just that lot were in here, wouldn't it?'

Harriet resented him praising the two younger women's looks, but understood what he meant. Workhouses were renowned for their toothless crones and pockmarked prostitutes; the girls – one dark haired, the other fair – were easy on the eye and reflected well on the master and mistress.

'Beauty's skin deep with Larkin,' Harriet sneered. 'If the visitors knew how shameless and defiant she truly is, those big blue eyes wouldn't get her far. They'd keep their distance, not queue up to be nice to her. It's high time *I* was matron. Things would be very different then.'

'I don't know what you've got against her. She'll be gone soon, anyway.'

The Board of Guardians would want to appoint a married couple to run the place, and Harriet was efficient and experienced. But Ben wasn't certain he wanted her permanently in his life. They'd been compatible lovers for several years but had little else in common. Her jealousy and bullying grated on his nerves. As did her drinking. He'd caught a whiff of sherry on her breath a moment ago. In time she'd be an obnoxious drunken shrew and try to rule him in the way she did the inmates. It had occurred to him that his parents might be delaying stepping aside to thwart Harriet's ambitions rather than his. He'd come to the conclusion it was high time to cool things between them. For some time Ben had realised there was friction between his parents and Harriet. Whenever he asked either side for an explanation, he was fobbed off with denials that anything specific was wrong. If his parents were to sack his girlfriend, Ben realised it would do him a favour, saving him the headache of getting rid of her himself when he took over.

'Larkin can't disappear soon enough for my liking,' Harriet said sharply. 'You don't have to deal with the little madam day in, day out.' She turned her back on the tea table to indicate it wasn't a subject worthy of further discussion. Yet the way Ben had stuck up for the girl irritated her.

'I'm going back to work,' he said. 'You should too, Harriet.' He'd noticed his father frowning at them to indicate they'd outstayed their welcome. Senior staff were invited to the sale but were expected to return to their duties once they'd applauded the master's opening speech. His father would expound the worthiness of Lady Brabazon's scheme to train and employ inmates in work best suited to their age and physical capability. Men were taught basket weaving or such like, and women various needlecrafts. Ostensibly the scheme's purpose was to give dignity and meaning to the lives of people no longer fit for hard labour. In reality it was implemented to discourage ageing paupers still on the outside from coming in and expecting an easy ride until they expired. No inmate, however ancient, was permitted to idle or take advantage of free board and lodging provided by a workhouse union. The money raised from these sales was supposed to go towards improving facilities in the wards; little that was new, or extra, turned up here . . . other than in the master's private quarters.

'Glad Miss Fox has left,' Lily whispered to Margie, having observed the two supervisors exit the room together.

'Keeping tabs on her meal ticket, she is,' another colleague hissed with a wink, making Lily and Margie suppress their smiles. Everybody knew about the lovebirds and that they would eventually take charge. At present the girls rarely encountered Ben Stone, running the male section. When they occasionally crossed paths, he tended to stare at Lily in an intense way that made her feel uncomfortable. Other than that, she'd nothing in particular to hold against him but, judging him on the company he kept, and the fact he got on with Harriet Fox, she reckoned he couldn't be a very nice person.

The woman who'd made the saucy comment had been fetching more milk from the kitchens a moment ago. Fanny Miller was a good few years older than Lily and Margie. She had a buxom figure and thick, unruly red hair that had been neatened into a plait at the nape of her neck in honour of today's posh visitors. Some springy locks had already escaped confinement to straggle on to her shoulders. Fanny had also been selected to attend today.

The master and mistress liked to parade their success in rehabilitating fallen women. Of the many prostitutes in the workhouse, Fanny Miller was the shrewdest. She was also the most presentable. She had turned up months ago with a swollen belly. After the baby was born, mother and son had been separated. Fanny was well enough now to discharge herself, and that's what she intended to do.

'I heard you're escaping soon, Lily. I won't be far behind you.' Fanny took the opportunity to have a gossip while they were unobserved. The master and mistress were toadying to a group of customers who were admiring the patchwork bedspreads hanging on screens by the sale table.

'Got a job to go to,' Lily said proudly.

'Yeah? Doing what?' Fanny cocked her head.

'Market work.'

'Lil's long-lost cousin's her new boss.' Margie sighed. 'Wish I had a nice cousin like that.'

'That's a turn-up, gel.' Fanny gave Lily's arm a congratulatory squeeze, looking impressed, and curious to know more.

Before the older woman could fire off more questions, Lily asked some of her own. 'So when are you discharging yourself? Are you taking the baby with you? If they'll let you, that is.' Fanny had told her that she'd not been allowed to visit the nursery other than to feed him. It seemed unbelievably wicked to Lily to ban a mother from caring for her newborn. But she'd been here long enough not to be surprised by the cruelty of the rules.

'Too bloody right I am. And if they try 'n' stop me having me son, there'll be murders.' Fanny defiantly tossed her fiery head and busied herself with the crockery

56

as Bertha Stone peered their way. 'Look lively ... the old cow's clocking us.'

Lily industriously stacked used cups and saucers and Margie did her best to help, one-handed. Once the mistress's attention returned to the visitors, Lily whispered, 'Where you going to live then, Fanny?' Lily admired Fanny and liked talking to her, though she knew what she did. Lily understood now how life treated destitute women and why some of them would prefer to 'look for sailors down by the docks', as Fanny termed her occupation, rather than moulder away inside a place like this. Fanny Miller had been in and out of the workhouse more than once. She was tough and resilient and never sounded sorry for herself, or for the way her life had turned out. Lily guessed that behind Fanny's brazenness was a tale of crushed hopes and dreams similar to her own. Yet Lily knew she was about to hear Fanny's plans for another go at surviving in the outside world, with another mouth to feed this time.

'Me sister's husband has run off. She's on her own with three kids now. I promised her, when I've had me baby and discharged meself, I'll move in with her and we'll sort things out between us. We'll hire a handbarrer and sell soap and soda and all that sort of thing, door to door.' She smiled. 'Our mum used to do that. She split profits with her sister after Dad died. Never knew him 'cos I was just a toddler when he passed on. Anyway, Mum 'n' Aunt Grace would share rent and they raised me and Lizzie between 'em. Me 'n' Lizzie always said we'd follow in their footsteps, but she let me down before we even got started.' Fanny snorted in disgust. 'She married *him*. He was always a wrong 'un. I warned Lizzie he'd up 'n' leave her for a fancy piece, but she wouldn't listen. Never could keep his trousers buttoned, that one.'

Lily and Margie exchanged a scandalously amused look.

'I hope my little sister comes to fetch me home when she's old enough and got a job.' Margie steered the conversation away from blue talk. She had been listening wistfully to tales of families and remembering the woes in her own past. Her father had been killed in an accident at the railway yard. Unable to support all her kids, Mrs Blake had dumped her disabled girl in the workhouse because she'd never be able to contribute to the family kitty. Margie had said she didn't blame her mother and was glad she wasn't a burden. Nevertheless, she dreamed that someday someone might turn up out of the blue to rescue her.

'Never seen him in here before.' Fanny was considering the young gentleman who'd turned up with the Stratton women.

'Don't think he's too happy to be here either,' Margie smirked. 'He wasn't 'arf effing and blinding earlier.'

The subject of their discussion was making no effort to disguise his boredom, pacing from window to window to stare out. He was a well-built, smartly dressed fellow Lily judged to be about nineteen. But however pleasant his looks, she had taken against him straight away. Not simply because he hadn't the good manners to at least feign an interest in the handiwork on display. She had been brought up to believe that gentlemen didn't swear in front of ladies, no matter what. Even at his darkest, she had never heard her father use bad language while at home. But she *had* learned that people who believed themselves superior often weren't.

Life, Lily reckoned, was down to luck. People like the

Strattons had been showered with plenty of the good sort. Whereas those like Fanny and Margie had been dogged from birth by misfortune. Lily knew she was blessed to have some very happy early childhood memories of her family to treasure. And once she was out of this place and reunited with Davy, they would make some more. They would chase their good luck until they had it cornered. And they had Mr Wilding to thank for giving them at least a chance to do that.

Chapter Four

'Oh, for goodness' sake settle down, Clive.' Mrs Stratton pointed exasperatedly to a chair, hoping her son would cease prowling and use it.

He jammed his hands in his pockets, continuing to stand and scowl. 'Must I stay longer in this blasted place? Surely one of your offspring accompanying you to look at this tat is adequate.'

'You know what your father said. You must remain for at least one hour and talk to some of the inmates. It will do you good. Perhaps you'll gain a necessary lesson from observing how the poor wretches live and improve your behaviour.' Mrs Stratton pursed her lips. She wasn't going to elaborate. But he knew to what she referred, although he didn't look remotely sorry for it. *She* was sorry that her husband had passed to her the burden of their errant son's company, when it was clear he was out to embarrass her this afternoon.

'Stranding him in the midst of paupers and fallen women won't cure him of chasing petticoat, Mama,' the woman's daughter scoffed. 'He's probably eyeing up his next doxy.'

'Phoebe! Really!' Mrs Stratton spluttered, turning pink. 'It's enough that I have your brother's vulgarity to contend with. Keep a civil tongue in your head. Go and look at the embroidery while I talk to Clive.'

The girl huffed and flounced off to finger some tray cloths.

'I'd as soon be back in Oxford than participating in this ghastly pantomime.' Clive was on a recess from university but wished he'd gone elsewhere for a holiday. His father's summons to return to London had seemed innocent enough. The moment he'd stepped over the threshold, though, he'd been threatened with having his allowance cut off. His latest slip had come to a head while he was away, but the housemaid he'd impregnated had been paid off by the time he returned. Now she'd been dismissed it was all at an end and forgotten as far as Clive was concerned. He couldn't see what the fuss was about.

'I'd as soon you were back at college, too,' his mother snapped. 'Learning about self-discipline. It seems your father and I have woefully failed to instil any of that in you.'

'I'll be damned if I'll stay here another minute,' Clive muttered beneath his breath.

'Before you leave you will purchase something from your allowance.' Mrs Stratton gripped her son's elbow, preventing him storming out. 'Go and show some interest in the lovely crafts and choose one.'

He ripped his arm free and sauntered off, but instead of looking at the display, he approached a window in the hope of taking another crafty nip of whisky from his pocket flask. Before he could position himself to do so unobserved, he was intercepted by the medical officer. Adam had just entered the boardroom, having missed the master's speech while attending to a sick child in the infirmary. Arriving late was a small mercy in Adam's opinion: it turned his stomach the way the Stones would puff up and take all the credit on sale day.

'Ah, a new face. I don't recognise you, sir. But I saw you talking to Mrs Stratton and believe I detect a family likeness.' Adam extended his hand and introduced himself. 'I'm the medical officer here. Is this your first visit to a Brabazon affair?'

Clive gave a nod. 'And the last. Not sure I could endure it all again,' he returned bluntly. But he shook hands and confirmed he was accompanying his mother and sister.

Adam misunderstood the reason for his disgust. 'All a bit much, isn't it?' he said conspiratorially. 'A person might be forgiven for thinking the Stones had stitched the stuff themselves the way they carry on.'

That finally drew a chuckle from Clive. 'I'm under orders to stay for an hour and purchase something.' He drew out his watch. 'Thirty-five minutes to go, so I'd better show willing and see what's on offer.'

Adam patted him on the shoulder. 'That's the spirit. A nice little gift for your mother perhaps?' He nodded at Mrs Stratton and Phoebe, who appeared to be on their way to say hello.

'Or perhaps not . . . ' Clive drawled, and glanced at the attractive girls serving tea. He looked smug as he strode off to avoid being saddled with his mother's company again.

Lily was aware they were under observation. She avoided the young man's eyes and looked instead at Adam, hoping he'd come over. She hadn't spoken to him for a while. She'd been wondering if he'd been avoiding her, feeling embarrassed that the master had won the argument over her future. Usually the medical officer would request her assistance in clerical duties at least once a week. Often there wasn't a lot for Lily to do. She guessed he was simply being kind, wanting to give her a short break from doing laundry and scrubbing floors, day in day out. Lily imagined he'd heard she was leaving, and she hoped to have a chance to say a few words to him today to reassure him that she was happy with the way things had turned out. She started to attention, conscious of people approaching.

'Mrs Stratton's coming over.' She murmured a quick warning to her chattering colleagues.

'Ain't putting up with that stuck-up cow Phoebe looking down her nose at me,' Fanny muttered. 'I'm off ...' She bustled away, carrying a tray to collect used crockery just as Mrs Stratton and her daughter came to a halt by the table.

'Tea for you, m'm?' Lily picked up a teapot covered by a cosy.

'Thank you, my dear,' the older woman said. She flicked the colourful bobble on the top of the cosy. 'Such lovely work you girls produce.'

'The older ladies are the ones who make it all. I'm no good at knitting, m'm.'

'No? Really?' The woman smiled, looking as though she wished she could have heard differently.

Phoebe was enviously eyeing Lily's thick chestnut tresses and large blue eyes. Her own hair was a gingery shade of brown and her eyes grey. It didn't seem fair to Phoebe that girls who used harsh soap had nice complexions. She had a dressing table filled with lotions and potions, yet still had a spot on her chin. 'You're a scholar, aren't you, Miss Larkin?

The medical officer just told me that you are a bright little thing and help him in his office.' Phoebe sounded as though she believed the man must have been exaggerating.

'Yes . . . I do some clerical work.' Lily gritted her teeth, wishing she was collecting dirty cups with Fanny, instead of being patronised by a woman not a lot older than she was. Phoebe looked about seventeen. Lily was proud that people thought her bright, so Phoebe could scoff all she wanted. Lily's mother – her father too, in the early days, before he lost interest in everything except a liquor bottle – had praised her for doing well at school. Adam Reeve had chosen her to help him tidy his office on his first day as the new medical officer. It was almost two years ago that she'd unpacked boxes for him, then sorted weighty tomes into subjects and alphabetical order without him asking her to. It was how they had got to be friends of sorts, talking about polio and diphtheria. Lily had always liked school. She believed her mother had been wise in understanding education was a way people – especially poor people – could better themselves. And then her thoughts turned to Gregory Wilding. She doubted that he'd liked school and wondered how he'd started off in life and what obstacles he'd overcome to end up successful. And obviously he was: few working-class men of his age carried so much cash in their pocket, she was sure of it.

Having taken a sip of tea, Mrs Stratton filled an awkward silence that had developed. 'Goodness me, Lily Larkin! You look rather big to be still at school, my dear.' She discreetly ran an eye over the girl's figure. The baggy workhouse uniform did nothing to enhance her shape, yet it was clear she had already developed a pretty bust and neat waist. 'How old are you, now?'

'Fifteen, m'm, and I don't attend school any more. I'm leaving South Grove, too. I've got a job.'

'Oh? What work are you going to do?' Phoebe butted in.

'My cousin has his own business and will employ me in his office.' Lily wasn't going to admit she might be hawking from a market stall and so suffer more of Phoebe's sneers. She wasn't exactly sure what her new boss had in mind for her, but doubted he needed a secretary when he filed all his papers in his pocket. He'd described himself as a costermonger and displayed an invoice for a load of fish, amongst other things. He'd also spoken of selling bed linen and having 'fingers in pies'. She hoped she wouldn't be expected to gut fish or make pastry. But she'd willingly throw herself into doing whatever task he set her. And so would Davy. Mr Wilding had given them a stepping stone to a future, one that eventually wouldn't include him. But for now they'd show their gratitude by working hard.

'Would you like some tea, sir?' Lily addressed the newcomer before Phoebe could interrogate her over her boast to be employed as a clerk.

'Oh, there you are Clive.' Mrs Stratton had turned about, all smiles as her eldest child sauntered up to join them. He appeared to have got over his sulks. 'Clive is my son, just back from Oxford University. He wanted to come today to show his support to the Whitechapel Union and all you hardworking people. As we all do, of course.' She gave Lily's sleeve a pat. 'This is Lily Larkin and her companion is ... what is your name, my dear?'

'Marjorie Blake, ma'am.' Margie shoved her lame hand further into her skirt.

'Would you like tea, Mr Stratton? Or a cake?' Lily politely repeated her question to take the focus off Margie.

Her friend had turned bright red now that all eyes were on her. Margie was no doubt remembering the incident earlier when this fellow had spotted them laughing at him. And so was Lily thinking of it, and hoping he'd not bring it up. She lifted the teapot, ready to pour his tea.

'If you've got nothing stronger to offer me, then I suppose tea will have to do.' He winked and gave an exaggerated sigh.

Mrs Stratton attempted to conceal her mortification by fiddling with her hat. Phoebe used her fingers to smother her spluttering laugh. Workhouse inmates – even those old enough to drink – were severely punished if found with any alcohol. It was strictly prohibited.

Lily's dislike of Clive Stratton strengthened. It had been years since she'd been close to somebody who'd been drinking whisky, but it was a smell she would never forget. He had no need to ask them for booze if he'd brought his own. Lily guessed his intention was to belittle them and make his mother feel uncomfortable too. But he'd amused his sister with his crude joke. A moment later even Phoebe looked shocked at what he did next. He drew from his pocket a knitted doll and with a flourish presented it to Margie.

'There, something for you, my dear. Girls like you don't get toys to play with, I suppose. But you can have it.'

For a second Margie seemed to freeze, then she stumbled back as though he'd hit her. In all her life she'd never received a gift, but she'd had plenty of insults and knew this was another of them, differently dressed. Margie had grown up amusing herself scouring gutters for cigarette cards, salvaged from discarded packets. Her favourite games had been playing hopscotch or Jacks with pebbles, thrown left-handed, on dirty pavements. At eleven years old she'd been brought here, and even those small pleasures were henceforth denied to her. She glanced up at a face, flushed and fleshy from good living, leering at her. Wordlessly she begged him to stop making fun of her and go away.

Clive noticed tears in her eyes and his expression changed. For the first time that afternoon he appeared faintly ashamed of himself. He'd not expected these rough people to be capable of having any dignity. If they had sprung from decent characters, they wouldn't be in a workhouse in the first place, was his thinking. It was an opinion shared by others, including his sanctimonious parents. They put on a good act, but he'd overheard them talking about inmates as though they were a breed apart.

'Here,' he barked, thrusting the toy at Margie. 'I bought it just now from over there. It's yours.' Clive's intention hadn't been to upset the workhouse girl, who was surprisingly pretty. Rather, in his arrogance, he'd expected to flatter her with his attention, and take a swipe at his phoney mother at the same time.

Lily nudged her friend, urging her to take the gift and bring the excruciating episode to an end. Margie pulled her withered hand from her skirt and clumsily fastened the thumb and stumps of fingers about the doll. 'Thank you, sir,' she croaked.

The Strattons hadn't been expecting to see that sight and several intakes of breath were audible. 'Welcome . . . ' Clive mumbled. 'I think it's time I went home.' He directed that at his livid mother, then strode away to say goodbye to Adam Reeve.

'What just happened?' The moment Mrs Stratton and

Phoebe had beat a retreat, Fanny whipped up to join them, crumbs on her lips. She'd found a half-eaten biscuit on a saucer and had hastily dispatched it before anybody noticed. She plonked down a rattling tray of cups and saucers and goggled at the pretty doll Margie had dropped on to the table. It had yellow woolly locks, bright button eyes and a long scarlet dress that reached right the way down the legs to rest on two brown shoes. 'Here, take it ...' Margie said, and pushed the doll towards Fanny. 'Give it to your baby.'

'Don't you want it?' Lily frowned. It was a lovely thing, skilfully made. 'They won't dare take it off you, Margie. They saw Mrs Stratton's son give it to you.' She slid a glance to the master and mistress.

Though obviously shocked, the Stones had kept their distance. Mrs Stratton was a wealthy woman and they intended to keep her patronage. They weren't about to rock the boat because her son had decided to show off in front of some young female inmates.

'He was trying to get me back 'cos he caught us spying on him and laughing at him,' Margie said angrily.

'The whole bloody family are bonkers, if you ask me,' Lily whispered in comfort. She could see Margie was trembling after being singled out. 'Why did you show him your hand?' Lily sounded perplexed. Margie had been at pains to conceal her disability all afternoon.

'Ain't ashamed of what I am. Being a cripple's not a crime, and it's not funny either.' She sniffed. 'Wish now I'd been in the laundry 'stead of in here.'

Lily felt incensed that a rare bright spot in Margie's life had been ruined by a man who didn't know what hardship was. Lily wished she could promise her friend that better things would come her way soon, but lying to her now would add insult to injury.

Fanny had been listening open-mouthed, wondering what the girls were looking so miserable about. In her eyes, if somebody gave you something you just snatched at it and didn't bother with the whys and wherefores. And that's what she did. The doll was already halfway inside her pocket when she said, 'You'll let me have this fer me baby then, Margie, will you?'

Margie nodded. She hadn't given the toy a second glance.

'Better hide it, or Miss Fox'll find an excuse to have it off you,' Lily warned Fanny.

The girls became aware their chatter was no longer being masked by a hum of conversation. They fell quiet too.

A new arrival to the gathering had arrested everybody's attention. Lily's gasp of recognition turned into a spontaneous smile, but before she could hurry over to greet him, Fanny stopped her.

'Oh, my good Gawd! Look who's arrived . . . '

'I'm going over to say hello.' Lily beamed.

'You don't know Greg Wilding, do you, Lily?'

''Course I do.' Lily frowned at Fanny, wondering why she was wearing that odd expression. 'He's my cousin . . . me new boss. I wish it was Friday so I could go off with him now. Not long to wait till I get out of here, though.' It had been a thoughtless thing to say in front of Margie. Lily felt rotten for making her friend upset again. She and Fanny would soon be gone, leaving Margie behind.

Yet excitement still bubbled in her as she gazed at the fair-haired gentleman stationed just inside the door. And he did look a gentleman, even if he didn't quite fit in with the others. In amongst the soberly dressed guests, his broad-shouldered, flash-suited figure stood out like a sore thumb. He beckoned her with a smile and a jerk of his head, and Lily proudly stepped out from behind the table to go to him. She barely knew him; he wasn't *really* a relative, yet just the pretence of kinship between them was enough to make Lily feel mellow.

Clive Stratton hadn't yet managed to make his escape from the boardroom. His mother had pursued him and inconspicuously scolded him for showing his family up in front of lesser mortals. In retaliation he'd not bothered being discreet when finishing the whisky in his hip flask. He was now quite tipsy, but finally the change in atmosphere penetrated his foggy mind. Intrigued, he turned away from the window to discover what had caused it. Having taken in the scene, his expression became grim. He started forward, rather unsteadily, glad he'd been delayed after all. The more whisky he'd shot back, the more he'd told himself the wretched pauper should have shown him proper gratitude for even noticing her, let alone spending money on her. Now he was feeling resentful over another girl who'd rebuffed him after he'd spent money on her. A little tart who had preferred Gregory Wilding to him. And finally he had an opportunity to get even.

Lily was aware of somebody else approaching Mr Wilding at the same time as her. Before she could speak, Clive Stratton did, and she almost recoiled from the stronger smell of whisky about him.

'Guessed it must be you, Wilding,' he slurred. 'Don't know anybody else who dresses like a rutting peacock. Shouldn't you have used the tradesmen's entrance?' Clive ran a disparaging look over the other man, wrinkling his nose as though a bad smell were assaulting it.

'Shouldn't you take more water with it, Stratton?' Greg returned with equal contempt, then turned his back on him.

Lily's smile faded. The hostility between the two men was abundantly clear. And she wasn't the only one worried by it. Mr Stone and the medical officer hurried closer to defuse the situation, but it was too late.

Being dismissed by an inferior as though *he* were the underling was the final straw for the drunk Stratton. Snarling, he balled a fist and threw a punch. Greg managed to dodge aside and the blow made contact with a shoulder rather than a cheek, but he was sent off balance. The craftswomen who'd been doggedly sewing shrieked in one voice as he crashed into the display table. One, nimbler than the rest, managed to get out of the way as the patchwork quilt was dislodged from the display screen and fell on to the heads of those inmates seated under it.

In the pandemonium that followed, Lily was steered away by Adam Reeve, while some younger gentlemen guests held Stratton's arms, preventing him lashing out again. He threw off the men restraining him and stalked from the room, with barely a glance at his white-faced mother.

Lily felt numbed by what she'd witnessed, but the moment she saw Matron's expression she livened up. The woman was glaring at Mr Wilding as though *he'd* started the fight instead of being a victim in it.

Adam had satisfied himself that all the women smothered by the bedspread were uninjured before speaking to Greg. 'Are you all right, sir?'

'Never better,' he said, brushing himself down.

'How did you provoke him into acting like that, Wilding?' Mr Stone strode up to spit out his question.

'This man did nothing wrong,' Adam interjected, outraged. 'I saw it all. It was unprovoked. Stratton's drunk. He's been taking nips from a flask. I saw him.'

Mr Stone glared at the medical officer for poking his nose in.

'Larkin! Stop goggling and help to clear this mess up,' Matron snapped before hurrying away to fuss over Mrs Stratton.

The woman was crying and being comforted by her daughter. The other guests seemed to be abandoning ship as fast as they could. Within a few minutes, only the staff and inmates and Gregory Wilding remained.

'I'll speak to you in my office, Wilding.' Mr Stone knew that somehow he must appease the dratted man. The other attendees were acquaintances and could be persuaded to keep quiet about the rumpus. The Strattons certainly wouldn't mention it. But Gregory Wilding had shown up out of the blue, as was his right, and if he complained to the police that he'd been attacked, with Reeve backing his story, an investigation would ensue. The scandal would result in philanthropists withdrawing their support. And the chairman of the Board of Guardians would demand some answers.

Greg had been righting the chairs that had toppled over, and assisting some of the jittery old women to sit back down. 'It *would* be wise to have a talk,' he finally answered Stone, who looked about to explode in fury for having been made to wait.

The master flung out an arm, indicating he was ready to go now.

'Come on, Lily . . .'

Lily had been folding up the crumpled quilt with one of the needlewomen while Fanny and Margie gathered up the crafts that had been scattered across the room. She saw that Mr Wilding was waiting for her to join him. Her friends stopped their work to dart her anxious looks as she went with the men.

Inside the office, William Stone launched immediately into, 'I trust you understand that the fellow meant you no real harm, Wilding. A youthful slip ... a silly incident because he had unwisely taken drink.'

'Oh, Stratton meant it all right,' Greg said.

'You know one another?' William sounded disbelieving. Wilding could be just a year or two the wretched trouble-maker's senior, but he seemed a decade more mature than Stratton in every way.

'We've got mutual acquaintances.'

William looked as though he expected a better expla-nation than that.

'Nothing that need concern you,' Greg told him bluntly. 'In the circumstances I'm taking me cousin with me now. Lily Larkin's not staying longer in this roughhouse.'

Mrs Stone had just entered the room, having seen the Stratton women out of the building. 'That's not possible. Things have to be arranged.' She wasn't having this flash Harry laying down the law in their domain.

'Think you'll find it is possible.' Greg sounded polite, but looked belligerent.

'Are you prepared to leave now, Larkin?' Mr Stone was furious that they'd been put on the back foot. But ridding himself of the girl was tempting him to swallow his pride. Once she was out, her cousin would have no further need to ever come here again.

Lily barely hesitated before saying, 'I am, sir.' Inside, her guts were roiling in a mix of emotion. This had been dumped on her so suddenly that she could hardly think straight.

'Wait outside in the corridor, then, while the necessary paperwork is done.'

Lily believed they were talking to her, but Matron grabbed her arm as she made for the door.

Minutes later, just Lily and the master remained in the office. He ignored her, scribbling away at his desk while she stood shifting from foot to foot. Soon Matron reappeared with Harriet Fox, carrying a bundle of clothes.

'Get undressed,' Matron snapped.

'What?' Lily backed away, wondering if they'd gone mad.

'Take off our uniform and those boots and put on your own clothes.'

Blushing furiously, Lily darted a look at the master, but he seemed uninterested in seeing a female inmate stripping in front of him. He continued writing.

Harriet held up the dress that Lily had arrived in five years ago. 'Here put that on.'

'It won't fit me,' Lily protested, looking at the small, faded garment she'd worn when ten years old.

Matron started forcefully unbuttoning Lily's clothes and yanking them off her until she stood stripped of even her underclothing.

Harriet ripped the back of the old dress and thrust Lily's arms into it. 'Fits you like that,' she said with a malicious glint in her eyes. She placed the piece of old blanket that had served Lily as a shawl around the shivering girl's shoulders.

'Go back to your duties, Miss Fox.' Matron could see that

the supervisor was enjoying herself rather too much. But they'd done nothing wrong in insisting that their property was left behind. Inmates were discharged in the clothes they'd arrived in.

'Bring Wilding in then, if she's ready to leave.' Mr Stone handed the completed forms to his wife.

At first Greg didn't notice the state Lily was in. He was distracted by the papers being thrust beneath his nose. Then he heard a faint noise.

Lily had smothered a sob, humiliated beyond endurance at him seeing her like this. Her face was scarlet but she lifted her chin. They wouldn't cow her; she just hated them more for their meanness. The dress barely reached her mid thighs and was tight across her bosom, even with the open panel down her spine. Her body was exposed by the gaping material so she backed towards the wall in the hope Mr Wilding wouldn't see her naked buttocks. She let the blanket slither from her shoulders to her waist and gripped it tightly, curling the toes of her bare feet.

Greg slowly looked Lily's waif-like figure up and down. 'Is this a joke?'

'Inmates leave in the clothes they arrived in. Those are the rules.' William Stone peered along his nose in satisfaction.

'Let her put the uniform back on.' Greg approached the desk and William Stone pressed himself back into his chair.

'Uniforms are the property of the Whitechapel Union and cost money.'

Gregory made a noise, almost like a laugh. He took out his cash from a pocket, peeled a note from the roll and, though he felt inclined to stuff it into William Stone's mouth, let it drop to the desk. 'Give her back those rags to dress in. I'll be waiting outside.'

Two minutes later, Lily had on her old uniform over the torn dress, and the boots on her feet. There had been no goodbyes with the Stones; they'd just shut the door behind her, though Lily had heard Matron's muttered, 'Good riddance.' But in the corridor she noticed that there were people waiting to say farewell. Adam must have heard she was leaving straight away. He hurried up to squeeze her fingers before extending a hand for Mr Wilding to shake. 'Take good care of her, please. Lily Larkin's an exceptional girl, bright and hardworking, and will do well at whatever she turns her hand to. She deserves to be happy.'

'I'd like to stay in touch, sir,' Lily blurted. It suddenly seemed rather daunting to be leaving all that had been familiar for five years. She certainly would miss this man. Since he'd come to the workhouse, she had daydreamed that if only she'd been older she would have fallen in love with Adam Reeve. And if he had ever felt the same way about her and they married, then she and Davy would always be safe. Doctors knew about the dangers of alcohol: Adam regularly came into contact with its dreadful blight in those who ended up in here. He would never get into trouble and turn to drink as her father had. Lily believed Charlie Larkin had loved his family but he hadn't protected them as he should have done. His beloved wife had spent her last wretched months alone on a workhouse bed until a dead baby joined her. Lily had been told the girl had been placed in her mother's arms for burial. A cold everlasting embrace was no comfort for the poor little mite she had thought. But Lily had at least been allowed to cross the road to the cemetery to watch

Maude Larkin and her stillborn baby being lowered into a pauper's grave.

Lily spotted her friends, hiding under the stairs for a last look at her. Margie briefly wiggled some fingers in farewell before wiping her eyes with them.

Fanny suddenly dashed over and drew Lily aside. 'You sure you know what you're doing, Lily, going off with *him*?'

Lily's apprehensiveness strengthened, but she nodded, concentrating on soon seeing Davy. 'You'd better go, Fanny, Miss Fox is on to you.' The sour-faced supervisor was lumbering in their direction, making Lily hate her even more. The cow couldn't even leave her alone to spend a few minutes saying a proper farewell to the two girls who'd been like her sisters. She wanted to promise Margie she would come back as soon as she had the money to do so. Lily knew now exactly what was required to satisfy the Stones and get them to sign the necessary discharge papers. What Lily *didn't* know was how on earth she would ever manage it.

'Don't trust Wilding,' Fanny hissed. 'You'll regret it if you do. When I'm out of this dump you'll find me at the Bow Bells tavern. If you'd like to keep in touch, that is.' Fanny looked diffident. Not many decent girls sought former prostitutes as friends.

''Course I'll come 'n' see you. First chance I get.' Lily meant it too. 'Tell Margie I'll not forget about her. I swear I won't.'

'I wish I was off today 'n' all,' Fanny sighed. 'Good luck, Lily.' She turned and trudged away.

'Ready?' Gregory Wilding was watching her with a knowing look in his bright hazel eyes.

'Yes ...' Lily said, and started walking behind him

down the long corridor towards the exit, their footsteps echoing on the hard stone floor. Before she followed him on to the step she hesitated, looking back at a silent, empty space.

Chapter Five

'Oi, darlin', don't forget these. There ... put an extra one in out the goodness of me 'eart.' The lad lobbed a long fat carrot on to the scoop that was cradled on a set of rusty scales. 'Come back 'n' see me tomorrer and I'll give yer summat else you wasn't expectin'.'

His customer elbowed her way back to the market stall, towing a grizzling child. 'Tell me 'usband about you, I will.' She was blushing and gamely acting up to his flirting as he shot the carrots into her shopping bag.

Lily turned red too as the cocky youth spotted her watching him and blew her a kiss. 'Got something fer you 'n' all, sweet'eart,' he called after her, as she hurried on. 'Come 'n' 'ave a squeeze of me onions. Won't find none firmer.'

That ribaldry was heard by Lily's companion, though nobody would have known they were together. Mr Wilding's long stride had taken him some way ahead of her. He halted and retraced some steps. The lad's grin drooped on realising he'd attracted some worrying attention. He dived into neatening a mound of cabbages.

Greg caught Lily's wrist to urge her on. But within

seconds he'd left her behind again, weaving in and out of the teeming shoppers at a pace she couldn't match in her ill-fitting boots. They'd rubbed raw places on her heels weeks ago, and the scabs would be bleeding again. She didn't want to lose sight of him in the swarm, so wriggled past some people and trotted on, hoping to gain some ground.

After they'd turned out of the workhouse gate, Lily had tried to talk to him, but her urgent chatter – thanking him, and rattling off question after question about her brother – had drawn little response. Then they had entered the market, and she'd imagined Mr Wilding might want to wait until they were away from this hubbub before having a proper conversation. It was hard to hear your own voice above the costermongers and housewives who were giving each other as good as they got.

Lily's petite figure dressed in a workhouse uniform had drawn few glances. But she, tagging along behind, had seen people turn and stare at Mr Wilding as he moved amongst them dressed in style. He was easily head and shoulders taller than the majority of the wiry men balancing wooden boxes on their heads, or pushing carts overflowing with fruit and vegetables. The gossiping women were eyeing him for a different reason, and making the navvies jealous.

Mr Wilding was handsome. Lily had thought that the moment she'd first seen him in the master's office. And it occurred to her again now as she trailed in his wake. She wondered, though, if he was embarrassed to be seen with her: a girl dressed in workhouse rags. Feeling indignant that he might have pulled ahead for that very reason, she put on a spurt to catch up with him. When in reach she grabbed at his hand and yanked on it. Greg stopped and looked down at her, freeing his fingers with a jerk as though she'd scalded him. 'What's up?'

'What's up?' she mimicked. 'I thought you were taking me to see my brother, and telling me about my job. Yet you've hardly spoken to me or looked at me. You're going so fast, it's as though you're trying to shake me off.'

He grunted a laugh, then inclined towards her so she would hear every word he said over the din. 'I'm not shaking you off, Lily Larkin. I won't be doing that until you and your brother have paid your dues.'

Lily chewed her bottom lip and slanted a look straight into his cat-like eyes, almost level with her own. 'Good,' she said, ''cos I've had me fill of charity. You give us work and we'll do it. You'll have back every penny we owe you. Don't you worry about that, Mr Wilding.' She gave him a firm nod that sent her untidy dark locks swaying about her pretty features.

'Right . . . glad we understand one another.'

She could see her attitude amused him. She would always be grateful to him for getting her out of the work-house, but she'd said enough thank-yous. He seemed to have no use for gratitude anyway. He'd just made it clear that he'd not helped them from the kindness of his heart. 'Sooner you take me to Davy, sooner we can make a start settling up with you. Then, when we have, we won't bother you again. We'll be all right on our own, you know.' That brave boast made him chuckle and it made Lily squirm for having come out with it. She didn't even have a decent stitch of clothing to her name, and she doubted that Davy was much better off. They were a couple of ragamuffins at this man's beck and call . . . for now.

He'd set off again and Lily did her best to keep up, while things buzzed around in her head. It seemed odd that a posh fellow like Clive Stratton held a grudge against him, and Fanny seemed set against Mr Wilding too. Lily guessed asking him for an explanation about why that was would earn her a rebuke for impertinence. But she'd not judge on hearsay and would take as she found. So far he had been good to her and she'd no complaints to make. He had bought her clothes to wear and given her a chance to walk out of that dump with her head held high. She'd scrimp every day to repay him the pound he'd spent. She would have died of shame being seen on the street in her old ripped dress with her backside on show. Yet still it niggled at her that she could have jumped from frying pan to fire when agreeing to go with him.

She shook off her doubts, concentrating on the bliss of being free. Once out in the air and putting distance between herself and the workhouse, Lily had savoured every sight and sound. The sun was trying to break through the clouds and somewhere in amongst the clamour of rattling carts and bawling market traders, she could just make out a blackbird's song. Her slight body was constantly taking knocks as people pushed past, but Lily loved the jostling. She was amongst *real* people; people with purposeful lives and families to go home to. A fragrance of baking bread was in the air she breathed instead of the stink of desolation and carbolic.

The noise of fractious children being urged along by their harassed mothers brought back poignant memories. Long ago, she would clutch her mother's hand, Davy holding on to the other, as they propelled their way through the crowds on market day. Sometimes, Maude would top and tail her twins in the pram, even when they were too big to ride in it – 'for quickness', she'd say, when Lily and Davy would protest they weren't babies any more and didn't like potatoes squashing their legs. Then, when old enough to help properly, and the pram sold off, Maude would give her children a bag each to carry home. Sometimes they would be heavy with vegetables and other times light, crammed with cotton threads and knitting wool; these would occupy their mother's evening hours in mending and making their clothes before bedtime. In those early days, before Charlie Larkin took to going out so they couldn't watch his decline, he would sit in the parlour too, and play a game of draughts or cards, then chivvy his children to prepare for school in the morning before they turned in.

If Lily had only known what lay in store for them all, she would have wrung more pleasure from every one of those glorious days.

Lost in wistfulness, she didn't notice Mr Wilding had stopped. She crashed into his side as he half-turned towards her. He pointed to a premises, barely visible behind the stall awnings. A pall of frying onions pin-pointed where the caff was, as did the customers emerging through an oilskin suspended over a railing, teeth tearing into doorsteps of bread wedged apart with bacon.

'I'm after somebody in there. I'm late 'cos you're a slow-coach.' He raised an eyebrow at her. 'When I've finished with him, I'll take you for that reunion with your brother. He's doing all right, and you will too, if you toe the line like him.'

Lily bristled at that but mumbled, 'Oh, right you are ... thank you ... ' She felt rather put in her place. If he'd told her he had to rush to a meeting before taking her home, she'd have understood. Perhaps he didn't think she was entitled to explanations. She followed him, stepping over boxes of beetroots, towards the entrance to a shop that had 'Keegan's Café' painted over the door. She'd been hoping to sit down and take off her boots, and perhaps have something to eat if he was still feeling generous. She'd missed her dinnertime meal at the workhouse – not that it was ever much to miss.

'Stay there. It's not a place for kids.' He held her at arm's length as she made to go in with him.

'I'm not a kid!' Lily retorted. A quick peer through the glass had revealed it looked a bit dingy inside, but that didn't matter when a savoury aroma was making her mouth water. 'Anyway, I've been in a caff before.'

'Not this one, you haven't.' He pointed to the pavement. 'Sit down there and wait for me.'

Lily bit her lip to prevent herself answering back. A kid, was she? She thought furiously. She'd be sixteen in a few months' time. She'd been expected to work as hard as an adult since she was eleven years old, when she'd been instructed how to use the washing coppers and airers at South Grove. The reason she'd been denied a place at the Cuckoo School was to keep a full quota of female labour at the workhouse after a flu epidemic had reduced numbers. As fast as the washing coppers were filled with dirty bed sheets, another mountain of soiled cotton would sprout on the laundry's stone floor. Lily still had the stench of it in her nostrils.

She sank down to sit on the pavement with her back against the brick wall. 'I'm old enough to work bloody hard. That's all you need to know,' she muttered below her breath. Then added with more volume, 'Don't be long.'

About to go inside he stepped over to her instead. 'Get one thing straight, shall we, Lily Larkin? You do as you're told and keep that tongue still and we'll all get along.'

'And if I don't?' she challenged him, squinting up mutinously through sunbeams.

He crouched down and took her chin in his fingers. 'If you don't ... we won't get along and that won't be any good, will it?'

Lily flicked her face from his hold. She wasn't fooled by his mild tone. He was threatening her. She ignored him and started easing off her boot, grimacing as the leather stuck to her blister. She was hoping he would go away now but he remained at her side.

'What did that tart say about me?'

Lily blinked but avoided looking at him. She knew he was talking about Fanny and she was angry that he'd insulted her, even if the name he'd used was valid. 'Fanny's me friend,' was all she said.

'Fanny Miller's everybody's friend ... if they've money in their pocket.'

'Don't talk about her like that!' Lily gave him a fierce glare. 'She's me friend.'

'What did she say?'

'Not to trust you. She didn't need to tell me anyway. I'd already worked that one out for meself.'

'Is that right?'

'Yeah ...' Lily cocked her head at him. 'You see ... it's not just us got to toe the line, so have you. Treat us fair and pay us fair or we'll just go and find someone else to work for.'

'That's what you'll do, will you?' He frowned to stop himself laughing.

'If you don't believe me, just wait and see, Mr Wilding.'

'Yeah ... let's wait and see,' he said.

He was looking at her with his foxy eyes in a way that made Lily tingle and remember the kiss she'd given him. 'Why do people think you're a villain?'

'I am a villain.' He made to stand up but sank back down to say. 'Stay away from Fanny Miller when she gets out of the spike, got it?'

'No, I won't! She's me friend. What do you know about any of it? You with your roll of cash to flash about?' Lily twisted her face away, knowing she'd been very unwise to backchat him. Some of that roll of cash had been spent on her. And at present she still needed him far more than he did her.

'Oh, I know about it, Lily Larkin,' he said quietly. 'I know so much about it it'd make your hair stand on end.' He shot upright. 'Stay there. I won't be long.'

Lily started using the hem of her skirt to dry the blood on her heel, wincing at even a light dab. She drew her knees up close to her body to let a fellow pushing a loaded barrow get past on the pavement. He bumped the wheel over some uneven cobbles and an apple slipped off the side. He hadn't noticed or, if he had, he wasn't bothered he'd lost it. Lily kept her eye on the rolling fruit as her belly grumbled a reminder that it needed filling. She grabbed the apple as soon as it was within reach, concealing it under her skirt just in case he came back for it. She'd not tasted an apple or pear since before she'd entered South Grove.

The sun was strong for April, and Lily filtered the dazzling light through her eyelashes. She was impatient to be with Davy, but forced herself to forget about him for a moment and to concentrate on the fellow who held all the aces. She was beginning to understand why Fanny had warned her not to trust Mr Wilding. Lily sensed he was a hard man beneath a thin coating of charm. She wondered what he'd meant about knowing things that would make her hair stand on end. If he'd endured hardship, he'd certainly pulled himself out of it now, and she and Davy would do well to watch him and learn how he'd thrived. Then Lily turned her thoughts to the workhouse. She really wanted to drive every memory of it from her mind, but while Margie was still stuck there, she couldn't. They had looked out for one another for years . . . grown as close as family. A lot of inmates became brutalised by their torment and turned on one another. With her and Margie it had been different, and Lily couldn't bear the thought of her best friend's misery and isolation.

With a sigh Lily found the apple concealed beneath her knees and bit into it, savouring its tart juiciness. She glanced eagerly at the café doorway as a man emerged. But it was a stranger, wiping his greasy lips with a handkerchief before striding off in the opposite direction. Nobody was paying attention to her, so she settled back more comfortably to wait. The sun's warmth was making her feel quite sleepy, so she folded the remnant of blanket that was her shawl, placed it on her knees, then lay her head down to doze. The musty smell of it was in her nostrils and she inhaled, trying to detect her mother's scent. She had nothing left that her mother had touched but this bit of bobbled wool they used to cuddle beneath.

Her eyes suddenly flew wide open as the sound of an argument startled her. Lily shrank back against the wall as two women started shoving one another, stumbling close to her feet. Suddenly the younger of them grabbed at her opponent's hair, causing the coiled grey plait on her crown to unravel. That attack produced some cussing and a retaliatory swipe of fingernails down a sallow cheek. They sprang apart to purposefully roll up sleeves in preparation for battle proper. Lily jumped to her feet as her sore toes got trodden on again.

A little jeering crowd was gathering, but a short chap suddenly elbowed his way through the spectators. He was wearing a flat cap and an oddly blank expression. Despite the fact that the older woman had twice his girth, he yanked on her arm, dragging her stumbling backwards to the tune of her opponent's cat-calls. The disappointed audience started to disperse and, as Lily was barged out of the way, she dropped her precious apple. She glanced about for it in a forest of legs, then saw a shoeless scamp retrieving it from the gutter. He knew it was hers and gave her a wide-eyed stare, waiting for a sign. She smiled her permission and a moment later he'd hared off, with his teeth already sunk into his treasure. She watched his dirty flying soles, and her smile faded. Her mind had been jolted back through the years to the night she'd walked barefoot on frost at ten years old. The memory of that Christmas Eve air spiking her lungs and freezing her body made her catch her breath as though she were again in its icy grip. Yet she would welcome it over this mild atmosphere, if she could turn back the clock to drag her mum and brother past that porter's lodge. Her blurry eyes focused on the urchin disappearing into the crowd, and she wished she'd yelled at him to keep scavenging on the streets of London. If the unsuspecting lad ended up in a workhouse, he might never again taste fruit or see his family.

About to settle her back against brickwork again, the sound of another rumpus made Lily quickly push herself to her feet. This time male voices were raised, and one of them she recognised. The crash of overturning furniture sent her hurrying to find out what was happening.

Her mouth dropped open as she squinted through the dirty windowpane. Mr Wilding had another fellow pinned against the wall by his throat. Equally astonishing was the fact that customers were still seated at the tables that hadn't been sent flying. Unperturbed by the fighting, they continued wielding knives and forks and gulping at mugs of tea. Lily dashed inside just as Mr Wilding ducked to avoid a fist aimed at his cheek. He spotted her then and his face contorted in anger.

'I told you to wait outside,' he roared, staggering back from a blow. His opponent had taken advantage of the distraction, but Wilding soon refastened a hand on his windpipe, driving the other into the choking man's pocket. He pulled out a wallet, then used a foot to swipe his opponent's legs from under him. After some banknotes had been removed, the leather was dropped on to the fallen man's chest.

Lily couldn't hear what Mr Wilding was snarling into the loser's ear, but she guessed it wasn't nice. She hastily retreated to her spot in the street. Just minutes later he was outside too. Instinctively Lily backed away from him.

'You're gonna have to learn to do as you're told pretty damned quick, my gel,' he growled, catching her jaw in a strong hand.

'You just stole his money.' Lily sounded shocked as well as disgusted.

'Did I?' he replied sarcastically.

'Yes, you did, I saw you and I wasn't the only one.' Lily anxiously glanced to and fro, priming herself to make an escape if he suddenly made a run for it. 'You'd better give it back,' she warned. 'If you don't he'll fetch the police and you'll be arrested.' She knew that was true. Her father had bankrupted himself to repay his boss and stay out of gaol.

'Don't think so.' Greg released her face and stuffed the pound notes into his pocket. 'Rule one ... round here we steer clear of coppers. We never tell 'em anything. We sort things out between ourselves. Got it?'

Lily was sending nervous glances at the caff doorway, anticipating the robbed man soon flying out to do battle.

'Better go,' she said urgently, and stepped off the kerb. She'd never find Davy if anything happened to Mr Wilding. She'd guessed he ducked and dived, but just an hour into his company, he'd proved himself to be a proper villain. She felt sad and foolish for being gullible; she and Davy would have to find other jobs. She wasn't risking swapping the workhouse for gaol, and that's where they might end up if they stuck around with him.

Greg was watching her. He shook his head, chuckling as she hopped agitatedly from foot to foot. 'Won't be taking you on heists then, Miss Lily-liver, will I?'

Lily overlooked the taunt to concentrate on something else. 'What work's Davy been doing for you?' she demanded.

'What I tell him to,' he said.

'Have you made him *steal* stuff?'

Greg studied her white face and his expression changed. 'Calm down ... I'm just having a joke.' He pulled a paper bag from a pocket and held it out. 'S'pect you're hungry.

Give that old miser his due ... he can knock up a decent bit of grub.'

Lily barely noticed the enticing aroma wafting from the bag. He thought stealing was a joke, did he? Well she didn't! Her father's fraud had cost his family a terrible price. Yet Mr Wilding had just mocked her for fearing an entanglement in his crime. She punched him in the chest before he could laugh at her again, and would have landed another, but he grabbed her fist before it made contact.

'You think it's funny, do you?' She tried to rip her hand from his and – when he wouldn't let go – kicked a booted foot against his shin. 'Well, I don't!' Suddenly freed, she staggered back, then leapt forward to slap the bag of food to the ground. 'And I don't want that. You've probably stolen it, you thief!' She rushed off into the crowd and kept going, pushing a path through people until her legs ached and her reason returned. By the time she was perched on a low brick wall for a rest, she was crying tears of frustration for not having held her temper. She should have waited until she knew where Davy was before exploding and burning her bridges.

'Here ... that's the last one I buy, you ungrateful little cow.' He'd come up unseen and dropped another paper bag on her lap. 'Eat it; it's not poisoned, and I need you fit to graft,' he said over a shoulder as he strode on.

By the time they were out of the marketplace, Lily had wolfed down every bit of the bacon roll, licked clean the greasy bag and sucked her fingers. She wasn't sure if he had slowed down or she'd speeded up, but she was again walking by his side. 'Thanks for the food ... sorry I wasted the other one,' she said stiffly. She hadn't forgiven him, but it pricked at her conscience that she'd thrown away a delicious meal that Margie would have loved to get her hands on.

He glanced at her. 'You're nothing like your brother, are you?'

'People say we *are* alike,' Lily returned in the same distant tone. She wasn't being contrary. Her mother had told her that when her twins were toddling, nobody could tell them apart until they started dressing differently.

'Didn't mean in looks,' he said. 'You were out in front when guts and manners were dished out.'

Lily knew Davy could be surly. If Mr Wilding was letting her know he'd still to tame her but that already he had her brother pinned beneath his thumb ... well, he'd soon find out he'd never cow her. And once they were reunited, she'd help Davy break free of Wilding. She didn't blame her brother for doing what he'd needed to, to survive. She'd thank Davy for being astute enough to coax his boss into being their ally. As a team she and Davy would be strong enough to fend off any enemy, even this one, if that's what Wilding turned out to be. Lily's sigh of determination was curtailed.

'Much as I like polite kids, if you lay into me again, Lily Larkin, I'll clump you back.'

'Sorry ... ' Lily mumbled, and meant it. She was ashamed she'd done that.

'I haven't stolen anything off Keegan ... just helped meself to what's rightfully mine, in the usual way we do things round here. He owed me for boxes of fish and spuds. I was done waiting for him to pay me, so had it out with him. He tried to stitch me up. Nobody gets away with that.'

Lily gave him a diffident look, which lingered and

turned to a frown as she noticed he had a bruise on his cheek from the fight.

'And that's the last time I'll ever explain myself to you. If you'd done as you'd been told and stayed put, you'd've been none the wiser, would you. So . . . learn from it.'

'Yes, sir . . . ' she said with a whisper of insolence. But she believed what he'd said and felt reassured that at least the police weren't on his tail.

'What's funny?' Greg had noticed Lily smiling to herself.

'Nothing really,' she said, screwing up the empty bag and putting it into her pocket. An irrepressible laugh erupted. 'It's just . . . you told Mr and Mrs Stone you weren't leaving me in their roughhouse after that pig Stratton whacked you. I've only been outside a matter of hours and almost got tangled up in two fights already. While you were gone, some women had a scrap and stood on me toes.'

'Bet you're glad you took the job now, eh?' He slanted her an ironic look.

'Remains to be seen about that, Mr Wilding . . . ' His dry tone had sent Lily into a fresh burst of giggling that was so infectious he chuckled too. She'd needed to let off steam and wiped mirthful tears from her eyes, pleased that they seemed more harmonious. 'Thanks for getting me this far, anyway. Me and Davy will work hard and settle up with you as soon as we can. But we only really need one another.' She held out a hand for him to shake. 'Pax?'

He looked at her extended fingers with studied suspicion. 'What's that mean?'

'It means no more fighting . . . a truce for now.'

He briefly touched her hand with fingers that had grazed knuckles. 'Your brother said you were clever. Cleverer than him, I reckon. Bet he loves that.'

'He does,' Lily whipped back. ''cos he knows he can match me in his own way.' She cocked her head cheekily. 'If Davy wasn't smart, *I* wouldn't be here with you now, would I?'

He grunted a laugh, seeming about to deny it, but instead of commenting he pulled some cigarettes from his pocket.

Lily kept watching him, expecting him to finish their conversation, but he lit the cigarette, flicking away the match.

A moment later all he said was, 'You've held me up running off like that. Should've been back by now. I've got stuff to do.'

Chapter Six

'Give over, Lil, you're strangling me.'

'Sorry ...' With a bashful chuckle, Lily removed her arms from her brother's neck. Seconds later, having gazed at his beloved face, relief and affection overcame her and she crushed him in another bear hug. 'Can't believe we're really back together,' she said against his jacketed shoulder. The material felt rough and smelled dirty, but she rubbed her cheek on it anyway. Even though she'd not seen or spoken to him in years, the scent of his skin was the same, the sound of his voice hauntingly familiar. 'I've missed you so much, Davy. I've got a million things to ask you and to tell you. We've lots of catching up to do.'

'Missed you, too,' he mumbled, easing himself from her embrace. 'I miss Mum 'n' all. Think of her all the time, I do, Lil. Did you manage to see her before she passed away?'

Lily used her knuckles on her bloodshot eyes, repeatedly swallowing a lump in her throat. Davy's sad blue gaze was pleading for some comfort, but she had none to give. And the burden of sorrow needed to be shared. 'I begged to be allowed to visit Mum as soon as I heard she was in the infirmary. Matron refused; the old bag said it could spread infection in the dormitory.' Lily had never believed that excuse; the meanness of spirit, designed to keep inmates in their places, was the reason she'd been denied the chance to say goodbye to her mother. And Lily had desperately wanted to cuddle and talk to her only remaining parent, so that she wouldn't endure a lonely, undignified death like her father's.

Davy would argue that Charlie Larkin had deserved what he'd got. But Lily still loved her dad and missed him. She wished she'd not been bound by a child's fear and had asked him why he'd done what he'd done while she'd had the chance. She'd been young – just nine – but it had occurred to her even then to challenge Charlie Larkin over his disgraceful behaviour. Duty, embarrassment: whatever it had been that had kept her tongue-tied had been stronger than her need to know why he'd risked destroying it all to steal from his boss. He'd had a good job and regular wages and, though they hadn't been flush, they'd always got by. And then suddenly it had all gone and so had her father.

As for her mother, she'd shouted and argued with Charlie but had remained loyal. Her children had never heard her speak ill of him, and neither had the nosy neighbours to whom Maude gave short shrift. Her only fault had been to neglect herself because she loved others too much. She could have abandoned her children to the workhouse, as Margie's mother had done Margie. Maude Larkin had been lovely outside and in, and could have attracted a man to care for her, if not her husband's kids. Lily's reflectiveness was interrupted by a growled question from Davy.

'Did those bastards at least tell you where Mum's buried? I'd like to visit her resting place, Lil.' His voice was breaking due to adolescence and his upset, making his words emerge unevenly pitched.

'I do know where she is,' Lily soothed him. 'They let me go to the funeral. I'll show you, and we can take some flowers.' Davy appeared eager to keep talking about it, but Lily didn't want to now. He believed their mother had died from bronchitis, but the struggle to bring their lifeless sister into the world had been the death of Maude Larkin. A family tragedy of such magnitude deserved to be reported solemnly, not to the accompaniment of raucous talk and a fellow playing a mouth organ.

'Are they your friends as well as colleagues?' Lily looked over Davy's shoulder at the two youths, squatting around an upturned orange box on which rested playing cards and beer bottles. They'd taken a breather from gambling to whistle and tap their feet along to a tune that one of them was tooting out on a harmonica. Every so often the lads glanced over, but so far had said nothing to her other than chorusing gruff hellos when she was introduced as Davy Larkin's sister.

'Bobby Smith and Fred Jenkins are me pals fer now,' Davy said. 'But I shan't be stickin' around here for ever.'

Lily nodded vigorously. She was glad he agreed with her way of thinking that they should cut loose once they were no longer beholden to Mr Wilding.

An hour ago, she and her new boss had eventually reached his home territory in Poplar. Lily had been expecting to meet Davy at his digs, but of course he'd still been at work – and would be until sundown, she'd been told, as Mr Wilding unlocked his warehouse.

He hadn't felt obliged to add anything else, or to entertain her in the interim. He had left her to her own devices

97

while he got on with his work. She'd been wrong thinking him too crude a businessman to own a desk. He did have one – a battered affair shoved up one end of the depot that was otherwise taken over by the tools of his trade: stacked pallets – some empty; some containing a few leftover wilting vegetables. There were barrows, too, of varying shapes and sizes, and long metal poles and canvases to erect market stalls. All were neatly arranged to make the most of the available space. Though Lily had itched to demand some answers about her job and her accommodation, she had been wary of disturbing him as he wrote things down and moved desk drawers in and out. They'd had no more run-ins, but she was getting to know him and was familiar enough with his character and her indebtedness to tread carefully. Don't trust him, Fanny had said. Yet oddly, Lily did. She hadn't once doubted that her brother would arrive after he'd finished work. And duly Davy *had* shown up, pushing a handcart in a line with his two colleagues.

At the first sight of her brother, she'd abandoned her aimless inspection of a costermonger's paraphernalia to dash to the doorway, dizzy with euphoria. Davy's huge grin of welcome showed he too had believed this day would never come. Then he had given her a frown. Lily had understood his warning and had held back on launching herself at him. She had stood aside to allow the convoy to park up. The trio had unloaded their unsold stock and received a bawling-out from the boss for having brought it back. But the real business of accounting for the sales money had taken up most time. Finally Davy had been free to turn in her direction. She'd needed no more permission to rush to enclose him in her greedy arms.

At some point Mr Wilding had left, but Lily hadn't

noticed him go. The moment she'd clapped eyes on her brother, nobody else had mattered.

'Do you sleep in here?' Twilight would soon fall, and with it the coldness of evening would close in on them. Lily's thoughts turned to practicalities. She glanced about at the cramped space. There was no obvious spot suitable to bed down, although a rickety-looking wooden stairway rose to a floor above.

'Nah . . . got a bedsit with those two.' He jerked a nod at the rowdy lads. Another game of cards was in progress, and it seemed some cheating was going on.

Lily didn't welcome the idea of sharing a bedroom with strange youths who looked older than she was. 'Be best if we get a room of our own now, Davy.'

He shrugged. 'I'll speak to the guv'nor when he gets back and pays us. Depends what mood he's in, though.'

It was the first reference her brother had made to Gregory Wilding. 'Is he a good boss?' She'd detected a worrying undercurrent in her brother's comment.

Davy pulled a face. 'Depends what you mean by *good*,' he said darkly.

Mr Wilding had done a lot for them, and Lily had expected a more favourable response. 'Where did you meet him?' she asked.

'Chrisp Street market.' Davy seemed reluctant to elaborate. Eventually he admitted sheepishly, 'I got caught pinching an old coat off a stall there. The old miser was gonna call the coppers on me until Mr Wilding stepped in. He gave him ten bob and offered me a job so I could work off what I owed.'

Davy read his sister's horrified look. 'I *had* to pinch it, Lil. It was wintertime and bloody freezing, and all I had

99

on was me school shirt and trousers, and they was in tatters by the time I reached the East End. I'd been sleeping rough on the way from Hanwell and had nothing to eat but carrots and parsnips. Almost tore out me fingernails digging those up; the earth was rock hard. I was in a right old state by the time I got here.'

'I know . . . I saw you, and thought you looked scrawny.'

'You should've seen me before,' he said ironically. 'I was on the up by then. At least I had a job and a bed to go to.'

Lily frowned; she'd believed he'd not long turned up in the neighbourhood when she'd spotted him on the Mile End Road. 'When did you get back here?'

'Over a year ago. I got away during that fire. Did me a favour, that lad burning down the barn; was hairy at the time, though.' Davy shivered his shoulders. 'About twenty of us was in there learning about blacksmithing. We were all congregating around the furnace and taking a turn on the bellows and tools. I could see one of the kids was up to something, so kept me eyes peeled. I soon guessed his game; he wasn't loitering by the fire to keep warm.' Davy hissed a noise of disgust. 'I shook me head at the stupid sod, warning him not to, but he just give us a grin like he was mental, then lobbed a burning cloth on some straw.'

Lily gasped in horror, covering her mouth with her fingers.

Davy widened his eyes to let her know he'd not stopped shocking her yet. 'Everybody was running round like headless chickens, getting in each other's way. The master was trying to get the boys in line, to file out properly, but a ruck started 'cos they all knew it was a waste of time. It was every man for himself.' Davy's expression turned bleaker. 'I just thought I'd leave 'em to it and sort meself out. So I squeezed out of some loose boards at the back of the barn. I never intended to scarper, just to get out of danger.' He paused. 'You should've seen it go up, Lil ... ' Davy circled his arms to show the spread of it and made a whooshing sound. 'Anyway, I made it as far as the lodge, and when I saw the front gates were open I ran out on to the road in a panic and kept going.'

'They told me you'd perished.' Lily closed her eyes at the memory of that terrible day. 'I was in such a state, thinking I'd nobody left.' She cupped his thin face between her palms.

'You won't get rid of me that easily ... though I did reckon at the time we was all goners.' He took up his tale again. 'I hung about close to the school for hours. Once I'd calmed down, I thought about going back in, but knew I wouldn't 'arf get a beating if I did.' He covered his face with his forearms as though to block out painful memories. 'They strap you down to a table over there to whip you, and the rotten swine don't stop till your back bleeds.' He sniffed. 'I'd already had a taste of it. I wasn't risking being flayed again. I guessed if I didn't turn up they'd think I was burned to bits, 'cos there was nothing left of the barn.' He screwed his fists against his closed eyes to block out grisly images. 'Don't know if all the other kids made it out. Hope they did ... even the nutcase that started it.'

'Thank heavens you kept your nerve that day.' Lily comforted him with a peck on the cheek. 'If you hadn't, you wouldn't have met Mr Wilding and I wouldn't be here with you now. It's a wonderful fresh start for us.'

'When I got to town and saw the markets and all the

food, it seemed like heaven. I snaffled the first thing I could get me hands on to eat.' Davy tutted. 'A bloody head of celery. But I grabbed some coppers and a sixpence too when the old girl on the stall had her back turned.' He paused. 'Them pennies kept me going for a couple of days, and I slept under a cart. Then it turned real cold and I had to get a coat of some sort ... and after that you know the rest. I met the guv'nor and here I am.'

'And here *I* am ...' Lily said with a smile, yet she felt a little uneasy about the way her brother glibly spoke of stealing. She knew she had to make allowances, though. He'd had to survive somehow until he found work. But the memory of her accusing Mr Wilding of theft niggled at her. She wished now she'd not acted so self-righteously about it all. He could have thrown in her face what he knew about her brother being light-fingered.

'It was a bright idea to get your boss to help rescue me from the workhouse.'

'Wasn't my idea ... it was his.'

'Oh?' Lily sounded surprised and disappointed.

'I'd have got you out of there eventually,' Davy said earnestly. 'I just couldn't until I was bringing in enough to keep us both. The master would've sent me away with a flea in me ear if I'd turned up to get you looking like a tramp without a penny to me name.'

'After he'd picked himself up off the floor.' Lily wasn't wholly joking. 'The master and mistress would've thought you were a ghost, Davy.'

'Giving those two heart attacks would've been a bonus,' he chortled wickedly. 'Anyhow, I told Mr Wilding that I needed a pay rise to support me sister. The Scrooge just said he'd get you out of there himself, and give you a job so you could pay your own keep. And that was that. If he says it, he does it: that's his way.'

A thought occurred to Lily. 'Was he with you on the Mile End Road that day? I didn't see him.'

'Well, he saw you.' Davy chucked his sister under the chin to buck her up. She still looked deflated that he hadn't been the one to charge to her rescue. 'Crying shame the workhouse didn't burn down on that day you climbed over the wall.' Davy playfully nudged her in the ribs to distract her from thinking he'd let her down. 'I won't forget that for as long as I live. The guv'nor and the lads had a laugh when I told 'em about how you broke the rules good 'n' proper.'

'It wasn't funny for long,' Lily said ruefully. 'I got the cane and solitary confinement. *And* they cut off all me hair again.' She twirled a thick brown tress around a finger. 'It's grown back all right now, though.'

The fire on that occasion had been found to have started accidentally in a kitchen where frying fat had ignited. The billowing smoke had made it all seem worse than it actually was and the inmates were all herded back inside eventually ... far too soon for those who'd relished the little drama and the break in the interminably boring regime.

'I stayed low when I first got to town in case I got carted back to school. Nobody'll bother about me now I'm turned fifteen and found a job.' Davy shrugged. 'Anyhow, Mr Wilding reckons the Guardians are just glad to be rid of the kids, dead or alive.'

'We'll work hard and save every farthing to pay off what we owe him. Then we can start our own business, Davy,' she said excitedly. 'Me friend Fanny is going in with her sister and selling door to door. How about if we try—'

'Don't want no dead-end capers like that!' Davy inter-jected. 'Need to think big. I'm not knocking me guts out for peanuts.' He sounded irritated. 'Anyhow, we can't pay off everything we owe; it'll take too long and keep us shackled to him. Guv'nor knows it too.'

Lily had expected Davy to show some enthusiasm for her suggestion, not find immediate fault with it. 'What's your plan then? Shall we leave and just bring him back money every week from what we earn?' Lily could see disadvan-tages in that, but she was keen to give Davy a chance to air his ideas. But he didn't answer her question.

'He got those two the same way he caught me. Down on their luck with nowhere to live.' He jerked his head at his workmates. 'Guv'nor makes out he's doing you a favour when really he's just out for himself. We're cheap labour, making him rich. So I ain't worried about short-changing him right back, in me own way.'

'You would've been worse off if you'd ended up in prison for stealing a coat,' Lily fairly pointed out. 'And can't blame Mr Wilding for wanting to make a profit. So, let's work hard and save up—'

'Work hard . . . save up . . . ' Davy mimicked.

Lily frowned at him for mocking her. Their reunion was barely an hour old, yet already the shine seemed to be rubbing off of it. But she'd not give up. The prayers she'd whispered into the darkness in her dormitory bed had been miraculously answered. Davy was with her and they had employment. Maude Larkin's kids had a chance to do all right after all, thanks to a Cockney costermonger, not the Cuckoo School.

Lily tried to catch her brother's eye but he turned away. It niggled at her that he didn't properly appreciate how lucky they were. He seemed different, but that wasn't surprising, considering what he'd been through. Perhaps unbeknown to her she'd changed as well. They might settle back into familiar ways once they'd left behind the sadness and bitterness of their parents' loss and their wasted years.

'Don't let's bicker over it.' Lily caught hold of Davy's hand. 'I know you're impatient to move on to something better . . . and so am I.' Her brother seemed to want to bite the hand that currently fed him. But putting their noses to the grindstone for their boss for a few months seemed a small price to pay to secure an ally. Lily was astute enough to know that good friends were hard to find, and that they might need Mr Wilding again someday. 'Just need to be sensible about it . . . '

'Being sensible ain't the way,' Davy scoffed, pulling his fingers from hers. 'Being crafty and mean like he is, that's how you get ahead. You'll learn that soon enough, now you're out in the *real* world.'

Lily's conscience wouldn't let her agree with her brother, though she knew he wanted her to. 'It's not mean of him to expect back what he's spent on us, Davy.'

'You don't know him, so why are you sticking up for him?' he demanded. His eyes darted past Lily as his workmates threw down their cards and jumped up. 'Shush . . . guv'nor's back,' he hissed, jerking a nod at the figure in the doorway. 'I'm getting me wages. I'm starving and me 'n' the lads go to the caff about now.' He took a step away from Lily, then hesitated, scrutinising her appearance. 'You can't work a market stall in those rags, Lil. You'll get laughed at.'

Naively Lily believed that he was about to offer to buy her some clothes from his pay packet.

'You'd better ask him to give you a sub so you can lay out for some second-hand togs. He'll just add it to your tally.' Davy tapped his head then muttered below his breath, 'He's got it all up here ... don't forget nothing, him.'

Lily caught up with Davy, curious to know the identity of the person who'd followed Mr Wilding inside. 'Who's that?' she whispered in her brother's ear. Her admiring gaze travelled from a dainty hat, perched on a coiffured head of fair hair, to a pair of stylish buttoned boots.

Lily had admired the elegant costume Phoebe Stratton had been wearing that afternoon, but this girl looked equally smart. Lily could detect a scent of violets. Being in the company of such femininity made her acutely conscious of her own bedraggled appearance. She tugged down her workhouse skirt, hoping to conceal her cracked leather boots beneath its hem.

'That's his girl, Jane Wright,' Davy muttered over a shoulder, and got in line with the others to collect his wages.

'Gawdawmighty! You wasn't kidding, Greg. Look at the bleedin' state of her.' The young woman might have looked angelic, but she spoke like a navvy. 'See what you mean about she needs summat to wear.' Jane wrinkled her nose and looked Lily up and down.

Lily stopped being in awe of this vision of loveliness. She bridled at being inspected as though she'd just emerged from beneath a stone. Her chin shot up in reaction to the heat flooding her cheeks. One of the youths was smirking. The other lad who'd been playing the harmonica looked embarrassed, and so did Davy, hanging his head. He'd not leapt to defend her, so a blushing Lily spoke up for herself.

'It's what they give you to wear in the workhouse. So, if you don't reckon it'll suit you, best stay outside.'

'I will, don't you worry. Rather go on the game than go in a spike,' Jane Wright trumpeted. She slid a glance at Greg, perhaps hoping he'd laugh, but he didn't and continued counting out coins.

'Well, some of those girls end up in there as well, so you might yet get a taste of skilly,' Lily snapped back. Then wished she hadn't, as Jane lunged at her and slapped her face.

'You keep yer place, you little maggot. Who d'you think yer talking to?'

'I'm talking to you ... ' Lily gasped out when she'd got over the shock of being hit.

'Enough!' Greg roared and swung a warning look between the belligerent pair.

Lily's cheek was stinging, but she refused to raise a hand to rub it. Davy sent her an angry look, as though she'd been the one to start trouble. When it was his turn to be paid, he received his cash without asking about them having their own room. Lily caught his eye and gave him a significant nod, but he glanced away. Once again Lily felt disheartened. Her brother had never possessed her gumption, but he needed to make some effort if they were to make a go of it. Her exasperation didn't last long; he meant so much to her that she found an excuse: he'd already been ticked off for bringing back unsold stock and might not want to ask his boss for favours just yet.

Lily had no such qualms; she'd sooner things were straight between them all from the start. 'Me 'n' Davy want our own bedsit, so if you know of one going, could we have a look at it, Mr Wilding?'

Greg turned to her with a quizzical expression. 'You want your own room?'

'Yes. How much does one cost?'

'How much have you got?'

Lily bit her lip at his sarcasm. She glanced at Davy, but it seemed she still couldn't rely on any help there. Her brother was larking around with his workmates, pretending ignorance of what was going on.

'Can I have an advance on me wages and pay our rent out of it?' Lily asked.

'Hark at her! Miss High and Mighty wants her own place,' Jane crowed.

'Even cheap rooms are expensive. We'll see how things go. For now you can bunk with Jane.' Greg was no longer teasing Lily.

'Do what?' Jane snorted. 'Ain't having some workhouse ragbag in me digs. Gawd knows what I'll catch.' She plunged her fists on her shapely hips and glared at her boyfriend. 'She can have the room and I'll move in with you.' Jane brightened, giving him a wink. 'You'll like that.'

'You'll stay where you are,' he said, extricating himself from her clutch. 'You'll have the place to yourself again soon. Larkin and his sister aren't intending to stop around here for much longer.'

It was a mild comment that drew Davy's attention. He glowered at his sister in a way that made Lily wonder what she'd done wrong now.

'She'll need something to wear for work tomorrow.' Greg spoke to Jane. 'Find her something plain you've no more use for.'

'Well, I ain't giving her a decent dress, that's for sure . . .

not unless you're taking me to Bond Street for something new. 'Bout time you treated me.' Jane's suggestion drew no more than a sardonic smile. She swung a thoughtful look between the waif-like drab and her boyfriend. 'She's just a kid ... got no figure ... might not have anything to fit her.'

'Find something. She can take it in.'

Lily had had her fill of being talked over as though she were invisible and still at Whitechapel workhouse. She wasn't putting up with it any longer. 'I don't want to live with her and I don't want any of her cast-offs either. I'll take a sub on me wages and buy my own stuff, thanks all the same.' She paused to control her temper. 'And as for lodgings, me 'n' Davy will live together,' she announced. 'We haven't got back together for you to separate us again after five minutes.' She glanced about. 'How about if the two of us bed down in here then, until we've enough put by for a proper place?'

'Don't be daft, Lil. I told you, I've got a place to kip with me mates.' Davy hurried over, red-faced and apologetic. 'Me sister don't mean to be a nuisance, guv'nor. She ain't used to how things go on outside a spike. She'd be much obliged to have a pallet on the floor of Jane's. Say sorry to Jane for what you said.' He dug his sister in the ribs with his elbow.

Lily stared at Davy, silently pleading with him to back her up, but he averted his eyes. Affecting not to see Jane's smug expression, she mumbled, 'Sorry.'

'I'm off with me pals to the caff.' Davy backed away now things seemed on an even keel. 'I'll let you settle yourself in and catch up with you in the morning, Lily.' He glanced at his boss. 'Night, guv'nor,' he mumbled.

The other two lads grunted similar goodbyes to the boss, and a moment later Lily was staring at the warehouse door as it creaked shut.

Chapter Seven

'I'll start work straight away in the morning, if that's all right?'

'It is.'

'How much is my pay, please?'

'Seven and six a week, Monday to Saturday. Start at dawn, finish when it's done. Lodgin' thrown in. Pay for your own grub.'

Lily digested her terms of employment as far as she'd understood the clipped list. Rather than raise questions just yet, she turned her mind to her lodgings. 'Your girl-friend doesn't want me staying with her.'

'She'll put up with it. Won't be for long, will it?'

'No,' Lily mumbled. He knew – as did she – that her hopes of being independent in the near future had been set back. Not by him, but by Davy. Her brother had moaned about being hard done by, and about wanting his own business. Be that as it may, it was obvious he'd not yet risk giving up the devil he knew to be his own boss. 'What's my tally so far, Mr Wilding?' Lily was concentrating on straightening her bootlaces, though she'd perfected the bows.

'We're quits.'

She'd been avoiding his eyes, but now brought her chin up and saw he was too occupied to bother with mockery. Davy had humiliated her, then swanned off with his pals without a backward glance. Shortly afterwards Jane – sighing heavily – had been dispatched to buy some beef and onion pies. Left alone with Mr Wilding, Lily had felt foolish for having given him the impression that Davy was as devoted to her as she was to him. Her brother hadn't even invited her to go to the caff to celebrate their reunion with a cup of tea. She'd felt tempted to ask if she could tag along, but in his present mood that would just have irritated him. She knew her boss was aware she felt crushed by it all.

'You said we had dues needed paying.' Lily cleared her throat to gain his attention.

'Your brother's got debts.' Greg turned her way and shrugged. 'As for you, a bacon roll won't bankrupt me. Have it as a welcome-home present.'

So he *was* feeling sorry for her after Davy's snub. She didn't want his pity or his charity.

'You bought me two lots of food. And Jane will want something for her old clothes. And you paid Mr Stone for this . . . ' She twitched her skirt, then regretted reviving the memory of another time she'd been humbled in front of this man, standing half-naked in the master's office.

'I'd be embarrassed to make you stump up for it.' He barely glanced her way. 'I paid Stone a quid for it to show the skinflint up.' While talking to her, Greg had been making his way along the neat line of carts jammed nose to tail. There were at least ten of them. Periodically he dislodged a stub of pencil from behind his ear, licking the lead and noting any damage in a book.

'Thanks … but if Davy has to settle up with you, so will I.'

'Oh, he has to settle up, all right.' He wobbled a loose wheel on the largest cart, testing its iron rim with a kick.

Lily's heart sank. From that dry comment she deduced Davy's debt was substantial. Little wonder her brother had hinted at doing a moonlight flit rather than paying it all off. Lily stared at the bruise on her boss's angular profile. She reckoned he would know how to find people who crossed him and how to deal with them when he did.

'I don't want favours off you.'

'The bacon rolls were fourpence ha'penny each. I'll take ten bob for Jane's old clobber and a quid for the uniform then.'

Her pride had cost her dear, and Lily wished she'd kept quiet. It would take ages before she was in a position to start squirrelling away some of her wages to do the things she wanted to do. Her goals now went far beyond keeping herself and Davy housed and fed. Despite her brother's faint heart and their grim financial situation, Lily felt quite invincible, overflowing with ideas of what she wanted to achieve. She wouldn't nag Davy to fall in with her way of thinking. Maybe he was wise to be chary of rushing to make changes they might live to regret. He was still the most cherished and important person in her life.

There were other relationships she wanted to nurture too. Margie had to be rescued from her miserable existence in the workhouse. Lily hadn't yet got a clue how to bring about her friend's freedom, but a solution wouldn't come cheap. Apart from that, Lily was determined to see Adam Reeve again. This time their meetings would be on an equal footing. From the start they had liked one another, but their difference in status had built a barrier between them. Lily Larkin, workhouse stray, was no more. She had a job and a brother. She even had a roof over her head. Although her sleeping arrangements weren't ideal, anything beat into a cocked hat a cold, silent dormitory. A mattress on the floor of Jane's was a start, and Lily was grateful for it. But she wasn't about to accept less than her due. If she didn't ask, she wouldn't get. Seven and six seemed little reward for long hours and hard graft, even for a workhouse apprentice. If her brother was getting paid the same pittance, she could understand his discontentment. 'Do we all get an equal rate of pay, Mr Wilding?'

He grunted in amusement. 'You forming a union on your first day, Lily Larkin?'

'Just asking,' she retorted. 'If I'm doing the same work and the same hours, don't see why I shouldn't get equal pay. Once I know the ropes, I'll work as hard as the lads. You'll see.'

'Reckon you would too ... but you're not all doing the same work.'

She was tempted to quiz him further about her colleagues' pay, but had a feeling she'd be told to mind her own business if she did. Her prickly brother might not like her prying either. She wished that she and Davy had discussed money earlier, but there had been no time. They'd spoken of more important things. The most vital news of all, though – about their lost sister – she'd still to reveal.

Lily trailed in her boss's footsteps along the line of barrows. They were of every shape and size. Some as small as the one her father had kept in the shed, many long years ago. A reminder of that garden brought with it a redolence of mown grass, and the music of her mother's laughter. A forgotten game they'd play popped into Lily's head. On hot days during the long summer holiday from school, Maude would throw over the washing line a candlewick bedspread to be pulled tight and weighted down either side with stones. Sometimes she would join her twins in their little tent. They'd have a picnic protected from the midday sun then, satiated with warmth and contentment, would curl up and drowse to bees' lullabies.

Enchanted by her sweet memories, Lily hadn't noticed Greg Wilding was watching her. When she did, she snapped herself out of the doldrums. 'So, which cart am I in charge of?' Her voice sounded husky with emotion. 'Don't suppose pushing a barrow loaded up with sacks of spuds can be worse than yanking wet sheets up to the ceiling.' She was annoyed at herself for continually slipping back into nostalgia. Her mother would be telling her now to gee herself up and make that fresh start instead of moping. 'At least I shan't get soaked while straining me arms. Sometimes we couldn't get a proper grip on the ropes 'cos of dripping water making our fingers slip.' She wished he'd stop staring at her as though he knew she was just a kid who wanted her mum. 'I'll take this one.' Lily clumsily grabbed the battered contraption closest to her. She sprang back, red-faced, as he had to use a hand and foot to prevent it overturning on her.

He lobbed the notebook on to the desk and stuck the pencil back behind an ear. 'I'm giving you a job here, in me lock-up, so don't act like a bull in a china shop or you'll bring a stack of pallets down on your crust.' He pulled from a pocket a handful of folded papers, much as he had on the day she'd first met him, and he'd shown the master his credentials. 'The medical officer vouched for

115

you and I need somebody with savvy to set my records straight in case the taxman comes callin'.' The bills went the same way as the book, landing with less of a thud on the desk. 'Apart from logging purchases, you can keep a proper note of all the hired stuff.' He tapped his skull. 'I keep it all up here, but it's about time things got written down. Half a dozen spare carts are rented daily, and extras as well.' With a swing of his arm he indicated poles, tarpaulins, ropes and other equipment that was propped, stacked and hooked all about the place. 'Customers turn up for stuff as early as three o'clock to get a head start at the markets. Billingsgate, Spitalfields, Smithfields – all open at the crack of dawn and me regulars know to be ready for the off.' He pointed at her. 'So you'll need to be up and have your wits about you. You're young and you're new and you're a girl, and they'll think that counts in their favour and try running rings round you. They'll probably reckon I've gone nuts for putting you in charge. They're probably right.'

'No, they're not!' Lily interjected with a sharp nod. 'I'll show you and them that I know what I'm doing. Adam Reeve wasn't just saying I'm clever to be nice. He *knows* me.'

'Does he? Not in every sense, I hope,' Greg said sourly. 'Never mind,' he followed up when Lily frowned for an explanation. 'Right, I'm putting me faith in you, gel, to hold yer own once you're clued up to the routine. First thing tomorrow I'll go through everything and teach you what's what and how to spot when a punter's trying to have you over.'

'I won't let you down, Mr Wilding.'

'Even if a lairy lad gives you some patter?'

'What?'

'You're a pretty gel, so don't give 'em the come-on or they'll try to weasel round you with a bit of flirting.'

Lily was quiet for a moment, taken aback that he thought her pretty when she knew she looked a mess and needed a bath. She felt enormously pleased by his offhand compliment but brushed it off. 'I'm not a fool, you know.'

'Neither am I.'

Lily felt rather strange as he continued staring at her with those wolf-like eyes. Then he said, 'Billy Tate is a customer of mine. You saw him earlier, selling off one of my carts in the market. He's hired it for the week. He'll be bringing it back at some time. He thinks he's Jack the Lad. Got a lot to say for himself.'

'So have I.' Lily remembered the cocky youth with his winks and innuendoes. 'He's just a show-off.'

'They all are. That's how they attract the housewives. Women like it. They come back for more and stay loyal to a particular coster.'

Lily snorted her derision. '*I'd* buy off the cheapest stall with the freshest stuff,' she said, ever pragmatic.

'That's why I couldn't let you loose out there, with your attitude,' he said wryly. 'Housewives who've had a bellyful of their old man like a bit of sweet-talk from a handsome lad down the market. And you're not a lad, but the costers will take to you. Besides, you're too honest. You wouldn't keep yer thumb on the scale while loading it, would you?'

'No! That's sneaky.'

'Yeah ... and there's bunce in it ... extra money,' he explained when she looked mystified.

Lily didn't want to seem prissy, so kept her thoughts to herself about the methods he used. Her boss wasn't squeaky clean. But she liked him. And she sensed that, for some reason, he felt the same way about her. Mr Wilding had presented her with a normal life, helping her even more than her brother had so far. So what if she was expected to duck and dive to pay him back? In time she'd run a business her way, and meanwhile anything was better than being stuck in a workhouse in Whitechapel. The thought of Whitechapel brought with it something that had been niggling at the back of her mind. 'Didn't think you'd be back until Friday to collect me. Did you come specially to get me today?'

He shook his head. 'I was passing and saw the banner up for the Brabazon sale.'

'Wouldn't have thought embroidery was your thing, Mr Wilding,' she teased.

'That's 'cos you don't know me.'

Lily took note of the change in his tone.

'Worked out well in the end.' His manner was light again.

'Worked out well?' Lily mocked. 'You got a thumping.'

'Stratton ain't got a decent punch on him. If he'd swung at me outside, I'd have shown him that.'

'Didn't expect Clive Stratton to know somebody like you,' Lily said.

'Somebody like me?'

Lily sensed she'd again touched a nerve. 'You're different sorts ... he's posh and horrible.'

He half-smiled. 'Take that as a compliment, shall I?'

Lily fidgeted beneath the look he gave her. Evening was drawing in and they were facing one another across yards of shadowy obstacles. She felt more self-conscious of her appearance since he'd said she was pretty. In the workhouse everybody dressed in ugly clothes, but being

118

around Jane had made her feel hideous in comparison. Lily edged behind one of the handcarts so less of her figure was on show.

'The master wanted to blame the ruckus on you.' She puffed disgust. 'He and Matron crawl to Mrs Stratton. It was good of Adam to stick up for you.'

'Reeve seems a decent sort.'

'He *is* decent . . . the best fellow I know. I used to help him in his office and we always got on well. He didn't look down on us inmates. He was especially good to me.' Lily's voice had softened when speaking of the medical officer.

'Why was that?'

'I took an interest in his books . . . I like to read. He felt sorry for me, I suppose, after he heard what happened to me mum and brother.'

Lily hadn't meant to mention her mum. But he didn't comment on it. 'You carrying a torch for Reeve?'

Lily was glad it was too dark for him to see her blushing. She'd not even confided in Margie about her daydreams of a romance with their medical officer. 'He's a bit older than me,' she said and turned away.

Once she was sixteen, the age gap between her and Adam wouldn't seem so great. Years ago she'd known a neighbour's daughter who'd got married at sixteen and had her first baby seven months later. Lily knew she was on the brink of womanhood, and felt as though today had seen her start to emerge from a stifling cocoon of childhood. She was determined to fly, too, and be happy. Anything was possible now.

'You'll get your heart broken if you wear it on your sleeve, Lily Larkin.'

Lily didn't get a chance to answer back. At that moment

Jane swept in, her expression sulky. She'd noticed her boyfriend staring intently at the scruff who was to be her unwelcome companion. Sashaying past Lily, she swung the bag of pies on to the desk. 'Hope you're not expecting me to settle fer one of those. You said you'd take me out for supper later.'

Greg took one out and bit into it, releasing an oniony aroma into the air. 'I will,' he said between chews. 'You'd better get going. When you get home, find Lily a dress and somewhere to sleep.' He shoved the remaining food across the desk. 'Feed yourself up for work in the morning. And get a good night's kip. You'll need it. Your brother will be by early to bring you into work.' He gave her a crooked smile, pointing to the bag she'd picked up. 'Imagine you'll want to know that'll be another one and six on your slate.'

Chapter Eight

The lodging was situated a short walk from the warehouse by the docks, so Lily had been told by her new roommate. That was all the small talk Jane would engage in as they turned on to the High Street. The only other attention Lily had received was a terse instruction to keep a few paces behind in case anybody believed they were together. Ordinarily Lily would have found something to say about being told she was an embarrassment. The day was catching up with her, though, and she begrudged wasting her breath. More importantly, her stomach was grumbling and the weight and warmth of the pies in her hand was harder to ignore than Jane Wright.

As a child Lily hadn't been allowed to eat in the street. The enjoyment of food had been given the respect it deserved. But gathering around a family dining table was a distant memory now. Silent lines of miserable people eating off pine trestles was Lily's recent experience of meal times. She opened the bag and took a hearty mouthful of meat and pastry.

In fact, few people noticed Lily's shabby figure as she walked along devouring her tasty supper; they were too busy gawping at beauteous Jane. And it wasn't just the men eyeing the blonde up and down. The women did, too, with slit-eyed envy as she sauntered past, chin up.

Soon they'd turned off the busy thoroughfare into a sparsely populated area with tall, grimy-windowed buildings facing one another along either side of a narrow central lane. Jane didn't seem bothered about being accompanied by a workhouse girl now. She glanced over a shoulder, urging, 'Don't dawdle! Come on, I'm off out this evening and I want to get meself looking nice.'

Lily continued at the same pace, eating and watching Jane sashaying along in front, her swinging hips setting her skirts dancing about her polished boots. Lily wondered how much nicer Jane Wright *could* look. She was attractive enough to grace the pages of a fashion journal, in Lily's opinion.

Having dispatched every crumb of the pies, she speeded up in response to another command to get a move on. Her full stomach hadn't boosted her energy; she felt lethargic and her limbs leaden. Beneath her trudging feet was a patchwork of uneven cobbles and wonky paving. Every ridge stabbed through the worn soles of her boots into her tender flesh. She'd been used to standing at a mangle for hours on end, or to crawling forward on wet hands and knees, whizzing a scrubbing brush in her hands. Walking to school or tramping around the workhouse corridors had exercised her legs. This afternoon she felt she had covered miles. Even so, the smile remained on Lily's face. No amount of Jane's scorn or blisters giving her gyp could dampen her contentment.

At last she was her own person ... or Mr Wilding's. But she hoped he'd liberate her the moment she asked him to.

And if she still owed him money, then she'd bring him what she could spare until the debt was cleared. He'd said she was too honest, so he would surely trust her to do it. She hoped he had a good heart. But until she was convinced he did, it might be wise not to trust him too much.

The alley was dappled with shadows, and she pulled her old blanket shawl about her shoulders to ward off chillier air, still engrossed in thoughts of him. She wondered if he had helped them because he knew what pitiless discipline was like. Something had happened to him, but she doubted he'd volunteer what that was, any more than she'd willingly relate her family's tragedy. She reckoned he hated wanton cruelty as much as she did. Every second spent at South Grove had been a torment she yearned to forget. But she'd never be able to. The stain of the workhouse couldn't be destroyed as easily as the uniform she intended to burn.

Lily snapped to attention. This time Jane's shout hadn't been directed at her, though. Just ahead, two women were lounging in a doorway of a dilapidated house, gossiping and swaying half-dressed toddlers on their stout hips. Another was up above at an open sash, elbows resting on the ledge. They all called out greetings in response to Jane having hailed them.

'Lily Larkin's stopping with me fer a while,' was Jane's bawled introduction as they passed, and she indicated her new roommate with a pat on the shoulder. The women waved again and so Lily raised her hand in acknowledgement. Jane slowed down to walk beside her. 'Friends 'n' neighbours, they are,' she explained. 'Eunice Smith up at the window, her Bobby takes out one of Greg's barrows. You met her lad; he was with your brother.'

'Oh, right ... I never got properly introduced to them.' Lily glanced back at the women. They might be neighbours, but they had nothing much in common with Jane, kitted out as they were in serviceable skirts and blouses with rolled-up sleeves. They all had similar careworn complexions and their hair was scraped up into untidy buns. Yet ... Lily imagined that fewer than five years in age might separate the youngest of those mothers from Jane. It had come as a surprise to know vain Jane got along with them. Lily realised there must be more to her companion than met the eye, and she started to see her in a better light.

'Sorry if you thought I was being rude earlier.' Lily's tone was conciliatory. 'I wasn't. I mentioned about fallen women ending up in the workhouse 'cos it's true. That's how me friend landed herself in South Grove.'

Jane sent her a sidelong frown before erupting in a snorting laugh. 'You don't look as though you'd know a good-time gel.'

'Well I do,' Lily declared. 'Her name's Fanny Miller and she's all right. I like her.'

'Fanny? You know Fanny?' Jane choked, eyes bulging.

Lily nodded. 'She's had a baby in there and will be bringing him home soon, then setting up in proper work with her sister.' Lily was about to add that Mr Wilding knew she was friends with Fanny, but realised that might not be wise. Jane seemed possessive of her boyfriend and mentioning him and a prostitute in the same breath could cause ructions. Lily had had enough of those. She wanted to keep things between herself and her roommate on a good footing. Most of all she wanted a bath and a long sleep. She hoped they were close to their destination and blurted that out to steer talk away from Fanny.

124

'Only just up there and round the corner.' Jane gestured wildly.

Lily took more notice of her surroundings, as much to get her bearings as anything else. She'd need to know which way to head home after a day's work.

The lane had a dip winding along its centre where silt and debris had collected. There were other dusty hollows that were brimming with rubbish, the identity of which Lily had no wish to contemplate. The smell was foul and the sound of scurrying could be heard in amongst a pile of decaying cabbage stalks. Jane hopped and skipped over litter, protecting her fine boots and the hem of her skirt from getting dirty. Lily didn't have a spring left in her step so simply skirted around what she could.

The light dimmed, the further into the neighbourhood they went. A strip of sunset-hued sky was above them, intermittently blanked from view by sheets flapping in a breeze. The washing lines strung across the narrow access were anchored from tenement to tenement, but Lily didn't want that sort of reminder so avoided looking up. Instead she watched a cat lithely padding along a fractured brick wall, keeping time with her. It froze and sank down, ready to pounce on an unsuspecting pigeon that had waddled into view further along on the ledge.

Jane had taken a sharp turn and stopped by a set of rusty railings fronting a red-brick building. Lily clapped her hands to scare the bird to safety, then hurried after her.

'This is us, then.' Jane started clattering down some stone steps, worn thin in the middle, that were located behind the railings.

*

'There, you can have that. It's the best I can do.'

Lily gazed at the blue cotton dress that Jane, with a faintly defensive expression, was holding up by its shoulders. It had a plain collar and buttoned sleeves and bodice. The colour was patchy where it had faded in places, and the cuffs were frayed. None of that mattered to Lily. She thought it was beautiful.

'Thanks,' she said gruffly, taking it and feeling tempted to hug the garment to her bosom. But she didn't. 'I'll pay you for it, of course.'

'No need,' Jane said airily, sitting down on the edge of her bed to remove her boots then roll down her stockings. 'Only wear it when I have a fit of spring fever and clean the place up a bit. While you're here you can do the chores.' She smirked. 'Anyway, Greg'll see me straight with a new frock.' She cocked her head, running an estimating eye over Lily's thin figure. 'Don't suppose you got fed much in that place. Ain't got much of a bust, have you? You might need a needle and cotton on it.'

'Don't mind if it's baggy,' Lily said, holding the length up against her. The hem wouldn't need altering. Jane was no more than an inch or so taller than she was.

'And while we're talking about me boyfriend: don't go getting in the way, playing gooseberry. We'll want to be left alone when he comes over, if you get my drift. So stay out of here.' Jane settled herself more firmly on her mattress, unpinning her velvet hat while giving Lily a warning look.

Lily nodded, wondering where on earth she was meant to sleep then, if not in here.

'Follow me.' Jane had interpreted Lily's frown and jumped up. She padded barefoot to the door and along a dim corridor, leading Lily to a small room. 'Ain't big, but it'll do you until you move on. And the sooner that is, the better it'll be.' She crossed her arms. 'No offence, but I like having the place to meself.'

'I like my privacy too,' Lily returned. 'And don't worry, me and Davy want to get going as soon as we can.' It was a confident statement, yet she was no longer sure about her brother's intentions. Davy had said one thing one moment then another the next. Realising she was still clutching the dress, Lily carefully folded it over to keep the hem from dragging on the floor. 'So ...' she swept a glance over the tiny space that smelled of coal. It had been swept of grit, she discovered, having tested the brick surface with a shuffle of her boots and finding it smooth enough. She approached the small window to peer upwards to a view of the railings and the gloomy lane. A huge cobweb strung between the walls moved in a draught, clinging to her cheek. She shuddered, pulling it off then shaking it from her fingers.

'You'll need to give the place the once-over with a broom, but it's a roof over your head and you can make it a bit more comfy,' Jane pointed out.

Lily smiled as her reluctant flatmate now tried to sell her the accommodation. 'I've no complaints. I'll need a mattress of some sort to sleep on, though.'

'I've got a couple on my bed. S'pose I'll have to let you have one of 'em and then suffer with me back.' She gave Lily a wink. 'He's vigorous.'

'Any chance of a bath?' Lily blurted. She didn't want to hear about that.

'Old lady upstairs might lend you her hip bath. Depends what mood she's in.' Jane grimaced at Lily. 'Best take off those rags. She'll not lend it to a workhouse girl. She'll blather about getting the itch.'

'They made us bathe every week, y'know.' Lily was irritated by these constant remarks. 'I haven't got lice or fleas either.'

'Well, you can't blame folk for thinking you might have, dressed like that.' Jane started scratching her arm. 'Anyway, I'm getting meself ready to go out. So if you want to shift your mattress into here, I'll find you a spare sheet and blanket in the cupboard. Moths might have been at 'em but better than nothing. After that you can see to yourself. You've been landed on me without my say-so, so I ain't running round after you.'

'Don't want you to,' Lily shot back, yet appreciated it must have been galling for Jane to suddenly find herself sharing her home with a stranger. She imagined that Mr Wilding thought he could do what he liked because he paid the rent. But Lily intended to be a good tenant. Keeping herself to herself suited her fine.

She managed to get the mattress along the corridor on her own when it became clear that Jane wasn't going to offer to take the other end and help move it. It was a flimsy, flock-filled affair anyway, and not too difficult to manoeuvre. She was just settling it on to the floor under the window when Jane reappeared in a dressing gown with her hair in curling rags. She was carrying the promised bed linen, but what caught Lily's hungry gaze was the pair of boots balanced on top of the pile.

'There ... found you these as well, right at the back of the cupboard. They need mending but I can't be bothered with that. The style's old-fashioned.' The black leather ankle boots had gathered so much fluff they looked grey.

They were dropped on to the mattress in a puff of dust, along with the bedding. Jane was at the door before she remembered something else she didn't want. 'Got a spare chair. Just gets in the way in my room. Stubbed me toe on it countless times. And you'll need a lamp. There's one either side of my bed. You can take the smallest.'

'Thanks. I'll have anything going begging.' Lily smiled in gratitude. 'And if you'd just show me where everything is, I'll get on by myself after that.'

Ten minutes later, Lily had a few more tatty items gracing her new bedroom and had received a speedy tour of the basement flat. It was roomier than she'd expected. There was a tiny scullery with a small cooking stove and a chipped china sink with a stiff tap. From that room, a door opened on to a crazy-paved courtyard where a short iron stairway led up to an outside washhouse and privy. Lily was keen to investigate it all but didn't linger in the malodorous shed. She glanced around the garden. There was a strip of cultivated land along the fence where a single pink flower had opened.

'Old gel upstairs keeps that flowerbed looking nice,' Jane said as Lily inclined to sniff the petals. The approaching dusk had made the scent intensely sweet. But Jane wasn't hanging around to appreciate it herself. She was soon back by the stairs with a, 'Bleedin' hell, time's getting on. Greg'll be here to take me out 'fore I know it and I haven't put me face on.' A church bell was chiming seven o'clock.

Back in the house, Lily carried on exploring alone when Jane disappeared. In addition to the rooms she'd been shown, there was a walk-in cupboard with a hanging rail jammed with stylish outfits. The moment Lily had pulled open that door, Jane appeared as if by magic on the threshold of her bedroom. She had one hand on her hip and was rubbing cold cream into her complexion with the other. 'And you can leave that lot alone. Don't touch any of it.'

'Sorry ... just getting me bearings.' Lily pulled her hand away from a yellow dress she'd been stroking. She knew she was here under sufferance and was prepared for Jane's mood to change like the wind. Lily suppressed her indignation; she was keen to satisfy her curiosity about something. 'Will you be off to work in the small hours, like me?'

'I don't work for Greg, if that's what you mean. And I don't get up early; I start at midday. Now's as good a time as any to tell you that I don't want your brother hammering on the door, waking me up at the crack o' dawn. Make sure you're already outside on the pavement when Davy turns up. I need me beauty sleep.'

'Will do,' Lily promised. 'So what's your job, if you don't mind me asking?' Her guess was that Jane was an assistant in a fancy West End store and had to look glamorous every day. That would explain her having so many lovely outfits: she probably got a staff discount. Lily would adore a job like that with perks; for now, though, she'd be happy for her boss to let her have buckshee a few bruised fruit and some wilting veg to take home for her tea.

'Me dad's a pub landlord down the Roman Road and I serve behind the bar at dinnertimes.' Jane put paid to Lily's fancy ideas about Mayfair. 'I sometimes do an evening shift as well. Been working there since me mum went, y'see.'

'Oh ... sorry about that,' Lily murmured.

'Don't be. *She* weren't. Selfish cow ran off and left us all to just get on with it. Caused a right bleedin' ruckus, she did.'

Lily made a noise she hoped sounded sympathetic.

'Four years ago that was, when I was sixteen and about to get engaged,' Jane resumed. 'Me older sisters had already scarpered, so that left just me to soldier on at home with Dad.'

'You and Mr Wilding were going to get married?' Lily hadn't expected to hear that. She reckoned he must have been sixteen then, too; they looked about the same age.

'Didn't even know Greg back then. Another feller proposed to me, though he was twenty-one.' Jane scowled. 'Rupert dropped me like a hot potato when he found out about me mother's fancy man. His family never liked me, especially his mother, the snooty old bag. She nagged him to throw me over. Heard Rupert married somebody else. She's welcome to him.' Jane chewed on the inside of her cheek for a moment, looking despondent, then she went into her room, shutting the door.

It seemed to Lily that her flatmate was putting on a brave face about being jilted, even if it had happened a while ago. So she decided not to disturb Jane again and ask for a flannel and towel, but make do without. She returned to the kitchen and fought with the stiff tap, placing under it an enamel bowl she'd found. The water suddenly spurted out, spattering her bodice and making her gasp it felt so cold. It continued dribbling and spitting but, though impatient, Lily waited until the bowl was half-full, then used both hands to turn off the tap. She carefully carried the bowl back to her room, with a beaker of drinking water wobbling in the centre. She'd also discovered a cracked piece of soap under the sink. The sliver smelled familiar and brought with it memories of helping her mother shave chunks of Sunlight soap into the copper on wash day. They'd take turns plunging the dolly on to the clothes to create a lather. That reminiscence brought spontaneous tears to her eyes; she impatiently wiped them away. 'Blubbing won't help,' her mum would be telling her. 'You're a grown-up now with a job and a home and responsibilities. And I'm proud of you.' Lily knew her mother would be jubilant that her kids had slipped off the yoke of the workhouse.

With no towel or flannel to use, Lily improvised. The edges of her bed sheet were a help in washing and drying herself, but she made sure to leave a centre patch dry to sleep on. Invigorated by the cold-water strip wash and rough towelling, she sat down on Jane's unwanted wicker chair and lowered her weary feet into the bowl to soak. To freshen her mouth she rubbed a little soap over her teeth, then swilled her mouth twice with clean water, spitting foam down into the bowl where her toes were being wriggled. Her hair felt gritty against her fingers as she used them to untangle it. It needed a good wash, and she promised herself that from her first pay packet she would treat herself to an hour at the municipal baths, where she could dunk her head down into a tub full of hot water. A wonderful indulgence, considering what she'd been used to. Shivering in a stone bath containing an inch or so of lukewarm water had been the norm, and no workhouse inmate healthy enough to stagger to the bathhouse escaped the ritual.

When her toes had stopped throbbing, Lily withdrew her wrinkly feet from the water and walked them dry on the edge of the sheet. Then came the most pleasurable part. She tried on her new dress and boots. The realisation that she had on proper clothes for the first time in five years started her eyes smarting again. There was no mirror, but she ran her hands and gaze over her silhouette. Jane had been right: the material was baggy around her bust and waist, but a nice belt would make it look and fit better; the market stalls would be filled with cheap second-hand stuff, and she was confident she'd manage to pick one up for pennies. Lily slipped out of the garments. She carefully folded the dress, straightening the material until she was happy it was neat enough to ensure minimal creasing. Then she polished her dusty boots with her workhouse skirt until they gleamed and tied the laces into dainty bows. Finally she placed them side by side under her chair, and turned her attention to her bed.

She spread the sheet on the mattress, formed a make-shift pillow out of her old shawl, then clambered on to her bed in her underclothes. She covered herself with Jane's moth-eaten blanket, closing her eyes and willing herself to drop off. Davy would be by to fetch her in just a matter of hours. But the excitement of the day and the prospect of starting her new job bubbled beneath her weariness.

Mostly her head was filled with images of people: those she'd just met and old friends she'd left behind. She wanted to cuddle Margie and repeat her promise that she wouldn't forget about her. Years ago, when Lily had been told her brother had perished, she had cried herself to sleep, sometimes in Margie's arms. Her friend would creep from her bed to comfort her. Once they'd been caught and both punished. Lily knew that Margie would be crying tonight . . . for her. In her mind, Lily put her arms around Margie, hoping her best friend knew she was missing her right back and thinking of her. More faces marched relent-lessly behind her eyelids. Mr Wilding's was the hardest to banish, and that surprised and frustrated Lily; she really wanted to concentrate on Adam Reeve and a way to engineer bumping into him. She knew she'd never get past the matron if she turned up to pay a visit. Adam didn't work full time at South Grove: he divided his time between the workhouse and other institutions where he acted as a medical officer. So if she could catch him leaving at the end of his shift, she could suggest they have tea in a caff. That way she could discover how Margie and Fanny were doing, and she knew he'd be eager to hear her news. After that he might suggest they meet up to go out again … perhaps to the flicks. And soon she'd be sixteen, viewed by everyone as a young woman, not a kid.

With that pleasing thought lulling her, Lily finally started to doze off and was soon gently snoring. About an hour later she rolled on to a ridge in the lumpy mattress and the awkward pressure on her arm gave her pins and needles. Still half asleep, she shimmied away from it to search for her comfortable spot. She was burrowing contentedly into it when the sound of a man and woman arguing rumbled into her consciousness. She pushed herself up on an elbow, straining to listen. She hadn't heard Mr Wilding turn up, but guessed he must have done, and that he and Jane were having words. After a moment, Lily realised that the raised voices weren't coming from along the corridor in Jane's room, but from up above, outside on the lane. She turned on to her hands and knees and crawled closer to the window to see what was going on beyond the railings.

A woman's skirt was visible, and Lily knew it was Jane's from recognising her flatmate's none-too-dulcet tones. The man's voice also sounded familiar, but the accent was too refined to be Mr Wilding's. Overcome with inquisitiveness, Lily inched closer to the glass, rubbing grime off the pane with her fingertips. It was quite dark now and the moonlight pale, showing her little other than a pair of trousered legs. By craning her neck, Lily had a better view of them both. Jane's fair hair was loose about her shoulders, but the fellow's face remained frustratingly just out of Lily's sightline. A moment later he obligingly struck a match and inclined his head to put a cigarette to it.

Lily's mouth dropped open in shock as the profile of a person she'd hoped never again to clap eyes on was illuminated by the flame. She jerked to one side using the cobwebby wall to hide herself, hoping that Clive Stratton hadn't noticed her spying on him for the second time in one day.

Chapter Nine

'Gawd's sake, Lily! This ain't the way to start off on the right foot with him. You've dropped us both in it now.'

Lily had been woken by her brother shaking her shoulder and yelling at her. She deserved his telling off too. His bangs on the street door had roused Jane, but Lily had slept on, blissfully unaware that she should have already been dressed and waiting in the lane for him. Once Jane had let him in, she had stormed back into her room, slamming the door.

Lily struggled up off the mattress, knuckling her heavy-lidded eyes and trying to get her bearings. Being woken from a deep sleep in unfamiliar surroundings had made her feel dizzy and disorientated. 'Sorry, Davy ...' she mumbled.

'Hurry up and get dressed. I'll wait in the corridor,' he blasted out.

'Promise I won't be long.'

'You'd better not be,' Davy flung over his shoulder. 'It'll be down to you if we both get the sack. Guv'nor don't like people turning in late.'

'Sorry ...' Lily apologised again, though the door had

already been crashed shut. She shoved her bare feet into her new boots, then crouched down to the enamel bowl to splash her face with some of yesterday's washing water. A quick drink from the beaker also helped liven her up, and she pulled her dress on over her head, drying her damp face on a sleeve. She was still fumbling with the buttons when she hurried out to find Davy pacing agitatedly to and fro. 'Be up tomorrow on time ... swear I will,' she said sheepishly. 'Just ... it took me ages to drop off. I must've gone out like a light when I did. Sorry, never even heard you knocking.'

Davy wasn't listening to her excuses, he was already opening the front door. Seconds later he was stamping up the steps to the lane.

He set off at once without waiting to walk with her. Lily closed the door and dashed after him, but kept a few paces behind, thinking it best to give him time to calm down before catching him up. She felt guilty and stupid for having overslept, especially as Mr Wilding and Jane had made a point of reminding her to be up and ready for work.

The dark lane was a minefield, and twice Lily almost came a cropper as her haste made her clumsy. Davy was speeding along, lighting his way through the gloom with a pocket torch, and hugging the tenements to shelter from the persistent drizzle. Every so often he swerved to avoid a pothole in his path. Lily tracked his footsteps closely. The mood her brother was in, if she tripped he might leave her where she fell. At last they reached the main road where the streetlamps put a glow on the dank buildings and a glitter on the rainy pavement. They had no protection now from the close-set buildings in the alley, but it was no use wishing for a coat to put on. She didn't own one, and she wasn't begging more cast-offs from Jane Wright. Lily crossed her arms over her middle to suppress her shivering and started marching at her brother's side. 'Won't be *that* late, will we?' She tried to break the ice with him.

'Late enough to start him moaning.' Davy adjusted his flat cap on his head, hunching his shoulders to his ears to try and keep dry. ''S'all right for you, taking it easy in the warehouse. I've gotta get loaded then set up me pitch in this weather.' He tutted in disgust.

Lily thought about what he'd said. 'Did Mr Wilding tell you I'm not going to be working in the market with you?'

Davy nodded. 'He met up with us in the caff for a while. He often joins us after work to give us our orders for the following day. He's not standoffish, give him that.'

Davy seemed friendlier, so Lily slipped her hand through the crook of his arm, hugging against him, for warmth as much as anything. 'I'll tell him it was my fault we're late.'

'Bleedin' right you will!'

Davy started crossing the road, and Lily trotted at his side with a jumble of things she needed to say to him in her head. But it didn't seem the right time to bring up the subject of their future plans, or to delve into the past. She was anxious about how he would take the truth of their mother's death. Thoughts of their sister often haunted Lily's mind while she lay in bed waiting for sleep to claim her. Last night no spectre had been responsible for stopping her getting back to sleep; that had been down to the antics of real people.

After witnessing the drama, Lily had concluded that Jane must be the mutual acquaintance Mr Wilding had said he shared with Stratton. Lily had also assumed Jane didn't like the horrible man either, and that was why they were arguing. She'd deduced that Stratton had come looking for Mr Wilding to resume their fight, and loyal Jane had been telling him to clear off. However, before they parted, Jane's meeting with Clive Stratton had taken an unexpected and eye-opening twist, and all Lily's careful reasoning had flown out of the window. Their bickering had suddenly quietened into whispers, and when Stratton had grabbed Jane and tried to kiss her, she'd made little effort to stop him.

In fact she'd put her arms round his neck and kissed him back.

Their canoodling didn't last long. Jane had probably warned him that her boyfriend was due any minute. She'd cut it fine, too; Greg had turned up shortly after Stratton had jauntily disappeared into the gloom in the opposite direction. Greg had let himself in and Lily had huddled on her mattress while a hum of indistinct conversation drifted to her ears from the adjoining room. She'd been feeling indignant on her boss's behalf, and in two minds whether to barge in on them and tell him what she'd seen. Shortly afterwards the couple had gone out, and Lily had watched Jane hanging on his arm, for all the world like a devoted sweetheart.

Lily didn't feel guilty for being a Peeping Tom when she'd had little choice in the matter. She wished she was still in blissful ignorance of their love triangle, though. It was no wonder the men hated one another if they were rivals for Jane. When all had become quiet in the flat, she'd agonised over whether to tell her boss tomorrow that he was being two-timed. Eventually Lily had drifted off to sleep, still undecided. She hadn't heard Jane come back, though obviously she had at some point, and had slept alone.

Relationships between men and women were complicated; Lily only had to think about her mum's loyalty to Charlie Larkin to know that. After her father had been sacked she'd overheard her parents arguing about a woman. She'd been nine years old and none of it had made sense then. Now she began to wonder if his cheating had gone beyond a swindle and he'd committed adultery too. She'd no proof that it was so, and if her mother had known about it, it hadn't stopped her loving him. Jumping to conclusions about such things could get her into trouble: Lily guessed if she went telling tales, her boss might react by telling her she was a kid who should mind her own business. She would soon be in his bad books, anyway, for being late. She daren't lose her job and her lodgings before she'd had them a full day, so she reckoned it was wisest to overrule her conscience and keep quiet about what wasn't her concern. Having made a decision, she pushed the incident to the back of her mind, and concentrated on her own problems.

'When we finish work later, Davy, let's meet up. There's something important to talk about.'

'What's that then?' He threw her a distracted glance as he rushed round the corner, Lily striving to keep up.

'Well, we should get a place to live together.' Lily shook his arm because he didn't seem to be listening. She wasn't going to break the *real* news until they were sitting somewhere quiet. 'I can't stay where I am. Jane's made it clear she doesn't really want me there.' Knowing what she did, Lily didn't *want* to stay there. The prospect of bumping into Clive Stratton hanging around filled her with dismay.

Davy suddenly raised a hand in salute, drawing Lily's attention to other early risers. So far they'd come across nobody at all in the deserted streets. She hadn't realised they were almost at their destination. Some flares had been lit by the warehouse gates where a group of men had congregated. These were Mr Wilding's quick-off-the-mark customers, she supposed. The ones he intended she would deal with ... when she turned up on time.

'We can't afford to pay rent yet, Lily,' Davy said, hurrying her along by the elbow. 'You'll have to wait a while and get some money together before you think of moving out of Jane's. Look, Bob and Fred are ready to set off. They're already loaded. Anything else to tell me 'fore I go and get me stuff together?'

'No ... it'll save till later,' Lily replied with a sigh. 'We got here sooner than I expected.' The working day was already under way for these market traders. A fellow emerged through the little crowd by the entrance and started towards them, pushing a handbarrow that had pallets and ropes piled on top.

'Mornin' Davy,' the fat fellow said from behind the roll-up stuck in his mouth. He briefly tugged his cap at Lily as he passed, quickly taking the strain of the barrow again with both hands.

A moment later they'd turned into the compound, the donkey-jacketed men separating to make a path for her to walk through while eyeing her up and down. But Lily wasn't bothered about any of them. Her eyes were drawn immediately to the tall fair-haired man watching her arrival.

'Afternoon ... ' was the dry comment she received.

'Sorry we're late, Mr Wilding. It's my fault,' she blurted, smearing rain from her bleary eyes.

'Guessed as much. Wait inside and I'll speak to you in a minute.' He turned his back on her and paid attention to a fellow who was trying to negotiate the cost of a particularly large tarpaulin he needed.

Davy had mumbled his, 'Mornin', guv'nor,' then whipped inside to appear willing. Lily caught up with him as he manoeuvred a cart then tossed ropes on top of it.

'I can help you with that,' she said, and grabbed one end of a pole he'd started wrestling with. She retreated when her brother simply frowned at her in a way that told her not to embarrass him but to clear off. So she did, and tried her best to keep out of the way as men trundled past, carrying or pushing stuff they'd hired. They all nodded or grunted at her in greeting and seemed affable enough. So she smiled back and chirped her good mornings, sure that being nice to the customers would be a mark in her favour with her boss.

'Met me mum yesterday, didn't yer?' The taller of the two youths Davy classed as his pals had strolled up to talk to her. 'She said you was walking home with Jane Wright.'

'Oh . . . yes, I did wave to her. Eunice Smith, isn't it?' This was the harmonica-playing lad who'd seemed sympathetic when Davy had made her look a fool yesterday. 'You must be Bobby, her son.'

'I am.' He grinned, pleased she'd remembered his name. 'And you're Lily Larkin and you look like a drowned rat.' He cocked his head, assessing her damp figure and stringy dark hair. 'Dress suits you though. Better than that bloody old uniform, eh?'

Lily nodded. 'You sound as though you might have had one on at some time.'

'Not for long, thank Gawd.' He looked diffident. 'I was in St Pancras for over three months but me granddad come and discharged me soon as he could. Mum was proper poorly in hospital then, and as for me dad ... well, never knew him really.' He sniffed. 'Anyhow, Mum's right as rain now.' He showed Lily two sets of crossed fingers.

'You *were* lucky,' Lily said wistfully, mirroring his gesture. She and Davy hadn't had any grandparents to take them home. Just the aunt her mother couldn't abide and rarely spoke about. If they did have real cousins, they'd never had a chance to get to know them. And it was too late to question her mum and dad about missing relatives. Now she was older and lonelier, Lily knew she'd love another chance to sit and talk to Maude and Charlie about their early lives and the people who'd figured in them.

'It was all hunky-dory for a few years till me granddad got sick and passed on.' Bobby carried on his tale. 'He had his own pitch in the market and I was working with him full-time when I turned twelve but ... ' He rubbed a finger under his nose. 'Anyhow, after that the gaffer took me on. He knew me granddad. So it all worked out all right in the end.'

'You're an old hand at costermongering then,' Lily said admiringly. 'Bet you've taught Davy a lot.'

'Him? Can't tell him nuthin'. He thinks he knows it all, does master of the market. But guv'nor's that, not him.' Bobby's chortle turned into a sniff. 'Didn't mean nothing by it ... just a joke. Forgot for a moment Davy's your brother.'

'It's all right,' Lily said with a shrug, though it wasn't.

She needed to consider what could be read into that criticism. She'd noticed an unfavourable change in Davy, and it seemed others were also aware of his shortcomings.

'Come to the caff with us after work.' Bobby tried to make up for his slip. 'I'll stand you a cup of tea till you get your wages. Then next week you can treat me, if you like,' he said.

'Deal ...' Lily put out a hand to shake, pleased that she might already have made a friend. She'd had her brother's opinion on their boss but, as he'd seemed resentful of Mr Wilding's success, she wanted to hear somebody else's view. 'Is your guv'nor fair to all of you?' Lily glanced over Bobby's shoulder to study him. He'd come in from outside with an elderly customer and was unhooking stuff on the wall to display it.

Gone was the smart suit and polished shoes. In their place Greg Wilding wore boots and a donkey jacket. With his flat cap and knotted scarf, he looked little different to the men begging favours. She'd heard them asking for discounts and a chance to pay out of profits when they brought the equipment back at the end of the day. From what she could hear, her boss wasn't budging.

'I think he's all right on the whole,' Bobby said. 'Not as good as some but better than most, is how I see it. People do call him master of the market. Could sell sand to Arabs, him ... got the gift of the gab.' Bobby gave an admiring shake of his head. 'Somehow he knows when there's gonna be a shortage of stuff and buys up extra. Last Christmas we was the only ones in Chrisp Street with Brussels sprouts on the stall. Housewives were queuing round the block to get served.' Bobby chuckled. 'Year I started with him there was a potato blight ... terrible shortage. He managed to get some, though. Another thing, he ain't worried about selling sheets one end of the table and cabbages the other to keep the cash rollin' in.' Bobby gave Lily a gentle nudge. 'Most important, he don't take no nonsense off this lot.' Bobby rolled his eyes at the navvies milling about. 'They moan about him but keep coming back, and they don't have to. There's other places they could go to hire stuff. Some of 'em are old enough to be his granddad, but they respect him, see, just don't fully trust him. And that's probably how us lot see him. Me mum's always had a good word for Gregory Wilding though.' Bobby finished on the best endorsement he could give to anybody.

Lily considered what she'd heard, concluding that it reflected her own ideas of the man's character as a canny operator who walked a thin line between good and bad. Reassuring as it was to know Bobby felt satisfied here, her ambition was still to join forces with her brother in their own venture as soon as possible. 'Have you ever thought of setting up on your own, Bobby?'

'Thinks about that all the time, ain't that right, Smudger?' Davy's other work pal had come up behind Bobby Smith to thump him on the shoulder. He gave Lily a wink then started prising the lid off a tin of tobacco. 'Trouble is, love, as you'll learn, setting up on your own takes more cash than any of us are ever likely to have in our pockets.'

'Well you won't, if you drink and gamble away your wages,' Lily pointed out. She'd seen beer bottles and silver and copper on the box yesterday when the two of them had been playing cards.

Bobby hooted a laugh. 'Got you there, mate,' he said, with a playful punch for Fred.

'Tell your Davy that then, will yer, Lily?' Fred smirked. 'Don't mind if I call you Lily, do you? You can call me Fred.'

'Right-oh,' Lily said, but knew already she didn't like Fred as much as Bobby ... or Smudger it seemed was his nickname. 'What did you mean by that? Why should I tell Davy about gambling?'

'He's just blowing hot air ...' Bobby tried to smooth things over.

'No I ain't. Davy's same as us. He likes a drink and a smoke, and he gambles worse than us two. Lily should know what he's like if she's planning on splitting bills with him,' Fred added. 'I'm still waiting on him paying me back his share of the coal we had months ago.' He glanced around, shouting, 'Move yerself, Davy.' He lit the cigarette, exhaling smoke in a showy way. 'I'll have a fight on me hands now to get on the door knockers 'fore the other geezer doing his round. If I don't sell out, I'll get a rollickin' off you-know-who.'

'You lot standing gossipin' all day?'

'Just off, guv'nor, if Davy's ready.' Fred jumped to attention, aware he'd been overheard.

'Reckon he can find his own way to Chrisp Street after all this time,' Greg said. 'I just told him to get going.'

Davy was in the process of pushing his cart through the open doors.

'See you later, Davy,' Lily called, curbing an instinct to run over to hug him goodbye. She got a whistle back from her brother and the two-tone salute reminded her of their father. As a child she'd creep to the top of the stairs in her nightdress and call to him when he came home after a late shift. He'd look up, grimy faced and slump-shouldered, but would give her a soft whistle, his way of letting her know she'd been in his thoughts too.

Fred and Bobby briskly followed Davy out, leaving Lily

with her boss and a few stragglers still loading up in the warehouse.

'Right,' said Lily, business-like. 'I'll start making some notes so I know what's expected of me.'

'Good idea. Top of the list is to get here on time.'

'Mmm ... sorry ... overslept ... won't happen again.' To avoid any more caustic remarks she hurried to the desk to look on its littered top for paper and pencil.

'To start, I'll want you to keep proper records of the hired stuff for me. Nobody ever borrows anything, so if I'm not here and they tell you they can, you say they can't. Everything's got a price. Extras like pallets or scales or tarpaulins and poles ... all cost money. Mostly a customer just wants the basics: a barrow to sell goods off and maybe a set of scales. We take a deposit on it all or it won't come back.' He paused. 'I've got rates up here ... ' He tapped his skull. 'Don't expect you to remember it all yet though.'

'I could do with a little notebook to write stuff down.' Lily hadn't found anything much on the desk under the stack of bills she'd shifted to and fro.

'Got one in the van.'

'Oh ... where's that?'

'Parked round the corner. Come on ... you can tag along and have a lesson in buying stock. Be handy for you when you're doing this on your own account.' He was heading for the exit, shooing the customers out in front of him.

Lily followed him, then waited in the flare-lit gloom while he fixed heavy padlocks into the hasps on the doors and locked the warehouse. Having extinguished the torches by the gates, he secured those too, then led the way around the corner to where a truck was parked. He opened the passenger door for her.

'Where we off to then?' Lily clambered on to the hard seat.

'If those likely lads are to earn their keep and me a profit, they're going to need something to sell. It's Friday so we're off to Billingsgate. You'd better hope we're not too late to make a killing.' He got into the van and pulled away from the kerb. 'If you've any sense you'll take more notice of what goes on at the business end of things than your brother did when I took him along for the ride.'

'What did Davy do then?' Lily sighed. She was getting fed up of hearing bad reports of her brother.

'Fell a-kip in the van and yawned his way round the market, then tripped over a guy rope and ended up in the drink.'

Lily gasped. 'He almost drowned?'

'He might have if I'd not collared the daft sod as he went down. As it was, he just got a soaking. Livened him up if nothing else.'

'I'm wide awake, and steady on me feet,' Lily vowed.

'You should be wide awake at just gone four o'clock. Billingsgate's already opened its doors and we'll be at the back of the queue instead of at the front.'

His reprimand came with a glimmer of a smile, so Lily turned away, folded her hands on her lap and decided not to answer that.

The only motor vehicle Lily had ridden in was a bus; long ago when her mum had taken her and Davy to visit Madame Tussauds and the Tower of London. They'd had a lovely day out sightseeing and visiting the parks during the school summer holiday. It had been the year before her father lost his good job. After that they'd walked everywhere to save the fare.

This morning Lily felt as excited as she had as a child on an excursion. She gazed through the windscreen as the wipers creaked and smeared wet over the glass. A faint blush was on the horizon, clearing away the rain clouds and heralding a fine morning. Yet spoiling her special first day as a working woman were thoughts of what Fred and Bobby had said about her brother. Mr Wilding's criticism also niggled at her. Her boss could have made more of Davy's mishap but had decided not to. Fred hadn't worried about upsetting her or about being disloyal to his pal, blabbing that Davy was a spendthrift. Lily wasn't sure she'd take to Fred, yet she sensed he'd told the truth about her brother's bad habits. And that was depressing.

She'd not have a chance to talk to him in private until after they finished work. She hoped they wouldn't end up arguing. As knocking-off time was many long hours away, there was no point fretting in the meanwhile. She might as well make the most of her day until then.

Chapter Ten

'Keep your wits about you and pay attention to what I do and say. You need to learn to talk sharp and think fast or you'll end up skint in a week. I won't be around to help you when you go it alone. Being a nice polite kid won't do yer no good, not with this lot. This is serious business and we're all in it to rifle somebody else's pockets. You have to see it that way as well or you'll never come out on top in a deal. Don't matter whether you're at Spitalfields or Billingsgate, the game's the same. Got it?'

Lily nodded, gazing up earnestly through grey morning light at Mr Wilding's stern expression. He'd parked up the van on the fringe of the market and they'd got out to be jostled by a stampede of people heading in the same direction. The determined-looking men were trundling every size and shape of cart or wheelbarrow. Lined up along the kerbs as far back as the Monument were motor vans and trucks, some making deliveries but most waiting with open doors to be loaded and take stock away.

Lily appreciated her boss's pearls of wisdom but believed she wasn't as clueless as he obviously thought her. She'd already guessed that being self-employed would bring her into the orbit of unscrupulous characters. Once Davy decided he was ready to strike out with her, and she was sure it'd be soon, they'd be a good partnership. Her brother had gained more experience, and a harder nose, and she had the sense to stop him frittering his wages, so the money they earned could be put to good use. She couldn't really blame him for buying himself some pleasures. In an effort to fit in with his new life and his new pals, he'd probably just done what they did and unwittingly overstepped the mark. She also reckoned Mr Wilding was overstating the case of bogeymen lying in wait to diddle them. He wanted to scare her, for her own good, which was nice of him considering they would be rival sellers at some time. There was no doubt in Lily's mind that life had made her boss a cynic. She'd had it tough but still believed in giving people the benefit of the doubt. Those folk who felt the same way as she did were the ones she'd sooner do business with. She hoped she wasn't being naive in thinking there were such people out there.

They set off into the throng, Lily fizzing with exhilaration as she strove to keep up with his long stride rather than trail behind. She felt extremely alert, darting interested glances here and there, drinking in this new experience.

Billingsgate market was situated right on the banks of the Thames and the salty smell of the sea was striking. They passed close to a mound of rotting fish heads dumped amongst a pile of broken pallets. A young scamp had spotted a meal in amongst the mess. He scrambled forward to beat a trio of mangy-looking dogs to a sizeable piece of fish. The animals were dodging kicks and inching closer to jump on to the pallets to feed. Lily held her nose as her cheeks ballooned, but her boss seemed unaffected by the stomach-turning stink. She skipped ahead of him to find cleaner air, forcing him to grab her elbow and steer her in the right direction. They entered a covered building heaving with people and ringing with din.

The noise was the most powerful part of this baptism of fire as a costermonger's apprentice. Buyers and sellers were hollering at one another, red in the face, sometimes in a language unintelligible to Lily. She guessed they were all arguing the toss over the price of the goods. Porters roared at everybody to clear their paths, as they marched through the crowds balancing baskets on their heads. The crash and crunch of equipment and merchandise being shifted from place to place added to the clamour, making Lily want to clap her hands over her ears. Yet still she smiled. She'd gone from the soul-destroying silence of the workhouse to this in less than a day! And she loved it.

Greg drew her close to his side to protect her from a colossus barging his way through the masses with a tower of baskets stacked on top of his squashed helmet. All the regular porters wore them. Lily gawped at the fellow in awe and admiration as he strode on, his expression as set as his burden. Not all the labourers were as strong as him, or as well equipped with leather hats and aprons. Scores of thin, ragged men and boys were wheedling to earn themselves coppers for carrying a customer's purchases to his vehicle. They looked like whipped curs, expecting cuffs from their more able rivals, or from the contemptuous buyers who haggled with them even when they wanted just pennies for their toil.

Davy could have ended up somewhere similar to this, Lily realised with a pang. A half-starved guttersnipe scrapping with mongrels for fish offal and begging a chance to be a beast of burden for tuppence.

Her boss seemed to know where he was going, and she stuck close to his side as they made headway through the crowd. She knew if they got separated, she might never find him again. They'd passed a lot of wholesalers standing on boxes, pitching their wares directly to him by name. Yet he didn't stop to speak to them or to inspect what they were offering. Lily, however, was fascinated by the buckets of slithering eels, and slabs filled with wiggling, silvery fish. Haddock, brill, herring and numerous other varieties were being displayed by their tails or weighed on a fishmonger's bloodstained palms. Be it a pail of cockles or a huge mackerel on offer, all were described in a bellow as being, 'the best you'll find'.

Greg had other ideas. He ignored every summons to 'Come 'ere and take a butcher's, me ol' cockle.' He entered a shed and, in the half-light, Lily could make out caged lobsters pushing claws through their prisons, and dozens of tubs brimming over with shellfish.

'They're still alive.' Lily shifted away from some fierce-looking pincers near her skirt.

'Better be, or I ain't havin' 'em.'

'Oi, Mr Wilding. Look. Won't get no fairer price nor fresher ... just in from Yarmouth. Bloaters. Ladies love 'em. You know that, doncha? You'll have this lot shifted and all be down the rub-a-dub for a reeb be ten, Greg, stand on me ... '

Lilly gawped at a gap-toothed fellow winking at her and shaking a fat brown fish by its tail. 'What did he say?'

'He says if I buy his bloaters I'll be sold out by ten and down the pub drinking beer, trust him on it.'

'Buy some of those then, shall we?' She eagerly moved towards the merchant.

Greg pulled her away. 'Selling's the easy bit, Lily. It's buying at the right price that's the art. We don't trust nobody and we don't tell him, or any of 'em, we'll buy until they're ready to take a third – a half at most – of what's being asked. Even if he says his sick kid won't get his medicine 'cos I'm a callous bastard, we stick to our guns. That's how it works.'

'Perhaps he has got a sick kid, though.' Lily thought it *would* be callous behaviour in that case.

Greg threw back his head and barked a laugh. 'You need to toughen up, my gel. Bartering's about who tells the best lies.'

Lily sent an apologetic look the vendor's way, but he was already shaking his fish at somebody else. She scooted after Greg as he strolled from the shed, hands in pockets, as though not interested in having anything at all and content to browse. As they got closer to the quayside, an invigorating blast of briny air whipped her rain-damp hair off her cheeks, helping to dry it and fluffing it about her animated features. She could glimpse masts and rigging silhouetted against the pink streaks in the sky. Then they were by the wharves where fishing boats were moored mere yards away. Baskets of oysters and shrimps were being unloaded. The fishy smell was now overlaid with diesel oil, and the beat of working engines added a bass note to the cacophony.

'Down there the oyster boats line up, and it's known as Oyster Street,' he told her, pointing ahead. 'This is where your brother took a tumble, so watch yer step, it's slippery.' He shifted aside some ropes and lobster pots with a booted foot to clear their path. 'Buying stock direct from this lot cuts out the wholesaler's premium. Understand what I mean?' He glanced down at her and Lily gave him a smile and a vigorous nod.

He chuckled at her enthusiasm. 'Like doing this, do you?'

Another emphatic nod and she said, 'Just wish I could understand what some of them are saying though.' Lily glanced back at the shed they'd exited. 'Double Dutch to me ... yet they don't look foreign.'

'Costers often use back slang to keep the customers and the coppers in the dark about what they're saying.' He sounded amused. 'It's not foreign, it's like a code, and as East End as you'll get.'

'Glad you talk properly.'

'Posh now, am I?' He quirked an eyebrow at her.

'Comparatively speaking, I suppose, guv'nor,' she teased him back.

'You know big words, Lily Larkin.'

'I do ... and I can use them to your advantage, and keep all your books straight.' She tilted her chin to a jaunty angle.

'He taught you the big words, did he?'

'What? Who?' she demanded.

'Your friend, the medical officer, taught you big words to confuse ignorant folk. A bit like those costers in your own way, eh, Lily?'

'*I'm* a coster now, so you can teach me back slang if you want,' she challenged.

'Nah ... you'll not be in the game long enough to need it.'

'Oh?' She tugged on his sleeve to make him look at her rather than a pile of cooked pink shrimp. 'What will I be then?'

'Married with a couple of kids in a few years.'

She snorted derision. 'I *will* not.'

Her vehemence made him smile. 'It's what most gels want.'

'Not me. I'm not ending up relying on any man.'

'That include your brother?' he dryly suggested.

Lily squinted at him. 'We'll be a team ... equal partners in it.'

'Straight down the middle, eh? Sharing losses as well as profits?'

''Course. Don't intend making losses though.'

'Those'll be famous last words unless you lose them rose-tinted spectacles and give your brother a kick up the backside.' He returned to a previous subject. 'You didn't say if your friend taught you big words.'

'I did vocabulary at school,' Lily snapped, feeling peeved. In his opinion she was too sentimental and Davy was too weak. 'Surprised you gave us jobs if you think we're useless.'

'Every so often *I* act daft.' He sounded self-mocking. 'Anyway, you've got time to shape up and I reckon you will if you take my advice. Now you gonna answer my question about your friend the medical officer?'

Lily realised there was no use in sulking or she'd cut off her nose to spite her face. There was some unpalatable truth in what he'd said, even if the delivery had been too blunt. She wasn't one to hold a grudge so let it go ... for now. 'Thanks to Adam Reeve I stayed on at school. The master would've had me skivvying every day, but Adam told him I had the potential to be a useful clerk and that improving my education would be beneficial to him.' Lily gingerly stepped over obstacles as they carried on along the jetty, side by side. 'He arranged for my friend Margie to get a day a week at school as well. Her right hand's deformed and makes her a clumsy needlewoman. She can't lift a bucket full of water without spilling it. But she can write nicely with her left hand. Adam told the master she'd eventually be a good enough scribe to get employment.' Lily gave a chuckle that was husky with affection for Margie. 'I knew she could sew if she wanted to. I hated sitting mending for hours on end. Rather be up on my feet.' She gave him a nudge so he'd see her grateful smile. 'You and Davy saw me coming back from school that day. Davy told me you decided to rescue me.'

'Yeah, I saw you. I saw that officer whack you 'n' all. Don't like bullies.' He put a hand on her crown, guiding her on to another wharf as she would have walked on by.

'You're right, though.' Lily resumed their conversation. 'Adam did help teach me big words. I know some medical terms from reading his books. Eviscerate ... there's one for you.'

'What's that mean?' Greg asked as they flattened themselves against a wall to let some porters get past on the gangway.

'What they're doing over there.' Lily wrinkled her nose at the sight of a fish being gutted.

'Right ... well, let's see what price he wants for his eviscerated mackerel,' Greg said. 'Then after that we'll have some oysters and shrimp from further along. First I've got to knock 'em down in price so they'll take what I'll give. Don't snivel if he tells us his wife's on her last legs.'

Lily ignored the jibe. 'I could find a porter to help us load up.' She had noticed an elderly fellow getting shoved aside every time he crept up to offer his services.

Greg's eyes had followed the direction of hers. 'You've not listened to me, have you? You're too soft-hearted.'

'You're too *hard*-hearted,' she whipped back at him.

She got no reply. Greg had already started to negotiate a deal with the master of the boat. The prices were written on a blackboard, but he didn't even give it a glance.

After some shouting, a deal seemed to have been struck. Hands that moments ago had been angrily gesticulating were offered and shaken. Lily started to understand what her boss meant about it all being a strategy. The two men had looked about to exchange punches but were soon friends again. Cash changed hands, and then they were off down the quay to another dock and another boat.

Up ahead was a florid-faced fisherwoman bawling out the price of oysters while filleting fish with such swift, concise movements that Lily barely saw her hands move. The woman threw down the knife and planted her slimy fingers on her hips. 'Come 'a see me, 'ave yer, Greg?' She sent him a wink. 'You know I always gives yer what yer want, don't yer?'

'Relyin' on it, Bet,' he said.

'Brought yer li'l sister along, 'as yer? Ain't seen her before.' The woman was weather-beaten and of indeterminate age. She could have been as young as the man she was bantering with.

'I'm Mr Wilding's assistant.' Lily inwardly cringed at having sounded too haughty. She'd bridled at the patronising look the older woman had given her.

'La di da li'l madam, ain't she?' the woman hooted in her gravelly tone. 'What's she doin' with you then, Greg?'

'I'm goin' up in the world, Bet,' he teased her. 'Need some classy people around me.'

The woman regarded Lily with renewed interest. 'Tha' right?' She cocked her head. 'Told Jane Wright about that, have yer?'

Lily slanted him a glance. She'd forgotten she had more than Davy's antics ruining her peace of mind. The more time she spent with Mr Wilding, the more Bobby's words rang true about their boss's nature. Mr Wilding had told her home truths and upset her, but she respected him and she hated the idea of his girlfriend cheating on him.

Greg ignored the fisherwoman's baiting and told her the price he was prepared to pay for her oysters. Once she'd stopped complaining and agreed to the deal, he started her off blaspheming again by adding that he'd only take the oysters if six trays of cockles and four of whelks were thrown in at two for one.

He turned to Lily who'd been listening intently to it all. 'What's the tally?'

Lilly chewed her lip while concentrating on doing the mental arithmetic and came up with two pounds ten and sixpence.

He tutted. 'What about the half knocked off the oysters?'

Lily blushed, and her confusion increased as the woman started sniggering. 'Classy but dumb, eh, Greg?' She cackled. 'Comes to two pounds one and six, lovey.'

'I'm not dumb.' Lily was determined to hold her own. 'I know what eviscerate means. Reckon you don't, yet you should in your game.' She crossed her arms and stared defiantly, though she was annoyed at herself for allowing this rough woman to make her act childishly.

Bet settled her chin on her chest and pursed her mouth. 'She off her rocker? What's she on about, Greg?'

'That.' Greg was laughing as he pointed at the pile of

filleted mackerel. 'Right, we're done here. Now back to the shed, and the lobsters 'fore they croak.' He gave Lily a nudge to move her on.

By five thirty it was properly light and they were done with buying stock. The frail old porter had been allowed to carry the shrimp and oyster boxes to the motor, and for his trouble had received the sixpence he'd asked for, and a penny tip. Another beefy fellow had been given the job of loading up the mountain of heavier boxes of fish for payment of a florin, which Greg told him was a diabolical liberty. Nevertheless, he handed it over.

When seated again in the van and heading away into a coral-coloured sunrise, Lily realised she was exhausted, despite so far having done very little but walk about and tax her brain with one sum. She was annoyed with herself for not working it out correctly, but her mind soon wandered to other things. At least it had stopped raining, so Davy would be dry while setting up his stall. Customers might already be out buying their suppers, eager to snap up the freshest produce, and he hadn't yet got any stock to sell.

The throb of the engine and the rocking of the vehicle as it travelled along was adding to her lethargy. She tapped her feet and hummed to keep herself awake, but eventually rested her head against the side window and dozed off.

The sound of her brother's voice made her snap to attention. He and his colleagues had gathered round the van in Chrisp Street to unload the stock. Lily opened her door and jumped down, attempting to help. She kept getting in the way, so gave up after a while. The lads worked well as a team with their boss. She proudly watched her brother as he decanted some of the shellfish into a pail to take to his stall. A moment later he hurried back to get an early bird housewife some bloaters she wanted. Once the woman had her fish wrapped in newspaper, Davy started again to load up the stall, neatening the display as he went. Bobby and Fred were piling on to their smaller handbarrows an assortment of merchandise. Between them, the lads had erected the tarpaulin-covered pitch while waiting for the fish to arrive. Greg left the boys to finish off emptying the van and went to an adjacent stall to buy fresh parsley and lemons. On his way back he lobbed the fruit at the boys, who deftly fielded it and juggled the lemons as though it were a regular game. Lily thought it was nice to see them all larking about together, and to see that their boss had a sense of fun beneath his businessman's exterior. Having given his salesmen a bunch of herbs each, Greg swiped his palms together and turned to Lily. 'That's us done, then. Time you was earning yer keep 'n' all.'

They got into the van and he wound down the window, shouting to Fred and Bobby, 'Right, I know you've had yer breakfast in the caff, so stop dawdling. Get started on your rounds. And don't bring none of it back, or I'll have yer. Goes fer you too.' He pointed a finger at Davy. The window was wound up and, after he'd lit a cigarette, taken a drag and exhaled with a satisfied sigh, they set off.

Lily was expecting that they'd head straight back to the warehouse, but after leaving the market behind he stopped at a caff on the Commercial Road.

'Don't expect you to work on an empty stomach, either.' He jerked his head at her, indicating they were getting out. 'Come on, brainbox, it's breakfast time. Best meal o' the day.'

Chapter Eleven

'Written it all down, have you?' Greg asked. He'd been giving Lily dictation while prowling about in the warehouse, tidying away items that his customers had pulled from racks to inspect, then discarded. At present he had a crumpled tarpaulin spread out on the ground to straighten it. 'Read it back so I know you've got everything,' he ordered, while bringing the sides of the canvas to the middle. The ends were then repeatedly folded over until they overlapped at the centre and formed a neat parcel. Finally the sheet was secured with string and put back in its place, the whole slick process having taken under a minute.

Lily consulted her notes. 'We take a deposit on everything, even little extras like sets of scales and weights, 'cos if we don't we won't see them again.'

'That's it. What else?'

'I write down in the book a customer's name, what he's hired and how much he paid, and the total amount of his deposit. That only gets returned when everything is brought back in one piece, and on time. All the cash is locked away in the desk or filing cabinet. Then you put it in the safe at the end of the day. Only you and me ever have the keys to the desk.'

'And if a customer says he'll divvy up at the end of the day rather than in the morning? What d'you say?'

'I tell them it's not allowed,' she answered. She wasn't going to tell them to piss off, though that was the blunt phrase her boss had used. She imagined her brother now knew some quite colourful expressions from the company he'd been keeping. 'If I ever hire out stuff, I'm going to let my customers pay on return,' she piped up. 'I reckon you're losing business. If a man's got empty pockets in the morning, he'll hire his equipment elsewhere.' Lily remembered her father never had a farthing to hand over on going to work. Her mother would pace about, waiting for him to return from the railway yard with his day's pay, so she could dash out and buy something for supper. When he was on late shift, they might not eat until nine o'clock in the evening. The corner shop would still be open for a stale loaf and a penn'orth of broken biscuits. During those final months together, after he'd lost his job as a solicitor's clerk and was drinking heavily, they'd existed every day hand to mouth. Lily thought her boss was being callous, but she hadn't swayed him with her argument.

'A coster who's not earned much won't hand over to me what little he has got. So it's up front or nothing.'

'You could keep a tally and charge interest when he's had a better day,' Lily suggested.

'Right . . . I'll charge you interest on your tally,' Greg said, hooking up a length of rope he'd just wound into a coil.

'No, you won't!' she said defensively, earning herself a quizzical look.

'Outfits that let punters run a tab go bust. They charge

double my rates 'cos they don't take deposits and their stuff goes missing. I'm running a business not a charity,' he said. 'I'm not waitin' in line behind the bookmaker and the pub landlord, or their missus, for that matter. When you go it alone you shouldn't either.' Greg approached the desk to look over her shoulder. He flicked over the notebook's pages, scanning her neat columns of figures listing prices of hired items.

'You seem to know what you're doing so far,' he faintly praised, then tapped the bottom of the page. 'At the end of each day you can add up the takings.' Before walking away he said, 'I'll have to get you an abacus for that, I suppose.'

Lily winced at that dig about her slip-up earlier. But her pride helped her rally. 'No need to go to that expense, guv'nor. In future I'll do me sums using all me fingers 'n' toes.' She had slipped into addressing him the way Davy did.

Her insolence made him smile. A moment later Lily was smiling too.

'You can knock off now and catch up on some sleep,' said Greg. 'Saturday's a big market day, so make sure you get here on time in the morning. Jane said she gave you something to sleep on; is the mattress uncomfortable?'

'No ... wasn't that ... it was the argument stopped me dropping off ... ' Lily froze and fell silent, darting a look his way. The good humour between them had made her gregarious, but the mood had changed now. She had almost blabbed out that his girlfriend and Clive Stratton were to blame for her oversleeping.

'Argument?'

Lily turned pale and chewed a corner of her lip, scouring

her mind for something innocent to say to explain away her remark.

'I opened Jane's clothes cupboard,' she burst out. 'I touched some of her lovely dresses. She didn't like it. It played on my mind and I couldn't get to sleep. That's all it was.'

'Right ...' he said. 'That blue dress suits you anyhow. Matches your eyes.'

'Thanks,' Lily murmured, self-consciously smoothing her skirt. She knew he didn't believe her. She was getting to know that sarcastic look. He wasn't even making an attempt to appear convinced by the tale. She hadn't told a complete lie, but describing that prickly exchange with Jane as an argument was definitely stretching the truth. She got up from the desk and walked quickly to the door, keen to escape before he questioned her again. 'See you tomorrow then, guv'nor. Thanks for ...' She wasn't sure what she wanted to thank him for; she just knew she'd been enjoying her first day at work before being careless.

'Thanks for what?'

'Thanks for the job and for showing me the ropes at the market. I appreciate it 'cos I want to learn. Won't be late tomorrow, promise.'

'Let's hope no more arguments keeping you up then,' he purred.

'Mmm ...' Lily shifted closer to the exit.

'Don't you want some wages?'

Lily blinked. 'Didn't think I had anything to come. I owe you for breakfast now as well as all the rest. Don't want a big debt building up, so take it off my tally, would you?'

'You'll need something to live on. Smudger said you're going to the caff later. They don't give grub away free at Mason's.'

'Bobby offered to treat me so I'm all right for now. Only want a cup of tea after that big fry-up.' She ignored her boss's outstretched hand with silver glinting on it. He thought giving her money was the way to delay and cross-examine her. Tempting though it was to have cash in her pocket, she kept her distance. She was a poor fibber and would eventually blurt out what she'd seen and heard last night. Then all hell might break loose. Perhaps he already had his suspicions that his girlfriend was a two-timer, and had planted her in Jane's flat as his spy in the camp. Whatever the truth of it, Lily didn't like the idea of being the bearer of bad news. Gregory Wilding had a ruthless streak, and Davy would blow his top if they both got the sack because she'd said something to send their boss into a temper.

Greg approached Lily and tipped a florin and a six-pence into her palm. She avoided his knowing hazel gaze, though she felt it burning into her skin.

'Right, see you in the morning.'

There were several parcels of newspaper-wrapped haddock on a shelf, shoved to the back where it was dark and cool. He had brought those in with him when they returned from the market. Lily had not long ago enjoyed a blow-out of bacon and eggs, washed down with a strong 'cuppa char', as the café proprietor called his liquorice-coloured tea. At the moment, food was the last thing on her mind. In a day she'd been fed more than she would have eaten in a week at the workhouse, and all of it delicious.

'Take that for your supper later. Know how to cook it, do you?' He seemed to assume she didn't, despite her nod. 'Put it in a skillet with some water for about fifteen minutes. Or stick it in a hot oven for about the same time. Tastes better done on the hob, though. Don't let it dry out.' He held out a package.

'Thanks very much, guv'nor.' Lily took the fish, stepping quickly to the door. 'Bye for now.' She slipped outside, then stood stock-still when she heard her name called. Reluctantly she turned back to see him walking after her.

'You'll need this. Jane won't be home to let you in; she'll have started her shift at the pub.'

'Right oh, thanks.' Lily grabbed the key he was holding out to her and fled. She was soon at the gate and heading along the road. She glanced back through the bars of railings and saw that he'd braced an arm on the open door of the warehouse, and was watching her.

*

'What in Gawd's name are you doing? Bleedin' stink woke me up. It's gone right through the place.'

Lily turned from the stove to see her flatmate in the kitchen doorway. Jane had a hand on her hip and her nose wrinkled in distaste.

'I'm cooking haddock fillet for tea. Want some? It's huge, so plenty for two if you fancy a bit.'

'No, I don't want none!' Jane said ungratefully, yanking tight the belt on her silky dressing gown. She had returned from her shift at the pub about an hour ago, and gone straight to bed without realising that Lily was already home. She'd left for work believing her unwanted flatmate was locked out. 'Greg's taking me out to eat. And how did you get in without a key, might I ask?'

'Guv'nor gave me his. He let me knock off early and knew you wouldn't be home.'

Jane looked deflated to hear that. 'Right, well give it here and I'll make sure he gets it back. You won't be living here long enough to need your own key.'

Lily pulled the heavy key from her pocket and handed it over. She could have returned it herself in the morning but it seemed her flatmate didn't want her to hold on to it a minute longer in case she felt too at home. She nipped back to the cooker to turn the gas off and let the fish cool in the pan. A chunk of white flesh had flaked off into the steaming water and, impatient to sample it, she fished it out, scalding her fingers. It tasted succulent and creamy. She used the palette knife she'd found in a drawer to tip the fillet on to a plate; it seemed done to perfection.

'The place looks different; you been tidying up while I was out?' Jane asked accusingly.

Lily nodded. 'I thought you wanted me to. Anyhow, I would have ended up with bad guts if I'd used the kitchen without cleaning it first.' She'd intended taking a catnap when she got home from work, but first had looked for a cool place to store the fish for cooking later. Her investigation had brought to light how filthy everything was. She'd peered into the rancid-smelling oven and spotted mice droppings amongst the congealed grease. There'd been some on the floor of the larder too, although it was bare of anything but chipped crockery and dented pans. Her search hadn't turned up any disinfectant, so her trusty piece of Sunlight soap had come into play again. Lily had boiled some water in a pot and dissolved half to make cleaning fluid, saving what remained of the soap to wash herself in later. The lino on the floor was cracked, but at least it was now spotless after she'd gone on to hands and knees to scrub it. She'd dunked the plates bearing indeterminate food scraps in soapy water too, scouring the china with more rag torn from her workhouse uniform. Lily had felt immense satisfaction at putting the hated garment to such use. When she'd finished and stood, satisfied, surveying her work, she'd realised she couldn't have been as tired as she'd thought.

'Nobody cooks at home, y'know.' Jane had turned huffy at the implication she lived amongst dirt. 'We all eat out in the caffs, so I never bother much with the kitchen.' She sashayed to the back door and opened it, dramatically waving her arms about to clear the air.

'You *never* cook?' Lily knew she wasn't spending all her earnings in caffs.

'What, here?' Jane gave a derisive snort. 'Last time I stirred a pot was when me dad was laid up with lumbago and the customers insisted on having their pie 'n' mash 'n' gravy at dinnertime. Dad said I had to serve 'em something or they'd scarper up the road to the Bull. Reg Wright can bake you anything you like, when he's on form.' She proudly praised her dad. 'I take after me mother, in that respect. She ruined every meal she stuck in the oven.' She rolled her eyes. 'The bakery delivered the pies, but I boiled up spuds for mash and made a jug of gravy to pour on top.' Jane basted imaginary pastry with a swing of a hand. 'Customers said it was just the job, so I surprised meself. Anyway, I've got a rich boyfriend so can eat in nice places and keep me hands pretty.'

Lily felt tempted to ask her boastful flatmate which rich boyfriend she was referring to, but held her tongue and turned her attention to her meal.

'Suppose in the workhouse they make you skivvy in the kitchen, do they? Noticed your hands are all rough.' Jane pulled a sympathetic face.

'Us younger women had to do cleaning and washing.' Lily crossed her arms, hiding her red hands beneath her armpits, though she'd never been self-conscious of them before. 'The master was probably afraid we might pinch extra rations if we got near the kitchen larders.' She picked up her supper. 'Sure you don't want half of this?' The idea of eating all the haddock made Lily feel greedy, yet her flatmate waved it away as though being offered poison. Lily carried her plate into the corridor, intending to sit down on her bedroom chair and savour her first home-cooked meal for five years. Before entering her room she said, 'Bobby Smith's asked me to go the caff. Do you know where Mason's is?'

'On the High Street.' Jane was examining her nails but she stopped to give Lily a sly smile. 'You didn't hang about. Found yourself a sweetheart already, have you?'

'No!' Lily tutted. 'He's treating me to a cup of tea so he can get to know me. He seems nice and friendly.'

'Boys always are when they want to get into yer knickers.'

Lily turned red and spluttered, 'Don't reckon he's like *that ...*'

Jane hooted. 'They're all like that, love.' She cocked her head, amused by Lily's discomfiture. 'How old was you when you went inside that spike?'

'Ten ...' Lily said rather defensively, wondering what was coming next.

'So you've not learned about men and their dirty ways, have you?'

'Fanny Miller told us a few things about you know ...
all of that ...' Lily's first conversation with Fanny had been
about how babies were made. Shortly after Lily turned
fourteen, she had been shocked to discover blood on her
underclothes on waking one morning. She'd dashed to
Mrs Windham to ask to see the medical officer urgently.
The woman had told her to stop making a fuss as it was
just a 'woman's complaint'. The dormitory officer had
given her rags to stuff into her bloomers. Later on Fanny
had been the one to explain what was happening to her
once a month. Lily had felt grateful and relieved that she'd
not waylaid Adam Reeve and embarrassed them both
because she thought she might be dying.

'Fanny's warned you, has she, to keep your knees
together until you've got a ring on your finger or the boy's
wearing a johnnie?'

'Umm ... yes,' Lily said, though she'd only understood
half of that. She'd not a clue about a johnnie.

'Bet Fanny wishes she'd taken her own advice then, if
she got herself knocked up and ended up in the workhouse.' Jane gave a shiver at the very thought of entering
such a place. 'If you need to know anything else about that
sort of thing, you can ask me. Ain't much I don't know
about men trying it on.'

Lily had a feeling she was about to be regaled with
tales of Jane's love life, and she didn't want to hear them.
Especially if they concerned Gregory Wilding. He might
be a hard-nosed Cockney, but he was handsome and kind
in his own way, and Lily reckoned he could do better for
himself than the cheating Jane Wright.

'Thanks ... I'll remember it.' She'd had enough of this
conversation. 'I shan't be gone more than a couple of hours,

but if I'm not back before you go out, would you leave me a key somewhere? I'm early to bed and up again at the crack of dawn.'

'Make sure you are up on time too! Took me ages to fall asleep again this morning after your brother woke me.'

'Sorry. Overslept ... couldn't drop off for ages.' Lily avoided her flatmate's eye.

'You *did* drop off. You was snoring when I poked me head round your door.' Jane gave her a penetrating look. 'Was you making out to be asleep then? Not been snooping on me, have you?'

''Course not ... Sorry about the disturbance. Would you leave the key out?'

'I'll put it under the flower pot.' Jane sighed heavily. 'I want it back straight away, though. You're not keeping it.'

Jane seemed to consider it a huge favour. Before the woman could have second thoughts, or probe into what Lily might have witnessed that she shouldn't have, Lily changed the subject. 'I hope Davy will be at the caff actually. We've got lots to talk about.'

'Well, if he *is* there and ain't expecting you to drop in, you might get a bit of a surprise.'

'What do you mean by that?'

Jane shrugged, already walking away. 'You'll find out for yourself soon enough.'

Lily stared at her flatmate's closed door for a full minute before entering her own room. Slowly she forked the fish into her mouth, but it could have been skilly for the enjoyment she now got from it. It seemed everybody had something to say about her brother. Jane had hooked her with a cryptic comment then clammed up. But Lily could guess what she had meant.

Her father had frequented a caff that had a back room for illegal gambling and drinking so he could hide his vices from his family. But Maude hadn't been a fool; Lily had heard her mother tearing him off a strip about squandering his wages at 'that dive'. Lily imagined at Mason's she might come across her brother acting like the father he despised.

The very thought exasperated Lily. They had been given a second chance at being a happy family, and the wonder of it still sent a thrill through her. She clung to the hope that her brother might also thank his lucky stars, once they'd had that talk and he knew their deceased little sister hadn't been allowed a single second of life or luck.

Having finished her tea, Lily washed up and tidied everything away, then carried a bowl of fresh water to her room. As she scrubbed her face with a cloth, she felt a tingle of anticipation. This was her first evening out as an adult. It might only be a trip to a caff with a friend, but she couldn't wait to do it, or any of the other ordinary things people got up to.

She would've liked to borrow Jane's hairbrush, but didn't ask in case Jane fired questions at her about why she'd overslept. Jane had looked shifty just now, as though she suspected she might have been rumbled kissing Clive Stratton. As for Jane reckoning Bobby fancied her flatmate, there wasn't much chance of that! He'd said Lily looked like a drowned rat earlier, and she hadn't felt offended. A simple friendship suited her because she didn't fancy him. But she liked Bobby and was looking forward to seeing him again.

She began loosening the snarls in her long thick hair with her fingers, and promised herself that tomorrow after work she'd stretch her two and sixpence as far as she possibly could, buying essentials. A trip to the municipal baths before they closed was at the top of her list, then she'd be off to the market to rummage on the second-hand stalls. She was polishing her boots with another strip of cotton torn from her uniform when she heard a loud knock at the door.

Jane got there first and opened up. Bobby had spied Lily along the corridor and gave her a wave. 'Thought I'd come and get you to take you for that cup of tea. Been visiting me mum so was over this way in any case.'

Jane poked her tongue to the inside of her cheek, sending Lily a wink for good measure. Lily stopped herself rolling her eyes, though she couldn't prevent herself blushing. She hoped Bobby hadn't a clue what the older woman was insinuating, or he might curl up with embarrassment.

'You've got here just on time,' Lily announced brightly. 'I've finished getting ready.' She brushed a speck from her dress, wishing she had a change of clothes. Yesterday she'd been glad to just have this one good garment. 'Early start again tomorrow, isn't it,' she said conversationally as she headed towards the front door.

'You'll get used to the hours after a while.' Bobby stood aside to let Lily go first up the stone steps. 'We sell fruit and veg on Saturday.' Bobby resumed talking about work as they began to stroll along the lane. 'I'll be back on my usual round and Fred's on the pitch in Chrisp Street instead of Davy.' He chuckled. 'We all like getting a turn on the stall. Pushing a loaded cart fer miles ain't much fun.'

'Can imagine, Lily replied, though she was only half listening. She was in two minds whether to ask Bobby what her brother was up to this evening, but she didn't want it to get back to him that she'd been checking on his movements. As they drew level with Eunice Smith's tenement, something occurred to Lily. 'Are you just visiting your mum then? Don't you live with her?'

'I lodge with the lads,' he said jauntily. 'I always call by and see Mum Fridays, though. Bring her in a bit of fish and she cooks us both a nice tea with fried spuds and mushy peas.' He glanced up to a first-floor window and waved. Eunice wasn't concealing the fact she was watching her strapping son out walking with a girl. 'I moved out so Mum could rent my old boxroom. She could do with the money 'cos charring don't pay much. The guv'nor pays the rent for the bedsit we all share, so it made sense for Mum to find a lodger. She misses me being there. I miss her too, but now I'm sixteen I prefer having me freedom, if you know what I mean.'

'I do.' Lily had the opening she needed. 'Davy likes being one of the lads and having his freedom too, I imagine?' It was a leading question but Bobby avoided answering it.

'Guv'nor don't pay generous wages, but we get benefits like our lodgings and a fish supper and a cotchel of fruit and veg once a week. I give Mum my share; the others sell theirs.' He grinned at Lily. 'Then best of all we get our bunce on top.' Bobby jerked a thumb to indicate they were turning on to Cotton Street.

'Bunce?' Lily had heard her boss use that word but hadn't got much of an explanation from him of what it meant.

'Extra cash we earn for ourselves from skimming. Like when we sell a pint of cockles or whelks and give a short measure. Do it on five pints and you've got enough spare to make another pint to sell for yourself. Bunce is important to a coster's lad, but you gotta do it right. A bit of flattery's needed on the doorstep; keep the customer occupied while you're doing some sleight of hand. A sidekick has to learn all the dodges 'cos an extra bob or two put in a jar gives him a chance to be independent of his guv'nor eventually.' Bobby shrugged. ''Course it's hard not to dip into a kitty when you know it's there. I had a ten-bob note put by from bunce then blew the lot in one go.' He regretfully shook his head. 'Good job me mum never knew. She'd have gone nuts. Deserved some sense knocked into me 'n' all. Tossed a coin half a dozen times and lost me savings and me good jacket. Bloody fool, I was.'

Lily indeed thought he *was* mad, but simply grunted in sympathy. Lecturing her brother was enough for her. If Davy also gambled to such an extent, she'd have a job on her hands stopping him. 'Suppose, as well as skimming, you keep your thumb on the scale when selling a pound of carrots, do you?'

'That's it.' He laughed. 'Davy put you wise to that trick, did he?'

Her brother had put her wise to very little, especially about what he got up to. 'No, the guv'nor did. I reckon he knows about you all pinching his stock for your bunce.'

''Course he does.' Bobby grinned. 'Guv'nor expects it. S'long as the customers are the ones getting short-changed, he's not bothered. If he was . . . ' Bobby whistled a caution through his teeth. 'Me granddad told me not to ever try crossing him. So fair warning, Lily.' Bobby gave a meaningful nod.

She remembered receiving similar advice from Fanny Miller about Gregory Wilding. Lily knew to heed it too, after seeing her boss throttling the café owner who'd tried to 'stitch him up'. Nobody did that, she recalled he'd said.

'Let's go to the Lyons Corner House. Ain't far to walk.' Bobby stuck out his elbow for her to take his arm.

'Aren't we off to Mason's caff?'

'Give that a miss on a Friday night. Gets a bit rowdy with all the market traders in there. Gel like you deserves a better welcome on your first day on the firm.'

'I would have liked to see Davy, if he's going to be at the caff. D'you reckon he will?'

'He sometimes goes to the dog track with Fred on a Friday night,' Bobby said, then started reeling off other little tricks of the trade that could help a fledgling coster build a nest egg.

Some of the stunts were quite ingenious and she couldn't help but chuckle. But Lily felt sorry too for the customers on the wrong end of the scam. When they fell into strolling along in amicable quiet, Lily's mind wandered to her brother again. She wondered if he was at the greyhound track or whether he'd told his pal to say he was, to avoid her. It was a sobering thought that such a thing had occurred to her when their reunion was barely a day old.

But there was loads of time for them to make things right.

Chapter Twelve

August 1914

'Don't you dare tip me out!' Lily squeaked as Bobby careered around a corner with her hanging on for dear life to the splintery sides of the wheelbarrow. Her long wavy hair was flowing out behind her like a conker-coloured flag as they raced along.

'We hammered you.' Davy punched a fist skyward in victory as he was trundled over the finish line round the back of the warehouse. He jumped out of his ride and held out his hand for his teammate to shake.

Fred was gasping after charging along pushing the barrow. He gave Davy's fingers a single pump, then rolled up his shirtsleeves to flex his biceps at the loser. 'Need muscles like these, old son, if you want to win a barrer race,' he breathlessly boasted, as Bobby crossed the chalk stripe on the concrete with Lily fanning her laughing face.

Bobby plonked down the barrow and she rose gingerly from her kneeling position on the scratchy base. The white-knuckle ride had left her feeling giddy, and she gratefully took Bobby's hand as he offered to help her alight. Having shaken the creases from her skirt, she patted his shoulder in thanks and consolation. 'I reckon a rematch is in order, Bob. They cheated coming round that bend, barging us out of the way like that.'

'Take you on again anytime you like.' Davy puffed out his pigeon chest. 'Right now, if you're up for the challenge.' He cocked his head at Fred. 'All right by you, skipper?' His question received a firm answering nod.

Lily sent Bobby a quizzical look. He appeared shattered after round one, let alone doing it all again.

'Give us a mo to catch me breath then, and I'll be with you,' Bobby wheezed, fumbling in a pocket for some cigarettes. He lit one, sucking on it repeatedly.

'You jump in this time and I'll push you,' Lily offered as Bobby coughed and thumped his chest with a fist.

Fred snorted a scornful laugh, retrieving a half-smoked cigarette stashed behind an ear. 'A gel push a bloke? You won't even make it halfway round the course, Lil. By rights Smudger should've won just now, being as I had more weight in me barrer.'

'Bet Davy doesn't weigh more than me,' Lily returned. Davy had always been slightly built. During their years apart he hadn't filled out much, although he had overtaken her in height by about an inch. 'Bet I do make it right round the course too.' Lily spat on her hand and held it out, copying what she'd seen the boys do when making wagers.

'You don't gamble so what you staking then? A kiss?' Fred taunted, giving her a lecherous wink before taking a drag on his newly lit dog-end.

Lily wasn't fazed by the dare though she'd seen him ogling her. She guessed she wasn't the only girl Fred Jenkins gave the eye to. She'd been working at Wilding's for over three months, but it had taken just a few days of his company to suss him out. He was the oldest and brashest of them all. He'd told Lily he'd already turned seventeen and was getting engaged to his sweetheart, or 'me doxy', as he termed her. Lily had come to realise that Fred used the word as a term of affection. Getting engaged or not, it seemed he'd no intention of packing in flirting. Bobby had never put a foot out of line, though Lily was aware he had a crush on her. They'd been to the Lyons Corner House several times, and she'd insisted on paying her way. She'd found an excuse when he asked her to the flicks. It wouldn't be fair if he started to read more into their friendship than there was. She was keeping her first-ever trip to a cinema to share with somebody else. She'd almost saved enough now to make an excursion to Whitechapel to see Adam Reeve and treat him to tea at a caff as a thank-you for all he'd done for her. But it was Margie who was top of her list to go to the flicks with. Fanny too, if she could find somebody to look after her baby. Lily missed Margie even more now than she had on the day she left the workhouse. But her savings jar had less than five shillings in it; that wouldn't go far in persuading the master that Lily Larkin now had the means to provide her crippled friend with board and lodging.

'You got an answer for me?' Fred sidled closer to Lily, dropping his cigarette butt and puckering up lips through which smoke drifted.

'Give it a rest,' Bobby snarled and elbowed Fred away, making him stumble.

'Oi ... who you shovin'?' Fred rushed back at him, but Lily stepped between them.

'It's all right, Bobby. I can handle him,' she said. 'Kiss

on the cheek, if you win.' She tapped the side of her face. 'That's your lot, Fred Jenkins.'

'You two still walking out?' Fred knew his pal was soft on Lily and would make digs about it. 'Eunice ain't scared Lil off then, Smudger?'

'I said give it a bleedin' rest, now.' Bobby had had enough of being taunted.

'We having a bet on this race or not?' Davy took a coin out of his pocket and flipped it. 'Tanner says me sister will get past halfway pushing Bobby.'

'You're supposed to be on my side,' Fred grumbled, matching the stake with a sixpence from his pocket.

'I can't nobble the race from where I'm sitting,' Davy pointed out with a grin.

'In you get, Bob.' Lily jerked her head at the barrow.

'I'll hang me legs over the side, Lil,' he hissed, climbing into it. 'That might make it a bit lighter for you.'

Aware Davy was watching and listening to their tactics, Lily poked out her tongue at him. He retaliated by gurning and twisting his ears, making her guffaw.

She adored getting glimpses of her Davy of old, which brought back reminders of their childhood closeness. Back then she'd almost known what he'd say before he said it. Now he constantly surprised her with what he came out with, and to have his company she'd learned to appear less eager for it. When run off her feet in the warehouse, dealing with customers wheedling for favours that she daren't give, her brother would loiter around to back her up. He still found excuses to avoid meeting up with her after work, though. Undoubtedly their bond was stronger on her side. When stuck in the Whitechapel workhouse with no bright outlook, she'd drawn comfort from glorifying the past. Her brother embodied every cherished family memory. But the future – even one that Davy might decide not to fully share – was becoming as important to Lily as harking back to bygone days. For Davy, living furiously in the moment was what mattered. And his pals were like-minded ... as though they were all fearful of their years being numbered.

On this warm August afternoon, the playful atmosphere had peeled away half a decade, returning the twins to the happy kids they'd once been. Lily felt optimistic that the long-overdue talk about their lost sister would finally take place today. With the passing of time its urgency had mellowed in her mind, if not its magnitude. But something else of magnitude had happened, and everybody was affected by it.

The news that they were at war with Germany had been shocking, and oddly exciting to the boys, but it all seemed very distant and unreal, especially on a glorious, carefree summer day such as this.

'Oi, daydreamer! Get on your marks.' Davy had seen his sister looking reflective and warned her that they were ready for the off.

In preparation for the effort, Lily undulated her shoulders, then grabbed the barrow by the handles. It was a struggle for her to move it up to the chalk mark. She had no intention of throwing in the towel, though, and called, 'Righto ... ready when you lot are.'

'*I'll* give the off this time,' Bobby growled. He hadn't forgotten Fred's teasing. 'You got an advantage last time, doing that, Jenkins.'

'Won't make no difference, lover boy. Still gonna give you both a hiding, even though I'm knackered.' Fred rolled the barrow about to show how easy he found the game. He might be Bobby's inferior in height and girth, but he had a wiry strength that the younger youth lacked.

Bobby stuck his shins over the side of their vehicle, then gave Lily's arm an unobtrusive squeeze to prime her. 'Go,' he bellowed.

Lily made a valiant effort, but was trailing the others before reaching the corner. By the time she could see the front gates, she was spent from exertion and laughing so much. Bobby was smacking the side of the barrow with an open palm, geeing her up as though she were a donkey.

Exhausted, Lily landed the barrow, then collapsed on to her backside in a fit of giggles. Bobby scrambled out of it and dragged her to her feet. She soon understood why he'd turned serious. Gregory Wilding was lounging against the warehouse door with a sheepish-looking Davy and Fred shuffling beside him. Their boss had gone earlier to collect some merchandise from one of his suppliers and they'd all believed the coast to be clear for a while yet.

The boys seemed to have collectively lost their tongues so Lily blurted, 'Just having a lark about, guv'nor, while we waited for you to come back.' Her arms felt like trembling lead weights hanging at her sides, so she crossed them over her middle to ease her pulsing muscles.

They all waited for him to say something. When he didn't, Lily got fed up with his silent treatment and marched towards the warehouse door, muttering, 'Nothing wrong with having some fun.'

'Ah ... that's where you're wrong, y'see. You have your fun on your own time, not on mine. You're not in a school playground now.'

'Finished our rounds, guv'nor. We all sold out,' Bobby piped up, trying to take the focus off Lily.

'Good ... let's have a count-up then, if you're done acting like kids.'

One of Lily's tasks was to tip each boy's takings into a separate labelled tin when they returned at the end of the day. The tins were locked in the desk. Their guv'nor then reconciled the purchases, profits and float before paying wages. In the filing cabinet there was a separate container for the collected hire charges. That was also dealt with by the boss and the money checked against the entries in Lily's accounts book after she'd gone home.

Lily had a funny feeling in her stomach as she went into the warehouse. She remembered locking all the tins away safely, and putting the key into the small filing cabinet as she'd been instructed to do if she went outside. The key to the locked cabinet was kept in her pocket.

Her uneasiness was merited: the desk key and the cabinet key were already in their locks. She yanked open the desk drawer and closed her eyes in relief. All three tins were present. With thumping heart she swivelled about to pull open the filing cabinet drawer and see that tin present too. Lily swivelled about to meet her boss's cool-eyed stare. 'I'm sure I locked everything.'

'She did, guv'nor ... remember seeing her do it.' Bobby looked at the others to back him up.

Davy and Fred nodded and mumbled in unison.

Lily had been flushed from running when she came inside, but the colour had fled from her complexion now. She felt an absolute fool ... she'd eagerly joined in larking about with the lads the moment they'd pushed their barrows into the warehouse earlier. The trio had returned from their rounds in high spirits, having sold out and made bunce. Believing themselves at a loose end until their boss returned, they'd not bothered tidying up but had started playing piggy in the middle with some sprouting potatoes. Bobby had immediately sided with Lily while the other two leapt about trying to intercept the flying spuds. Then Fred had suggested they take two wheelbarrows outside for a race. Starved of games and enjoyment for so long, Lily had been lapping it up. But ... had she rushed outside before going through the motions of locking up?

'If I've been careless, I'm sorry, guv'nor ...'

'Never mind about that now.' He snatched at the tins, lobbing each one on to the desk in a rattle of metal. 'Why isn't this lot back where it should be?' he shouted, swinging an arm to indicate the tarpaulins and scales that still lay in a jumble on the floor and barrows. He slung a glance at Davy. 'Get on with it. Make extra space 'n' all for the stuff I've brought back. There's two-score boxes of mixed linen needs stacking.'

'I'll help, Davy,' Lily immediately offered.

'Yes, you will,' her guv'nor told her while still glowering at Bobby and Fred. 'You two, outside and help me unload. Bring a couple of carts with you.'

'Wasn't expecting *him* for an hour at least,' she hissed at Davy when they were alone.

'He's probably sneaked back early to catch us out,' Davy sourly muttered, squashing canvases one on top of the other on the shelf to make extra room.

Lily sat down at her desk but got up again straight away. She peeped round the half-open door to watch Bobby and Fred dumping cartons on to the carts. Their boss seemed occupied too, opening lids and counting contents. It seemed to Lily they'd be outside for some while yet.

She glanced at her brother then blurted out, 'I must talk to you, Davy, about Mum and what really happened to her.' She pushed the door closed to give them as much privacy as possible. But stood close to it so she would hear if somebody approached. Then, as he swung towards her, she started to tell her tale.

*

'Ain't true! It's a load of fucking lies!'

'It *is* true, Davy.' Lily rushed to her brother, comforting him with a hug. She knew she'd shocked him, but she'd not expected him to react like that. She'd thought he'd be distressed not angered by the news of their lost sister. She hoped his outburst had been drowned out by the noise being made unloading the van. In the mood their guv'nor was in, she didn't want him barging in to investigate.

'That officer lied to punish you 'cos you climbed over the wall to find me.' Davy jerked himself free of her embrace, his grimace deepening until it was impossible to read his feelings.

'It's not a lie,' Lily stressed gently. 'I asked Mrs Windham about it. She denied it at first, but in the end confessed that Mum and the baby had been taken to the mortuary. She was nicer than the other officers and warned me that if I made a fuss the master wouldn't let me attend the funeral. He'd say I was too hysterical to be trusted out in public.' Even before she'd had a chance to confront Mrs Windham, Lily had worked things out for herself. The final hours spent with her family on that fateful Christmas Eve had played over and over in her head as she'd lain in the dark, banished to solitary confinement for breaking the strict rules of segregation. Pieces of a puzzle had slotted into place, making her howl with grief as she made sense of something her mother had said.

'I've two children you can see and another you can't.'

In her innocence, Lily had imagined her mother to be pretending to have abandoned one child. But Maude Larkin hadn't been lying to make the porter pity her. The *'little 'un'* she'd accused him of condemning to freeze to death hadn't been one of the twins shivering at her side, but the unborn baby in her belly.

The cruellest thing he could have done was be merciful. Her mother and sister might still be alive had he sent them packing. Taking their chances on the street couldn't have turned out worse for them than entering that place. The separation from her twins had broken Maude's spirit, contributing to her decline. In the end she had been too weak and heartsick to bring a healthy baby into the world.

'Why've you been keeping this to yourself anyway?' Davy demanded, swiping at his glistening eyes. He'd been furiously restacking pallets while composing himself.

'That's a bit rich!' Lily burst out. 'You know very well I've been trying to talk to you since I turned up here. You kept avoiding me and making excuses about meeting up after work.'

He looked sulky at that complaint but didn't deny it.

'Shall we visit the cemetery on Sunday afternoon?' Lily offered an olive branch.

'Don't know ...' Davy said.

'You said ages ago you wanted to.' Lily guessed his half-hearted attitude was due to him having nothing spare to contribute towards flowers. 'I've enough saved to buy a posy,' she coaxed.

A noncommittal grunt answered her, and exasperated her in the current tense atmosphere. 'Why can't you ever give me a straight answer?' she demanded. 'I take it you won't be coming to the cemetery, and if you've changed your mind about us being business partners, just tell me. Not going to say I don't mind, 'cos I do. I thought that's what we both wanted and to share a place of our own . . . '

'Well I don't!' he exploded. 'I ain't a kid now. I'm nearly sixteen and got me own life. Don't need me sister nagging me.' He growled in frustration then tried to make amends. 'We're still family, Lil, but I ain't ever going to be the little boy you remember or want me to be. We're grown-ups and got to go our separate ways.'

Lily felt as though he'd slapped her, but despite her shock she was still alert to approaching footsteps and the noise of creaking axles. 'Shhh . . . they're coming back.' She mumbled a warning.

Davy started industriously rearranging equipment on the shelf as the loaded carts were wheeled into the warehouse.

Lily sat down at her desk, while the others piled up the merchandise. She checked her figures in the account books through blurry vision, wondering why her brother had turned on her like that. She'd only told the truth. She got up and started putting the invoices away in the filing cabinet, continuing to neaten folders long after the job was done. The others had all congregated around the desk and she didn't want to go back there and sit down. The sales tins were emptied and the tally done. They received their wages from their boss, then Davy stepped away and she was aware he was sliding brooding glances at her.

Shortly afterwards, the three lads were heading for the

exit with gruff goodbyes. They were all subdued, now they'd been caught out skylarking instead of finishing up the day's chores. For Lily, though, that incident was forgotten; her melancholy was due to her brother having just cruelly shattered her dreams. She trudged to the open door, watching Davy walking with his friends to the corner. He was smoking, as they all were, and Lily noticed they were laughing again ... perhaps congratulating each other on having got off lightly. She wasn't sure she had.

Her brother's donkey-jacketed figure had disappeared round the corner before she turned away. She sniffed and briskly rubbed at the tears smarting her eyes, then waited for her boss to finish dredging the desk of coins that were cascading noisily back into the tins. She wanted to be paid so she could go home to lick her wounds.

'You want anything docked?'

'What?' Lily frowned, lost in thought.

'Do you want anything taken off your debt?' He spelled it out.

Lily shook her head, glancing at the door and wondering whether she could catch Davy up and try to make up with him.

'What's happened? You two fallen out?'

Lily had believed her boss to be too preoccupied to have noticed she was upset.

'I'm all right, thanks.' She put out her hand to take her wages so she could quickly get going. But he kept the money enclosed in his fist.

'Don't want any unrest in the camp, so you might as well own up. Heard him shouting before. Did Davy have a go at you for not locking up?'

189

'No, he didn't; and I'm not sure I did forget to do it,' she retorted then shrugged. 'We had words – something private – about our mum, that's all.' She was hoping he wouldn't pursue it but he did.

'Davy told me your mum died in the workhouse just as he was sent to the Cuckoo School.'

'Yes, she did . . . ' Lily murmured.

'That's a real shame. Ain't the place to spend your last days, that's fer sure.'

He sounded kind and the lump in her throat thickened, making her turn away to blink back fresh tears.

'Davy said she'd been suffering with bad bronchitis the winter you went in.'

'She couldn't work 'cos of it.' Lily said bitterly. 'Wish I'd been older . . . just a couple of years would've done. They'd have given me a job at that bloody laundry if I could've pretended to be thirteen. Mum went there every day, looking like death warmed up. She always got turned away. We never had a chance to earn enough for a room or food. Just a few years older, and me 'n' Davy could've helped out so Mum could rest till she felt better . . . ' Lily's voice broke and she suddenly sat down at the desk, cupping her face in her hands.

Greg pushed the tins away and hunkered down beside her.

'No point beating yourself or your brother up about it now, y'know. You was just two kids at the time.'

'Should've been three of us.' Lily thumped a hand on the desk in despair. 'That's what I was telling Davy. He didn't want to hear it. Our Mum didn't die of bronchitis. She had a baby in there.'

Greg looked thoughtful for a long moment then asked,

'What happened to it?' He placed a callused hand over hers in comfort.

'Same as what happened to her . . . ended up buried in a pauper's grave.' She wasn't sure why she'd confided in him just like that when she'd kept it to herself for so long. She pulled her hand free and stood up. 'Didn't tell you about it to make you feel sorry for me. If you want to believe I forgot to lock up, go ahead.'

He slowly rose to face her. 'If you locked up, who opened up?'

Their eyes held and she read in his ironic expression just what he was thinking. One of the boys had been rummaging for some reason. And what would they be after, but money? Yet he'd checked their tins in front of them and paid their wages. He wouldn't have done that if the cash didn't tally. All hell would have broken loose.

'Don't know what's happened,' she mumbled. 'Perhaps me brain's playing tricks on me lately. I must've been to blame.' She wouldn't drop anybody in it, although she had a good idea who might be responsible. Fred had disappeared into the warehouse for several minutes before the start of the barrow race. He'd said he'd left his fags on the shelf when they'd started chucking spuds. He'd come out with the Woodbines and smoked half a cigarette before sticking the stub behind his ear. They all knew the desk key was locked away in the cabinet. And often when it was just staff in the warehouse, she left the cabinet key in its lock. But earlier she could have sworn she'd put the cabinet key in her pocket.

At first Lily had been surprised that her boss had no reservations about his workers seeing where the takings were kept. As she came to know him better, she realised he didn't trust their honesty, just knew that they'd be terrified of the consequences when he discovered the theft. The only liberty the guv'nor allowed was the taking of bunce. He would know too if money went missing; he was able to swiftly calculate a balance sheet down to the last farthing.

'Can I have me wages now, guv'nor? I want to go home,' Lily said.

Greg gave her the cash then plunged his hands in his trouser pockets. 'Very sorry to hear what happened to your mum and the baby.'

'Thanks,' she said hoarsely, putting her money away in her bag. 'I am too ... but you know what, I'm glad me little sister never lived a second in that place. Poor little mite would've been stuck in a cold orphan's cradle with no mum to love her. The mean pigs would have separated them, even if Mum had survived.' She shook her head, incensed. 'They did that to Fanny and her little boy.'

'Real shame about your dad too.' Greg paused. 'Davy told me he was found dead by the canal.'

Lily nodded, amazed that Davy had mentioned that to his guv'nor. But she was coming to realise she didn't know Davy as well as she thought she did. 'Everything was fine when we were little. We were happy. Then it all went wrong, and don't even know why.' She shook her head. 'S'pose Dad felt ashamed after what he did. Then he started drinking and couldn't stop.'

'What did he do? Davy just told me something bad happened.'

'Dad was accused of stealing. Don't know why he would have done that. He had a good job. Maybe it was something to do with the woman.'

'He was playing around with someone?'

'Don't know. I overheard Mum yelling at him about a woman. And I saw him once with a lady in the street. They didn't see me; I was about nine and was coming home from school. They didn't look lovey-dovey. Dad seemed to be trying to get away from her, as though she was getting on his nerves. I didn't think any more of it at the time.' Lily hung her head. 'But I've been thinking a lot about things just lately. And I'm sure he loved my mum and she loved him.' She shrugged. 'Anyway, once he'd passed away and Mum got bronchitis . . . ' Lily's voice tailed away. Her guv'nor knew where the Larkin family's disaster had eventually led and she didn't want to mention the workhouse again.

'Where was your stepfather in all this?'

'Did Davy say we had a *stepfather*?' Lily had turned to go but swung back with an astonished expression.

'No . . . just assumed . . . after what you said.' Greg stacked the boys' tins and turned his attention to the hire charges tin, tipping out a stream of silver and copper and a ten-shilling note on to the desktop.

Lily sensed he was trying to cover something up now. 'Why would you assume something like that?'

'Forget it. Get off home. And no more larking about. I expect more sense from you. Know those three are a lost cause, though.'

He'd started counting the cash but Lily wasn't finished. 'Tell me what you mean by it,' she insisted fiercely, grabbing his arm to make him look at her.

He planted both hands on the edge of the desk, sending her a sidelong frown. 'Your father had been dead a while before you went inside that place, hadn't he?'

'We managed to get by for four months without him.'

193

He stared at her, as though waiting for her to make the connection he had. But she continued raking his face with vivid blue eyes, hoping to detect a clue to his meaning.

'Your mum must've had another man in her life then, wouldn't you say.' His tone was soft.

Lily's eyes narrowed on him in outrage. 'What d'you mean? What're you saying about my mum?' Her mind had whipped back through the years to a bristly faced officer who'd leered at her while, in the background, smoke choked the air. He'd told her she'd be a fallen woman like her dead mother. And Lily had whacked him as hard as she could. Now she lashed out with a hand that glanced off a lean profile as her boss reared back, having seen it coming.

She backed away towards the door. 'You're just saying that to be spiteful 'cos we've been larking about and I forgot to lock up!'

'Fuck's sake!' he roared. He was raising a hand as he strode towards her. 'I warned you not to hit me again!'

Lily stopped in her tracks, letting him come right up to her. But the fist aimed at her face didn't hurt, instead opened to grip her chin.

'Why would I be spiteful to you? Think about it. You're not a kid,' he gritted out through his teeth and gave her a shake before letting her go.

'You said I was before!' she stormed.

He sat down at the desk, shoving his fingers through his fair hair, looking like a man who wished he knew how to keep his mouth shut. 'Look, if your dad died and then your mum had a baby about a year later ... doubtful it was your dad's child, isn't it? Maybe Davy's realised it and that's why he's just blown his top.'

He'd started to move his knuckles back and forth on his jaw where she'd slapped him. Lily didn't care if she'd hurt him ... she didn't care if she got the sack. She didn't care about anything but defending her mother. Maude Larkin had been the best, most selfless person Lily had ever known and she wouldn't hear one word against her. But a glimmer of understanding was strengthening into a blinding stream of memories ... too many to cope with. She'd been about to blame him again but, instead, she dashed to the door. Once she'd turned out of the front gate, she started to sob, and to run.

Chapter Thirteen

The chill damp air didn't bother Lily, and not simply because she now had a jacket to huddle into. Her excitement had caused her heartbeat to flutter and race, making her uncomfortably hot despite the worsening weather. She was sheltering from the drizzle beneath a canopy of leaves. The sycamores had been planted long ago and were now gnarled with age. As a breeze dislodged rain droplets from foliage, the cool shower felt pleasant on her complexion. Nevertheless, she shifted closer to the trunk. She didn't want to appear a drowned rat, today of all days. She'd taken trouble with her appearance, dressing in her best and brushing her hair until it shone and curled neatly on to her shoulders. Yesterday she'd splashed out on a bar of Pears soap, then had spent an hour at her local baths luxuriating in the scented water. Her most expensive treat had been something she couldn't barter for: a small bottle of lavender water purchased from the chemist. Before setting out for Whitechapel earlier, she had shaken it liberally on to her skin.

For almost half an hour she'd been loitering across the road from the premises that had housed her for so long.

She'd reached her destination deliberately early so as not to risk missing Adam's departure. Working as his clerk, she'd learned a bit about his weekly routine. Sundays, he would arrive before eight o'clock in the morning, visit the infirmary to check on the patients, then report to the master's office. If any emergencies needed to be dealt with, he'd be delayed in leaving at his usual hour of two o'clock. Lily guessed it must be almost that time now, and the anticipation of soon seeing him, talking to him, caused another rush of blood to flush her cheeks.

When a schoolgirl, she'd taken little notice of the workhouse she was leaving or entering. She could study the building dispassionately now and concluded it wasn't as huge or as intimidating as it had seemed when she'd walked its stone-cold corridors. A 'spike' held no terrors for her, since she knew she'd sooner starve than enter one again as an inmate. But she'd bang on the door of South Grove workhouse the moment she had the means to apply to discharge Margie. Confronting the master and mistress didn't bother her, and neither did being brought face to face with Harriet Fox.

If her friend were in the dormitory today – a possibility, as it was the Sabbath and a day of rest – Margie wouldn't be able to see her from those high windows. But it was easy to imagine her friend's melancholy face behind the rain-spattered glass. How Lily wished she could march in there right now and take her friend home with her. Lily started to attention as the gate swung open ... but the man emerging wasn't the one she'd hoped to see. She recognised the fellow, though, having caught a glimpse of Ben Stone before he shielded his face with an umbrella and strode off towards the High Street. Lily retreated beneath her insubstantial shelter. A moment later, and with a small joyous sound, she was again on the move.

Adam had stopped by the lodge to speak to the porter. He had no umbrella, just his hat to keep the rain off. She fondly watched him pull up his collar and continue chatting. He was the best sort of gentleman – always finding time for everybody, even if it meant getting drenched.

Lily waited impatiently for a horse and cart to pass, then sprinted across the road after him, catching up with him as he was about to enter a tobacconist's. He spun about as she called his name and her heart soared. Genuine delight had creased his face into a smile the second he recognised her.

'Lily! What a lovely surprise!' Adam drew her into the shop doorway, out of the rain. 'I've been thinking of you, hoping you were faring well in your new life. Let me look at you.' He ran his eyes over her. 'My, you've blossomed, and only a short while spent on the outside. It's obvious your cousin is caring for you.' He gave her fingers a fond squeeze, his smiling eyes continuing to admire the change in her.

'Will you come to a caff and have tea with me, please?' Lily blurted, hanging on to his fingers as he would have withdrawn. 'I've so much to talk about.' He seemed lost for words by her invitation. 'I want to treat you as a thank-you for everything you did for me in that place,' Lily coaxed.

'Well ... I haven't finished work for the day. I've the wards in Pentonville Prison still to visit.'

'Oh ... sorry, didn't realise you were still on duty.' Lily looked crestfallen. There was a question spinning in her head and she'd ask it right here if she had to, even though it was a sensitive subject and they were blocking the shop's doorway, so that people were trying to squeeze past them. She couldn't go home without knowing the truth about her sister. And who better to ask about birth and death than a medical officer? There had been a brief opportunity yesterday to talk to her flatmate, but Lily hadn't asked Jane's advice. Lily might hear old wives' tales from a woman who'd never had children. But Adam would know plain facts.

'I daresay a quick refreshment break won't delay me that much,' he kindly agreed. 'I can buy cigarettes later.' He steered her towards the kerb. 'Let's go to the nearest caff. It's a bit of a greasy spoon, but the tea and buns are nice. If we make a dash for it, we won't get too soaked.'

Lily smiled happily and gladly took his hand when he held it out to hurry her across the road with him.

*

Greg had been emerging from the house of a business acquaintance who lived on the Mile End Road. The fellow had a knack of knowing when merchandise bound for Selfridges was likely to fall off the back of a truck. He was too timid to sell it on himself, but Greg didn't mind taking it off his hands and putting it on his barrows, if the price was right. Today he'd concluded a sweet deal and had been about to drive off in the van. But he'd stopped whistling the moment he spotted Lily hand in hand with Adam Reeve.

He sat back in the seat, an odd feeling in his guts as he watched them go into the caff. From the moment Davy Larkin had pointed out his sister in a group of workhouse girls, Greg had felt fate was having a game with him. She wasn't exactly like Catherine: her hair too brown, and eyes too blue. But Lily Larkin was similar enough in looks – character too, now he'd got to know her – for him to ache inside when she was close to him. His cousin – his real one – had been a year older than him, and would've been twenty-two now had she survived the spike.

Greg took out a packet of cigarettes and lit one, staring across the road. They'd taken a table by the window and he could see them talking animatedly. Lily was gazing at Reeve in a way that twisted the knife and made him want to leap out of the van and drag her out of there. Yet she was with a good man, somebody she seemed to love and trust. Her brother notwithstanding, she was nobody's fool in Greg's estimation. But she was young and inexperienced around men ... easy prey. Perhaps Reeve loved her back ... despite their age difference. Greg guessed the man was a few years older than he was, so being a doctor didn't mean he was a paragon of virtue. Greg had vowed to keep his hands to himself where Lily Larkin was concerned, telling himself she was just a lovely, gutsy kid. But he lay awake at night, thinking about her instead of the woman by his side. He took a hefty drag on the cigarette, watching them through a smoke haze. Despite the tug on his heartstrings, he couldn't be sure she wasn't a sly cow who'd started to steal, impatient to set herself and her brother up on their own. She was devoted to Davy, yet he wasn't worthy of it. He certainly wasn't worth serving time for. But if she thought she could smile and act the innocent with Gregory Wilding, then have him over, she was wrong. He tossed the half-smoked cigarette out of the window and drove off.

He wasn't the only person who'd noticed the couple

together. Harriet Fox had followed Ben Stone out of the workhouse, hoping to catch him up and have it out with him. For weeks he'd been avoiding her – even at bedtime – and she was afraid he was about to throw her over. Well, she wasn't going to let him do that, when for years she'd pinned her hopes on being his wife, enjoying the perks his parents had as master and matron of South Grove. Ben no longer spoke about their future plans and ignored her when she brought the subject up. The unexpected sight of Lily Larkin – looking annoyingly attractive – had reminded Harriet that *all* the Stones owed her a debt of gratitude because of that bloody family. If they thought they could edge her out of the picture now a few years had passed by since she'd helped avert a scandal, they'd discover she had different ideas on that. A few pounds paid wasn't nearly enough when a life of ease was at stake. She chuckled to herself as she saw Lily gazing adoringly at the medical officer. Pretty as she was, Lily Larkin would get nowhere with him! He'd already shacked up with the love of his life. Harriet snapped up her umbrella and walked on. She'd loitered for too long watching Lily; she was too late to follow Ben and demand some answers. But the pubs were open and she felt in need of a strong snifter before going back inside the workhouse.

*

'Now tell me all about what you've been up to,' Adam said, stirring sugar into his tea. 'I can tell you've been earning some wages and eating good food. You've filled out and look very pretty in your new clothes.'

Lily blushed at his compliment, pleased that he'd

noticed her blossoming figure. The work dress Jane had given her now fitted perfectly. Lily no longer needed to use the belt she'd bought down Chrisp Street market. It had been from the same second-hand stall where she'd haggled with the merchant for her Sunday best, worn for the first time today: a smart, navy blue costume and the first handbag she'd ever owned. As Adam reached across the table, squeezing her fingers, Lily's optimism soared that he'd ask to see her again before they parted today. She felt like an attractive young woman on a date with her boyfriend. And it was wonderful.

She'd never been awkward with Adam before, but their changing relationship made her self-conscious about bringing up the subject of carnality. She'd fantasised about him kissing her, now nothing but a half a dozen or so unimportant years in age separated them.

'I'm sixteen soon,' she said shyly.

'Well, you look quite the young lady too,' he replied.

Lily glowed beneath the warmth in his eyes. 'Has Fanny Miller been discharged with her little son?' Talking about babies could lead to a mention of her mother's pregnancy.

'She has indeed. Fanny looked elated to finally have the little lad all to herself. I found her a shawl to wrap him in to take him home, and told her to make sure never to come back.'

'She won't.' Lily stoutly put her faith in Fanny. 'She's got plans for her future.' Lily settled her chin on her fist. 'I've missed seeing Margie so much. Think about her all the time, I do. Is the master still allowing her to go to school?'

Adam's smile drooped. 'I'm afraid I have bad news about Margie Blake . . . '

'Is she ill?' Lily cried, forgetting about turning the conversation back to workhouse babies. 'Is Margie in the infirmary?'

'Nothing like that, Lily.' He patted her hand in a calming manner. 'The master *had* allowed her to continue studying one day a week. He knew it would be beneficial if she took over the job you used to do, copying out dockets and so on.' He sighed. 'Shortly after you left, Margie gave Miss Fox the slip and absconded on her way to school.'

Lily's teacup had been hovering by her chin, but it found the saucer in a rattle of crockery. She didn't know whether to whoop with joy or groan in despair. It was wonderful that her friend was free and had got the better of the officer. But what of practicalities? Margie's mother didn't want her, and her siblings were too young to help. Who would employ a disabled fifteen year old with no references? How on earth was Margie getting by?

'Not only that,' Adam carried on bleakly, 'the master made a fuss, although Margie was entitled to apply to discharge herself. It's true she went about it the wrong way but that wasn't the issue. He was more concerned with the loss of her uniform and reported a theft to the police.' Adam tutted his disgust. 'I made my feelings known on that.' On hearing Lily's gasp of dismay he added comfortingly, 'I'm sure the police have better things to do than harass a young woman to recover some worthless clothes.'

Lily wasn't surprised that the master had stooped so low. She remembered how she'd been humiliated so he could save the cost of replacing her uniform. She felt guilty for not having attempted to visit Margie and reassure her she *would* be back the moment she'd saved enough money. She knew she must track down her friend before the authorities did, then they'd muddle through the best they could. But where to start the search?

'Don't be down in the dumps, Lily.' Adam chucked her under the chin. 'I expect Margie had a plan in mind when she ran off.'

He was trying to ease her mind . . . but Lily knew Margie better than anyone. Her friend wouldn't have had a plan, just a raging need to escape. Margie had told her she'd be lonely and depressed when on her own. After Fanny got out, it had probably been the final straw for Margie. Lily knew that she would have been tempted to snatch at a chance to have her freedom as Margie had. Gregory Wilding had saved her needing to take such a risk. She owed him so much, yet had treated him dreadfully, slapping him like that. Soon she might feel even more ashamed of herself if Adam confirmed what her boss had told her about her sister not being Charlie Larkin's.

'I really must scoot over to Pentonville now. I've promised to meet up with a friend later.' Adam drained his teacup then turned to ask a bored-looking waitress for the bill.

Lily waited patiently while he settled up. He'd insisted on treating her when she offered again to pay. He was keen to get back about his business, but she wasn't offended: he was a conscientious man who would fulfil every duty before taking time for himself. 'Would you mind if I quickly asked you something?' she blurted. 'It's rather a sensitive subject . . . ' It was now or never, she realised; she wasn't going home none the wiser. 'I'm sure you know about such things . . . I expect older women do as well but I . . . umm . . . don't . . . '

'Ask me anything you like,' Adam interrupted mildly. 'I

won't blush, I promise. I know you've no mother or older sister to talk to. If you're a bit in the dark about women's ailments and want advice, don't be embarrassed to come to me.'

Lily gave him a grateful smile and started, 'I wanted to ask about my mother and my sister, actually. I know you didn't treat my mum in the infirmary as she'd already passed away when you arrived at South Grove.'

Adam hadn't expected the conversation to take this turn and he settled back in his chair, intrigued.

'She had bronchitis for months, but she died giving birth to my little sister.'

'I recall you told me about that tragedy when we were working in the office.'

'And my father had died before we were admitted.'

Adam indicated with a nod he remembered being told that too.

'Dad passed away four months before we entered the house. Could my sister have been *his* baby?' Lily rattled off the vital question very quietly. She didn't want the waitress, hovering close by for a tip, to hear what was being said.

Adam contained his surprise then, after a lengthy pause, asked, 'How long was your mother an inmate before she died?'

'Eight months and ten days.'

Lily felt lead settle in her belly. Adam's expression was similar to the one she'd seen on Gregory Wilding's face when he'd wanted to extricate himself from a difficult conversation. 'Mum only ever loved my dad; she never had a boyfriend,' she insisted. 'I swear it's true. Me 'n' Davy had to pack up school. Mum couldn't get work. We were

205

all together night and day until we entered the house. I would've known if she was seeing somebody.' Lily's vivid blue gaze was imploring him for reassurance. 'Couldn't the baby have stayed inside her longer than usual 'cos it was trying to get stronger?' It seemed logical to Lily that an infant would wait, hoping to be born healthy enough to survive ... even if fate still denied it a chance at life.

'Babies are often born overdue, Lily, but not by that amount of time,' Adam said carefully. 'From what you've said, it seems the child was your half-sister.'

'But ... it's not possible! Mum was segregated from the men in that place. I don't understand.' Lily sounded annoyed as well as distressed.

'I agree it is odd,' Adam soothed. He'd heard of female inmates being abused by male workhouse staff. And if Mrs Larkin hadn't been pregnant on entering the place, there seemed little else to go on. It was a horrible conclusion to have to come to, and without proof he certainly couldn't voice his thoughts. Braving a talk about menstruation would have been easier than this, Adam ruefully realised. 'Are you ready to go now?' He smiled apologetically. 'I must get a move on.' He pushed back his chair.

Lily stood up and approached the door. When they got outside she glanced up at him. 'Sorry I had to ask you about that but ... '

'We've always been able to talk to one another. I don't want that to change, Lily,' he said.

'Shall we meet up again? I'm going to try to find Margie and do all I can to help her. I'll let you know if I have any luck.' Lily held her breath while waiting for his nod. 'And would you look for my mum's infirmary records and see what was noted at the time? There must be some sort of mistake.' Lily wasn't giving up yet. She had a strong intuition the workhouse held a clue to solving the mystery. The frustrating thing was that, had she known about this sooner, she could have searched for the file herself. She would have had to break into the cabinet where inmates' confidential records were kept, but she would have done it without a second thought. Her clerical duties had been restricted to the mundane: copying purchase orders for routine medical supplies and huge quantities of disinfectant and soaps and soda, then filing away the paperwork in its designated folder.

It had already occurred to Adam to search through the archives. He hadn't intended to let Lily in on it yet, in case nothing came to light ... or, worse, something dreadful did. Telling her it was possible that her mother had been assaulted would be no easy task to tackle. 'I'll see what I can dig up, Lily, but it might take some weeks. And bear in mind that the midwife might have left just basic notes that reveal nothing you don't already know.'

'It is a long shot, but thanks anyway.' Lily went on to tiptoe to kiss his cheek. Then feeling bashful for having done it, she blurted, 'Davy was flabbergasted when I told him we nearly had a sister.'

'Davy? Your twin brother?' Adam frowned as though believing he'd misheard her.

'Oh! I forgot to tell you the wonderful news that Davy survived the Cuckoo School fire and made his way to London. He's been working for Mr Wilding. He's not our proper cousin, but he feels like family because he's been such a good friend to us.' The moment she said it she realised she meant it. They might fight and argue, but Gregory Wilding was her mainstay. She owed him a humble apology now she knew he'd spoken the truth. She'd been in shock when she lashed out, but it was no excuse and she felt miserable for having done so.

'What excellent news about Davy. I knew Mr Wilding was a good sort. He could have punched that fool Clive Stratton on Sale Day, but instead he helped settle down the old ladies after the rumpus. A lot is learned about a man's character from random acts of kindness.'

Lily beamed agreement, deciding not to let on that shortly afterwards that kind man had punched a fellow who owed him money. Lily would have loved to stay longer talking to Adam. The rain had stopped and a weak sun was trying to push through the clouds. But she could see he was itching to get going. 'Shall I meet you here in a few weeks' time then? Will that be long enough for you to find out something?'

'I expect so. I'll look forward to seeing you again, Lily.' He cupped her face. 'Now take care of yourself. Work hard and be a good girl for your boss.'

'And you take care too, Adam. See you soon,' she called as he strode away.

He raised a hand in acknowledgement but didn't turn round.

Chapter Fourteen

'So you're back at last, are you?'

Lily was wearily unbuttoning her jacket in the corridor when her flatmate's bedroom door was swung open and she received a curt greeting. Lily had grown used to Jane's snappiness but she was surprised the older woman seemed bothered by her long absence. Lily had her own key to come and go, courtesy of her boss who'd handed it over saying it was hers to keep. She no longer needed to hang around on the doorstep waiting to be let in when Jane swanned off unexpectedly with no thought for Lily's predicament. The two of them were like ships in the night now. Her boss's girlfriend had also seemed more accepting of sharing her flat; but Lily sensed that might be about to change.

'Didn't think I'd be missed.' Lily bent to ease her boots from her aching feet. She'd saved the bus fare and walked home, tormenting herself picturing Margie sleeping rough and stealing food to survive. Davy had started out that way, but at least he'd had two strong hands to use. Every penny Lily could put by might assist in dragging poor Margie out of the mess she was in.

'Ain't missed you.' Jane sounded scornful. 'Been like the

good old days having the place to meself all afternoon. Just warning you that Greg was after you earlier. He was in a right mood. Didn't even stop for a cup of tea.' Jane was in a huff, having been slighted. Greg had given her seduction the brush-off, even though they had time alone. 'He said he had business in Whitechapel. So what've you been up to then?'

'Met a friend and had tea in a caff on the Mile End Road. Then went to visit me mum's resting place.'

'Didn't mean *that*! I mean what have you been *up* to? I smell trouble brewing.'

So did Lily. Her boss had never previously come here looking for her. Everything that needed to be said between them was dealt with at work. She didn't need a crystal ball, though. He was going to tell her she'd gone too far this time, then sack her. And in truth she couldn't blame him after the way she'd behaved. Yet it couldn't have come at a worse time. She needed her job more than ever now she'd learned about the dreadful scrape Margie was in.

'I knew having you here was a mistake,' Jane said crossly. 'Greg's not stayed the night with me since you moved in, and he's not the only one fed up of you cramping his style.' Jane would have gladly upped sticks to his plusher digs, but more often than not he brought her home after they'd made love.

'It was his idea,' Lily pointed out. Then she sighed. 'Look, you know I want me own place but—'

'Why not get it then?' Jane sharply interrupted. 'You and your brother were supposed to set up together ages ago.' She followed a barefoot Lily, who was carrying her boots, along the corridor. 'Suppose Davy's more interested in shacking up with Angie than with you, ain't he?'

Lily swung around, open-mouthed.

'Oh, right. Still ain't told you about his girl, has he?' Jane looked sheepish to have let the cat out of the bag. 'Well, the three of you will have to work it out, 'cos I ain't losing me boyfriend over this.' She slammed back into her room.

Lily sank down on to her bedroom chair. The news about Davy hadn't come as a complete shock ... he was turning into a man and liked adult pleasures. She should have guessed he'd have an urge to chase girls. Naively she'd assumed her platonic love was enough for him. Oddly, it was a relief to know it wasn't. The reason for Davy's evasiveness had become clearer: he might have made plans with Angie, including setting up in business with his future wife rather than his twin sister. Perhaps this might also be for the best; Lily wouldn't want to choose between him and Adam. He had looked at her with such admiration and affection that she glowed anew with the memory of it. Now Adam knew she'd soon turn sixteen, he might admit his feelings for her went beyond friendship.

Lily's secretive smile soon faded away: she had another man on her mind, too, and her conscience was badly troubled where he was concerned. Lily rubbed her palms over her tired face. She'd never rest until she'd apologised to her boss and discovered if she still had a job. If she asked Jane for his address, she'd probably be told in no uncertain terms that she couldn't have it. But Bobby might know. There was an outside chance he'd paid a weekend visit to his mother and was sitting drinking tea just down the road. It was worth a try finding out. If she were to eat humble pie, she'd sooner do it privately on Sunday evening than turn up on Monday morning to face the sack and a public drubbing. With a sigh she wriggled her feet back into her boots and rebuttoned her jacket.

*

Lily had been unlucky at Eunice's. The woman had told her she'd not seen her son since Friday, but she had invited Lily in for a cuppa and a chat. Lily had made her excuses, guessing from the older woman's calculating gaze that Eunice intended to quiz her about her relationship with Bobby. Though there was nothing but a friendship going on, Lily didn't have the time to impress that on his mother.

Rather than return home to her cantankerous flatmate's company, Lily kept going towards the High Street. She'd decided to head for Mason's caff in case any of the lads were in there. If not, she'd track them to their lodgings as a last resort. She knew where the room was, although Davy had never invited her to visit. Neither had the others. She guessed they got up to high jinks deemed unsuitable for her eyes. She'd not be welcomed in ... especially if her brother was with his girlfriend. Yet it might be as well to get that bridge crossed too, so they all knew where they stood.

Lily trudged along, occupied with jumbled thoughts of kith and kin, and almost passed her place of work without realising that the gates were unlocked. Then she noticed the van parked. It was probably no later in the day than six o'clock, but the rain-heavy heavens had brought a premature gloom and a sticky atmosphere. She hurried over the road; on getting closer she realised the warehouse doors were ajar and lamplight was visible.

She slipped inside, the creaking of the door masked by a sudden loud banging.

212

She'd not expected to fortuitously come upon her boss and hadn't properly prepared what she wanted to say, other than: sorry, won't do it again, and please let me keep my job. Nor had she expected to see him stripped to the waist. He had a damaged four-wheel cart upside down and was crouching by it, hammering at the broken axle. He'd obviously been working on it for a while as a pile of parts were scattered on the floor.

'Guv'nor . . . ' Lily meekly called to him as she approached. An odd sensation stirred in the pit of her belly as she watched him working, biceps bunched and his long fair hair falling across his face. She was in two minds whether to sneak out again and bang loudly on the door to properly announce her arrival.

He hadn't heard her, so she moved closer . . . then stopped and stared. The stronger lamplight was illuminating a number of raised scars undulating on his sweat-sheened back as his muscles rippled and flexed.

'What *happened* to you?' It was an unnecessary question. She knew; and furious sadness washed over her as her fingertips touched his beaten flesh.

He sprang up and spun about, as though that featherlight stroke had stung.

Lily had immediately tottered back at his violent reaction.

'What d'you want?' he snarled. He grabbed at his shirt discarded on another barrow, immediately shrugging into it.

'Jane said you wanted me.' Lily watched him warily, for the first time a little afraid of him. They'd crossed swords before, but he'd never looked so cold and aloof.

'Yeah . . . so I did.' He shook a cigarette out of a pack that was thrown back down on the cart, and started smoking it.

A silence ensued.

'You waiting for me to guess what you came round to see me about?' Lily was unable to decide whether to humour him or be bolshie.

An indolent gesture with his cigarette told her to go ahead if she wanted.

'I know I owe you an apology. I know you were right . . . what you said yesterday about my mum and the baby.' She paused, hoping for a show of conciliation. None came. 'I was wrong to hit you and I'm sorry for that as well. I won't ever do it again and to make up for it I'll work a day next week for nothing.' She'd thought of that on the spur of the moment, and hoped it was a good inducement for a man who adored making money.

He sat down on the side of the upturned barrow, tilted up his head and chuckled. 'You think I'd bother coming to find you about that?'

Lily looked bewildered. 'What else have I done then?'

'You tell me . . . ' He ground a boot on the dog-end.

'Don't know what you mean, guv'nor.' Lily made it clear her patience was wearing thin by sighing heavily.

'I'll help you out then,' he said, standing up. 'The hire tin is eighteen bob short. Any idea why?'

Her mouth dropped open as she battled with her disbelief and indignation. 'Are you accusing me of *stealing*?' she finally burst out.

'Not yet. D'you know who's taken it?'

'No!' Lily exclaimed. 'It's only you and me go near the filing cabinet.'

'You suggesting I stole me own money?'

'Don't be stupid!' Lily immediately regretted that outburst. A nasty smile was distorting his mouth.

'You left the cabinet open yesterday. See anybody hanging around by it?'

She shook her head.

A slow shrug of his shoulders demonstrated he'd be forced to draw his own conclusion in that case.

She pointed a condemning finger. 'You soon changed your tune, didn't you? You sounded sincere when you said you thought me honest.'

'Yeah, I've thought a lot about you – believe me I have – but you've changed, too.' He looked her over in her fine clothes, worn for Adam Reeve. A hint of flowers was in the atmosphere, the scent strengthening as she swung her body in irritation.

'What's that mean?' She made another wild gesture. 'Don't understand bloody riddles . . . '

He took another cigarette and struck a match. 'It means nobody makes a monkey out of me.'

He started to walk towards her and Lily backed away. 'Don't they? Well I know your girlfriend does!' she yelled, hoping to stop him stalking her down with a peculiar look in his feral eyes.

'Ah . . . right . . . wondered if you might tell me about that.' It wasn't a sour laugh this time. He sounded amused. 'Decided where your loyalties lie on that score, have you, Lily? Bit late in the day.'

Lily felt even more confused but was glad she seemed to have distracted him. He wandered off to sit down at the desk and swivel the battered chair to and fro on its pedestal. It was then she noticed why he was acting strangely. He'd been drinking. There were at least half a dozen brown bottles on the desk, and she reckoned most were empty. He picked one up and took a swig. She felt her trust and respect for him withering. She'd witnessed her mother being on the receiving end of a drunk's temper. Charlie had never raised his hand to his wife, but he'd known how to make her cry anyway.

Lily put up her chin. She wasn't crying, or pleading, or apologising for blurting out the truth about Jane's two-timing. Not that it seemed to bother him. 'You knew she was cheating on you, didn't you?'

''Course I knew.'

'Don't you care?'

'Not really.' He leaned his head against the chair-back, then slammed one then the other of his boots on the edge of the desk, continuing to raise the bottle then the cigarette to his mouth. 'Stratton had first dibs on her, after all.'

Lily continued watching him. 'You're not as nice as you seem at first, are you, Mr Wilding?'

'No ... I'm ... not ...' he softly drawled. 'So, do you know who's had their fingers in my till, Lily Larkin? 'Cos I'll have to assume it's you if you don't grass him up.'

'No ... I don't know. Don't even know if you're just spouting rubbish,' she said. 'You're drunk and no point talking to you.'

'Find something else to do then, eh?' He shoved back the chair and stood up.

'Can't do anything with a drunk,' Lily scorned. 'They're fit for nothing but trouble. I know. A drunk ruined our lives.' Tears dribbled on to her cheeks and were immediately rubbed away. 'Was the death of my mum ...'

She stared blearily at him until he turned away.

'Get out of here ... go on ... piss off,' he rasped, and prised the top off another beer.

The lamp flickered in a draught made by the closing

216

door. He lifted the brown ale to his mouth, but instead of tasting it he hurled the bottle at the cart he'd been mending.

Lily whipped along the street. Her boss had seemed on the point of doing or saying something to her that had nothing to do with unfairly branding her a thief. She had been more aware of him as a virile man, not just as her angry boss. Though a thrill of anticipation was still making her tingle, she knew she wasn't going back there to ask if she should turn up for work in the morning. But she knew where she *was* going, and right now.

*

Lily was breathless by the time she reached the boys' lodging. She knew the main entrance to the tenement had no door on it, as she had passed by at other times and stared into a bleak, black hallway. On those occasions she'd lost her nerve and decided not to knock Davy up and make him listen to what she had to say. The talk about family was now done, but heaven only knew she had something of similar importance on her mind. Whether Davy and the others liked it or not, she was unburdening herself right now. It could be that none of them would have a job in the morning if the culprit didn't own up to the theft. Though she'd told her boss he was drunk and didn't know what he was on about, she knew he did. He always knew what he was doing where money was concerned.

The boys' room was situated on the first floor, and she hurtled up the dank, rickety stairway and hammered on the door.

'Lily! Wasn't expecting you ...' Bobby awkwardly blocked her way, peering over his shoulder into a dim, candlelit space. He was unsure how his pals would take to her barging in on them.

Lily shoved past him with, 'When you find out why I'm here, you'll all be bloody glad to see me. Don't worry about that.'

Davy had been reclining on his mattress in his pants, and Fred had been scooping out of a bowl what looked and smelled like jellied eels. If Lily had had the time or inclination to take notice of Davy's home, she would have been unimpressed by it. The room reeked of mouldy male sweat, and discarded scraps of food and clothing littered the floorboards, along with old candle stumps and an unlit oil lamp. But no girls were present, and for that Lily was grateful. What she had to say should be kept between the four of them.

'What've you come here for?' Davy sounded peeved as he jumped up, yanking on his trousers.

Fred patted his belly and stood up. 'Come to give me that kiss you owe me, ain't yer, gel?' He burped and took a swig of beer, then eyed her up and down. 'Looking swell too, dressed up to the nines like that.'

Lily took no notice, and launched straight into, 'Guv'nor's on the warpath 'cos somebody's stolen eighteen shillings out of the hire tin.' She planted her hands on her hips and looked from one to the other of them.

'*What?*' The chorus of disbelief was as she expected.

'None of us ever gets near the hire tin ... just *our* tins, when we get paid,' Bobby said.

'That's right. Hire tin's always locked away,' Fred backed him.

'The desk and the cabinet were unlocked yester-day while we were all outside. But you went into the warehouse while the rest of us lined up the carts for the race,' she told Fred.

'What you trying to say?' Fred snarled.

'You can't go suggesting things like that, Lil.' Davy slid Fred a wary look. Of the three friends, Fred had the shortest fuse and the hardest punch.

'Davy's right ... don't prove nothing, Lil, just 'cos Fred went to fetch his fags.' Bobby frowned at her, warning her to tread carefully.

'I'm not pointing the finger, just saying what happened. Somebody's a thief,' Lily said bluntly. 'Guv'nor thinks it's me and I know it isn't. I'm not losing me job for something I didn't do.'

'You won't lose yer job,' Davy soothed. 'Guv'nor likes you ... always has, from the start.'

'Well, he doesn't now!' Lily yelled. 'He's been drinking and ... has turned funny. I reckon he was about to clump me just now.' Lily had sensed the tension building between them in the warehouse and she still felt wound as tight as a spring because of it. He'd told her to clear off in case this time it was him, not her, who lost control and let fly.

'Give over, Lil.' Davy put an arm round his sister as he heard her suppress a sob. 'He wouldn't do *that*. He'll calm down. Just tell him you done your sums wrong in the book and that's why it don't tally with the tin. Or could be a stranger sneaked in while we was all round the back larking about and helped himself.'

That *was* a possibility, but Lily didn't think it the right one.

'If he won't wear it, then we'll all have to pay it off between us.' Davy looked to his pals to agree. Bobby gave a nod; Fred continued to glower at her.

'I ain't chippin' in. And you ain't sayin' *I* did it!' Fred roared. 'You've got a bleedin' cheek, putting me in the frame.' He started advancing on her. 'What about him?' He jabbed a finger at Davy. 'He's always hanging around by your desk.'

'Well I would do. She's me sister and I talk to her while she's working.' Davy shoved Fred in the chest for trying to shift the blame.

Bobby sprung between his pals as they squared up and intercepted Fred's punch for his pains. Then everybody started shouting.

Lily was about to add her two penn'orth, but her shoulders slumped and she left them to it. She didn't have any proof that Fred had done anything other than what he'd said he'd done: taken a packet of fags from the warehouse. She clattered down the stairs and out into the street, wiping her eyes.

She was turning into the alley when Bobby caught her up. 'I'll walk home with you, Lily. I'm gonna stay with Mum tonight,' he said. 'Won't get no sleep with those two going at it hammer 'n' tongs.'

She nodded, turning her tear-stained face aside.

'Eighteen bob's a lot o' money. D'you reckon we'll all get the sack?' Bobby sounded glum.

'Don't know,' she said huskily. 'Probably, when he's found new people to take over.'

'I think I know who took it.'

Lily immediately squinted through twilight to read his expression. He looked bashful and rubbed the bridge of his nose while building up the courage to begin. 'Before you started work, there was a pack of johnnies in the desk and Fred would sneak one out every so often when he was seeing his gel.' Bobby cleared his throat. 'You know, rubbers . . . to stop her getting pregnant.'

'Oh, right . . . ' Lily recalled Jane having used that term, but she didn't ask for any further explanation. Bobby was embarrassed as it was. 'I've not seen those in the drawer.'

'Ain't none been in there since you turned up; guv'nor must've moved them,' Bobby said. 'Few weeks ago, Fred got Davy to keep you occupied by the door while he searched for 'em.' Bobby sighed. 'Ain't happy telling you this, I ain't a grass, but then again it's not fair if you get the blame when you've done nuthin'. So, could be Fred had a shufti in the drawer while he was getting his fags, 'cos he knew he was seeing his gel later. If he saw the cabinet was open, he might've thought, why not try me luck in there . . . ' Bobby shrugged that she could work the rest out for herself.

'Thanks . . . I'm glad you believe it wasn't me.'

'If the guv'nor sacks you, I'll jack it in, 'cos it wouldn't be fair if he did that.' Bobby gave a firm nod.

Lily turned and smiled at him. She took his arm as he poked an elbow her way. Bobby Smith was a good person . . . a true friend. Since she'd left the boys' lodging, she'd been doing a lot of thinking, and was coming to the heart-breaking conclusion that her brother was neither of those things.

Chapter Fifteen

'What the hell are you lot doing standin' around? Waiting for Christmas? Get going. Time's getting on.'

Davy, Fred and Bobby sprang into action with such alacrity that they started getting in one another's way and their carts locked wheels.

They'd all turned up early for work, on tenterhooks. In fact, they'd been so early that their boss hadn't yet arrived, and while waiting for him to unlock they'd started sniping at one another. Since they'd learned about the theft, their camaraderie had vanished.

When he eventually showed up, some grunted 'mornin's' were exchanged as they trooped in behind him. Instead of setting to work, the trio of youths had shuffled about uneasily, anticipating an explosion. But it hadn't come. Their boss had only hollered when a lack of customary noise had caused him to glance over his shoulder and notice them idling behind him.

Lily arrived in the road when the boys were heading in the opposite direction. She called and they all turned round. Davy and Bobby stopped, dropped cart handles, and stuck up their thumbs to reassure her things seemed calm. Fred simply stared for a second, then spat on the ground and carried on without giving her any other acknowledgement.

She watched them disappear into the distance, then spotted the first of Wilding's customers bowling along the street. It was the lairy lad with the gift of the gab; she didn't feel like bantering with Billy Tate today. Then a couple of other regulars turned the corner, chatting together. Soon she'd be surrounded by bluff costers, barking questions at her and tipping coins on to the desk. They all chivvied her to put them first, arguing they were in more of a rush than a rival. It was always hectic, logging their money and filling out chitties, sometimes through yawns and with sleep still in her eyes. Yet she loved her job, and she knew she was good at it; the thought of her days here being numbered put a lump in her throat. Today, though, she hadn't wanted to come into work, despite lying awake all night imagining what might occur when brought face to face with her boss.

'All right, gel? Nippy this morning, ain't it?' Billy rubbed together his palms, swaggering up to the door. Remembering his manners, he stepped back and – with a sweeping flourish – invited Lily to go in first.

She understood her boss well enough to know he'd never mention he'd been robbed in front of his customers. It would put him and his business in a bad light. And might give them ideas. She'd rather get things off her chest right now but knew she'd have to wait until they'd all gone to get a conversation out of him.

Just over an hour later, Greg had accompanied the last departing customer on to the forecourt and hadn't come back. Lily knew he was still about, though. She peeped around the door to see if he'd finished tinkering under the bonnet of the van. If she didn't know better, she'd think he was avoiding her – he'd been messing about with it for so long. These mornings were still quite bright at four o'clock, and instead of a dawn chorus she could hear a single robin's merry chirrup. The sweet sound did nothing to improve the strained atmosphere between them, palpable even though they were yards apart. Pulling open the door, she marched out to stand beside him.

'I've something to say,' she announced when he didn't stop what he was doing or look at her.

'So have I.' He wiped his oil-smeared hands on a rag. 'Ladies first,' he added after an expectant pause.

Lily was about to suggest they go inside, but realised it didn't actually matter where this conversation took place. Now she'd started, she'd rather just carry on. Nobody was about, and perhaps being in the open might work in her favour if fireworks started.

'I borrowed the money,' she rattled off. 'I found out my friend's absconded and the police are after her. The master's accused her of stealing her uniform.' Lily paused. 'I can't let Margie go to prison; she's disabled, and anyhow she's me best friend and I'm helping her, and that's that. If I pay the master off, he'll leave her alone.' She glanced at her boss's profile as he carried on using a spanner. 'You'll get the money back, promise. Just put it on my tally.' One whole minute later she added, 'Did you hear what I said?'

His single slow nod indicated he had.

Quiet ensued, and she imagined he must be mulling over the pros and cons of giving her a second chance. 'What did *you* want to say?'

'I had a recount. Nothing's missing from the tin.' He removed the prop, letting the bonnet fall into place. 'Seems one of us is wrong. Perhaps we both are.' He walked past her into the warehouse.

Lily remained outside for several minutes, pacing to and fro while wondering what possible reason he had for calling her bluff like that. She went back to her desk with no idea how to proceed. She sat down and tried to pencil entries in the ledger, but couldn't concentrate and kept using the rubber. She had one eye on him and could tell he was preparing to go off buying without anything else being said. She couldn't bear the idea of fretting all day. Once again, she'd sooner get this conversation over and done with.

'Why are you lying?' she demanded.

'Why are you?'

'Yesterday you practically accused me of stealing from you!'

'Yeah ... well, like you said, drunks spout rubbish. I'm sober now.'

'What d'you want to say now you're sober?' she prodded. 'Can tell you've got something eating at you.'

'It's time you moved on. Your job here was never meant to be permanent. You said you'd go your own way.'

She'd accepted the risk of being fired the moment she took the blame; nevertheless she felt forlorn. He'd guessed she was covering up something, so was punishing her for not siding with him rather than with the boys. That idea helped her keep her spirits up. 'You're sacking me then.'

'Yeah ... sorry ... '

She gave a harsh laugh. 'That's another lie. You're not sorry.'

'I am ... that's the truth.' He turned to look at her. 'It was my mistake bringing you here.'

'Why did you then?'

'Because if I hadn't, you'd still be stuck in that dump in Whitechapel. And you know it, don't you? Davy never saved a penny to discharge you. Don't reckon he ever would've, either.'

Oh, she knew it, and the hurt was like acid, burning beneath her ribs and gnawing at her heart. 'Will you let me stay until I find something else?'

'End of the month ... that's it.' He paused, took out his cigarettes and lit one. 'You're too good for this anyhow. You're clever – you could get something better in a regular firm. If you want a reference, I'll sign it. Write your own. You know where the headed paper is.'

Lily smiled bitterly. 'You really do want me gone, don't you?'

He didn't answer, just said, 'your doctor friend'll find you something. He recommended you to me. Educated man like that probably knows lots of people who need a clerk. I'll speak to him if you like.' He paused, looked at her. 'Or you could go and see him, couldn't you?'

Lily nodded and a smile softened her anxious expression. 'Already met up and going back to see him again soon.'

'Good ... well ask him then,' Greg said harshly.

Lily suddenly felt she was floundering, out of her depth. She *could* ask Adam to help find her an employer, but for some reason she didn't really want to. She wanted what she'd got. She felt at home here. A memory of walking to the workhouse exit, filled with foreboding, burst in on her. Gregory Wilding had been a trusted stranger then. But he wasn't a stranger now, though they acted distant. 'I know the money's gone, and you're right I'm lying too ... but not

226

about Margie. Adam told me she's in trouble. And he told me about my sister being a half-sister.'

'You didn't believe me when I told you though, did you?'

'He's a doctor!' Lily defended herself. 'He knows more about that sort of thing than you, so I checked what you said.'

'I wasn't being spiteful, was I? A kid would've acted like that.'

Lily blushed and winced. She deserved his sarcasm, but wasn't getting side-tracked into a row. 'Anyway, I promised you'd get the money back that's missing.'

'You still don't get it, do you? It's not about the money.'

'It's always about the money with you.' She shot upright.

'You don't know me, Lily Larkin, so keep your thoughts to yourself.' He unhooked his donkey jacket and picked up his cigarettes and motor keys.

'Don't you walk out before we've finished this,' she shouted.

'It is finished. Get yourself another job and leave me alone,' he growled.

'I'm truly sorry that I hit you,' she blurted. 'I never used to be a horrible brat when I was little. Mum said I was a sweet girl . . . ' She pulled a face and made him half smile.

'It's what those places do to you . . . make you violent. If you don't fight back, the bastards grind you into the dust.'

Lily knew he was talking about his own experience, but she agreed with it wholeheartedly. She'd seen inmates too intimidated to raise their eyes, let alone their fists to stick up for themselves. 'You got caned by a master.'

That halted him and he turned to look at her as she traipsed towards him. 'You were in a workhouse. I guessed it from the start. That's why you helped me and

Davy ... you know what it's like to be starved and beaten, don't you?'

'Yeah ... I know. But don't go thinking I'm a soft touch for waifs and strays. I gave Davy a job 'cos at the time I needed a hired hand. He's outgrown his usefulness. As for you ... you remind me of somebody I used to know. I felt sorry for you, like I did for her. That's all it was.'

Lily was intrigued. 'You knew somebody like me? A relative, was it?' She could see she was starting to grate on his nerves with her questions, designed to keep him gentle. He'd snapped his eyes skyward in exasperation.

'If you want paying later, get to work, or I'll change my mind about letting you see the month out.' She was too close to him, still smelling faintly of lavender and challenging him with that powerful blue stare. He'd thought he'd never forget Catherine, but Lily Larkin's raw beauty was eclipsing the memory of his gently pretty cousin, and that just added to it all, making him feel wretched. He owed Lily an apology, but didn't know how to start to say he was sorry that he'd almost drunkenly kissed her yesterday, and that hadn't been the worst of it. He had wanted to take her home with him. In her own way she still liked and trusted him, thought him honourable, and he couldn't destroy something that precious. In a few years he wouldn't be a creep wanting to go to bed with a kid. And perhaps when she'd seen a bit of the world, kissed a few boys, she might remember she'd liked him enough to be familiar and follow him around. She might come back to him.

For now she had to go; he couldn't stand feeling like this every day, jealous of Adam Reeve because she had a crush on him, avoiding being at the warehouse in case he gave in to the urge to touch her and she lashed out in disgust this time. Fifteen or not, she was shaped like a woman, and it was hard when she had a sweet figure that even a faded cotton dress couldn't disguise . . .

She'd come right up to him again and he opened the door and walked outside before pointing at her desk. 'Get to work, Lily, I'm not joking . . . ' You're the joke, mate, he mocked himself, obsessed with a girl when you've got a few proper women to choose from.

With a defeated sigh, Lily went back to it and sat down.

'You're not doing him any favours, you know.' Greg spoke from behind his wagging cigarette while shrugging into his jacket. 'Keep covering up for him and he'll try it again on somebody else and risk a blade in the guts, or a good kicking if he's lucky. If you want to help Davy, turn your back on him.'

The planked door was creaked shut, blocking out the morning light, and just minutes later Lily heard the motor start up.

*

There had been no need for Lily to beg her brother for five minutes of his time after work. He was waiting by the gate for her with Bobby, both boys looking nervous. Fred was still in high dudgeon and had taken his pay then stomped off straight away with just a glare for his colleagues.

Lily hadn't bothered trying to engage her boss in any more conversation on the subject of the theft or the loss of her job. She'd done what she'd done and accepted that his retaliation had been fair, if hard to swallow. Not that there had been much opportunity to talk to him anyway.

He'd come back to the warehouse only a few minutes before the lads turned up with their empty carts. They were later than usual, having put extra effort into shifting their odds and ends of stock. Regular tattered stragglers turned up as the market was being dismantled, to slouch around for a bargain or sift through the bruised fruit that had rolled into the gutter. Then there were the canny housewives who'd wait until the last minute, intent as they were on never paying the going rate for anything.

'How di't go?' Bobby put a comforting arm around Lily's shoulders as she joined them. 'You look as though you've been put through the mill. We didn't get a peep out of the guv'nor about the money this morning, did we?'

Davy confirmed with a shake of his head.

Lily hadn't realised she looked as wrung out as she felt, and she tried to rub some colour into her cheeks. 'I've still got me job, for the moment ... ' She feigned brightness, glad she hadn't lied. She *did* still have her job for the moment. She didn't want Bobby to know more in case he handed in his notice in sympathy. She'd enough on her conscience, without that adding to it. She gave Davy a significant look. 'We were going to walk part of the way home together so I can talk to you about visiting Mum's resting place.'

'Yeah, that's right ... I'll come as far as the alley with you.' Davy had got the message that she had something important to say just to him.

'I'll leave you to it then,' Bobby said.

'Thanks ... ' Lily was grateful he'd been sensitive and not tried to tag along.

'What happened then? Guv'nor must've said something about it this morning.'

'Oh, he did.'

'What did you say?'

'What you wanted me to,' Lily said quietly. 'I told him I was to blame.'

'See, told you nothing would come of it,' Davy crowed. He stopped and turned towards her, grinning.

They'd been walking slowly in the direction of the alley, but Lily could see her brother thought he'd done his bit and could now dash off home. What she said next soon stopped him in his tracks.

'He knows I was lying and covering up for you.'

'You told him *I* took it?' he raged, marching closer.

Lily shook her head. 'Didn't need to. He knew anyway. Same as I did.' Her boss had guessed she'd only shield one person.

Davy started to bluster his innocence, exasperating Lily. 'Oh, for heaven's sake, stop lying! I worked it out from things you said, and I remembered you took my jacket to hang it up for me. The key was in the pocket and you had enough time to open the desk and the filing cabinet before joining us in the yard.' It was such a hurtful thing to have done that tears stung her eyes. 'How can you be so selfish? You were happy to let me take the blame for everything, weren't you!'

His affronted look didn't last long; differing emotions shaped his boyish features: annoyance, defensiveness and finally shame. But there was no apology. 'Guv'nor won't do nuthin' about it. Not where *you're* concerned. And I needed it urgent, Lil.'

'For what?' she blasted.

'Mind your own business.' He swung away and started jogging home.

231

'Just you hang on a minute!' She raced after him and grabbed his arm, yanking him back. 'Don't you dare try to swan off without explaining after causing me such trouble!'

'What trouble?' Davy scoffed, wrenching himself free. 'You're his blue-eyed gel. I've seen the way he looks at you.'

'What?'

'Guv'nor fancies you . . . don't make out you don't know.'

Lily shook her head in disbelief at her brother stooping to that. 'We both know he's got a girlfriend. Don't try to wriggle out of this by talking rot.'

'Jane Wright ain't his *only* gel. We've all seen his others. She's just the one who's been around the longest.'

Lily believed that could be the truth and she was taken aback by it. Little wonder then that he wasn't bothered about Jane cheating on him, when he was clearly just as bad. She wasn't letting Davy squirm out of anything, though, or run away with the idea that she'd not suffered for what he'd done. 'If you think the guv'nor's let me get off lightly, you're wrong. I got sacked today.'

'No, you didn't . . . you told Bobby you didn't . . .' Davy laughed.

'Go back and ask the guv'nor then. Dare you. Go on!' She wrathfully pointed in the direction of the warehouse. 'Only nice thing he said to me was that he'd let me stay till the end of the month and I could write me own reference on a bit of his paper.' She could tell that at last Davy understood that what he'd done had had serious consequences. She bit her lower lip as she felt it tremble. She'd not cried over it yet, and she wasn't starting now. 'So you can own up to what you've done that took eighteen bob to sort it out. Whatever it was has cost me a job and a home. I'll get chucked out of Jane's place as well.'

Davy licked his lips then croaked, 'You sure he knows it was me?'

'He's no fool.' Lily couldn't be bothered to shout at her brother, though it was apparent he was only concerned with saving his own skin. She'd not needed to tell him what their boss had said about Davy having outlived his usefulness. He'd guessed he was next in the firing line. 'What've you done? Gambled with the money, or spent it on Angie?' She slung a look at him. 'Yeah I know about her, too.'

'Smudger been blabbing, I suppose?' Davy agitatedly shoved both his hands through his hair.

'He's done nothing. Jane Wright mentioned your girl-friend in passing. She thought, as your sister, I'd already know about her.'

Davy stopped prowling and leant against a wall, hanging his head. 'What a fucking mess.'

His swearing no longer bothered – or shocked – Lily. 'It's that, all right.' She gave a hoarse laugh. 'Have you got a few shillings left to return to the guv'nor? That might show willing and sway him to think you really are sorry for thieving off him.' It was a faint hope and they both knew it.

'Got nothing.' Davy gave a defeated shrug.

He looked pitiful and she was tempted to comfort him. She crossed her arms to stop herself hugging him. Their boss had been right about that, too. Killing her brother with kindness was a risk she wouldn't take. 'What's happened to make you do something as gormless as this?'

'If I tell you, you won't tell the others, will you? If it gets about, it'll just make things ten times worse.'

''Course I won't.'

'Angie reckons she's in the family way,' he blurted, looking relieved to be unburdening himself. 'She's trying to get rid of it before her stepfather finds out.' Davy rubbed his face with his hands. 'He's a big brute and he already knocks her about. She reckons he'll kill her and come after me 'n' all.'

Lily leaned back against the wall for support next to her brother, winded by that news. 'Did Angie want the money to buy johnnies?' Lily had remembered Bobby saying they stopped girls getting pregnant.

'Too bloody late for using those!' Davy snorted. 'She wanted the money to buy some pills off a woman she knows, but they've not worked. There's another woman who does operations, but it costs three quid. Angie won't stop nagging 'cos she's frightened her belly'll start to stick out and her stepfather will notice.' Davy frowned at Lily. 'Mum died having a baby . . . I'm scared, Lil. What if Angie dies? It'll be my fault for knockin' her up. Her old man'll kill me and then we'll all be dead and the baby too . . .'

'Shhh . . .' Lily caved in and hugged him tightly. 'Panicking won't help.' She understood now why he'd reacted badly when she'd told him about their mother and baby sister. He'd not been fretful over who might have got their mother pregnant; the girl *he'd* got pregnant had been worrying the life out of him.

'Got any ideas how to help sort Angie out?' he asked hopefully. 'She's going on and on at me about it, but how would I know? And I haven't got a clue how to get three quid to give her, now the guv'nor's on to me.'

Despite his frustration, Lily reckoned that Davy understood far more about it all than she did. Adam would be the best person to ask about abortions, but she didn't relish

234

bringing up the subject with him. Then she thought of Fanny Miller. Though Fanny had chosen to keep her baby and enter a workhouse, she would know friends in her old profession who'd wanted to unencumber themselves as soon as possible to keep working.

'I could go and see somebody who had a baby in the workhouse. I said I'd stay in touch with her when she discharged herself.' Lily gave her brother's arm a pat of encouragement. 'Worth a try.'

'Angie said she'll have to go to a spike if she can't get rid of it. If her stepfather don't kill her, he'll turf her on to the streets anyway, the moment he finds out. She'll lose her job in the drapery and, even if the guv'nor don't sack me, I don't earn enough to keep us all.' He rubbed his glistening eyes. 'Can't let her go in one of those places. Not now I know what it's like. No kid of mine is starting life like that. Just wish we could be a family. But it's too soon; I'm too young fer all this, Lil.'

'Let me speak to Fanny Miller,' Lily said calmingly. He was getting more and more agitated, and she could understand why. Although her brother had done wrong, his motives had been right. 'Fanny might have some handy tips to pass on.' After a pause Lily added, 'You might as well get going home now.' There was nothing else to be said and suddenly she wanted to be on her own. Davy nodded despondently but still loitered, stepping on and off the pavement, kicking at the kerb. When he eventually ambled away, Lily realised it was the first time she'd felt relieved watching her brother walk away from her.

Chapter Sixteen

'Got an appointment in Highgate ... be back later.'

''Bye ...' Lily glanced up from her work but her boss was already gone. It was how they went on now. Just a few necessary words spoken between them during the day. He only told her where he was going in case somebody called while he was out. Occasionally canvassers – some smartly dressed, some in overalls – might stroll in asking for Mr Wilding and leave a business card for her to pass on. A few went in his pocket; most ended up in the wastepaper bin beneath the desk.

Lily had come to the conclusion he couldn't wait for her to leave, and that he was regretting having said she could see the month out. Davy was already looking for other work. He didn't want Bobby and Fred to cotton on to it, but Lily reckoned they already had. Just as they knew who'd had their fingers in the hire tin. What nobody could fathom was why their boss was biding his time doing anything about it. Lily believed Gregory Wilding was fair in his own way, and wise. If a boss demanded dishonesty from his apprentices, he might consider it just deserts when one of them took it too far. That was Lily's theory, anyway, convinced as she was that Mr Wilding wasn't a vengeful hypocrite. Her brother, though, continued to disappoint her, and prove that the apple hadn't fallen far from the tree. He still bought beers and cigarettes, despite Angie's urgent predicament, and constantly whispered to his sister that they had to get money 'to do something about helping Angie'.

Lily felt ashamed that she and her brother were responsible for causing a bad atmosphere to affect everyone at work. She had never warmed to Fred Jenkins, but Bobby Smith had been a different matter. They had been good friends until the theft, and though they still spoke to one another, their conversations were now stilted. Fred bore a grudge and wasn't going to let it drop, despite Lily's tentative overtures to try to heal the rift.

None of the market traders Davy had approached would offer a job that came with a lodging. In any case, those after apprentices didn't want sixteen year olds, but tykes wet behind the ears who could be moulded into their guv'nor's ways, as Mr Wilding had shaped his crew.

Since his pals had cold-shouldered him, her brother was now keener for them to live together. Lily knew they'd little option but to share rent, but she had got used to her tiny private sanctuary below stairs. She'd even got used to her strident flatmate and would miss Jane. Mean fate hadn't favoured the Larkin twins for long, but Lily refused to sink into self-pity when she still had so much to be thankful for. She'd brought on herself her first hard lesson about working life, and reckoned Davy also rued not fully appreciating what he had until it was too late.

If forced to choose, she'd probably do exactly the same thing again, though. Right or wrong didn't come into it; the blood bond with her twin – her only remaining family – still outweighed everything else, including her feelings for Adam. She couldn't wait to see him again, though, and discover if he'd traced those infirmary records. Thoughts of her mother and sister were never far from her mind, despite everything else vying for her attention. But Davy hadn't mentioned his family again.

Acting on her boss's advice, Lily had already drafted her reference in pencil. In a quiet moment, she'd use the rubber on it when a better phrase occurred to her to convince somebody she was the perfect candidate for a clerical post. She hoped he wouldn't burst out laughing when she asked him to sign it and he read the bit about her trustworthiness. She'd prove she was honest, to herself as well as to him. Everything would be paid back, even if it meant them doing it at the rate of sixpence a week. Family loyalty was one thing, but if Davy was under any illusion she'd pitch in the eighteen bob he'd stolen, he would have a rude awakening coming.

Having completed the day's entries into the ledger, Lily opened the drawer to retrieve her half-finished reference and burnish her credentials.

'That's a bloody relief. I hoped I'd find you on your own. Wasn't going to hang about if Greg Wilding was around.'

A familiar coarse voice made Lily forget about her reference. Pushing the drawer shut she jumped up, beaming a welcome. 'Fanny Miller! Oh, what a lovely surprise! You don't know how pleased I am to see *you*.' She meant it too. Lily hadn't realised just how much she'd missed having some female company, surrounded as she was by men all day long. At home Jane was never much of a friend to her. 'Oh, you've brought the little 'un.'

Fanny, fiery hair straggling about her shoulders, was loitering just inside the warehouse door. Lily dashed over, eager to get her first glimpse of her friend's baby. Pulling back an edge of threadbare woollen shawl, she gazed at a chubby pink face.

'Crikey! He's bigger than I thought he'd be,' Lily exclaimed. 'He looks so bonny and content. What did you call him?'

'Ronald ... he's nigh on four months now; the little blighter's a whopper 'cos he don't stop feeding.' Fanny chuckled fondly, tickling her son's cheek. The boy immediately turned, mewling, towards his mother's touch. 'See what I mean?' Fanny held the child out for Lily to take, then yanked up her blouse.

'Come and sit down.' Lily smothered her embarrassment at the sight of Fanny unceremoniously exposing a swollen breast and concentrated on cuddling the wriggling bundle.

'Don't mind if I do, me dogs are barking. I walked all the way. Miles it was, too.' Fanny let out a sigh as she took the weight off her feet.

'I'll make you a cup of tea.' Lily hastened to the Primus stove on the shelf and lit it with a match, giving Fanny some privacy.

'Got all the comforts of home then?' Fanny sounded impressed.

'Guv'nor got a Primus for me so I could have a drink during the day. He brings me in a pie for me dinner usually,' Lily explained as she spooned tea into the pot. 'There's a standpipe out in the yard so got water on tap.'

'Lucky cow ... ' Fanny sighed.

'So ... how have you been? How's your business going?

Not working with your sister today then?' Lily rattled off her questions as she waited for the kettle to whistle, then poured boiling water into the pot.

Fanny's expression turned dark. 'Me sister's let me down again. Should never have trusted *her* to keep to her word. Her husband came crawling back and between 'em they're doing the round *I* helped to set up. Sauce of it! Only lasted a month before Lizzie stabbed me in the back.'

'Oh, I'm so sorry, Fanny ... so will your sister be if he mucks her about again.'

Lily picked up the two teas and placed them on the desktop, then perched on the edge of it. She'd let the nursing mother have the only chair. When in the yard or the warehouse, the men would sit on upturned orange boxes.

'Me brother-in-law's a coward and a parasite; always hid behind Lizzie when times got tough. It's the war that's brought him running home. He's making out he's a devoted family man with responsibilities, just in case it ain't all over by Christmas and he gets asked to join up.' Fanny snorted in contempt. 'I don't need her anyway. I'll do all right on me own once I've got some essentials sorted out.'

Lily knew how it felt when a sibling took but gave little in return. 'If – please God – the war *is* over by Christmas, he'll probably scarper again. Your sister will be back knocking on your door in the New Year.'

'I wouldn't give her the time of day. I've got the chance of taking over a better round and I need a reliable partner. Two brothers do it now and they've given me first refusal on it 'cos they're enlisting. They're younger than me ... probably seventeen and eighteen. They've already been down the recruitin' office and done training. Once they've got their shippin'-out dates, the round's mine. They want it back, though, when they come home.' She shrugged. 'Fair enough . . . it'll be a start for me at least to learn the ropes.' She beamed. 'I'll sell everything: polish and pegs, soap and soda and all that sort of stuff. You watch me. I'll make me fortune. Just need to get set up first. The lads only hire a cart so haven't got any equipment to hand me on, you see. But they've told me where they go to buy wholesale at rock-bottom prices. I reckon I can get a better deal than what I was getting with Lizzie. She won't like that.' Fanny sounded chirpy but her face told a different story.

Lily pondered on the news that brave young fellows were already going to fight. She'd seen a few recruiting posters out on the streets, but it all seemed quite distant and unreal. Despite reports of Allied casualties in the paper, the consensus of opinion was still that it was just a storm in a teacup. Lily prayed that it would be.

To cheer herself up she said, 'I saw Adam Reeve the other day. He told me you'd discharged yourself. I was going to come to the pub and see you as soon as I could get the time off.' Lily frowned. 'Did you know Margie scarpered? I'm so worried about her.'

Fanny grimaced that she did. 'The pigs set the coppers on her.'

'So I heard; I've got to find her and do something to help.' Lily jumped off the desk in agitation and started pacing. 'I would've gone back for her when I had enough put by and a place for us to live.' Lily felt guilty and selfish for spending on a set of best clothes. That money could have gone towards helping Margie. 'Perhaps she's gone home to Stepney and her mum took her in,' Lily said optimistically.

'She tried her luck there, but Mrs Blake didn't give her

that.' Fanny clicked her fingers. 'She showed Margie the door and told her to get herself back to the workhouse.'

'You've spoken to Margie then?' Lily brightened up.

'I have at that.'

'Has she found some work? Is she all right? Can't believe her mum would be cruel enough to turn her away.' Lily beckoned to take the boy again so Fanny could button herself up now she'd finished the feed.

'He'll sick on you if you jiggle him.' Fanny gave a timely warning as her son burped and dribbled milk.

Lily ceased bouncing Ronald on her forearm and used her hanky on his wet face before handing him back. She sensed her friend was reluctant to say more about the runaway. 'Margie *is* all right, isn't she?'

'She's as well as can be expected,' Fanny said evasively.

'What aren't you telling me?' Lily cut to the chase.

'Oh, all right ... but don't go bonkers. On the day I left South Grove, I told Margie to look me up at the Bow Bells if she got the chance, same as I told you to. Bugger me, wasn't even a week later that I spotted her hiding round the corner to ambush me. She was in a right state and urgently needed a place to stay. I'm camping out at a friend's, so couldn't help her there.' Fanny continued rattling off her tale. 'Just so happens, though, that I'd heard on the grapevine of a woman wanting somebody to write some letters for her. No pay involved unfortunately, but she's got a big house and a room going begging. Now we both know that writing's something our Margie *can* do, so I introduced them.'

'Bloody marvellous!' Lily gleefully clapped her hands.

'Not quite ... ' Fanny sounded cagey. 'Gladys is a madam and she wanted somebody she could trust to keep shtoom as this stunt of hers is a bit dodgy. Well Margie ain't about to tell tales, is she, when Old Bill is already on *her* tail.' Fanny read Lily's horrified expression and shrugged. 'Beggars can't be choosers. Margie gets her board and lodging free while she's of use to Gladys.'

Lily felt like putting her head in her hands now. But she was also intrigued, so gestured for Fanny to tell her more about this Gladys.

'She's been a brothel-keeper for donkey's years. Gladys is like me, never did much schooling, so never properly learned to read or write. Margie can't be blamed for taking dictation though,' Fanny reasoned.

Lily was alive to Fanny trying to minimise a hazard. 'Sounds like a bad idea. Margie won't be accused of doing anything criminal, will she?'

''Course not.' Fanny waved that away. 'Margie ain't got money for a stamp to post a letter. Gladys does that.' Fanny put her son to her shoulder and started rubbing his back. 'Margie won't pack it in, anyhow. She's adamant she'll do whatever she has to 'cos she's never going back to that spike. Can't say I blame her either.'

'Is she still wearing her uniform?'

Fanny nodded. 'Margie might eventually get a cast-off dress if Gladys takes to her enough. But she's a real miser, even though she's rolling in it. I know her of old and I reckon she's gone too far, blackmailing punters.'

'Blackmail! Gawd! What a confounded mess.' Lily had echoed her brother's recent lament and had almost used his rude swearword, too. 'There must be *something* Margie can do that's above board.'

'She wants to be my sidekick . . . but she'd hold me back,' Fanny explained. 'I'll feel rotten telling her no, but she can't handle a loaded cart. And she's not got a farthing to add to the kitty to buy stock.' Fanny stroked her son's downy head as he started to doze and her voice became softer. 'I'd sunk some cash into the business with me sister, and the cow won't give it back. I'm back to square one and need to save a few bob before I can start again.'

Lily chewed on her thumbnail, mulling things over.

'I'm helping a neighbour out with childminding so she can do a shift in a laundry,' Fanny continued, bringing Lily up to date. 'She returns the favour and has Ronny for me while I do mornings at the rag shop. Had a belly-full of laundries, so I wasn't going there.' Fanny gave a wink. 'I'm on the straight and narrow, doing regular work. I managed to get me 'n' Ronny a roof over our heads too. Me friend's wife ran off, so he took me in. We were sweethearts at school so it's not really business ... just doing each other good turns. He and his missus never had kids, so he's not used to a crying baby. He hasn't moaned yet though.'

'Is he Ronald's dad?' Lily was curious about who'd fathered the little boy. She could tell Fanny had a yen for her old flame.

'Wish he was ... I should've snapped him up when I had the chance.' Fanny sighed. 'I had a few gents buzzing around when I fell pregnant, so can't say for sure who's responsible.' She shrugged. 'Don't care anyway. My Ronny's the important man in my life now.'

Fanny had an intensely protective look as she cradled the infant slumbering on her shoulder. Lily recalled a similar ferocious glint in her mother's eyes on the perishing night she'd begged the porter for entry to the workhouse. Maude had fought, kicking and shoving, to get inside the lodge and persuade the stranger to give her twins a chance at a better life. And she had succeeded.

'Out of all of us, you look to have fallen on your feet, gel.' Fanny cocked her head, assessing Lily's filled-out figure and shiny chestnut hair. 'I was wrong about Greg Wilding then ... seems you was right to trust him. Working for him suits you.'

'I'm moving on shortly. He doesn't need me any more.'

'The bloody git!'

'No ... he's not.' Lily jumped to his defence. 'He's been good to me and I knew it was just a temporary job from the start.' Mentioning him had reminded Lily that time was getting on. She didn't want him coming back and catching her idling with Fanny, or hearing any of this conversation. Before her friend left, there was something she needed to bring up. 'Actually, I've something to ask you.'

'Let's hear it,' Fanny bluntly invited. She had deposited her sleeping son on the chair and was inspecting the solitary parked cart. It hadn't been hired that morning due to a wobbly wheel.

'Do you know of an abortionist?' Lily blurted, thinking there was no point in beating around the bush.

Fanny swung about, mouth agape. 'The dirty beast! I told you not trust him, Lil! No wonder he wants rid of you.' She scooped up her son, startled awake by her bellowing.

'Not for me! For somebody else ... ' Lily hissed, scooting to the door to make sure nobody walking past had heard Fanny's explosion. 'My twin brother has turned up out of the blue and, though it's been wonderful to be back together, we've had some problems. Biggest one is that Davy's girl's up the spout. The pair of them are worried sick about her stepfather finding out and knocking them

245

both black and blue.' She gave a hopeless shrug. 'I thought you might have some advice.'

'I do know of a nurse who moonlights; she don't come cheap, though, so it's lucky she owes me a favour. We lost touch when I went into the workhouse. But I'll find her and remind her she owes me one.' Ronald was drowsing again, and Fanny tucked him into his shawl, securing the ends about her body and tying them at her waist so she could easily carry him home. She glanced at Lily with a sheepish expression. 'Actually, I didn't just come here to moan about my sister and tell you what Margie's up to. *I* want a favour off *you*, Lily. Looks as though I got here just in time, too, as you're leaving this place.'

'On one condition.' Lily had guessed Fanny was going to ask for a cart to start her round because she couldn't afford to hire one and buy stock. 'We throw our lot in together and take Margie in with us. Then, somehow or other, the three of us will have to make it pay.'

'You'll let me have a cart buckshee? *And* you'll be a partner?' Fanny sounded disbelieving. '*Promise* you will?'

'Promise . . . but the cart's not buckshee – we'll have to rent it. Best do everything properly.'

'I never for a moment thought you'd want to join forces with somebody like me,' Fanny choked out.

'Why ever not?' Lily said stoutly, though she was already reflecting on whether she'd regret her impulsiveness. 'I've got nothing else lined up and reckon it's worth a go, don't you?'

Fanny gave a firm nod, still beaming with joy.

'I hoped me and Davy would be business partners, but he's got other ideas right now.' Lily shrugged. 'He's had to consider being a father. It's made him realise he might need to put a new family first.' The idea that little Shrimp could be a dad was hard for Lily to take in. If only circumstances had been different and there was no need for talk of abortions! How wonderful it would have been to look forward to welcoming a little niece or nephew to swell the Larkin numbers. Not so long ago, she had believed herself quite alone in the world.

A surge of optimism quietened her collywobbles over what she'd let herself in for. In front of her was an exciting – if risky – venture. Being faint-hearted from the start was sure to doom it to failure. But she wouldn't go behind her boss's back about the cart. He'd been lenient, but that could change if she pushed him too far. She believed he would agree to let her have a vehicle and pay him back later out of profits. Although it went against his ruling, he might be swayed to relent for a member of staff he wanted out from under his feet. He'd promised to sign her reference and offered to contact Adam about clerical vacancies to help get rid of her. There would be plenty of time in the future to look for office work if she failed at being her own boss. For now she was tossing fate to the wind and sticking by the people she cared about. Margie and Fanny had been like her family when she'd believed she had none.

Chapter Seventeen

Adam Reeve had purposely left the door of his office ajar so he would hear when the man in the next room went out. Once a month, the master and his wife would spend half a day meeting members of the Board of Guardians, ostensibly to address workhouse matters. The local hostelry at which they convened was renowned for serving prime Scottish beef and lobster, and the feast was paid for out of Whitechapel Union funds. Disgusted as Adam was of the obscene hypocrites stuffing their gluttonous faces for hours whilst discussing rationing bread to poor children, he was glad to see the back of the couple. In their absence he had some snooping to do.

He heard a door slam along the corridor and stood loitering by his desk, tossing some keys in his palm while waiting for William Stone's footsteps to die away. On starting work at South Grove, the medical officer had been given the set for emergency use. They opened all the main rooms, other than the Stones' private quarters, he'd been told. He'd never had reason or desire to enter the unoccupied master's office before. Today he certainly did, and hoped one of the assortment of iron implements suspended on the ring fitted that lock.

Adam had been intrigued when Lily told him about her mother's mysterious pregnancy. At the time he hadn't wanted to promise her too much, in case he turned nothing up and had no answers for her. He'd already searched the archives for Mrs Larkin's infirmary records. They were missing. His suspicions had been aroused that they'd been deliberately removed after the file had not come to light in any place an officer might have innocently and erroneously left it. There was only the master's private filing cabinet left to rifle through.

It was a warm day in late August, but that wasn't the reason Adam felt a trickle of perspiration on his back as he sidled out of his door to stride the few yards to the master's office. He had a morbid intuition he was about to unearth abuse and fornication, and wasn't sure what he'd do with the proof of it. Glancing left and right, he started ramming one key after the other into the lock, his jerky movements accompanied by an inmate's staccato howls. It was the same woman who'd attempted to commit suicide a few weeks ago by drowning herself in a few inches of bath water. The pathetic soul understood in her own demented way that only death could reunite her with the children she cried for and who had perished from diphtheria two years ago in the infirmary.

At last Adam felt a key start to yield to the pressure he was exerting. With a flick of his wrist he spun it around. Seconds later, he was inside William Stone's office, closing the door behind him, and vigilantly locking it.

Remnants of a snack of tea and biscuits were on a tray on the desk, next to a depleted whisky decanter. Adam skirted the furniture and, on approaching the heavy wooden cabinet set against the wall, was relieved to see the key had been left in the escutcheon.

He set about flicking through buff folders, jerking some up to better inspect their contents. Most of the documents related to financial matters. Bank letters and purchase dockets and investment bonds. Adam imagined those would be sure to make interesting reading. He concentrated on the job at hand. If he found what he was after, he intended to quickly remove the file to his own office to thoroughly study the notes. The Stones would have no need to go back to the file, so it wouldn't be immediately missed, giving him time to replace it. His fingers increased speed as they worked through the drawer. He wanted to be gone from here in case one of the newer staff members, ignorant of the master's regular beanfeast, banged on the door, looking for him.

Harriet Fox had also been impatient for the Stones to go off on their jaunt so she could nose around in the master's office. She, too, was on a mission to locate Mrs Larkin's notes, but for a different reason. Harriet had no need to read them to know what had gone on. She'd been present during Maude Larkin's final hours, struggling to expel a child from her exhausted body.

Whereas Adam had decided to forgo investigating any fiscal irregularities, Harriet certainly intended to. She knew William and Bertha Stone were up to their necks in it, and she was after the evidence.

Last night Harriet had had a violent argument with their son when he told her he'd finished with her. She'd sensed it coming for a while, but was nevertheless seething from having been scorned. Knowing she could wreak revenge had helped her keep a cool head. She had something to say to him, and was hoping to find the document that would back up her words. If he still refused to marry her, then she'd take proof of his fornication and his parents' corruption to the chairman of the Board of Guardians. The Whitechapel Union would be desperate to keep the matter hushed up. There might still be a chance of doing a deal and gaining a key to the master's apartments, with or without Ben Stone. Plenty of men would be willing to toe her line to share in the perks of running South Grove workhouse as master and matron. But first she needed to break into the office ...

Harriet halted outside the door, glancing to left and right while working a hairpin free from the fat bun on the crown of her head. It wasn't the first time she'd picked a lock, but this was a more intricate affair than those on the medicine cupboards she'd robbed in the past of morphine to sell. The scrape of metal on metal as she worked at the lock initially masked the sounds coming from within the room. Eventually the noise of a drawer being slid shut made her quickly withdraw the pin and push it back into her hair. It wasn't the Stones inside; she'd loitered on the landing and watched the couple leave the building. Ben could be in his father's office if he'd found a way of gaining access. Her erstwhile boyfriend had once resentfully complained that he didn't have a key, yet the medical officer did ...

Harriet moved away a few yards then flattened her back against the wall. She didn't have long to wait before a white-coated figure emerged and relocked the door.

Noiselessly she strode up behind him. 'And what might you be doing, sir?'

Adam quickly recovered composure and secured a buff folder beneath his arm. 'I ... I ... not that it's any of your concern, but I've collected some necessary paperwork, Miss Fox.' He was stuttering and trembling from being caught out. He quickly calmed down; helped by suspicions of his own. 'I might ask you the same question. You're surely aware the Stones are at a meeting all afternoon. Don't you know the rota? You should be patrolling the female wards with the other officers.' He could see that his set of keys had drawn her eyes so dropped them into a pocket.

'Oh, never fear ... I know what I'm doing, sir, and I know what you're up to as well. What have you got there?' It was an unnecessary question. This man's meeting with Lily Larkin, their animated conversation in the café that Harriet had witnessed weeks ago – it all made sense now. Larkin had always been too sharp for her own good. Since leaving the workhouse, the girl had obviously been pondering on her mother's passing and, smelling a rat, had asked Reeve to poke around to see what he could find. The interfering doctor had dug up the midwifery report that only the master and mistress were supposed to have sight of. She had feared the Stones might have decided to destroy it to protect themselves and their son. Now Harriet was ruing that they hadn't done that. It had fallen into dangerous hands.

'Give that to me.' Harriet impatiently beckoned and clicked her fingers. The medical officer was a weedy individual and she felt confident she could overpower him and snatch the folder if he refused to hand it over. She guessed he'd taken it to read at his leisure and had little idea of what it contained. She wanted to get her hands on it before he did.

Adam barked an astonished laugh. 'Why on earth would I do that?' He started towards his office, but she dodged in front of him to block his path. 'What do you think you're doing? Move aside. I've patients to attend to in the infirmary.'

Harriet didn't budge. 'I said give me that! I warned you before about crossing me. I can ruin you.'

Harriet's tone and expression had become sinister, making Adam hesitate before pushing past. Her unmerited aggression was making him even more determined to get inside his office to read the report. With an enraged grunt, Harriet shoved him in the chest, sending him off balance. She was a strong woman, a necessary asset in a job where inmates often needed to be restrained, or a cane was required to be wielded in punishment.

Adam steadied himself against the wall and used an elbow to keep her at bay. A second later, running footsteps could be heard in the corridor.

'Miss Fox! You're needed urgently in the sewing room.' Mrs Windham panted to a halt. 'Two of the women have started fighting. One of them is threatening to stab the other in the eye with a darner. There won't be enough of us to subdue the lot of them if they all join in.'

Harriet glared at the woman but she knew there was nothing more to be done. The interruption had given Reeve an opportunity to lock himself in his office.

Adam knew she'd not simply give up and go away without having the last word.

'Let's have that talk later then, about why you were dismissed from a hospital in Doncaster, shall we?' Harriet hissed through the keyhole.

Adam didn't respond but he started shaking again. Now

he knew she wasn't making empty threats, the coward in him was tempted to chase after her and give her what she wanted.

First he needed to discover if he held in his hand a bargaining chip of his own. He opened the folder and saw the document it contained had been written in Harriet's spidery scrawl. Mrs Bertha Stone had countersigned it at the bottom. Adam didn't bother to sit down; he leaned back against the closed door, immediately turned the page and started to read.

*

The lads had finished work and gone home half an hour ago. Lily had been hanging about in the yard, hoping to talk to Mr Wilding about the cart she wanted to have to start her new business venture. He had a visitor with him in the warehouse; it was obviously a successful meeting as they'd been at it for ages. Usually salesmen were turfed out after a few minutes.

The late summer weather was humid with a rumble of thunder in the sullen air. Feeling hot and bothered and in need of a drink, Lily gave up waiting. She pushed herself off the wall she'd been lounging against while fanning her face with a hand, and walked out of the gate, intending to speak to him in the morning.

Since Fanny's visit, no opportunity had arisen for Lily to corner her boss about the equipment she and her friends needed to get up and running. He was out on business so often that sometimes they spent mere minutes a day together. When he was around, he seemed unapproachable. The closeness between them that had been there from the start, and had allowed her to be blunt and cheeky with him, had vanished since the big bust-up. She sensed he now wanted a distance kept between them, and Lily had respected the tacit ruling. She wished she didn't have an awkward favour to ask, but refused to dwell on it. She had plenty of things on her mind keeping her spirits up as she headed homewards.

She couldn't wait for Sunday to arrive, already savouring the moment she'd catch up with old friends. She'd see Adam at the caff; then afterwards she was meeting Fanny and Margie. Lily was praying Adam would have news to pass on about her mother but, if he didn't, the joy of a long-awaited reunion with Margie would sweeten the disappointment. The anticipation of her best friend's company perked her up so much that she started to hum and do a little jig . . . until she spotted Davy across the road with a girl.

Lily was keen to meet Angie Clark, so speeded up towards the kerb to go and join them. On getting closer, it became obvious from the girl's gesticulating that the couple were arguing. Lily had told her brother of Fanny's promise to contact the moonlighting nurse. It shouldn't be long to wait now for news of an appointment, but perhaps a panic-stricken Angie was impatient to get things moving and was taking it out on her boyfriend.

While Lily had been waiting for a bus to pass so she could cross the road, the couple had parted. Davy had shot off one way and Angie was now trudging along in the opposite direction with her head down. Lily still wanted to speak to her. They hadn't been introduced but could be sisters-in-law in the future. Besides, the girl looked miserable, and might welcome some reassurance that help was on the horizon.

'Angie?' Lily called out on gaining the opposite pavement.

The girl twisted around, looking hostile at first. Then she burst out, 'Blimey! You must be Davy's sister, Lily. Don't you look like him?'

'That's twins for you.' Lily smiled, pleased they'd got off on the right foot. 'It's lovely to meet you at last, by the way. I saw you with my brother just now.' Angie looked about seventeen, and was fair-haired with pleasant, plump features. Lily discreetly eyed the older girl's waistline. Thankfully her condition wasn't yet obvious as her figure was naturally rounded.

'Well ... nice to meet you, Lily, but can't stop. Me stepfather's waiting on me to help with a pile of washing up. Don't want an ear-bashing for being late.'

'Is everything all right between you and Davy?' Lily hurried after her. 'Well I know everything isn't *all right*. Davy has told me about ... you know.' Davy had told her something else as well, and that *did* show. The girl had a fading bruise on her cheek, no doubt courtesy of her stepfather's fist. It wasn't just ear-bashings that Angie was getting.

Angie touched her face, conscious of what had drawn Lily's eyes. 'No, everything's not bloody well all right,' she muttered. 'Your brother promised he'd have some money for me to sort things out, but I've not seen a penny today. This is all his fault, but look! I'm the one paying for it.' She pointed at her injury.

Lily thought that was unfair as it had taken the two of them to make a baby. She kept her thoughts to herself though. 'He's already handed over eighteen shillings for pills. That cash wasn't his to give and he doesn't have more.'

'Eighteen? I got fifteen bob. He said that was all he had.' Angie sounded cross.

Creaming a bit off the top for himself was the sort of thing Davy *would* do. He'd probably gambled with it in the hope of increasing it. He and his pals remained convinced that the next toss of the coin would bring winnings, despite experiencing regular losses to prove otherwise. 'I know the pills didn't work, but Davy told you the good news, didn't he?'

'What good news? When I found out he didn't have any cash, I told him to clear off and leave me alone.' Sulkily, Angie crossed her arms.

'My friend knows somebody,' Lily explained. 'A nurse who'll help you as a favour.' She had anticipated being treated to a thank-you, and a relieved expression. But she didn't receive either.

'What d'you mean a favour? Davy promised me three quid.' Angie seemed agitated.

'No ... you don't understand. You won't *need* money. The nurse won't charge, you see.'

'I *do* bloody need it!' Angie had turned pale. 'Me stepfather knows somewhere better to take me for an operation.' She pointed at Lily. 'You'd better tell your brother I must have that cash. He said he'd do it the same way as before. He better had 'n' all, or me stepdad said he'll swing for us both.' Angie fiddled nervously with her hair, pushing it behind her ears. 'Greg Wilding never caught Davy out last time. He short-changed his guv'nor, easy as pie ... ' Realising she'd said too much she stopped smirking. 'Have you got anything? A few bob'll do for now.'

Lily ignored the hand stretched out to her. Finally she'd realised that Angie had no use for a nurse ... money was all she was after. Lily was on to her now. 'I thought your stepfather didn't know about you being in the family way?' She cocked her head, waiting for an answer.

Angie licked her lips. 'Yeah ... well he's found out, and he's gone bonkers and landed me one.' She thrust her head forward so Lily got a better look at the bruise. 'I'm getting off to the caff before I get another right-hander for being late. I've got a stack of washing up waiting and I'm worn out. I've already done a shift at the draper's.'

Lily followed her along the street. 'You're not even pregnant, are you?' She put on a spurt and got in front of her, staring deliberately at a roll of fat at Angie's waistline. 'You wicked cow! Why would you make up something like that?' Enlightenment wasn't long in coming. 'Is your stepfather called Keegan? Has he got a caff in the market?' She blocked Angie's path as the older girl turned scarlet and attempted to barge past. 'Keegan's told you to get Davy to thieve from his boss, hasn't he? And he's clumped you to make sure you do!'

'You don't know what you're talkin' about,' Angie shrilled. 'Anyhow, who asked you to poke yer nose in? I'll end up in a spike if Davy lets me down. He hates the idea of his kid growing up in a workhouse. You ask him.'

'Oh, I know he does. And I know you've got him wound right round your finger. You'll do and say anything to pluck at his heartstrings, now you know how he feels about you. You've just been using him, you callous cow!'

'You mind your own business.' Angie jabbed a thick forefinger against Lily's nose.

'It *is* my business.' Lily stood her ground rather than be shoved into the gutter. 'I've lost everything over this. Over *you*.' Lily grabbed hold of Angie's arm, with every intention of dragging her round to Davy's place right now to make her own up to being in league with her stepfather.

Angie kicked out, wrenching herself free. For good measure she raked a set of fingernails down Lily's cheek before bolting off up the road.

The cuts stung, yet didn't bother Lily much because the extent of the swindle had started penetrating her mind. Could Davy have been in on it? Had he lied to his sister to get her sympathy and support? She backed against a wall feeling winded, barely aware of the growling thunder or the slow rain spots hitting her clammy complexion. She believed her brother was innocent of scheming against his boss. He'd been gullible because he loved Angie ... heaven only knew why when she was so horrible. Davy had been tearful when speaking about his girlfriend dying in a workhouse, as their mother had. Angie Clark and her stepfather had reeled in the love-sick fool hook, line and sinker, by using those fears against him. As for Lily, her devotion to her brother had led her to destroy her life for a pack of lies.

Davy really had trodden in his father's footsteps, thieving from his employer and standing to lose his livelihood. Lily knew she'd been the bigger fool in abetting him. If she hadn't covered up what he had done, Gregory Wilding would have got to the bottom of it by now.

Nobody stitched him up, he had said after fighting to recover a debt from Keegan. He'd been protecting his business and his reputation that day. Keegan would be congratulating himself on having the last laugh. And she and Davy had been his unwitting accomplices. Lily felt a stab of foreboding.

The rain was lukewarm and heavy, drenching her

head and shoulders, but she stayed where she was, an urge to let out a furious scream of frustration tightening her throat. She could race round and warn Davy that more calamities were piling up, but she'd have a job on her hands convincing him he was besotted with a nasty piece of work. Was Davy even at home? He might have immediately headed to a usual gambling haunt to try to raise the money his conniving girlfriend said she desperately needed.

At first the steaming downpour and a lightning flash prevented Lily noticing the van drawing up at the kerb.

'What the hell are you doing, Lily? Lily, what's up?' Greg strode towards her, yanking up his collar.

She stared at him, white-faced and startled. 'Nothing, guv'nor ... just off home,' she threw over a shoulder, breaking into a run. She had to avoid him until she'd spoken to Davy about this awful new development.

Greg grabbed her elbow, spinning her about and frowning at the scratches on her face. 'I said ... what's up?'

'Nothing ... just need to get out of the storm.' She tried to set off again but he tightened his grip on her.

'Get in the van, I'll take you home. You're soaked through.'

She shook her head. 'Thanks, but don't want you to.'

'What's happened?' He nodded at the red weals on her cheek. 'Hope the other fellow looks worse.'

She hadn't realised Angie had left her mark. 'A girl did it.' Lily rubbed her face and saw a smear of blood on her fingers. 'I'll get her back. That's all there is to it.'

'So your brother's not involved then,' he said drily, swiping rain from his eyes.

Rather than lie she kept quiet, face lowered, and concentrated on trying to slip her arm free.

'You might as well tell me what he's done. When he stirs shit, some of it always lands on my doorstep.'

'It won't, 'cos it's nothing much and I'll sort it out.' She attempted to sound breezy.

'You're a bad liar, gel. Looks like your scrapping's not up to much either.'

A huge thunderclap made Lily hunch her shoulders to her ears while Greg swore. He ushered her to the van and forced her to get into the passenger seat.

Lily considered jumping out while he dashed round to his side, but there was nowhere to shelter and she didn't fancy getting struck by lightning. The fight suddenly went out of her and she slumped back against the seat.

He got in, flicking rain from his slick fair hair with his fingers. Then he settled back too and they stared at one another. She glimpsed a spark of tenderness in his wolfish eyes. He was looking at her as he had at the beginning, when he'd been sympathetic and had wanted to help her. Lily experienced the same odd thrill she'd felt on the day she'd come upon him stripped to the waist and had seen the scars on his back. He'd looked vulnerable then and she'd wanted to hug him ... until she'd realised he was drunk. Even then she'd had an urge to reach out because he'd seemed in need of comfort. And she couldn't hurt him now by telling him that men in pubs might be laughing at him behind his back because Keegan had tricked him out of money with the Larkin twins' help.

'You gonna tell me about this, Lily? I'm this close to knocking your brother spark out.' He held thumb and forefinger an inch apart. 'And I don't care if he is only fifteen.'

'He's sixteen. We had our birthday a few weeks ago. And no need to worry about this, guv'nor. I'll deal with it.' She dragged hair that was hanging like damp rats' tails off her face.

He smiled at her fleetingly before diverting his gaze. 'Sweet sixteen eh? Time you got yourself a boyfriend. Get him to keep your brother in line and save me a job.'

'Boyfriend?' she scoffed in a defeated way. 'Men are just trouble . . . ' Lily was thinking of Keegan and her brother and father. 'Not you, though,' she said earnestly. 'Or Adam Reeve. You're both sensible people.'

'Sensible, am I?' He almost choked in amusement. 'You really don't know me, do you.'

'I reckon I do. You're fair and kind though you pretend you're not. I appreciate what you've done for me. Honestly. I want you to believe that, whatever happens.' She was tempted to tell him the whole story, and risk the uproar. But they'd be parting ways soon and, when they did, she'd like this quiet interlude to be what she remembered. She wouldn't ask her favour either. There were other places to hire carts, and pay out of profits.

'What's likely to happen?'

She shrugged. 'I should get home now and get out of these wet clothes.' She peeled from her skin the saturated material of her skirt. 'I'll see you tomorrow then.'

'Yeah . . . time you went home.' He'd already noticed her shivering and the shape of her firm breasts and hard nipples beneath her sodden bodice. The contour of her thigh was equally enticing beneath the cotton she was playing with.

'You sorted out a job yet?' he asked gruffly, staring out of the window and occupying his hands with his cigarettes.

'I'm going into business with some friends. Seeing them on Sunday. And Adam as well. Got lots to tell him now.

You don't need to worry about me, guv'nor. It's time I stood on me own two feet. I'll always be grateful to you, you know. You will remember that, won't you?'

He struck a match and took a drag from his cigarette. 'How about Davy? Is he in on this venture or is he sticking with me?' His lack of enthusiasm about the latter option was made intentionally clear.

'You ought to be glad he's staying,' she championed Davy. 'He's a hard worker and been selling out for you most days. He's been doing better than the others ... accounts prove it,' she said truthfully.

'Not a good employee though, is he?'

Lily rolled her eyes. 'It was just a one-off slip 'cos he was desperate. He thought he'd got a girl in the family way.' Lily knew she'd said more than enough now. 'I need to get home. I'll catch me death ... ' She reached for the door handle, ready to jump out, but he pulled away from the kerb.

When the lane became too narrow to negotiate in the van, he slowed down. The rain had lightened to a drizzle and though the thunder still grumbled and electricity still winked in the purple heavens, the storm was starting to move away.

'Thanks, guv'nor.' She sensed tension building and awkward questions coming. 'I can make a dash for it now.' She jumped to the cobbles, slamming the van door before the vehicle had properly stopped, then darted off, jumping puddles.

He watched her lissom fleeing figure until she'd disappeared.

Even then he sat there, staring at nothing but raindrop trails on windscreen glass. He'd told her to go and leave him alone and now she was doing just that. And he didn't want her to. He knew it was the best thing ... the right thing to have done, for them both. But it wasn't as though doing wrong was beyond him; it had put him where he was today.

And she'd turned sixteen. She was a woman now, in most people's eyes. Not in his, though. Not while he had an image of a sweet kid in workhouse uniform stuck in his head. And he wanted rid of it. He wanted rid of all of it.

He punched the steering wheel, rammed the gears into reverse and sped backwards out into the main road.

Chapter Eighteen

Last night Lily had intended to pay Davy a visit before turning in. But the storm had started up again and – having dried herself off – she'd not fancied another soaking. Nor had she believed that waiting a few more hours was going to make worse a catastrophe already weeks old. Speaking to her brother was vital, though, so she planned to ambush him along the road before they went into the warehouse.

Lily pulled a hairbrush through her sleep-tangled locks and, while staring out of her little windowpane at a new dawn brightening the alley, wondered if Davy would choose to have the good news or bad news first.

Hearing he'd not got Angie into trouble was sure to be a huge relief; hopefully it would help soothe the hurt of her treachery. The fallout of the feud between their guv'nor and Keegan was harder to assess, but it seemed pointless agonising over it. She and Davy might as well own up to having been patsies. Lily had lived amidst the meanness of human nature in the workhouse, yet had kept her rose-tinted view of the streets of London being cosy. She'd been naive. Malice and enmity were alive and well in the East End, and she needed to learn to spot tricksters. Gregory Wilding's cynicism wasn't a character flaw, rather a tool of his trade. She'd have to learn to think his way, now she was going into business on her own account.

Lily was halfway through tugging on her boots when she was startled by a loud banging on the door. She heard her brother's voice and rushed in an uneven gait to open up before he woke Jane. By the time she'd let him in, her flatmate was in the corridor, loudly complaining in colourful language. Unusually the older woman didn't make too much of it, though; she'd whipped back inside her bedroom before Lily had a chance to apologise for the disturbance. There was no time for Lily to poke her head round the door and try to smooth things over with Jane. Davy had started shaking her arm to gain her attention.

'I've got sacked and it's your fault! And Angie's not speaking to me and that's down to you 'n' all,' Davy snarled by way of good morning.

'What? Shhh ... ' Lily grabbed his wrist, dragging him along the dim passage to her room.

'Guv'nor turned up last night and give me the sack and a thump and told me to get me stuff out of the room by the weekend.' Davy looked distraught. 'What's started him off? Thought it had all blown over.'

'So he's worked it out for himself.' Defeated, she sat on her chair to put on her other boot. 'Should've known he would.'

'Worked what out?' Davy bawled.

'Angie's stepfather has stitched him up – with our help. If I'd known she was related to Keegan, then I might have

266

put two and two together sooner.' Her brother's bewilderment came as a great relief; proof enough that he'd not been involved in the scam. In less than a minute, Lily had brought him up to date with what had happened yesterday after he'd left the scene.

'You're lying,' he said hoarsely. 'Angie wouldn't do that to me.'

'Well she has,' Lily bluntly differed. 'Keegan's a bully. I expect Angie had little choice: go along with it or get whacked.'

Davy paced to and fro. 'I thought the guv'nor had gone nuts. I didn't understand what he meant when Keegan's name came up.'

'Didn't you bloody ask then?' Lily snapped, at the end of her tether.

'I didn't hang about. When he burst in and clumped me, I just scarpered up the road, hoping he'd calm down. D'you reckon he has? Shall I turn up for work and hope for the best?'

'Gawd knows . . . ' Lily sighed.

'You could persuade the guv'nor to let me stay. I've *got* to until I find another job and lodging—'

'I'm not asking him,' Lily cut across him. He sounded desperate, and even though the oil lamp shed meagre light, the bruise on his chin was visible. She ached to say something comforting but knew not to. 'We got what we deserve, Davy. Have you said sorry to the guv'nor for taking the money and causing trouble?'

'You told him you took it.' Davy sounded defensive.

'And I told you he knows I didn't. For heaven's sake, own up and apologise. It wouldn't be before time either, would it?'

He turned on his heel, shouting, 'Thanks fer nothing! Fine help you are.'

'Davy!' She had seen his bottom lip wobbling. By the time she'd finished tying her laces, she'd heard him slam the front door.

At first Lily intended to race to catch him up. She turned out the lamp, collected her jacket and bag and sped up to the street door, but then hesitated. She'd learned the hard way that snapping in two the rod she'd made for her own back was long overdue. He obviously wanted some time alone to come to terms with the consequences of Angie's betrayal. Lily wasn't going to be a hypocrite and make excuses for that girl so her brother felt better. The cow deserved to be paid back for the trouble and the scratches she'd dished out.

Lily leaned back against the wall, closing her eyes and thinking she could have done without this rotten start to the day. The sound of a woman's throaty giggle caused her lids to spring open again. If Jane had cheered up, there wouldn't be a better time to apologise for the disturbance, and Lily knew she ought to, rather than risk a week of snide remarks. A faint lamplight leaked from beneath the door; she imagined that having been woken up, the older woman had decided to read and something had tickled her fancy. About to knock, Lily's hand dropped to her side. She held her breath, straining her ears. She was sure she'd heard a man's voice intermingling with her flatmate's, then seconds later came the squeak of bedsprings. Lily felt her face growing hot as the human noises from within became more guttural. She had a good idea who was sharing Jane's bed and it wasn't Gregory Wilding. A few days ago she'd found two unwashed glasses that smelled of whisky in the sink. Only one had lipstick marks on the rim. Gregory couldn't have visited Jane as he'd been in Kent looking at a second-hand van to buy.

It seemed disrespectful to Lily for a woman to sneak her fancy man into a bed paid for by a regular boyfriend, even if he was as much of a cheat as she was. When that fancy man was as well-to-do as Clive Stratton, it seemed even more of a liberty that he hadn't shelled out on a hotel room! Lily always turned in early to make sure she was up for work on time, so she seldom heard her night owl flatmate arrive home, with or without company. In a fit of pique, Lily knocked on the door. The bed stopped rocking and some urgent whispers followed, then came a scuffling sound. A moment later Jane opened up an inch.

'Thought you'd gone out just now,' she gabbled, sounding flustered.

'Davy did; I stopped behind to say sorry for waking you up. But reckon you were already awake, weren't you. Anyhow, won't happen again. I'm off to work.' Lily turned on her heel and let herself out into the pale dawn light.

In the lane, Lily could just make out her brother's wiry figure trotting in front. Instead of chasing him, she settled into walking and thinking. She wasn't wholly surprised to discover that Jane had become more involved with Stratton. She was a rare visitor at the warehouse these days, and Lily had heard the lads talking about bumping into Gregory Wilding at the pub with a different girl. Lily knew it was no business of hers what he got up to ... still she felt an odd pang of emotion. She didn't like the idea of him being the sort of man who easily went from woman to woman.

Davy had disappeared by the time Lily rounded the

corner and the warehouse was in sight. Autumn was already in the air and the mornings were taking longer to brighten. The flares were lit and she noticed Bobby was loitering by the gate, smoking. As soon as he spotted her, he dropped the stub and strode towards her.

'Just wanted to warn you there was trouble last night, Lily. Guv'nor didn't clump you too, did he?' His tone had sharpened in disbelief the moment he spotted the marks on her face.

'I had a ding-dong with Angie Clark,' Lily explained. 'Just spoken to Davy. I know he's been sacked and chucked out of his lodging.'

'What's he gonna do now?' Bobby sounded concerned.

'He'll have to try and find a job and a room, I suppose.' She glanced about. 'Is Fred on his way?'

'He'll be along in a minute. I didn't wait for him. There's been a bad atmosphere for weeks in our place. I'm thinking of moving back in with me mum, anyhow, now the other two are off.'

'*Fred* got sacked as well?'

'He's jacking it in but he ain't broadcast it yet. When the guv'nor finds out he might calm down and let Davy stay on. Just be me on me tod otherwise, and that'll be a big drop in profit for him. Guv'nor'll have to go back on the barrow himself.'

'Davy might benefit from a clean break and a fresh start, same as me,' Lily said, hunching her shoulders against the breeze.

'Reckon you're right. It's time us lads carved out our own little manors.' Bobby booted a stray potato off the pavement and into the kerb. 'Can't be Greg Wilding's side-kicks for ever more.'

'Is that what Fred's doing?'

'Nah … He's gone all gung-ho and has been talking about joining up for weeks. He reckons he's really doing it this time, after what happened over there at Mons.'

'He's not old enough,' Lily exclaimed. She'd read about the Allied losses at the Battle of Mons in the paper, but the news that Fred was volunteering had come as a shock.

Bobby chuckled. 'He's gonna pretend he's nineteen so he can be a hero and give the Hun a good thrashing.'

Lily blew out a sigh. 'He doesn't look seventeen, even though he is. Doubt he'll get away with it.'

'I told him to draw on some whiskers before he shows up.' Bobby grinned and gave Lily a nudge. 'Oh, here he is, marching along.' He waited till Fred was in earshot before ribbing him. 'Left, right, left, right … Getting in some practice for them parade grounds, mate?'

'Shut it, Smudger.' Fred sounded jaunty and puffed out his chest even further.

As he seemed amiable, Lily joined the conversation. Fred had continued to be frosty with her, but they were both moving on and she hoped bygones could be bygones. They'd been colleagues for months and Lily would sooner part as friends. 'Good luck then, Fred. Keep your head down.'

'Wouldn't be jacking if it hadn't been for you 'n' yer brother. Ain't been the same at Wilding's since you two troublemakers showed up.' He strutted past into the warehouse.

'Good morning to you too,' Lily said with a sigh.

'Don't take no notice of him,' Bobby said kindly.

But Lily had taken notice, and she felt sad because she knew there was truth in what Fred had said.

The last of the customers had disappeared into the early morning light to start work. Bobby and Fred had been the first to leave, loaded up with the equipment to erect the market stall, the pitch Davy usually took charge of. The moment that quiet reigned, Lily had settled down at her desk to write up the day's accounts. She was interrupted after just a few minutes by her boss depositing a fistful of cash under her nose.

'What's that?' She eyed the heap of silver on the open ledger.

'Eighteen bob. Put it back in the hire tin. Make sure it stays in there this time.'

It was then that she noticed the torn and bloodied skin over the knuckles of his right hand. The mark Davy was sporting wasn't bad enough to have merited that damage. Taken together, it all told its own story.

'You got it back off Keegan ... *you* put it in the hire tin.' She scooped the coins up and held them out, staring challengingly at him.

'You giving me lip?'

'No ... I'm standing up for meself. I didn't take it out in the first place.'

'That's not what you told me.'

Lily shot to her feet. 'I'm past playing these games. If you want to make a point, go ahead, instead of being sarcastic all the time.'

He gave her one of his looks then walked away, and Lily laughed. 'Thought you might do that, instead of clearing the air once and for all. Well, so there's nothing more to say on the subject, *I'll* get it out in the open: Davy got taken for a ride by someone he thought cared about him, and I thought I was helping him keep his job by covering up his mistake. We're a couple of hopeless mugs – there, I've said it, so you don't have to. And sorry, I didn't learn how to spot a swindle in a spike; I was too busy yanking up an airer till me arms wanted to drop off.' She paused, flushed in the face with temper.

'And I'm sarcastic?' he queried.

'Yes, you bloody well are! I did wrong for the right reason, and I'll take me punishment without moaning and, as far as I'm concerned, that's that. Soon I'll be gone from here and I'm bloody glad! You won't have to see me any more and I'm glad about that too.'

'What about him?' Greg jerked a nod at the door.

Lily snapped her head around to see her brother goggling at her as though she'd taken leave of her senses for back-chatting the boss like that.

With two pairs of eyes on him, Davy started to shuffle about. 'Sorry for what I did, guv'nor.' He cleared his throat. 'Can I have me job back? Swear I'll not do it again. Me 'n' Angie's finished anyhow. She's thrown me over.' He sniffed, averting his glistening eyes from them.

Lily turned her attention back to their guv'nor, thinking if he so much as smirked, she'd hurl the handful of silver at him. He didn't; he simply looked at her in a way she couldn't fathom. It wasn't triumph, more a sort of satisfaction.

'So we're both sarcastic . . . could be worse. Good to have things in common. Put the kettle on then, Lily. Three cups.' He beckoned to her brother. 'You. Want a word. And you'd better fucking listen.'

*

On Sunday afternoon, Lily didn't need to hang about for Adam to show up as she had last time; as she strolled along the Mile End Road, warmed by balmy sunshine, she spotted him stationed outside the caff. He noticed her trotting towards him and waved, hurrying to meet her.

Lily had expected her beam of pleasure to be returned. He did smile a welcome, but it was soon gone and a serious, quite harassed expression replaced it. She was on the point of asking him what was up, but he beat her to starting a conversation.

'Let's have tea in a different café today.' He'd assumed she wouldn't object and took her arm to urge her past the premises. Adam didn't want to stay in the vicinity of the workhouse in case his nemesis spotted them together. Harriet Fox would rightly suspect what their meeting was about. Lily shouldn't suffer the officer's malice anew. The poor girl had been picked on more than enough as an inmate.

Since Adam had discovered Harriet Fox was privy to very sensitive information about her superiors, it had become clear why the Stones tolerated her, and had given her a senior post. Fox was also privy to sensitive information about him. How she'd found out, though, Adam had no idea. Yet he imagined she was the sort of character who made it her business to snoop and harvest information that might be of benefit to her. Following their clash outside the master's office, they had been circling one another like boxers waiting for an opening to floor an opponent.

Obviously Harriet hadn't yet used her killer blow where her employers were concerned either, and that's why they continued to put up with her. The Stones would have been instantly dismissed had it been brought to light that an inmate had been impregnated on their watch. A double disgrace when the culprit was then identified as the couple's son. The child's sire hadn't been named in the midwifery report, but Adam had guessed who'd fathered Lily's half-sister. He'd even worked out how the opportunity for fornication had come about. While checking back through the infirmary records, Adam had discovered the regular porter had been an influenza patient over the Christmas period in question. Ben Stone had temporarily filled the vacancy and had admitted the Larkin family into the workhouse on Christmas Eve 1909. Equally damning was the fact that the master's son had taken a posting up north and not returned to South Grove until after Mrs Larkin was in her grave.

Adam had to decide whether to keep what he knew to himself. If Harriet made good on her threats, he could lose his job . . . or face a prison sentence. His overriding anxiety was to protect the person he loved, and the prospect of failing in that made him start to sweat.

'Shall we try in here?' Lily shook her companion's arm, drawing his attention to a tearoom they were approaching. She'd been chattering about the pleasant weather as they strolled, but could tell Adam hadn't really been listening. 'Don't you feel well? You look peaky, you know.' She hoped he'd not caught an infection from a patient.

'I'm all right, my dear.' He smiled his thanks for her concern, holding the door open for her to go inside.

Lily glowed beneath his endearment, though wishing it hadn't sounded quite so paternal. 'You're rushed off your feet again at work, aren't you?' She had put her own interpretation on his pallor and preoccupation.

He led the way to a window table and pulled a chair out

for her to sit down. 'I am, Lily; there's always too much to do and never enough time to do it. I miss my clerk, you see. She was a wonderful girl ... a godsend to me.'

'I miss you too ... all the time,' Lily said, smiling. 'But I'm glad I'm out of there.'

He squeezed her fingers. 'And so am I. With all my heart. I was only joking. You're blooming, and I'd never want to see you back near that revolting Miss Fox.'

His concern pleased Lily, although his vehement dislike of the officer had been unexpected.

'Apart from feeling exhausted, I've got something on my mind as well.'

'Does it concern my mum?' She rested her elbows on the table and settled her chin on her knuckles, gazing at him with large, soulful blue eyes. 'Did you have any luck finding her records? I've not been able to stop thinking about it.'

'Yes, I found them. Your mother passed away on the same day a fire started at South Grove. Staff were evacuating the building and moving patients outside in case the blaze took hold. A shortage of nurses in the infirmary was noted in the report.' Adam believed that had been logged to excuse the lack of a qualified midwife in attendance. Now he knew what he did, he suspected the labour ward had been cleared on the matron's say-so, to prevent a delirious woman being heard naming the father of the baby sapping her life. Mrs Larkin would have known how and when she got pregnant. What Adam couldn't be certain of was whether it had been a brutish deed and whether Ben Stone was unaware he'd fathered a child.

'I remember that day!' Lily exclaimed. 'Did my mum

die because there wasn't anybody to care for her when the baby was coming?' She sounded outraged.

'There were people with her,' he gently reassured. 'Miss Fox had successfully delivered babies before and I'm sure she and Matron would have done their best.' He believed that to be true. Neither woman would have wanted a fatality on their hands. 'Your mother had grown too weak from recurring illness to safely deliver the baby, though the infant was small.' That reported information Adam also took to be accurate.

'My sister was small?'

'Premature, according to the notes.'

Lily thought about that quite logically, surprising herself by not being overwhelmed with emotion. 'So she came before time ... not after ...'

Adam confirmed with a nod. 'Not unusual when the mother's health is failing.'

'That means my mum *must* have met somebody inside.' The idea that her mother had found a friend in that diabolical place filled Lily with wonderment. But how Maude and this fellow had managed to strike up a conversation, let alone more than that, remained a mystery. Although the knowledge had come as a shock, it'd also contented Lily. Maude had been denied the comfort of her twins' company but if she had gained consolation elsewhere, that was something to be thankful for.

'She did meet a man on the premises. It couldn't have been an inmate, though ... segregation is too strict, even for husbands and wives.'

'The waitress is on her way.' Lily obliquely warned him to wait before saying more. 'I'd just like some tea, please. I'm not hungry at all.'

Once their order had been taken and the waitress had gone, Adam resumed their conversation. 'By my calculations, your mother would have fallen pregnant around the Christmas that you were admitted.'

'We rang the bell on Christmas Eve,' Lily confirmed. 'I shan't ever forget it. We could hear a choir singing carols while we waited for Mum. It was the worst Christmas ever ... worse even than those afterwards spent inside. We only had Christmas and Boxing Day together, then we were separated and ... ' She bit into her quivering lip, unable to voice that neither she nor Davy ever saw their beloved mother again.

'Why were you waiting for your mum, Lily?'

'The porter wouldn't let us in. It wasn't our district, but Mum wanted us to attend the Cuckoo School and said we'd have a chance to at Whitechapel. She was so sure the Cuckoo would benefit us if we could only get to it. But of course in the end I never went there, and it was almost the finish of Davy. Anyway, Mum was determined and was kicking and shoving at the lodge door to make him open up. She got the better of him in the end and slipped inside so she could have a conversation.' Lily could recall her mother's phrasing. That night had changed all their lives and would always occupy her mind, as would her beloved mother's impressive strength and daring, considering how ill she'd been. Lily's wistful expression faded away. 'You don't think ... ?' Her eyes widened, then focused on Adam's face.

'Yes I do ... ' he answered gently.

'She was only gone about twenty minutes, that's all. It was snowing. We were freezing, and hungry. Me 'n' Davy talked about wanting some toast and dripping to eat while we waited.'

Adam knew twenty minutes was ample time for a horny man to impregnate a woman but he couldn't say as much.

'Don't be embarrassed.' She'd guessed at what he was keeping back. 'We can talk about anything, can't we?' She echoed some of his words from their last meeting back at him.

He gave a wry grimace of agreement. 'Your mother was gone long enough to conceive a child.'

Their teas were placed down; by the time the waitress had gone again, Lily had composed herself. 'Mum would have done anything for Davy and me ... even that.' Her voice throbbed with a mixture of sorrow and adoration. 'She pretended to be pregnant to sway the porter, and told him that if he didn't let us in, he'd find us dead on his step on Christmas morning. Didn't work. She had to force her way in ... it was all she could do.' Lily took a gulp of tea to disperse the lump hardening in her throat.

'I think that's our answer then,' Adam said softly. 'It's probably not of benefit to look into which man was on duty that night. I discovered the regular porter was too ill to be at his post and had been replaced.' It seemed a rape hadn't been committed, and Adam was glad about that. Stone had simply been too weak to refuse what he'd been offered.

'Don't want to hear his name,' Lily said. 'Doesn't matter now. Both the Larkins he might have been important to are gone. He's not important to me. My mum would have wanted it kept a secret. Even if my little sister had survived long enough to be put in a workhouse cradle, Mum wouldn't have liked Davy and me knowing what she did for us. I'm not ashamed of her. I'm proud.' Her voice broke and she waited a moment before continuing. 'Maude

Larkin was the best of women. The best mother anybody could ever wish for.'

'She loved her children dearly, that's clear.' Adam sat back with a sigh, glad that was over with and Lily had taken it so well. But his relief was short-lived.

The bell on the door had clattered as a couple entered the tearoom. Without meaning to, Adam crashed his cup on to its saucer. The subject of his thoughts had materialised in the flesh.

Lily turned her head to see what had startled Adam. 'Crikey! Didn't expect to run into him this afternoon,' she whispered. 'Glad he's not with his vile girlfriend.' She leaned forward to add, 'Perhaps he's got rid of her for this one. Can't say I blame him ... goes without saying she must be much nicer than Harriet Fox.'

Ben Stone had seen his colleague, but it took him a few seconds longer to recognise the doctor's companion. Then he stared at Lily and his features became quite still. The girl had grown up, become a woman. Her similarity to her mother was astonishing, causing a pang to tighten his chest and buried memories to surface. He escorted his lady friend to a table then approached them.

'Dr Reeve ... Miss Larkin, this is a surprise, meeting you like this.' He smiled at Lily. 'It's good to see you looking so well, Miss Larkin. Things are obviously on the up for you.'

'I believe they are, sir,' Lily said politely. She'd never seen a great deal of him in the workhouse. But she paid attention to him now, realising he was as fair as Mr Wilding but not as tall or as handsome. His eyes weren't as striking: brown rather than the colour of autumn leaves. She flicked a glance at Adam, who seemed ill at ease.

'Miss Larkin has been keeping me up to date with what

she's been up to recently. She's secured a position as a clerk and is a credit to the Whitechapel Union, wouldn't you say, sir?' Adam broke the quiet, hoping to stop Stone staring at Lily. She wouldn't understand what Ben saw in her, but Adam reckoned he did: her mother's image. The interest and tenacity in the fellow's gaze was an eye-opener. Perhaps there had been some compassion in that venal transaction between Mrs Larkin and Ben Stone.

'Indeed I would.' Ben collected his thoughts. 'We need more such success stories.'

Lily blushed, in pleasure, but she was also squirming a bit. If the two men knew *all* of what she'd been up to recently, they might be disappointed in her.

'It's a good afternoon for a stroll and I don't think we should waste it.' Adam drained his cup and purposefully scraped back his chair. Ben seemed unwilling to go away without a push.

He did take the hint then. Having said his goodbyes, Ben returned to his companion who looked pleased that he'd stopped ignoring her.

Lily preceded Adam out of the tearooms, wishing she had more time to spend with him. Once they were strolling along, she remembered she must tell him she was seeing Margie and Fanny before she went home.

'I must dash off actually, Lily. I have another appointment to get to.'

'So have I,' Lily informed him. 'I have some wonderful news. I'm meeting Margie Blake. Fanny Miller's seen her and she told me Margie has a roof over her head and is doing all right.' Lily knew that wasn't quite true; but she couldn't give Adam more to think about. He seemed to have enough on his plate already.

'I was worried about the girl. Give her my best regards, won't you?'

Lily nodded. 'I'll have more to tell you about Margie next time. We will meet up again, won't we? Say in a few weeks?' she suggested.

'Let's do that. Same place, same time.'

Impulsively Lily kissed his cheek. 'I'm so grateful to you for finding out about my mum. I'd sooner have known the truth, and I know it wasn't easy for you to tell it to me. Thank you.'

'You deserve the truth, Lily. You're a good girl. I hope you'll always be happy.' He turned and walked briskly away. After a few yards he glanced over his shoulder at her, feeling fondness wash over him as he watched her hurrying off with a spring in her step. He thanked his lucky stars he hadn't let on that Ben Stone had been the man who'd had more than a conversation with her mother. The fellow had put in an appearance at an excruciating time; it was impossible to predict how Lily would have reacted to seeing him when so emotional. Yet in a way, Adam was glad Stone had turned up; the man's reactions had proven he hadn't a clue he'd fathered Lily Larkin's half-sister. There'd been no awkwardness when he was with Lily, just admiration. The man couldn't be that good an actor.

For some reason Harriet had never told her boyfriend she knew he'd had intimate relations with an inmate. Perhaps that might soon change; Ben had looked very cosy with the young lady just now. If he'd dumped Harriet – and who could blame him? – she'd have no reason to protect him and possibly every reason to punish him.

Chapter Nineteen

'We can't go into a pub, Fanny!' Lily protested. She'd thought at first the older woman was joking when she'd suggested it. But she was completely serious. 'I'm sixteen and Margie's still fifteen ... we'll get chucked out.'

Fanny waved that aside. 'You two weren't old enough to be filling washing coppers for all the hours God sends at eleven years old, but you did it. Anyhow, I'm nineteen and I know the landlord. He'll turn a blind eye if we sit up in the corner. Might even let us have one on the house for old times' sake.' She winked, beckoning the younger girls to follow as she jauntily headed towards the Bow Bells.

Lily exchanged a dubious glance with Margie, who was twitching her old skirt in disgust. She had tried to keep herself shielded between her two companions in the hope of passing unnoticed in the street, decked in the detested uniform.

'I ain't going in there like this and getting laughed at, Fanny.' Margie dug her heels in, shrinking back against a wall and crossing her arms. 'And I'll be in trouble if an off-duty copper's in there and spots me.'

'Oh, sod it. Could've murdered a gin.' Fanny sulkily

trudged back towards them but soon cheered up. 'Little Ronny would've liked it too. Gin goes straight to me milk and knocks him sparko. He kept me up last night, teething. Me feller's bound to get narky about him crying before long. He has to be up early to start his shift.'

'Where is Ronny?' Lily asked, in the hope of diverting Fanny's attention from the pub. 'I would've liked to see him again. He's such a little dear.'

'Me neighbour said she'd have him for an hour, to give me a rest. Can't be gone ages; she won't offer again if she thinks I'm a liberty-taker.'

'I'd better not stay out long either,' Margie said drearily. 'I'm never sure if Gladys will let me back in when I go out. She's a moody so-and-so. Can't chance upsetting her, though, until I've somewhere else to live.'

'I'm up at the crack of dawn for work so need to turn in early.' Lily let them know she was also conscious of time passing now the weekend was drawing to a close. As was August. Tomorrow was the start of her last week employed at Wilding's. A pang of some emotion flipped her insides whenever she thought about it. Lily knew it wasn't just the idea of leaving Davy behind she found upsetting. 'Shall we sit in the park for a little while then?' she said, to stop herself dwelling on it. These were her new colleagues now and they had a lot to talk about.

'Yeah ... let's.' Margie smiled. 'Got so much to tell you, Lily.'

'Can't wait to hear it.' Lily gave Margie another squeeze, overjoyed to be reunited with her. She looked shabby but clean and well-fed. The moment Lily had spotted her friends waiting for her, she had dashed up to spin Margie about in a bear hug. A breathless Margie had declared she wasn't ever going back inside South Grove, no matter what. She'd sooner die, she'd said, prompting both her friends to tell her not to talk daft and to forget about the rotten place once and for all.

Lily linked arms with Margie, and Fanny took up position the other side of her, keeping her more or less inconspicuous as they strolled along.

'You look so smart now, Lil.' Margie cocked her head, admiring Lily's get-up. 'Can't hardly believe it's really you.'

'Well, it is. And we'll smarten you up too, and get you out of that bloody workhouse stuff. You can take it back and dump it on the master's desk. Then you won't owe that miser a penny and he'll have no right to hound you.'

'Ain't setting foot in there again, even to do that.' Margie shuddered.

'Well, I'll take it then. That place doesn't scare me,' Lily declared.

On reaching the park, they chose a bench set in a secluded spot beneath a tree, to settle Margie's nerves. The youngest girl was constantly on her guard, peering about for nosy parkers who might report her as a workhouse escapee. Although it wasn't quite the end of summer, some leaves had turned russet and fluttered to the seat. Lily brushed them off before perching on the wooden slats and her friends sat down beside her.

'Now tell me all about this Gladys you're working for.' Lily was agog. 'These letters you're writing sound a bit risky, you know.'

'They bloody well are,' Margie admitted, torn between laughing and groaning. 'Can't wait to start a regular job with you two. We getting a room between us?'

'I'm stopping where I am for now,' Fanny said quickly.

'Me friend's giving free house-room to me and Ronny. Some landlords won't take kids. 'Course if his wife decides to come back, it'll be a different matter.' She pulled a face.

'I'll get a place with you, Margie,' Lily said. 'I'll lose me lodging when I leave Wilding's, and anyway, I'd far sooner set up home with you.'

'Is your brother Davy sharing with us? Just the two of us might struggle paying the rent while we start this business up,' Margie sensibly pointed out.

'Davy's stopping with his pal Bobby; he's still got a job at Wilding's. S'long as he keeps his nose clean.' Lily added that last under her breath. She didn't feel up to elaborating on her brother's misbehaviour, although she'd already told Fanny the need for an abortionist had thankfully been a false alarm. She'd also brought Margie up to date with all of it, including how happy she'd felt to discover her brother had survived the Cuckoo School fire. Lily just hoped he'd survive the roasting from his boss after his mischief. She hadn't sympathised with Davy after hearing the guv'nor bellowing at him that he'd had his last warning. One more slip and that would be it as far as Davy Larkin's job and home went.

'Ain't gonna be easy for the three of us, making this little venture pay, you know.' Fanny's heavy sigh was accompanied by a sidelong look at Margie's deformed fingers.

Lily ignored the hint that her best friend would be a burden on them. As far as she was concerned, they either all pitched in together or didn't have a crack at it at all. That had been the deal with Fanny at the start and she wasn't going back on it now. 'So why's Gladys blackmailing people?' She was curious to hear more about this woman.

'Money . . . ' Fanny snorted.

'Big money at that,' Margie emphasised, her eyes round as saucers. 'She wants twenty guineas off one of the blokes, and you'll never guess who *that* is.'

'Who?' Lily and Fanny chorused.

'Clive Stratton, Esquire,' Margie whispered.

Lily's mouth dropped open. 'You're joking ... '

Margie shook her head. 'I didn't let on to Gladys that I knew him. He's one of the clients who likes young girls. *Too* young ... ' She gave a significant nod.

'She's blackmailing Clive Stratton?' Fanny sucked her teeth. 'Gladys wants to watch her step. Rich family like that won't take no nonsense off the likes of her.'

'Gladys never mentions blackmail. She calls 'em "reminder" letters,' Margie said, and started to mimic her employer's snide tone. 'Just want you to do me some reminder letters for a few nice gents, Margie. Let the randy sods know they shouldn't be fiddling with my little girls and getting them into trouble.'

'Does she get you doing anything else?' Lily knew writing letters wouldn't take all day. Gladys sounded the sort of woman who'd want her pound of flesh in return for giving Margie board and lodging. Lily hoped her friend wouldn't be persuaded to join Gladys's 'little girls'.

'She asked me to teach her the alphabet so in future she can write her own letters.' Margie giggled. 'That could take years. She's no scholar that one.'

'You take your time and make sure you keep a roof over your head,' Fanny said pragmatically.

'And make sure you don't let her push you into getting into the same trouble as her girls, if you get my drift,' Lily warned.

'She reckons I'm no use to her there ... with this ... '

Margie flicked her deformed hand. 'It'd put clients off. I hide meself in the attic when the girls are working.'

'Well, you won't need to hide soon when we get our own place.' Lily gave Margie a hug.

'Me days are numbered with Gladys anyhow,' Margie said. 'She's a funny woman, is Gladys Ratcliffe. She's free with the grub; don't think she wants to seem greedy and scoff the lot. She's a real glutton. When I asked if I could have one of her old dresses, though, she looked at me as though I'd begged for a gold ring.'

'Would've swamped you, anyway, she's so fat,' Fanny pointed out.

'Don't care. I'd put on a nun's habit . . . anything's better than this.' Margie dismally eyed her patched skirt.

'I'll get you something to wear. Promise.' Lily had already decided to sell her best clothes and her beautiful leather handbag. Today was her costume's last outing. She only made use of her finery at the weekend and could make do with Jane's faded cotton cast-off in future. She wouldn't need fancy clothes pushing a barrow; then, when things were on the up, she could buy something nice again to go out in. It wasn't just for Margie's sake she'd part with her pride-and-joy outfit; some capital would be needed to start off their business. Lily guessed she'd be the one to put the first money in the kitty. But she expected her partners to divvy up their fair share as soon as they were able.

'Have you asked Greg Wilding to lend us a barrow? A set of scales would come in handy too, and anything else you can lay your hands on in the warehouse.' Fanny got down to brass tacks.

'I haven't yet,' Lily owned up.

'He's yer cousin and he's looked after you. I reckon you could sweet-talk him into giving us all our equipment for the first month, being as you're family. It'd help us get a head start.'

'He's not a real cousin; he took a shine to Davy a while back and helped him find his feet. That's how I got to know him.' Lily thought she'd better get that explanation out of the way to stop Fanny playing on a nonexistent kinship. Lily was glad when the church bell chimed and diverted everybody's attention.

'Crikey! Six o'clock. I'd better shift meself or me neighbour'll have my hide.' Fanny stood up.

'Me too . . . I'd better get going,' Margie dolefully agreed.

'Shall we meet here next week to talk about starting up the following Monday then?' Lily received nods from her colleagues. 'I'll have quit Wilding's and should have a bit of cash to use as a float.'

As they walked back to the road, an animated business conversation started. The excitement of what they planned to do now took precedence over the joy of their reunion.

'I know where we need to go to stock up on everything,' Fanny said. 'The wholesaler will give us a good discount and let us fill our own containers with soap and soda for a bit extra off. I've already got some pails. Didn't let me thieving brother-in-law get his mitts on 'em. He would've taken everything that I'd laid out for, given half a chance.'

'I'll turn up with the cart; I'll get one from somewhere,' Lily promised. 'As soon as we've got enough profit to reinvest, we should buy some fish on a Friday. Bloater or shellfish . . . you can get a better deal on those than some of the other sorts. All the housewives want a bit of fish on a Friday. We could branch out into haddock and cod if things take off. The guv'nor taught me how to barter with the dealers at Billingsgate.' Lily sounded proud.

'Reckon we'll be as big as Wilding's one day, Lil?' Fanny asked, giggling at the unlikelihood.

'Be his biggest rivals, we will,' Lily answered drolly.

'He won't like that,' Margie chipped in with a grin.

'He's fair, so I don't think he'd begrudge us. Could take a while before we can test that theory, anyhow.'

'About five years,' Fanny spluttered. 'That's if we're lucky.'

'Half a crown says we'll do it in three,' Lily declared. 'Shake on it.' She held out her hands, one either side of her, for her friends to shake. After that they all burst out laughing. It was a wager every one of them knew would never need to be paid.

She and her team would never be a serious rival to Gregory Wilding or to any other established traders. It was as well they accepted that and could chuckle about it. Just making a living would do Lily for now, and she knew the other girls felt the same way.

One short business meeting was enough to make her doubt whether their partnership would last months, let alone years. It was utterly worth a go in Lily's opinion, even just to give Margie a start at proper employment. But she could read between the lines; Fanny intended to go her own way as soon as possible. Lily understood that a new mother needed to be selfish and put her child's welfare above that of her friends. In Fanny's position she would do the same, just as her own mother had done whatever she had to for her twins' sake.

Perhaps Fanny might settle down with her childhood sweetheart and set up a business with him. As for Margie . . . Lily realised that the best thing for her would be to meet a nice, caring fellow who accepted her, faults and all. Margie was a beautiful soul and deserved to be loved after suffering rejection for most of her young life.

Lily knew she couldn't provide for herself and her best friend. It would be a struggle keeping her own head above water. But she wasn't abandoning this plan for a group of ex-workhouse girls to strike out and have a good go at making their own luck. A surge of affection made her sigh. She put her arms round her friends' shoulders to give them both a cuddle as they walked along.

At the corner they stopped, each of them having different ways to go. Lily wanted to squeeze every last drop out of her reunion with Margie. 'I'll walk back with you to your digs, before I head home,' she offered.

Margie looked delighted to have her company. 'Not far . . . so won't hold you up for long,' she said. Once they'd had their hugs and said their farewells to Fanny, the two younger girls set off arm in arm, Margie keeping herself concealed between Lily and the hedges that edged the front gardens of the houses they passed.

'Fanny reckons I'm getting in the way already, before we've even started,' Margie said dolefully.

'No . . . she's just fretting over her bloke's wife coming back and upsetting the applecart for her. Fanny's always got her little 'un on her mind. Must be hard, trying to find a lodging when you've got a crying baby.' Excusing Fanny's barbed comment in that way didn't completely wash with Margie, who nevertheless gave her a smile to show she appreciated the attempt at reassurance.

'Here we are . . . told you it wasn't far.' Margie pointed at a large villa a few yards ahead. It stood on its own in the street behind some high, messy hedging.

Lily reckoned that it had been left untrimmed so the neighbours didn't see all the comings and goings. As they drew closer, they could hear voices drifting from somewhere behind the privets. Margie stopped at once and put a finger to her lips. She tugged Lily backwards towards a small gate that was practically concealed by foliage. Carefully she eased her body behind the overhanging branch to open it.

'Can get into the kitchen this way. Don't want anybody to see me,' she whispered in Lily's ear.

Lily was about to quickly say goodbye and take off, but the conversation grew louder, startling them. Lily was put in mind of another time when she'd overheard a posh-voiced man and a coarse-toned woman arguing. The noise had woken her up and made her late for her first day at work.

Margie had also recognised the fellow's cultured bark. 'Stratton,' she mouthed, her eyes widening in shock. 'Let's have a look ... ' She beckoned Lily to follow her up the path.

From their vantage point behind a screen of greenery, they could glimpse what was going on. A fat woman of about fifty with bleached ringlets had her arm about the shoulders of a girl with a protruding belly, keeping her face shyly turned aside. Lily guessed the older woman was Gladys. She appeared to be urging Clive Stratton inside the house, doubtless to keep this business away from the neighbours. He knocked aside her pudgy hand and stood his ground on the step. He held a piece of paper in his fist and suddenly ripped it in two then threw it in Gladys's face.

'Looks like I've got me job for a bit longer. I'll be writing

292

him another letter,' Margie squeaked from behind her hand, then her mouth dropped open to convey her disbelief. 'He don't mind showing himself up, does he?'

Lily's expression mirrored her friend's astonishment. But she reckoned Clive Stratton didn't believe he had shown himself up. He was so horribly arrogant that he probably believed he could act any way he liked and get away with it. It hadn't worried him to cause a scene at the workhouse and embarrass other folk. He'd nearly made Margie cry, then had instigated a fight. At the end of it all he'd walked off scot-free. But perhaps not this time ...

Lily nudged Margie, drawing her attention back to Stratton by jerking a nod. He had whipped out his wallet and drawn a banknote from it. With a careless flourish, he suddenly stuffed it down the girl's bodice then started to laugh. A moment later he turned on his heel and was soon lost from sight. But they could hear him whistling as he went off down the street.

Lily exchanged a look with Margie while they waited for the sound of a closing door to indicate the coast was clear.

'Glad none of 'em saw me. Better get inside,' Margie said.

Lily nodded agreement and, after giving her friend a quick hug and a kiss on the cheek, she slipped back on to the street and hurried off towards home, thinking about what she'd witnessed. She wondered if Jane knew how sordid her fancy man was. And if she did, why on earth did she give him the time of day, let alone share a bed with him? Perhaps it was simply because Stratton had money to throw around.

Just like that, he had found a ten-pound note to use as an insult. When three workhouse girls started their business next week, they'd think themselves lucky to share out a ten-shilling note in profit. But Lily didn't brood on it for long . . . the spring was soon back in her step. She'd long known that there was little justice in life. But she had good friends and family. She was lucky and blessed in her own way.

*

'What's going on, Jane?' Lily had got home to find suit-cases cramming the hallway. She squeezed past them to poke her head round her flatmate's door. Jane had another open trunk on her bed and was in the process of upending a drawer-full of lacy camisoles into it.

'I'm moving out, that's what's going on.' Jane's announce-ment was snappy but couldn't disguise the fact she was upset. She carried on hurling fistfuls of stockings and underclothes into the open case, then turned her attention to some bottles of perfume on the dressing table. Those went the same way. 'Got meself a better place and a better boyfriend,' she announced.

If she was going up in the world, she didn't look very happy about it in Lily's opinion. Lily stepped into the bed-room. She'd had no idea she'd be coming back to this when she'd set off earlier. Her flatmate had already gone out and Lily had assumed Jane was doing a dinnertime shift at her dad's pub. 'You've had a bust-up with Mr Wilding, that's obvious. But if it blows over, you'll be unpacking that lot.' Lily gave her an optimistic smile.

'Ain't waiting around to find out,' Jane said. 'I'm off and I ain't sorry it's finished. I've had enough of him cheating on me. So that's the end of it.' She pursed her lips. 'This other girl lives on her own like I used to. He can come and go as he pleases with that bitch.' She sent Lily an accusing look. 'Sally Diamond's welcome to him.'

'Now hang on a minute,' Lily said. She wasn't taking the blame for this. And Jane was a fine one to talk about being cheated on. 'Perhaps it's nothing to do with me being here. Perhaps he's had enough of *you* cheating on *him*.' She reckoned it was time for plain speaking.

Jane paused in the process of lobbing a tin of talcum powder to join the rest. She narrowed her eyes on Lily. 'You *have* been spying on me, haven't you, you little maggot?'

'No, I have not,' Lily hotly defended herself. 'I wouldn't have known anything about it if the two of you hadn't woken me up with your arguing. When I looked outside, I saw you kissing Clive Stratton. Then the other morning . . . well, I knew he was in your room with you.'

Jane closed her dropped jaw with a clack, guilt flushing her pretty face.

'Before you ask how I know him, I'll tell you. He visited the workhouse with his mother and sister, Phoebe, and I served them all tea.'

'So you know those stuck-up cows, do you?'

'I hardly know any of them, and I wouldn't want to either.' Lily wrinkled her nose.

'Ain't you got stuff to be getting on with?' Jane turned a shoulder on Lily at that slight to her new man.

Normally Lily would have gone away, but she realised she didn't need to now Jane was no longer ruling the roost. Besides, there was a new vulnerability in Jane, and Lily wanted to offer some sisterly support. At times her flatmate had been kind to her, donating bits of furniture and clothes to make her life more comfortable. 'This better boyfriend you say you've found *is* Clive Stratton, isn't it?' Lily asked gently.

Jane gave a nod, her expression still veering between defensiveness and belligerence. 'Have you told Greg about me and Clive?'

'He knew about you and Stratton before I did,' Lily countered quite truthfully. 'I reckon you knew they'd been fighting over you for a while, didn't you?' The dust-up at the Brabazon sale seemed a long time ago now. 'On the last day I was at the workhouse, Clive threw a punch at the guv'nor during a craft sale. All hell broke loose, with stuff flying everywhere and some of the old girls going into hysterics.'

Finally a smile brightened Jane's face; Lily realised her soon-to-be-gone flatmate liked the idea of men causing a commotion over her.

Jane resumed her packing and became quite chatty. 'I've known Clive a long time ... longer than I've known Greg. Clive's family moves in the same circle as my ex-fiancé's and they're just as toffee-nosed.' She pulled a comically haughty face. 'Even before I got jilted by Rupert, I knew Clive fancied me, though he couldn't have been more than sixteen then. I'd agree to marry Clive just to put some noses out of joint and put meself in clover.'

'Has he proposed?' Lily asked in surprise. A man who visited prostitutes didn't seem the settling-down sort to her.

'Never stops going on about it. P'raps I'll say yes, now he's done with university and I'm done with Gregory Wilding.'

'I see ... ' Lily knew she couldn't warn Jane that her future husband was a horrible pervert whose penchant for young prostitutes had made him a blackmail victim. If she did, she'd put Margie in jeopardy; her role in it all was sure to be uncovered. Besides, Jane might already know what sort of character her upper-crust boyfriend was and be turning a blind eye to 'put herself in clover'.

Jane started emptying the cupboard in the hallway of garments, folding them into the trunk. One dress she held up to examine, then discarded it, letting it fall to the floor.

'Don't you want that?' Lily pounced, shaking it out.

'Take it, if you want,' Jane said, without giving the bottle-green drill another glance. 'Clive's promised me new stuff.'

'Have you got an old pair of shoes you don't want as well?' Lily blurted, thinking of Margie. 'It's not for me,' she explained, seeing Jane's ironic gaze branding her a brazen cow. 'Me friend's just got out of the workhouse and urgently needs clothes to start work. She can't wear this smashing dress with a pair of old workhouse boots.'

Jane bent down and pulled a pair of scuffed lace-up shoes from under the bed. She handed them over.

'Thanks, Jane.' Lily gave her a spontaneous hug of gratitude, eagerly folding the dress and placing the shoes on top. She turned to leave the room then hesitated, telling Jane, 'I think you're too good for Stratton, but anyhow I hope you'll be happy wherever you end up.' Lily meant it. She'd tasted Jane's temper on the first day they'd met, when Jane had slapped her face. But the older woman could also be sweet when the mood took her.

'Islington,' Jane announced. 'That's where I'm ending up for now. Clive's got us a love nest. Soon as he turns twenty-one and can marry who he wants, I'll make sure I'm living it up in Mayfair as Mrs Stratton. Then I'll make sure me husband *is* good enough for me or I'll cut his balls off.' She gave a smile that showed her teeth but didn't light her eyes. 'See how Gregory Wilding likes finding out I'm a society wife.'

Lily realised that Jane wasn't fooled one bit by Stratton's character. She obviously thought it was worth marrying such a nasty piece of work to get where she wanted to be. Lily headed for her room and Jane followed her along the corridor.

'Suppose you're pleased you've got this place to yourself, aren't you?' Jane planted a hand on the wall and glanced about at the home she was leaving.

'It'll only be for a week. I'm off too. I'm quitting Wilding's and setting up a little enterprise with the friend I just told you about and somebody else.' Lily thought it best not to name Fanny Miller and attract comments on her poor choice of business partner. 'We're selling door to door to start. Might get a pitch in the market if it goes well.' Lily hadn't mentioned to Jane she'd got sacked, and she saw no point in doing so at this late stage. Conversations between them had tended to be desultory and had mostly concerned Jane's news.

'Where's all this taking you to then?' Jane arched an eyebrow.

'Straight back to Whitechapel,' Lily said with a rueful expression.

Chapter Twenty

'I wanted to say a proper goodbye and thank you as it's my last day.'

Lily had loitered outside the warehouse until Greg came out and locked up. He had paid her wages as usual, but not wished her good luck, making her think he'd forgotten it was the end of the month. The bust-up was behind them, and they were getting along harmoniously enough that she thought he might spare a minute to wish her well.

He leaned back against the locked door with his hands in his pockets. 'You're quitting then?'

'You sacked me,' she begged to differ.

'And you believed I meant it?'

'Well, yes. Why wouldn't I?'

He shrugged. 'We always get over our differences; have done from the start when you chucked a bacon roll at me.' He chuckled under his breath.

Lily's recollection was that neither of them had thought it funny at the time. But it was a fond memory for her too, and her lips twitched.

He dislodged a half-smoked cigarette from behind his ear and relit it, exhaling smoke. 'I didn't intend you to leave. You're a good worker and keep things running smoothly for me when I'm not around. I'll pay you another five bob a week to stay on as me secretary.'

She stared at him in disbelief. She had desperately wanted to keep her job when he'd fired her, but had been unwilling to beg, accepting she'd got her just deserts. Now things were different: she'd made other plans and promises. 'It's too late. You should have told me you'd not meant it. Why didn't you say?' she demanded.

'Didn't think I needed to. You know me well enough by now.'

'You're always telling me I *don't* know you! And you're right!' Lily gestured her frustration. 'Me friends are relying on me to pitch in with them. We've sorted everything out and are starting our round on Monday.'

'Tell them things have taken a different turn. You can speak to them tomorrow. Come into work late on Monday if you like, since we've had a misunderstanding.'

'Just like that. You've had a change of heart and expect me to let them down.' She knew there'd not been a misunderstanding. When he'd said it, he'd meant it. But he'd expected her to back down and approach him, rather than the other way around.

'You'll let me down instead, will you?' He flicked the dog-end, walking away from her to grind a foot on it.

'Let you down?' She laughed. 'You don't need me. You were doing all right before Davy and me came along and you'll do all right after we've gone.' She paused to control her temper. She didn't want another row to ruin the memory of her final day at Wilding's. 'I'll miss you, guv'nor ... will always be grateful to you. But my friends are relying on me and I can't leave them in the lurch.'

'No point calling me guv'nor now, is there?'

'Sorry, Mr Wilding,' she said with a hint of familiar insolence.

'Reckon we're past you calling me that 'n' all.' He waited. 'Don't you know my name, Lily?'

''Course I do, Gregory.' She repaid his teasing. She was glad they'd cleared the air. He was right in saying the hostility that sometimes sprang up between them collapsed just as quickly. 'I'll pay rent until I move out. Me and Margie've found a place but we can't move in until the end of next week when the bloke's evicted.' She paused. 'Feel bad about taking somebody else's home.'

'He wouldn't care about taking yours. You'll never make a profit thinking like that.'

'Watch me,' she retorted.

'Oh, I will ... don't worry about that.' He gave her an indulgent smile. 'You can't change how things are; it's just how the world is.'

'World needs changing then,' Lily said sharply, though she knew he was only telling her for her own good. The lodging wasn't even worth fighting over; another square basement space, barely bigger than the coal bunker she now occupied alone. But she and Margie would have to manage, as it was the cheapest they could find. She hoped they could afford a shilling a week rent, or they'd end up back on the street like their predecessor. 'See you then ... be back at the weekend to pay something off me tally.' She extended her hand. He briefly shook her fingers, firmly, not in a patronising way.

'Forget about your tally and the rent. No need to come back. Call it a leaving present.'

'Is that your way of telling me to stay away?' She only

had a view of his profile, so shifted position to face him again. She studied each of his features in turn to impress them on her mind and subdue a sense of anxiety.

'You're partners with Fanny Miller, are you?' He asked a question of his own rather than answering hers.

She nodded. 'And my best friend Margie Blake. We're starting off selling soap and soda and that sort of stuff, door to door. We're going to branch out into other lines when we've enough capital.' She wanted him to know her plans and was hungry for any money-saving tips he had for her.

'It'll be hard work making a living if you're splitting profit three ways. Hope you're prepared to squabble and lose friends.'

'We'll stay friends,' Lily avowed. 'We want the best for each other as well as for ourselves. We'll make it pay ... we've got to.' She glanced away. She'd wanted other advice, not for him to bluntly bring her attention to hazards lying in wait to trip them up. They were real dangers too.

'You know what people will think about you, don't you, if you're seen keeping company with a brass?'

Indignation and embarrassment caused the colour to rise in her cheeks. 'Yeah ... they'll think we're a bunch of women who've got to try and earn ourselves a living together. If they're decent folk. If they're not, you're welcome to keep them as your customers.'

'That's not the attitude, is it?' He shook his head, mocking her now. 'What've I taught you, Lily Larkin? Nothing, it seems. You take anybody's money, fast as you can, and give 'em a beautiful smile while you're doing it.' He stroked a finger down her cheek.

302

'Yeah ... and keep me thumb on the scales when I'm weighing stuff.' She winked saucily. 'That's why me friends need me, you see, guv'nor: to pass on the pearls of wisdom from the master of the market.' On impulse she darted forward to brush her lips against his lean cheek before skittering back. She'd felt his hands jump to trap her and knew it was time to go. 'I'd stay with you if me friends didn't need me. Thanks for everything ... bye then ...'

She walked to the gate with the weight of his eyes on her. She'd taken for granted that he'd always be there, a mainstay; somebody to guide and protect her when times got tough. The idea of them losing touch made her insides lurch again with that horrible panicky feeling.

'I need you, Lily. Stay with me.'

He said it quietly but she heard it ... she'd been expecting it. She glanced back at him, well aware he wasn't just asking her to keep his books straight. Perhaps she'd known for a long while that Davy had been right when he'd told her the guv'nor fancied her. Perhaps she'd battled with Gregory Wilding and had let him know she had feelings for Adam to keep him at arm's length. She still did have fondness for Adam. But Gregory Wilding affected her differently: exciting and alarming her at the same time. She knew the bittersweet heat was to do with fancying him, whereas with Adam the warmth was nicer ... comfortable and mellow. She wasn't ready for the sort of relationship that required johnnies to keep a girl out of trouble. How could she be, when she wasn't sure what it entailed? Until she did, she wasn't taking Jane's place in the big bedroom, or risking having to pack up and leave as Jane had, pretending lying and cheating didn't matter.

'Can't ... not yet ...' she said, and walked out of the gate.

*

The money raised from selling her decent clothes had produced a small profit on what Lily had paid for them. She'd haggled with the totter who travelled the backstreets of Poplar with his horse and cart, clanging his bell. Finally, with much cursing, he'd agreed to give her the figure she'd wanted. Lily reckoned that first small business victory was a good omen for the future.

She was kneeling on her mattress, counting out the silver and copper from the sale. When added to her savings and her final wages, the grand total she had to her name was one pound seven and sixpence halfpenny.

She knew that hiring equipment on her first day would put a big hole in that, so she'd have to pay the dealer's premium for settlement on return, and hope he'd forgo a deposit. She calculated they might need at least a quarter of the kitty to buy stock on the first day. Then, if they took all of the first week's profit as wages and split it three ways ... they'd have to work dawn to dusk and sell a mountain of soap and soda to get a few bob each. She sighed in defeat. A moment later she'd bucked herself up. It wasn't as though any of them were unused to hard graft, and they were all aware of the pitfalls and had still decided to give it a go.

Having tipped the coins back into her savings tin, she stood up and wandered through the quiet flat, looking into the empty rooms. She wouldn't be sad to leave and start afresh. She and Jane hadn't been bosom pals, but Lily missed her now she'd gone. Jane hadn't been sure which day Clive would come to collect her; as the days had passed she'd increasingly seemed raring to go. During Lily's final week at Wilding's, her guv'nor hadn't mentioned a word to her about finishing with Jane, though he would have been aware Lily had seen her flatmate preparing to leave. Lily hadn't brought it up either, thinking it wasn't really her business.

The afternoon she'd got home and found Jane and her suitcases gone, Lily had felt oddly bereft. She'd wished she'd had a chance to say a proper goodbye. She'd spotted the old gossip who lived upstairs, pruning back the rose in the yard, and had hurried out of the kitchen door to ask her if she'd seen Jane set off. The elderly woman had crossed her arms while recounting that a posh fellow had pushed a handcart down the lane with all the luggage piled on top. 'Looked like Lord and Lady Muck, they did,' she'd snorted. 'Her in her glad rags and him togged out in his brogues and fancy titfer.'

Lily had picked up lots of Cockney rhyming slang from the lads, and knew that a titfer was slang for 'tit for tat', meaning hat. She'd chuckled too at the scene the old girl had painted. But later she had realised that it was possible Stratton did love Jane to lower himself for her. Perhaps Jane Wright would realise her ambition to knock him into shape and make him worthy of her to live it up in Mayfair, putting noses out of joint.

Lily had been gazing out of the kitchen window, lost in reflection, when she heard a bang on the door. She hoped it might be Davy, come to wish her all the best for next week. She'd not got much of a farewell from him, just a promise to come round and see her before he'd scooted off, mumbling about things to do. She pulled open the door to see Bobby grinning at her.

'Only come to say good luck and I brought you summat as well.'

Lily ushered him in, feeling mean to be disappointed to see him, not her brother. 'Want a cup of tea? Think I've got a drop of milk left to make a couple of cups.'

'That'll do nicely. I've got a thirst.' He followed her to the kitchen and propped himself against the wall.

'Gonna miss you, Lil. Wish you wasn't leaving.'

'Miss you too,' she said truthfully, putting the filled kettle on the stove. She set the cups while it boiled, asking him to fetch the chairs from the bedrooms so they could sit down.

'All right if I come and see you at your new place when you get settled? We could still have a trip to the Corner House or the flicks once in a while and catch up on old times.' Bobby set the chairs facing one another.

'I'd like that,' Lily said. 'Perhaps Davy might come along.' She raised a dubious eyebrow. Knowing her brother, it was unlikely, and his pal knew it too. She poured boiling water into the teapot, while keeping one eye on Bobby. 'What is it? What's he been up to now?' She had noticed the change in Bobby's expression when she'd mentioned her brother's name.

'He was gonna come and see you but he's got a black eye and didn't want to set you off worrying.'

'Guv'nor's whacked him again?' Lily felt more shocked than anxious. Surely Gregory hadn't taken it out on Davy because she'd turned him down?

Bobby shook his head. 'Guv'nor don't even know Davy's got a shiner 'cos it only happened last night. Old man

Keegan went for him. I warned Davy it'd happen if he didn't stay away from Angie.'

'I thought they'd broken up for good,' Lily cried.

'Perhaps they have, now her stepfather's proved his point.'

Lily poured tea, handing Bobby a cup. They sat down, sipping at the strong, scalding brew. There'd been just enough milk left in the bottle for a few drips each. Lily reckoned she'd spent more than enough time and energy worrying about Davy. There was nothing she could do for him when he persisted in bringing trouble on himself. She put him to the back of her mind and turned her thoughts to somebody else who'd been a colleague. 'Wonder how Fred's doing?' Fred had travelled to Dover at the beginning of the week to board a troop ship bound for Calais.

'He'll be in France by now,' Bobby said soberly. They didn't make jokes about Fred enlisting any more. It seemed unreal that he'd got away with it, being just seventeen. But he had, and so had other underage youths. Lily had heard people talking about boys rushing to take the king's shilling without due consideration. It didn't seem right to Lily that they were facing the same dangers as experienced men, some of whom were twice their age.

She'd stood in a bakery queue just the other day and overheard two women talking about a neighbour who'd lost her mind to grief after her eldest son was killed in action. French place names were no longer foreign; everybody was talking about Mons and Charleroi and the reports of Allied casualties that continued to appear in the papers.

'Knowing Jenkins he's already chatting up them mademoiselles.' The pensive atmosphere was broken by

Bobby's bright observation. 'Almost forgot; I brought you summat.' He put his cup down to pull his hanky from his pocket. 'Here ... for good luck, Lil.' He opened the linen to display a small silver horseshoe on his palm. 'Belonged to me granddad. He was a superstitious old sod. Had a rabbit's foot and a St Christopher and never would pass by a gypsy selling heather. He give me this horseshoe when he knew he was on his last legs. Said it wasn't doing him no favours any more, but it might bring me better days.'

Lily was touched by Bobby's sweet gesture. 'You should keep it yourself if it was a gift from your granddad.'

'Nah ... want you to have it. Don't believe in all that; anyway, I'm doing all right where I am. You'll need a bit of luck on your side though. Ain't easy what you're planning on doing.'

'I know ...' Lily gave a wry smile. 'Thanks.' She placed a kiss on her fingertips and patted his face, making him blush. She knew he still had a crush on her; she didn't want to tease him or jeopardise the friendship they had when she valued it so highly.

'Better get off now.' He drained his cup. 'Told Mum I'd call in on her on me way home after I'd parked up the cart.'

'The cart?'

'Guv'nor said you'd need a cart. Asked me to bring you one round.' Bobby frowned. 'Thought you knew. Anyway, I've parked it by the railings, but I'll take it into the yard and put it under cover. Some of the tykes round here'll nab anything given half a chance, the little bleeders.'

Lily smiled. 'I didn't know he'd do that ... I hoped he might. It's good of him.'

After Bobby had gone, she went out into the washhouse

where he'd stashed Gregory Wilding's gift. She stroked the splintery timbers as though they were silken.

It was an olive branch, and a link to him, while she made her own way and learned a bit about life without him. He'd given her a reason to keep in touch. He'd called her a nice polite kid; he knew that eventually she would go back to say thank you.

Chapter Twenty-One

'Oi . . . stay away from me 'usband or I'll have yer eyes out.'

'I ain't after your old man, Ma. But if you are, you'll find the miserable git down by the docks with his regular tart.'

The women surrounding the cart seemed to appreciate Fanny's novel sales patter. They started chortling, and continued to inspect the merchandise. The heckler went inside, slamming her door, letting her neighbours know she didn't appreciate them giving round one to the opposition. Lily wasn't amused either; the last thing she wanted was to alienate potential customers when they'd only been up and running just over a month. They'd made good sales in this lane so far, but that would change if they upset folk.

Occasionally, Fanny got recognised from her old profession and had insults slung at her. Lily knew it must be hard for her to cock a deaf 'un; Fanny was entitled to turn a new leaf and to give as good as she got if people dragged up her past to throw in her face.

They rarely sold out, and for each of them to take regular wages, they needed to. Even without hire charges to contend with, the fledgling business was constantly on a knife edge between profit and loss. If the cart hadn't come gratis, they would already have called it a day. Backstreet women were the toughest customers, and Lily understood why when they had to make every farthing count.

She sent Fanny a speaking look, begging her to tone it down, and received a careless shrug in return.

'Can do you a pail of soda for ninepence,' Lily told a housewife with a toddler clinging to her skirt and another in her arms. The girl settled on her hip had been playing with her mother's hair, and the strands yanked from the untidy bun on top of her head now draped her harassed face. 'I'll carry it to your door for you,' Lily offered. 'Can see you've got your hands full.'

'Ta, love. Throw in some of them soap chips, would you?' The woman plonked down her bucket for Lily to fill. 'Ain't got a shaving left to get me washing started early. Me husband likes his overalls clean 'n' dry by the evening.' She glanced up at the overcast sky. 'Bugger. Reckon it's coming on to rain soon.' She nudged Lily's arm. 'Could you do us a little bit more than that, love?' She gave Lily an appealing look.

Lily dredged up a smile and tipped a few more free soap chips on top of the soda. Every customer wanted extras thrown in when they made a purchase. Lily found it hard to refuse; she'd watched her mother trying to stretch sixpence into a shilling. But she was on the other side of the counter now, and every small generosity dispensed ate into her livelihood and that of Margie and Fanny. And that's why Fanny was looking daggers at her.

'That ain't Sunlight soap.' The troublemaker had crept back into the street to sidle up and sneer into brimming containers on the cart. 'That's cheap soap; it'll put holes in me sheets. I bought some of that last week and it ain't no use. Don't lather.'

'It *is* Sunlight!' Fanny planted her hands on her hips and jutted her chin. 'And I know 'cos I chipped it up meself off the big bars so you don't have to. Want any of it or not, Ma?'

'Ain't giving yer no more'n a tanner; it's imitation stuff. I know. I've been a laundress in me time.'

A neighbour grabbed a handful of flakes to sniff. 'Smells like Sunlight.'

'That's 'cos it is,' Fanny crowed. 'Tanner'll get you three washes' worth if you go easy with it. Take it or leave it, Ma.' She turned her attention to her son, grizzling in Margie's arms, stroking his small red cheeks covered in teething rash.

'I'll walk up the road with him again,' Margie said, and set off, rocking the child in her arms to try to settle him.

'How about you, missus?' Fanny was shaking a small tin as she approached another woman. 'This Windolene works a treat. Don't need no water with it. New thing now, cleaning winders without water.'

'How much?'

'Can do you a deal on it. This size'll cost you sixpence halfpenny in the hardware shop. 'My price: fivepence and I'll throw you in a duster.'

'Nah ... ' The woman shook her head. 'Vinegar water and me old man's newspaper's good enough fer me.'

Lily had put the bucket of soda on her customer's doorstep, then trotted back to the barrow to join forces with Fanny. 'This is the best furniture and floor polish you'll find.' Lily held out a tin of it to a housewife in a dirty apron. She had her sleeves rolled back and a pair of beefy tattooed forearms on display. 'Regina Cedar Wax. Doesn't 'arf smell nice too.' Lily prised off the lid and wafted the tin to and fro until a clean, pleasant scent mingled with the reek of overflowing gutters.

'She ain't got a stick o' furniture worth polishin',' one of her neighbours sniggered.

'Who you talkin' about, yer snide cow?' The tattooed woman turned on her. 'I ain't the one had the same old bits of net up in me windows fer years. Wouldn't hurt you to take 'em down and stick 'em in the copper, would it?'

As the sniping and shoving increased and some others took sides, Lily and Fanny exchanged a glance. They grabbed a cart handle each, knowing business here was done.

Fanny's nemesis kept pace with the vehicle as they started up the road. 'How much is yer washing line?' She picked up the wound ropes one after the other to inspect them and see if one was longer than the others.

Fanny grabbed the line out of her hand, throwing it into the cart. 'Piss off. Ain't dealing with you.'

'Ain't buying nuthin' off you lot. The boys should never have let the likes of strumpets take over their round and mix with decent women.' Her yelled abuse followed them up the road.

'What're you playing at?' Lily glared at Fanny as though she had gone bonkers. 'She would've bought a washing line.'

'Well she ain't having one,' Fanny said succinctly. 'I know what I'm doing.' She winked. 'Just you wait a few minutes and see what happens. Monday morning ... washday ... we'll be asking what we want for those ropes, and selling out.'

'Oh, Gregory Wilding,' Lily groaned with very little irony. 'Where are you when I need you?'

'We could all do with a bit of his magic touch,' Fanny agreed. 'And I ain't just talking market business, neither.' She gave a lascivious shimmy.

Margie had caught them up, Ronny dozing against her shoulder. She'd been using his little knitted toy to soothe him, and it had brought reminders of Clive Stratton and the Brabazon sale day when he'd bought the doll for her. Any memory of the workhouse made her nervous, so she tucked the grubby toy beneath Ronny's shawl, out of sight.

On turning the corner, a curious sight met the girls' eyes. Lily and Margie seemed taken aback. Fanny looked gleefully satisfied to see at least half a dozen women having an angry mothers' meeting on the pavement.

'Got any washing line?' one of them called out, on seeing the cart being trundled towards them. She marched over, swinging her arms in temper. 'Never guess ... some little bleeder has been in our back yards last night and cut every one of our washing lines into bits. Whoever he was, he needs more'n a clip round the ear. If I catch up with him, he won't sit down in a week!'

Fanny made a disgusted sound. 'Toe-rag deserves a strap across his back. What's the world coming to, eh? Need any pegs to go with yer line? Lucky we put a few extra on today. Send your neighbours over; first come first served.'

The woman hurried off, yelling to her friends.

'What the bloody hell have you done?' Lily hissed, wide-eyed and scandalised. It wasn't really funny, but she was having a job stopping herself laughing.

Lily and Margie had pushed the empty barrow round to collect Fanny to start work, as they did every morning other than Sunday. Their colleague had been ready and waiting, talking to a lad. Fanny had handed him some coppers before joining them and laying her son on the cart for a ride, saving her arms for the real work to come. Lily had assumed the coins had been payment for babysitting when Fanny explained the boy was her neighbour's eldest son. She had also said he was 'a big help'. Lily feared the nature of his help had just become clear to her. As had the reason for Fanny's insistence that they add washing lines and pegs to their range of stock, on loading up at the wholesaler's at first light. Lily repeated her question in a sharper tone. 'What on earth have you done, Fanny?'

'Drummed up a bit of business.' Fanny looked and sounded defiant. 'Either we pull a stroke now and then, or we throw in the towel. You two know it 'n' all. I said from the start there weren't enough in this lark to pay three wages when only two's workin'. And one of them's givin' stuff away free.'

Lily winced, knowing that the barb was directed at her, and she couldn't deny it.

'Gawd! You done what I think you've done?' Margie squeaked, ignoring the hint she was skiving. Her contribution amounted to little more than taking money and counting out change, or looking after Ronny. On the days that Fanny's neighbour did her shifts at the laundry, Fanny had no option but to bring along her baby and let Margie take charge of him. The younger girl was keen but lacked the dexterity to fill and carry buckets or prise lids off things. 'What if these people go to the coppers about vandals causing damage?' Margie pertinently pointed out. 'If Old Bill goes on the beat round here, I might get recognised.'

'Stop making a bleedin' fuss. You're in civvies now,'

315

Fanny said, narked. 'Nobody's gonna know you're a work-house runaway.'

'This might give it away.' Margie raised her deformed hand. 'The master would have provided a description. Until me uniform goes back to the workhouse, he can still accuse me of stealing it.'

'Soon as I've got a minute, I'll take it, promise.' Lily calmed things down. Margie's fear of being arrested and ending up back at South Grove was very real, and it wasn't fair of Fanny to trivialise it. Lily knew she should have already taken the rotten rags back, but she felt dog-tired from working long hours. Sundays were spent resting her weary limbs . . . and musing on how cushy she'd had it sitting at a desk, filling in ledgers for a living. 'Shhh . . . they're coming back.' She warned the others not to resume bickering.

The housewives started drifting over to buy their wash-ing lines, and in ten minutes Fanny was proved right: they sold every one and turned a decent profit. Most of the pegs went as well. But nobody wanted Windolene or Cedar Wax.

'Odd coincidence you lot turning up with all these lines the morning after we suddenly ain't got none.' A woman with a colourful scarf knotted over her wiry curls cocked her head at them.

Margie darted a wary look at Lily. Fanny adopted an expression of mystified innocence, as though she'd not got a clue what the customer was getting at.

'Bloody lucky for you lot we decided to extend our stock this week, that's all I can say.' There was nothing for it but to front it out, in Lily's opinion. But it would be wise to dis-cover if the scam might be traced back to them. 'Anybody catch a glimpse of the little blighter, did they?'

'Me neighbour heard a noise about midnight and looked out of her window. A big lad was climbing the fence. She reckoned he could've been about twelve, though she didn't see his face.' She raised a fist, shaking it. 'If he comes back, we'll be waiting for him next time. The sod.'

Lily coughed, hoping to disguise Margie's phew of relief. 'Any soda or soap needed?' Lily speedily changed the subject. 'What about step polish?'

'I'm out of soda. Just get me bucket,' a woman called out.

'Me 'n' all,' another voice joined in.

Half an hour later, having done some good business at last, the trio were seated on a low brick wall having their dinner break. Fanny had concealed herself behind some protruding bushes, away from the gaze of passers-by, to nurse her hungry son.

Lily was counting out their takings so far while eating a cheese sandwich. 'Doubt if we'll shift the polish round here. It's my fault saying we should try selling that, and the Windolene. People who want that sort of stuff have got decent furniture and don't need to buy off street barrows.' She spoke her thoughts aloud.

'I'm worn out already . . . and me belly's grumbling. Pass me a sandwich, Lil, would you?' Fanny started buttoning herself up.

Lily handed over a doorstep of bread and cheese.

'That old bag who was glaring at Fanny was giving me the evils as well,' Margie said. 'I reckon she's heard the coppers are after a disabled girl like me. She kept staring at me hand.'

'Chrissake's, everybody stares at your hand! Shut up about it, Marge!' Fanny exploded beneath her breath, startling her son into whimpering.

'I think we've stuck to just selling hardware for long enough.' Lily defused things by changing the subject. She knew they were all getting frustrated because of the constant struggle to make a go of this business, but it was a mean thing to have said. She made her feelings known by frowning at Fanny. 'How about we go to Billingsgate this Friday, and if it pays off, do a fish round once a week from now on.'

'Don't fancy handling stinky fish,' Fanny said pithily. 'Fruit and veg . . . I'll do that.'

'We'd need another round,' Lily warned. 'This one's already taken.'

While tramping the streets, they often passed two middle-aged men pushing barrows loaded with fruit and veg. The costers always glared threateningly, as though to warn them not to encroach. At Wilding's Lily had learned that poaching somebody else's patch could be a hanging offence. But she hadn't spotted anybody selling fish on their beat. It was autumn now and cooler. The race to sell fast before stock went off wasn't as vital as in the summer months. If they worked the day through, they'd have a good chance to shift all the fish, still fresh.

'I reckon trying something different is a good idea, Lil,' Margie said.

'Give it a go, I suppose.' Fanny sounded unenthusiastic. She was still smarting. She'd expected her colleagues to be grateful for the washing-line tactic instead of finding fault with it.

'Right! That's that then.' Lily folded the cloth her food had been wrapped in and stood up. She dejectedly eyed the cart's contents. There was a lot left. There was no prospect of an early day and, like Fanny, she already felt tired. Gregory Wilding would have known to take the Windolene and Cedar Wax on sale or return. It was too late now to renegotiate. The old miser at the wholesaler's would charge for restocking it. 'You two ready for the off? Those bigger houses down Burdett Road might have good furniture needs polishing.'

As they started off again, Lily and Fanny pushing the cart and Margie carrying the baby, Lily gave Fanny a wry sidelong look. 'The laundry pails *are* filled with Sunlight soap, aren't they, Fanny?' Lily had her suspicions; they took it in turn in the evenings to chip up the bars of Sunlight soap and fill the containers for sale. They also stocked a cheaper brand for floor cleaning. To give Fanny her due, she'd done a good job. The laundry pails *did* smell of Sunlight rather than cheap tallow.

'Half of it's Sunlight,' Fanny said, and started to laugh.

Chapter Twenty-Two

Following Lily's eye-opening first foray into Billingsgate, she'd accompanied her boss a few more times to the fish market and also to Spitalfields to buy fruit and vegetables. Her last trip to Billingsgate had been months ago, but she remembered which dealers he'd used and how to locate them in the maze of people and merchandise. The clamour was as deafening, the smell as pungent, as she remembered. But Fanny seemed to be taking it all in her stride.

'Which way we heading then?' Fanny asked, gesticulating rudely at a porter who'd barged her out of the way.

'Over here ... outside down by the water.' Lily guided her by the elbow. 'We'll buy some shellfish off Bet first, then see what money we've got left for mackerel and bloater. Her boat's moored in a place called Oyster Street. She'll usually give a good deal eventually, after she's finished moaning about it.'

Fanny looked impressed by Lily's knowledge and confidence in this new environment.

'Mind your step along here,' Lily cautioned, as they negotiated the obstacle course of lobster pots and sticky

320

tarred ropes that cluttered the jetties. 'My brother took a tumble and fell in once.'

Fanny took heed, lifting her skirts clear of her boots and proceeding daintily.

Lily was relieved to hear Bet's raucous cries drifting on the tangy air. It was gone five o'clock in the morning, and she'd feared the fisherwoman might have already sold out. Lily's intention had been to arrive as Billingsgate opened, but they'd been delayed. Ronny had been fractious, and his doting mum had refused to leave him until he'd settled down. Added to that, Fanny's neighbour had complained about being landed with the boy so early in the morning, even though Fanny insisted she'd told her about it.

To make up for lost time, the girls had raced through the dawn-streaked streets like kids, taking goes sitting on the cart for a breather. It was slow progress when it was Margie's turn to grip a handle, although her legs were as strong as theirs. In the end the two older girls had decided to allow the youngest to have more than her fair share of rides. By the time they'd arrived at the Monument, they were breathless and giggling, excited at trying something new. Apprehensive too; none of them had said as much, but they all knew that if this enterprise failed to bring good results, they would have no option but to disband. Fanny had already hinted at going back to her old job at the rag shop. Lily hoped she could return to Wilding's ... and in truth yearned to do so. She was worried about Margie's prospects, though, pinning her hopes on a recommendation from Adam being the key to finding her friend a position as a scribe. Margie had found employment before writing letters; she just needed it to be above-board next time.

While Lily and Fanny made a sortie into the market, Margie had remained outside, minding the cart in case it got pinched.

'Fanny Miller? Well I never. What're you doing here, gel?' A big bluff porter, empty baskets stacked on his head, had called out, stopping Fanny in her tracks.

'Sod it! Hoped that wouldn't happen,' Fanny whispered to Lily. 'I know him. Won't be a mo . . . just go and say hello for old times' sake.'

They'd been drawing attention as they moved amongst the throng. Unaccompanied women were a rare and unwanted sight here, as fishmongering was a trade dominated by men. Lily had hoped that would account for them being stared at. She couldn't kid herself any longer, though: some of the fellows had recognised Fanny, and it wasn't from her having sold them soap and soda.

After a few minutes Lily grew impatient waiting for her colleague to return. She started craning her neck this way and that to try to catch Fanny's eye and hurry her along, without success. Lily carried on alone towards Bet's mooring.

'Mornin' . . .'

Lily would never forget that drawled greeting. She'd heard it almost every day for many months, and hadn't realised until this moment just how dear to her his voice had become. She swung around, beaming. 'Guv'nor . . .' she gasped joyously. Then corrected herself on seeing his ironic look. 'Gregory. How have you been?'

'Better than you by the looks of it, Lily.' He'd watched her for a while before making his presence known. She'd lost weight and looked scruffy. The fullness had gone from her face as well as her figure, making her vivid eyes seem larger and bluer, and her cheekbones more prominent. Strands of her thick dark hair had escaped confinement and, though she was no less lovely, the bedraggled style made her look waiflike again. Perhaps, he mocked himself, she was missing him as much as he was her. She hadn't taken her gaze from him and hadn't faked her happiness at this chance meeting. He stuffed his hands into his pockets to prevent himself dragging her out of there and taking her somewhere to feed her up.

'I don't sit at a desk all day like I used to. We get lots of exercise ... walk for miles and miles some days.' She self-consciously excused her unattractive thinness. The bodice of Jane's old dress had barely buttoned up over her rounded bust by the time Lily had quit Wilding's. There was no fear of those buttons bursting open today. The belt was back round her waist as well, to pull in the loose material that was more faded and worn. 'You're usually gone from here by this hour.' She turned the focus on to him to divert his attention from her appearance. 'I didn't expect to see you.' She'd hoped to arrive as the market opened, knowing there'd be a chance of bumping into him if they were prompt. She'd thought she'd missed her opportunity, or she would've at least had a go at neatening her straggling hair.

'How's business going? Are you making it pay?' he asked bluntly.

'We're diversifying ... that's why I'm here. On Fridays, we're fishmongers.' She wasn't going to admit failure or answer questions he already knew the answers to.

'Diversifying, eh?' he said with a nod of approval. 'How is your friend the educated doctor?'

She knew he was mocking her for using big words, but

his mild teasing had brought a smile back to her face, and a fond memory of old times. 'I mean we're branching out, and Adam was fine last time we had tea together. Don't get so much time to socialise now I'm my own boss.' She'd seen Adam just once since the afternoon they'd spoken about her mother's death. He had seemed more distracted than ever, informing her he'd applied for another job. Lily had told him he deserved a position that allowed him more time to himself, winning herself a rare chuckle from him. Their outing had lasted barely an hour before he'd rushed off. Lily had also been glad to get home to concentrate on other matters. Preparations for the start of a new week took place on a Sunday. Fanny would come by the basement room, place Ronny on the bed to wriggle around with his dolly, and then the girls would get down to discussing how best to eke out their small profit. The older woman invariably wanted to take more in wages than her younger colleagues, who voted to invest. Another stumbling block was agreeing which new products to put on the barrow in the hope of improving sales. Lily had owned up to her mistake with upmarket brands last week; finding a way to put it right was again on her mind. 'Where do you live, Gregory?'

'I'll show you later if you like ... after work.'

'I wasn't being nosy ... I just wondered if you've got any nice furniture in need of a polish, or windows in need of a clean?'

'You're not charring as well, are you? Ah ... ' He'd cottoned on to her tactic and it amused him. 'Got stuff you can't shift, have you, Lily?'

'Windolene and Cedar Wax. Do you a good deal on it.' She started laughing as well.

'I'll think about it,' he said. 'We could meet for a bacon roll for breakfast one morning, and talk business.'

She nodded, though she knew she wouldn't be able to take time off to do that. But it was a lovely idea. 'I miss you, guv'nor . . . ' she suddenly blurted.

'I miss you, too.'

'How's life been treating you all at Wilding's?' She sounded brisk, stopping herself getting too emotional and pleading for her old job. Perhaps, in another week, it might be time to do that . . .

'Things have been changing. The hire takings are down. Billy Tate's joined the Navy; others might go the same way now that bachelors are being chivvied to do their duty. Posters are going up all over the place.'

Lily knew that was true; Fanny had got their round from two patriotic lads. When in the backstreets, Lily would overhear housewives gossiping about their own or neighbours' relatives having gone off to military training grounds.

'If business drops off any more, I might not need to take on staff to make up the numbers,' Greg said.

'*You're* not going to join up, are you?' she demanded anxiously. The idea that he might go away had dried her mouth.

He shook his head. 'I've still got a business to run.'

She gave a sigh of relief and he gave her a lengthy, penetrating look.

'You've spoken to your brother recently, haven't you?'

'He came over with Bobby a few weeks ago and we went to the flicks. Not caught up with him since, though.' Last Sunday she'd made an impromptu visit, hoping to see him, but had got no answer when she'd banged on the door. She hadn't been surprised to find nobody in; Davy and Bobby spent the majority of the weekend enjoying themselves if they'd cash in their pockets.

'You know Davy's signed up, don't you? He said he'd told you.'

Lily stared at him, then laughed rather shrilly. 'He's mucking you about, guv'nor. He can't; he's sixteen.'

'He's done it, Lily.' Greg sounded grave. 'I would've stopped him. But he didn't own up until after he'd done it. He swore he'd told you. Smudger backed him up on that.'

Lily couldn't find her voice for a moment. Then she burst out, 'Well, he'll have to undo it. The daft sod's made a mistake; I'll go and tell the recruiting officer he's sixteen, if he won't. What is *wrong* with him to keep doing stupid stuff all the time?'

Greg tugged her closer to him, rubbing his hands on her arms to calm her down. 'It'll be all right ... Lily ... hush, don't fret ... ' He tightened his grip on her as she started violently shaking her head, as though inwardly arguing with her brother.

'When you said about replacing staff, I thought you were talking about Fred Jenkins, not Davy.'

'Who's this?'

Greg let Lily go and turned to a young woman who'd pushed through the crowd to stand beside him with her hand on a jutting hip.

'Have you engaged a porter?' he asked her.

'Yeah, he's on his way to get our stuff. Now tell me who *she* is.' The newcomer had narrowed her eyes and pursed her mouth and was giving Lily a thorough looking over.

'Go and wait in the van.' Greg jerked his head at the exit.

Lily thought the blonde might refuse to leave, but she

stalked off. She was similar to Jane Wright in age and looks, but taller and less graceful. Her clothes were stylish but she didn't wear them with the same panache.

'When you quit I needed a clerk.' He pre-empted Lily's question.

'You gave her *my* job?'

'You turned it down, didn't you?' he said. 'I'm keeping proper records now. I don't have time to do all of it myself.'

The news that he'd replaced her came as another shock, before Lily had properly digested the first about Davy. The blonde was jealously watching them over her shoulder and something dawned on Lily. 'What's your clerk's name?'

'Sally Diamond.' He told her in a tone that let her know he knew why she'd asked.

So he'd employed his girlfriend ... Jane's rival. Lily stepped away from him. 'I'd better get on now, won't be anything left worth buying,' she said.

'She's not you, Lily. She's just a girl doing your job.'

'Yeah ... we're all just girls doing jobs for you, aren't we?' Lily slipped out of his reach seconds before he could fasten a hand on her and started weaving through the thinning crowds. It didn't take long to spot her colleague's unruly red locks.

Most traders were heading away from the market and setting out on their rounds, not buying the dregs of merchandise from yawning dealers who were already packing up their stalls. Lily felt like heading for the exit as well, but she didn't want to admit to her partners that this had all been a waste of time. She needed to buck herself up; put from her mind her brother and Gregory Wilding until she got home later. And perhaps, with any luck, she'd be too dog-tired to fret over either of them and would fall into a good deep sleep. She didn't want to dwell on why she was jealous of Sally Diamond for having her job, or why she didn't want the hard-faced blonde to have her boss either. She had turned both down. When Gregory Wilding had been with Jane, it hadn't bothered her so much . . . Jane had been on the scene first, after all. Lily felt guilty, too, for failing to thank him for the cart that was parked outside, waiting to be loaded with their purchases.

In hindsight Lily wished they'd just carried on with their usual round today. It was too late to buy the best fish . . . it was too late to stop Davy acting dangerously stupid . . . it was too late to have her boss and her job back. It was all too bloody late!

Fifteen minutes later, they were outside with a few boxes of mackerel and some pails of mixed shellfish.

Margie jumped off the cart when she saw her colleagues on their way with an elderly porter limping behind. He was balancing the trays of fish on his head while the girls lugged the buckets

'This it?' Margie eyed the sparse selection with un-concealed disappointment. She'd watched all the other fully loaded barrows and vans leaving the area, and had hoped her colleagues were getting some good bargains.

'We arrived too late,' Lily said. 'Most of the best stuff had gone. No point paying good money for poor quality.' Bet had told Lily straight she'd nothing much left. She'd done a deal on small oysters and thrown in some whelks and mussels to sweeten the deal. Lily could tell the woman felt sorry for her and thought her clueless for turning up as she was clearing away.

'Don't you go looking at me like that,' Fanny blasted as Margie turned an accusing look on her for causing the delay. 'I said from the off this was a bad idea. It's *all* been a bad idea. Wish I'd kept me job at the rag shop and me regular wage.'

'Let's talk about it later,' Lily said, hoping to calm things down. 'We've bought the bloody stuff now; let's try and sell it.' She gave the porter his coppers just as a younger fellow bowled up balancing some boxes of bloater and brill on his helmet.

'The gaffer told me to bring 'em to you,' he announced, dumping the boxes unceremoniously on their cart. 'He's gone now but said you'd know it was in exchange for the polish 'n' stuff.'

'You can take that away! Don't want his damn fish,' Lily said hotly.

'Thanks fer bringing it,' Fanny quickly interrupted. 'Don't hang about waiting for a tip, mate; ain't got a farthing for you,' she roughly told the hovering porter.

He turned on his heel, muttering something about women giving the place a bad name.

'You gone nuts, Lily Larkin, trying to turn down this little lot?' Fanny gave a gleeful hoot. 'Don't know how you pulled that off, but well done, gel.' Fanny rubbed her palms together. '*Now* we're in the fishmonger business. Come on, get a shift on you two. And *you* ain't sitting on the cart all the way back.' She pointed at Margie.

Chapter Twenty-Three

'Sorry to call early ... wanted to catch you in. Not sure if you remember me, I'm Gregory Wilding. We did meet once.'

'Oh, I know you, sir. You were at the Brabazon sale on the day Clive Stratton acted the fool.'

'Yeah ... that was it,' Greg agreed with a rueful smile. 'Seems a long time ago now.'

'Indeed it does. So what can I do for you, Mr Wilding?'

'We've a mutual acquaintance in Miss Larkin. I wanted to talk to you about her.'

'Lily? Shouldn't you speak to her direct? She said you would keep in touch after she left your firm—'

'Can I come in?' Greg cut him short. 'Won't take a minute.'

He was standing on Adam Reeve's doorstep, but had no intention of discussing Lily in the street. Reeve had always seemed a polite enough fellow, not too uppity to allow a lesser mortal over his threshold. But the doctor appeared nervous about inviting him in.

'Umm ... it's rather inconvenient. I'm off out shortly,' Adam said, sending a look over his shoulder towards the stairs.

'Won't take long. I've things to do as well. But this is important and I want to speak about it now.' Greg's tone had cooled.

'Just briefly then.' Adam reluctantly held open the door. His visitor had a persistence that was hard to evade.

'Can't offer you tea, sorry,' Adam rattled off as he indicated a chair in his small sitting room.

Greg moved a hand, rendering the apology and the seat unnecessary. He guessed the man was agitated because he wasn't alone, and that was why he'd peered anxiously up the stairs on passing them. Greg felt like reassuring him that the sight of a woman in a nightdress wasn't about to shock him. In fact, he'd be happy to know Reeve had a girlfriend. He wasn't a bad-looking bloke and it would be odd if he didn't attract female company.

'I'll get down to it then. Lily's struggling since she went street-selling. She's too good for it anyhow. She was an able clerk and kept everything straight for me. You'd know all this; you told me she was bright and hardworking. What I'm saying is I want you to find her an office job. It'll take her off the streets for the winter and give her a fair chance in life. She deserves it more than anybody I know.'

'I see ... well, of course, I'd always give her a reference and it sounds as though you'd happily do so too. Does she know you've come to see me about helping her find work?'

'No, and I don't want her to. She's proud ... stubborn ... likes to do things her own way.' He stopped smiling to himself when he caught Reeve looking at him with renewed interest. 'She's a kid who's too bloody stubborn for her own good. So ... can I leave it with you to sort her out something suitable?' Greg moved to the door. 'That's all it was. She trusts you and will listen to you. I just want to know you're looking out for her.' Greg took a business card from his pocket and handed it over. 'If you want to talk about this again, that's where you'll find me. I'll let you get on now.' He jerked open the door and came face to face with a young man of about his own age, fair-haired and sporting a colourful silk dressing gown.

The fellow sprang back and blanched before his face turned scarlet. 'Beg pardon . . . wondered where you'd got to with the tea,' he mumbled. 'Thought you were talking to yourself, Adam.'

The trio of men endured a silence for a moment. Then Greg asked mildly, 'Aren't you going to introduce us?'

'Yes . . . of course . . . ' Adam said in a suffocated voice. 'Ralph Villiers, this is Gregory Wilding.'

Greg held out his hand, poker-faced. 'Pleased to meet you. Well, I've got to be somewhere.' He turned to Adam before opening the street door. 'Don't forget about Lily's job, will you?'

Adam hurried down the hall after him as Ralph disappeared into the sitting room. 'He's a friend . . . '

'Glad to hear it,' Greg said. 'No really . . . I am. My only concern is Lily. And perhaps you should put her straight about things where your friend is concerned . . . kindly as you can. 'Cos that girl likes you.'

Adam looked puzzled for a moment before a glimmer of jealousy in the other man's eyes enlightened him. 'I . . . I've never encouraged her, I swear it,' he spluttered. 'I like the child very much but . . . '

'I know . . . but she's not a child, is she? She's sixteen now. She's naive but starting to find her feet in the world after being tormented in that fucking place. You know people . . . you can help her go in the right direction. And

I wouldn't want to have to come here again and remind you of it.'

Adam frowned. It was a subtler threat than those that Harriet Fox issued, but he recognised it all the same. 'I'm starting a new job soon . . . I'll do what I can about making enquiries for her, but there's not much time. I'm off at the end of next week.' When his secret was out, courtesy of Harriet's spite, a reference from him wouldn't be worth the paper it was written on.

'Off where?' Greg queried.

'I've joined the Royal Army Medical Corps, stationed in France. I'm sailing next Friday from Dover.'

*

'You're not telling me what to do any more, Lily. It's my life and I'm living it. I'm going overseas, and that's that.'

'Why?' Lily pleaded for an explanation from her brother but didn't get one; he tucked into his currant bun instead. She turned to Bobby. 'I thought we were friends. Wrong, though, wasn't I, about that? You lied to the guv'nor and told him I knew about Davy enlisting. Why did you do that?'

'Smudger did it 'cos I asked him to and he's me pal,' Davy butted in, then gobbled more bun and stared defiantly out of the window.

Lily had ambushed Davy and Bobby at the top of the road after they'd finished work. Her brother had agreed to go to the caff with her to avoid a scene in the street. Bobby had tagged along, offering to treat them to tea and buns, as he'd done all right on a dog at the greyhound track at the weekend.

'I would've told you, Lily, but perhaps your brother's got a point.' Bobby pushed his plate away, having finished his food in two wolfed-down mouthfuls. 'I think he's gone bonkers as well, but it's up to him what he does. Ain't as though you're his *big* sister, expected to mother him.' Bobby shoved his mousy fringe off his forehead. 'Mostly I kept me mouth shut 'cos I knew you'd be upset and it ain't fair him doing that to you all the time.' He blushed after his heartfelt speech and drained his teacup before standing up. 'I'm off home,' he mumbled, and sloped out of the caff.

'Smudger's still soft on you,' Davy said with a chuckle. He used the back of his hand to rub crumbs from his mouth. 'Look, Lil, I wouldn't have just gone off without coming to see you, you know.' He could see the tears in his sister's eyes spilling on to her lashes. 'I need to be the one in charge now. You've got to let me just get on with it. It's always been you telling me what to do. I know Mum and Dad favoured you and expected you to look out for me 'cos you was the brightest. "*Listen to yer sister . . . let Lily do it for you . . .* " That's all I ever heard off them. Dad told me once he wished his daughter had been his son. If he could see me now, he wouldn't be ashamed of me. I'm as good as any of those lads who was in the recruiting office. I got taken on, no problem.' He sat back proudly.

'I didn't know you were worried about that,' Lily said, wiping her dribbling eyes again.

'I thought they'd suss me out as only sixteen, being as I'm small . . . '

'No, I didn't mean that. I didn't know you resented me looking out for you.'

'Don't blame you,' he said earnestly. 'They kept on at

you to fuss round me 'cos they hoped some of you'd rub off on me.'

'Didn't know Dad had said that to you either.'

Davy shrugged. 'He was pissed at the time; doubt he'd have let out the truth if he'd been sober.'

'He didn't mean it, Davy.' Lily grasped both sets of his fingers, clinging to them as though she'd never let him go. 'When he'd been drinking, he wasn't himself. He talked rubbish. He was proud of you, so was Mum. And I'm proud of you for being brave and wanting to do your duty . . . but please don't go.'

'Can't back out. Don't work like that, Lil. All signed up now . . . done and dusted.' He chucked her under the chin. 'Look on the bright side: I'll get free grub and regular pay. Might even get a lie-in once in a while 'stead of getting up at the crack o' dawn.'

She sniffed back more tears and tried to laugh. 'Yeah . . . there's that to it, I suppose.'

He studied her pale, hollow-eyed face. 'You need to ask the guv'nor for your job back, Lily,' he said urgently. 'Bobby might not say anything 'cos he's still looking at you with moon eyes, but I'll tell you 'cos you need telling. You look a bleedin' state . . . like you've just come out of the workhouse again. And it's a crying shame when you was pretty as a picture not so long ago.'

'Thanks for the compliment,' she said with a punishing tap at his fingers. But she knew he was right; she felt a state too: hungry and exhausted most of the time. But she was content with it. She'd done what she'd wanted to do and stuck by the friends who'd seen her through her darkest days in the workhouse. That decision had left its mark on her, as it had on both of them. She wasn't alone in looking haggard from the effort of trying to carry on supporting one another as they had at South Grove. But it was out of her system now. Out of Fanny and Margie's as well, she reckoned. But Lily knew they'd always stay friends, no matter what else life threw at them. And they'd never forget.

Lily was relieved that they were closing up shop without rancour. The Friday fish sales had given them a temporary boost, but even if the persistent rain hadn't put a spoke in the works, slowing them down, they'd all come to the conclusion that they would need a barrow each and an extended round to make the business worthwhile. Fanny, as expected, had been the first to jump ship. She'd said she wasn't risking dragging her son round the streets in the winter months to catch his death. At the rag shop she could pick her hours to fit in with her neighbour childminding Ronny.

Fanny had said she wouldn't object if her two colleagues took the round over, but Lily hadn't wanted to do that permanently. As much as she loved Margie, she felt too physically weary to pull weight for the two of them. But they were carrying on just long enough to shift the remnants of stock before calling it a day.

Margie had approached her old boss and been told by Gladys she'd have her back temporarily to teach her to write her letters. Margie had seemed happy enough with that outcome for the time being.

'Are we friends again?' Davy asked his pensive sister. 'I want you to wish me luck in me new job as a rifleman, Lil.'

''Course I wish you luck! All the luck in the world! I'll write to you every week as soon as I have your address. And I want lots of letters back.' She sipped her tea to prevent herself again begging him not to go. Perhaps another woman might have better luck in that. 'What does Angie have to say about you going?'

'Proud as Punch, she is, that I'm doing it. She said she'll wait for me.' He grimaced. 'Not sure I want her to, though. Keegan's not the sort anyone'd choose as a father-in-law.' He changed the subject. 'What you said about Mum and our sister, Lil ... I've been thinking—'

'I found out a bit about it,' Lily interrupted. She wanted to put a lid on that subject now. It would be dangerous for Davy to fret over something like that when he needed to concentrate on keeping safe. 'Mum met a fellow ... a boyfriend, perhaps she would've called him, inside the workhouse. Don't know his name. It was Mum's secret, anyway, and she'd want it kept as such.' She used Davy's phrase next, 'All done and dusted there. Mum and our sister, God bless them, are at peace.' She'd given her brother a sanitised version. She couldn't tell him that their beloved mother had sold herself in exchange for a chance of a better life for her twins.

Davy looked shocked for a moment, then plonked his elbows on the table and cupped his face in his hands. 'Blow me down! Don't know how she managed that when the men were kept one side and the women the other.'

'I managed to come and see you.'

'You did 'n' all,' he said admiringly. 'No point dwelling on what happened to Mum; can't change things now.' He paused, fiddling with his teaspoon. 'Will you come to the cemetery with me before I leave? I want to lay some flowers, just in case I don't come back.'

'Don't say that!' Lily fiercely squeezed his fingers. 'We could go next Sunday. Me and Margie are finishing the round at the end of next week. You could collect the barrow from my place on that day and take it back to the guv'nor for me. It's been parked in the back yard overnight and the bloke upstairs moans about it blocking the privy.'

Davy crossed his arms, looking chuffed. 'Guv'nor's throwing me a leaving do at the warehouse. Few beers and so on. You will come, won't you, Lil?'

'Don't think so; rather we said our private goodbyes. Don't want to start blubbing in front of everyone.' It was a valid excuse, although she had other reasons for staying away: she didn't want to see Sally Diamond, in her smart clothes, sitting at her old desk. Lily didn't own a decent dress any more and she knew if she turned up in her work clothes the blonde would give her a scornful once over as she had at Billingsgate. Lily wiped the heel of a hand over her eyes. 'I'll come and wave you off at the railway station.'

'You better had! You're me sister. Got no other family but you to come and kiss me goodbye.' He bucked himself up. 'If I run into old Fred when I'm out there, I'll say hello from you, if you like.'

'Do that ... and remind him I know he cheated at that barrow race. When he comes back we'll have a rematch.'

'I won't be gone long. We'll all be home after Christmas when it's over and we've won the war. Guv'nor said we can both have our jobs back in the New Year.'

'Yeah ... not long and you'll be back home for good.' Lily wished she believed what she was saying. She knew Davy didn't believe it either. He was shipping out on the twenty-third of December. She had wanted this Yuletide to be memorable for them both; and it would be, but not in the way she'd hoped. It should have been a wonderful celebration of their first Christmas back together after all those long years apart. Instead it would be the start of another separation for the Larkin twins.

*

'Is it all right if I keep these clothes, Lily?' Margie smoothed her skirt. She had been thrilled when Lily gave her the bottle-green dress and the boots. Every night when she undressed, she brushed the twill carefully before neatly folding it. The leather boots were buffed up and placed side by side on the floor next to the mattress the girls shared.

''Course you can keep them. They're yours.' Lily gave her friend a hug. 'Dark green suits you, being so fair.'

Margie knew that her new clothes were superior to Lily's outfit, and it was good of her friend to let her hold on to the best set. 'Bet you miss having your lovely costume, don't you?'

Lily shrugged. 'Buy another one better than that sometime.'

The girls had been sorting out their few possessions in readiness to quit their room. The rent was due in a few days and they intended to be gone by then.

'What're you gonna do?' Margie asked anxiously. Of them all, Lily had been doing the best before they started this venture. Joining them and sinking her savings into the business had cost her dear.

'Fanny said I can go to the rag shop where she is if I want. They're always short-staffed and it'll give me a chance to earn wages while I sort something better out.'

'Rubbish job like ragging won't pay rent. It's all right for Fanny, living free with her bloke. Where're you stopping?'

'I'm going back to my old address.' Lily still had the key to the basement she'd shared with Jane. She'd gone there the other day to peer in the window and knock on the door. She'd got no reply, and everything had seemed as it had been when she'd left. She guessed it was vacant and Gregory was still paying rent on it in case he and Jane got back together. In Lily's opinion it seemed a waste to leave it unoccupied, and she might as well camp there while looking for somebody who needed a lodger. She knew if she asked he would let her stay there alone; she just wasn't sure that she wanted to ask when the relationship between them was volatile and Sally Diamond was in the background.

Lily glanced around the small brick-walled basement space. The first lodging she'd found for herself and shared with a flatmate of her choosing. It had been an adventure living here with her best friend, and she'd be sad to go.

Margie guessed Lily's thoughts. 'Been a good lark, hasn't it, living together – even if the place is a dump.'

Lily giggled. 'Yeah ... and it's a better dump than that bloody workhouse any day.'

Margie gave Lily a spontaneous hug. 'Love you, I do. Gonna miss you.'

Lily plonked a kiss on her fair hair. 'Yeah, and I love you, and will miss you; but onwards and upwards. Just the start of the next chapter for us. And you make sure you keep your job at Gladys's. We can still meet up, y'know, and go to the park or somewhere like that. Perhaps we might even come up with a better idea for a business. We've learned a lot and won't make the same mistakes again now we've got experience.' Lily let her friend go and picked up the string, winding it around her few underclothes and her nightdress, all bought while she had been at Wilding's. Last to be included in the bundle of possessions was the piece of blanket that would always travel with her as a reminder of her brave, beautiful mother.

Margie also tied up her things, then turned her attention to her old workhouse uniform. It had remained in the corner of the room from the moment they'd moved in. She stared at it as though it was a pile of festering ordure.

It was obvious why Margie had turned pale and fallen silent. Lily started neatly folding the uniform. She put the old cracked leather boots on top, then secured it all tightly with twine. When she'd finished, she threw the ball into the air and caught it one-handed. 'One of our better lines, these were.'

'Sold a lot of that twine,' Margie agreed. She turned an apprehensive gaze on her neatly packed uniform. 'Will you get rid of that for me, Lil?'

'I'll take it back to the workhouse,' Lily reassured her. 'I said I would, and I will.'

Chapter Twenty-Four

'I recognise you, miss, don't I?'

'I used to be an inmate. I've come to see the master, if that's all right.' Lily used a hand to shield her eyes from the glare of the flame. A naphtha flare had been lit by the workhouse gate. It wasn't much past four o'clock in the afternoon, but it was almost Christmas and the December days short and the atmosphere dank.

The elderly porter sucked his teeth. 'You've turned up on the wrong afternoon, miss. He's gone out, mistress too. They won't be back till after supper.' He could have added that when they did arrive, they'd both be sozzled, and argumentative. The Stones weren't folk made merry by drink.

Lily felt deflated. She didn't want this to be a squandered effort. It had taken nerve to come here. And some preparation. She'd made the best of her appearance, wanting the Stones to believe she was doing all right for herself, even if it was no longer true. She'd neatly styled her hair and given her old clothes a good clean and brush. Her shoes had received new laces and been given a hefty polish. She might no longer own a decent outfit, but she did have at her disposal the scraps of household paraphernalia to smarten herself up. Then, when she'd finished her business here, she had the most important appointment to keep: Davy was catching his train from Charing Cross later. Every time she thought about waving him off, her eyes stung and her heart thumped erratically, making her feel giddy. She was aching to tell him she'd be thinking of him on Christmas Day, and every other day that they were apart. And that she couldn't wait for him to come back on leave.

'There must be somebody in there who can write me a receipt for some stuff I'm returning.' Lily concentrated on the job at hand. 'I can't hang about waiting for them, I'm afraid.' She gave the porter a smile, shrugging her shoulder to indicate the bundle of clothing secured beneath it.

The old fellow took pity on her. He remembered her as an inmate and had always thought her a pretty kid. She'd grown up, and looked to be a backstreet girl just about holding her own on the outside. And God help her if she didn't. Once was more than enough in a place like this, in his opinion. 'The medical officer's inside. And the supervisors. They might be able to help you out.' He opened the gate, letting her through.

*

'Just wanted to wish you all the best for the future. I heard about you joining the military medics.'

Adam had been exiting the infirmary on his way back to his office when Ben Stone intercepted him to wish him well. Though Adam knew Stone had his faults, he rather liked the man. Besides, he was hardly in a position to stand in judgement on others when it came to resisting illicit carnal desire. He shook the hand extended to him. 'I'd be lying if I said I'm going to miss this place, or anybody in it. Oh, present company excepted, of course.'

'You've not given offence, actually,' Ben said. 'I'm leaving as well, and feel exactly the same way about South Grove as you do.'

'You're leaving the workhouse?' Adam was astonished. He'd thought this fellow was in line to take over.

'My fiancée is a registered nurse and I've signed up with the Voluntary Aid Detachment as an orderly. We'll be travelling to France together to do what we can to help the war effort.'

'Fiancée?' The surprises were coming thick and fast. Adam was sure he'd not meant Miss Fox. She would have been looking like the cat with the cream, sporting her ring. When Adam had seen her that morning, she'd been her usual sour-faced self.

'Penelope was with me when we met that day in the café. I would have introduced you, but I recall you and Miss Larkin were in a rush. It's been quite a whirlwind romance, and the engagement isn't yet official. But I'm glad my life is taking off in a different direction. I've hoped it would for a while.'

'I see ... well, congratulations. And the best of luck to both of you over there.' Adam shook hands again. 'How are your parents taking it?'

'Better than I expected. They're firmly entrenched here; my presence waiting in the wings was annoying them, I think.' Ben knew *he'd* not been annoying them as much as had Harriet. The prospect of her being matron had stuck in their craws. There wasn't much about his parents to admire but he liked their perspicacity. They'd seen through Harriet straight away, whereas he hadn't until he'd lost interest in sleeping with her. He felt ashamed that he'd allowed his life to be dominated by his parents and by a woman who'd had nothing to recommend her but her wantonness. He'd nobody to blame but himself for his weakness, and a tendency to take what was given to him on a plate. But he felt differently now he'd met Penelope: stronger, yet also as though a weight he'd not realised he'd been carrying was gone from his shoulders.

The men set off together towards the head of the stairs.

'Before we ship out, perhaps we could have a drink to toast better times ahead,' Ben suggested.

'I think I can find time for a swift half with you.' Adam smiled. 'Let's hope there *will* be better times and a speedy end to the conflict. This damned war has opened up new opportunities, but at what cost?'

He had something else on his mind: there were still problems to solve on home territory. He believed Ben Stone was basically decent, and could cope with knowing he'd nearly had a connection to the Larkins. Adam wasn't simply keen to unburden himself of keeping a secret. Lily was in need of assistance, according to Gregory Wilding. That forthright fellow expected him to provide it; yet Ben Stone was the one who owed the girl a duty of care. Stone had impregnated Maude Larkin; if he hadn't, the woman's health and fortunes might eventually have improved. She might have discharged herself from South Grove and been in a position to care for her children herself.

If Lily had developed an infatuation for him, Adam would sooner withdraw from her life than get further entangled in it. He was fond of the girl, but his heart and future lay elsewhere.

'Can you spare a moment to come to my office?' Adam said. 'There's something else I think we should talk about.'

*

The smell was the same ... sour and stomach turning. Lily walked the dimly lit, echoing corridor to the accompaniment of an inmate's howl. Her pace didn't falter; the sound was far away, or perhaps she'd simply muffled it, from habit.

She hoped Adam was in his office, rather than still in the infirmary. She'd timed her visit to coincide with the end of his rounds in the wards, hoping he'd be writing up his reports and they could talk for a few minutes. Life was changing for her again and she wanted to tell him about it, just as she wanted to hear his news about his new job.

She tapped on his door, then tried to enter, but the office was locked. Lily walked the short distance to the master's room, even though she knew he had gone out. She'd write her own receipt on a bit of official paper if it came to it, just so she could quickly leave. She'd seen William Stone's signature – Bertha Stone's too – plenty of times on dockets she'd filed and she knew she could make a fair copy of either. She didn't care if it was illegal. She was keeping her promise today and that was that; she'd been boastful declaring this place didn't terrify her as it did Margie. She gazed back along the shadowy, gas-lit corridor. She was never setting foot in here again.

She tried the handle and the door opened an inch. Her stomach had butterflies ... unpleasant ones that made her feel she wanted to be sick. She'd had this sensation every time on entering the master's office, knowing full well that a beating would be the result of her audience with the couple within. And Harriet Fox would smile.

She didn't this time. In fact, for a few seconds she didn't even realise she had company. She spun away from the open filing cabinet and gawped at Lily.

It was too late to back out of the room, though Lily would have chosen to stay outside had she known she'd be brought face to face with this old foe.

'What the hell are you doing, Larkin?' Harriet whispered. Her face was mottled, not just from alarm at having been caught rummaging in the drawer for incriminating documents. She'd been drinking, and a half-full tumbler of whisky, poured from the master's decanter, was on top of the cabinet. 'I said, what are you doing here?' She pulled herself round the desk and turned up the lamp.

'Might ask you the same thing,' Lily retorted. In poor light it had taken her a moment to digest the scene, but she knew now she'd disturbed Harriet Fox doing what she shouldn't. 'While the cat's away the mouse will play, eh?' She nodded at the glass of booze.

Harriet smiled nastily and deliberately picked up the drink, gulping at it to prove she wasn't bothered at being caught out. 'What've you got there, Larkin?'

'Margery Blake's old uniform. And I want a receipt for it. Going to write me one?' She certainly wasn't letting go of the rags without having something in exchange. This cow would deny she'd ever returned it just to get Margie into trouble.

'You might as well keep it, Larkin.' Harriet chortled. 'You'll need it soon enough when you beg to come back in. You won't give me lip then, I promise you that.' She sauntered unsteadily up to Lily, then circled her, looking

347

the girl up and down. 'You don't appear quite so chipper as when I last saw you cosying up to Reeve over a cup of tea.' She put her lips close to Lily's ear to whisper, 'Wasting your time there, dearie. He's a nancy boy. You're not his type.'

Lily jerked her head away from the sickly alcoholic smell of her breath, wondering what the drunken idiot was on about.

Harriet returned to the whisky and took another swallow. 'You're more that spiv's type. Thrown you out, has he, now he's had his fun? More fool you for trusting him. I knew he wasn't your cousin. He looked a filthy villain.' She upended the decanter again, thinking she would have liked a bit of that handsome rogue's rough treatment herself. She didn't just miss the status of being girlfriend to the master's son. She'd not had a man between her thighs in a long while.

'Don't you talk about Mr Wilding like that! You're not fit to polish his boots.' Lily's fists began clenching. She'd suffered at this officer's hands and felt tempted to throw the contents of that refilled glass in the woman's sneering face.

'Go on then ... dare you ...' Harriet taunted her. 'Not got the guts, have you, you little slut ... just like your mother.'

'Don't you dare say a bad word about my mum!' Lily shouted.

Harriet was boiling up as she looked Lily over. With her thin pale cheeks, dappled with angry colour, and her abundance of dark hair, she *was* just like her mother. The years seemed to have peeled away to bring her again face to face with Maude Larkin. Even when in the agonies of labour and calling for Ben Stone to come and take his daughter, the woman's eyes had kept a fiery, defiant brightness. It had dimmed eventually as the blood continued to leak from her, warming and giving life to the scrawny infant at the foot of the bed, and making the little bastard give a cry.

Lily could see Harriet was too drink-sodden to be of use to her. She turned away, intending to find Adam to write her receipt.

'Running away, Larkin, are you?' Harriet jeered. 'Don't you want to know about your sister? She didn't look like you; she was fair, like her father.'

Lily immediately swung back. Harriet was repulsive but could tell her things she desperately wanted to know. 'Tell me more about the day my sister was born.'

'Why should I?' Harriet slurred and turned back to the filing cabinet to pick through the papers.

'Tell *me* then. I want to know what happened to my child.' Ben Stone had burst into the room with Adam Reeve. Ben was ashen-faced from a mixture of shock and rage. In the space of a few minutes, his exuberance at the prospect of a rosy future had been shattered. He didn't blame Reeve for telling him, but it hadn't been his place to do so. His parents, Harriet Fox: they were the people who should have disclosed to him that he'd sired a child years ago. But they'd deliberately withheld the news.

For five years, the encounter with Maude Larkin had remained locked in a corner of his mind. He wasn't sure what had happened on that Christmas Eve to cause him to turn her to face him, or to kiss her. He'd needed some warmth as well as passion on that cold, lonely night when carols had been a distant accompaniment to their coupling. He'd told her his name and she'd said hers was

Maude. It hadn't been brutal. When it was over, she'd brushed her lips on his cheek – gratitude, he imagined, for unexpected kindness – then tidied herself and sped outside to gather her children into her arms. And he'd been forgotten again. He knew she'd been desperate, and any man would have served her purpose, but still he was sure that something finer than lust had fleetingly sweetened something sordid ... before reality set in and he opened the gates to let the family through. How he wished now that he'd never weakened and let her into the lodge; it had been no kindness. He should have sent them on their way. It would have been better for all concerned.

She'd told him she was already pregnant, and he'd believed her. He'd tried to see her again and get her privileges, but that hadn't worked and – once his parents had grasped the reason for his interest in her – he'd been sent away; a promotion to broaden his knowledge, he'd been told, when he'd ended up supervising a workhouse in Yorkshire. He'd been twenty-three and too callow to object. But he'd never forgotten about Maude Larkin; when he returned to South Grove and asked what had become of her, they'd told him the truth: she and the child she'd been carrying had perished in labour. He'd never suspected it could have been his child, though with more interest and better knowledge of such things he might have worked it out. He wanted to know how *they'd* worked it out ... or whether Maude had told them.

'Ah, the gang's all here. How nice and cosy.' Harriet revelled in seeing the anguish on the face of the man who'd rejected her. She hoped to twist the knife and wound him as deeply as he'd humiliated her. Yesterday he'd said he thought it his duty to tell her he was getting engaged and travelling overseas with his future wife. Now she felt it was her duty to tell him something. She tossed Maude Larkin's file across the desk. But the papers needed to prove his parents' corruption she kept hold of.

'There, read what happened to your workhouse doxy, if you like.' She grabbed the edge of the desk to steady herself as the drink started to take effect, making her sway. 'She wanted you to take care of your bastard, but your mother had other ideas.' Harriet tilted back her head and cackled. 'Now I wonder how your fancy fiancée would've liked the idea of putting up with a cuckoo in the nest? No better than I would, I reckon. She'll dump you, anyway, when I hand this lot to the Board of Guardians and your parents end up in court.' Harriet began to fan her flushed cheeks with the papers. 'Oh, gracious me! The shame of it!' she goaded.

'What d'you mean?' Lily found a small voice she barely recognised as her own. When Adam put a comforting arm about her shoulders, she shrugged him off and swung a glance between the room's other two occupants. 'My sister's dead . . . isn't she?'

Harriet put up her chin and stared triumphantly at Ben. 'It would've been better if the brat had perished, then I wouldn't have been landed with the task of getting rid of her.' She started to laugh.

Adam jerked himself out of his daze. Had he known Lily was here and about to get dragged into this, he would have kept his mouth shut and never opened this can of worms. The moment Ben Stone had heard Harriet's voice coming from the master's office, he'd charged out of the medical room to tackle her. A furore was likely to erupt when his parents returned. 'What in God's name *do* you mean?' Adam strode up to Harriet. 'Has the child *survived*? What have you done with her?'

'What they told me to. I took their son's by-blow away to be farmed out.' Even drunk Harriet was chary enough to keep to herself that she'd sold the child rather than found a foster mother. She'd no idea where the girl had ended up. She hadn't wanted her future husband to ever trace his bastard and bring it home, should he at some time discover what had gone on and decide to do so. His parents had shown no interest in their granddaughter's fate, just in knowing she'd been disposed of and their hands were clean.

'Where is she?' Lily gasped, rushing forward to confront the evil woman across the expanse of desk. 'What have you done with her? You'd better own up or I'll go to the master and make him tell me, then you'll really be in it.'

'You can ask all you like but he can't tell what he doesn't know ... never wanted to know. It was a sickly infant anyway, and probably didn't last the week out. I told them to leave her next to an open window and let the night air do its work. Then she could have really gone in the coffin with her mother.' Harriet gave a tipsy snigger.

Lily remained quite still and silent for a moment while it all sank in. Ben Stone had been her mother's secret man; her sister hadn't been buried, she'd been smuggled out of the workhouse and given away. Harriet Stone had wanted the baby dead and buried and had laughed as she said it. As the woman came round the desk to unstopper the decanter once more, Lily launched herself at Harriet, pummelling and kicking at her, while tears soaked her face and the hair that flew wildly about her face.

Ben tried to prise them apart and eventually succeeded,

only for Harriet to turn her fists on him. When he parried the blows, pushing her away, she grabbed the letter opener from the desk and lunged at Lily with it. Ben leapt between them to protect Lily, but wasn't quick enough in dodging aside. He yelped in pain. Forcefully he shoved Harriet backwards, then squeezed a hand over his forearm to staunch the bleeding.

It was some minutes later that Lily and the two gentlemen were calm enough to become aware of the remarkable quiet from the room's other occupant.

Lily broke free of Adam's comfort, and all three of them turned to stare at Harriet, sprawled on the floor with her skull on the stone hearth.

Adam sped to crouch down and take her pulse. He tried the other wrist then the point in her neck. He shot a frantic look at Ben. He put his ear to her chest, then tried her pulse points again with unsteady fingers.

Ben calmly walked forward and, taking his arm, hauled him up.

'You acted in self-defence; I saw it. It was an accident,' Adam said so hoarsely that the words were barely audible.

Lily had her face in her hands, too shocked to cry. She didn't give a thought to Harriet being hurt; her mind was filled with the image of a fair-haired baby. 'I have to tell Davy. Our sister didn't die, I have to tell him and together we'll search until we find her.' A memory jolted into her consciousness. 'Davy!' She twisted agitatedly on the spot. 'My brother's leaving to go to war. No!' she howled. 'What time is it?' She didn't wait for a reply, she bolted from the room and along the corridor, straight out of the door and past the porter who tried to say goodbye.

It wasn't until Lily had given the cab driver instructions

to take her to Charing Cross that she realised she'd dropped Margie's uniform during the fight with Harriet and had come away without obtaining the receipt she'd gone there for.

Chapter Twenty-Five

The constable tapped his teeth with his pencil. 'So this is how you found her, is it?' He eyed the corpse with a thoughtful grimace, then turned his attention to the two fellows.

Ben Stone nodded, then licked his lips before commencing his rehearsed speech. 'We knew my parents were out and the master's office should have been vacant. When we heard a noise coming from in here, we knew to investigate. At the time we were having a meeting in the medical room, just along the corridor.'

The constable inclined towards the body then reared back. 'Crikey Moses! You're right ... she reeks of booze. Little wonder she couldn't keep on her feet. Was Miss Fox known for drinking heavily?'

'Unfortunately, yes,' Ben said.

'Well, the silly lass has taken a tumble while under the influence and given herself a bad crack on the back of the head.' He used the end of his pencil to disturb her hair and find the source of the mess on the floor. Why would she be in here if the master was out?'

Adam picked up the depleted decanter, as though to indicate the answer to an unnecessary question.

'Dearie me; the demon drink's done its work well this evening. Not much to do other than leave you to clear up now.' The officer carefully wiped the end of his pencil on his handkerchief, then made a final scribble in his notebook before putting it away. He reckoned he'd be driven to the bottle as well if he worked in a gruesome place such as this. 'At least the lass has got all she needs close by.' A mordant smile undulated his moustache. 'You've got a mortuary, I take it? And there's the cemetery just over the road.'

'I'll do the death certificate and make arrangements with the undertaker.' Adam was praying the policeman had no more questions or tasteless jokes, and would just clear off and let them take a stiff drink each. Then they'd have to set about moving the body.

'Does she have family need informing?' The officer retrieved his notebook from a breast pocket.

'Her parents are both dead; she has an older brother and a sister ... both estranged. I don't think they've been in contact for years. I couldn't help you with an address.' Ben made a conscious effort to stop touching the throbbing wound in his arm. Adam had bandaged it earlier while they were waiting for this fellow to arrive. But he could feel it still bleeding.

'Right ... done here then, gentlemen.' The constable snapped shut his notebook with an air of finality.

When the porter had come puffing into the station and said an officer was required straight away at South Grove workhouse, following an accident, the rest of the boys had soon found something urgent to do, leaving him to draw the short straw. He couldn't wait to get outside into the December mist to get rid of the shivers. A nice mug of hot sweet tea was required after this.

Adam noticed the stain spreading on Ben's sleeve and widened his eyes on the darkening material, indicating he must conceal it. The injured man crossed his arms and shifted position, standing with his back to the constable. With his head bent and his shoulders hunched, he appeared lost in contemplation of a tragedy.

Though Ben had done nothing but defend himself against Harriet, they had decided the best thing would be to tell an economical version of the truth. If they recounted it all, enquiries and investigations would follow. It would delay them both in realising their plans, perhaps even blight their futures for good. Worse still had been the real concern of Lily being dragged into the mess. Young and hot-headed, she'd not the guile or experience to protect herself from a grilling and might admit to having instigated a fight.

If a miscarriage of justice occurred, Ben might face gaol or a noose. It had been Fox's intention to maliciously ruin both men's lives, and the idea that she might still achieve that ambition was intolerable to her victims. Neither of them had said so, but they knew Harriet Fox's death had left the world a better place.

Adam believed the master and mistress deserved their comeuppance. They'd sailed close to the wind and, when they found out about this, they would be fools to continue on the same larcenous path. All their son was guilty of was trying to protect Lily and himself from a she-devil disguised as a workhouse officer.

'I'll see you out, sir.' Adam quickly opened the office door and prayed the constable would take the hint. He did, eagerly.

A few minutes later, when Adam rushed back into the

office, Ben had poured himself a drink and was gripping the glass with quivering fingers.

'Do the staff know to avoid this area and to make sure the inmates do as well?' Adam asked. The moment Ben finished with the glass, he made use of it, draining the decanter of whisky.

'I've given the porter instructions to pass on. Colleagues will have plenty of questions.'

'Your parents will have to deal with those. It seems they're used to covering up things where you're concerned,' Adam said pithily, then knocked back his drink in a couple of swallows. 'I'll put a fresh bandage on that arm. It's soaked through. I can stitch it if you like.' He put down the empty glass and fussed at the limb, pulling up Ben's sleeve.

'Doesn't matter. It'll keep for later. More important to get this lot cleared up.' He thrust a hand through his hair, trying to avoid looking at Harriet or going near her. 'Thanks for your help in this.' He leaned back against the desk, taking a livening breath as though preparing himself for the task ahead.

'Harriet was the vilest person I knew,' Adam said. He had his own reasons for wanting all traces of the catastrophe wiped away. He knew that Fox had been on the point of exposing him as a homosexual. In fact, he couldn't be certain she hadn't already done so, or had letters ready to post to the newspapers or to the Board of Guardians. 'We should check her room for anything that might arouse suspicion. Was she given to writing stuff down that might prove useful to her?'

'She was too lazy for that. But it wouldn't hurt to make sure in a minute. I have a key to her apartment. I can't believe she knew about my daughter for five years.' Ben sorrowfully shook his head. 'I feel so ashamed ... '

'You mustn't. It wasn't your fault. You were defending Lily, I saw it all ... '

'No, I'm not ashamed of that,' Ben interrupted, glancing at Harriet. 'I should have done more ... would've done more to help Mrs Larkin and the child had I known the extent of my responsibility to them ... '

'We saw a policeman turning out of here ... what's happened?' William Stone had stridden into his office with Bertha wobbling close behind, making a valiant effort to keep up. 'What in God's name ... ' William tottered back against his desk to support himself on seeing Harriet's body and the pool of blood congealing on the hearth.

Bertha clapped her hands to her mouth and goggled at her son over the top of them. 'What's gone on? What are you all doing in here? What was *she* doing in here?' Bertha took a grimacing peek at the dead woman. Intuitively she knew there was bad trouble, and her quick wit had helped her guess what it was. Her eyes darted to the filing cabinet drawer that hadn't been properly closed.

'She was in here drinking. And gathering evidence of your corruption and my fornication. She intended to blackmail and destroy us.' Ben continued regarding his parents with despising eyes. 'Why didn't you tell me about my daughter?'

William and Bertha exchanged an aghast look.

'Harriet told you about *that*?' William finally managed to eject some spluttered words.

'And more besides.'

Bertha licked her lips. 'We couldn't be sure that Larkin woman wasn't lying, dear.' She approached her son, hand outstretched, but he evaded her as though her touch were poisonous. 'There was no proof the child was yours. She was delirious ... ' Bertha tried again to persuade her son that their actions had been taken in his best interest. 'The scandal ... accusations of rape and abuse of inmates ... we didn't want you to suffer.'

'I have fucking suffered!' Ben roared. He knew then quite clearly that he would have accepted the child as his ... Maude as his, too, had she survived. He would have removed the family ... made them his family. Not for love ... though perhaps in time it might have come. He would have done the right thing for the first time in his life.

'Just tell the boy the truth,' William interrupted wearily. 'The time for lies has passed.' He tried to meet his son's eyes but couldn't. When his wife remained silent, he said, 'The child has a birthmark on her ribs. A patch of freckled skin. We knew she was yours. And so did Mrs Larkin. She asked for you ... at the end. She wanted you to care for your offspring.' William shook his head. 'We did what we thought best, son, I swear that's true.'

A thin white line appeared around Ben's clamped lips. 'Well, now you have more than a child of mine to hide. That bitch stabbed me.' He unclamped his hand from the wound allowing blood to drip to the rug. 'And in defending myself, that happened.' He pointed to the lifeless figure. 'She was so drunk she lost her balance and cracked her head open. Now *that* is a secret to keep.' He turned and quit the office. Adam hesitated for a moment, wondering whether to speak to the master and mistress about moving Harriet's body. They'd gone into a huddle, so he left them to it and hurried after their son.

'Will you look for the child?' Adam asked as they marched along the corridor.

Ben shook his head. 'It's too late. She's settled somewhere, I hope. I'm settled too, with any luck. Why dig it all up?'

'Lily Larkin won't let the matter of her sister rest. Family means everything to her,' Adam warned.

Ben frowned. He'd forgotten there had been three of them in the room. 'Will you go after her and tell her to keep quiet? It'd be the wisest thing for her to do after setting about Harriet like that. Lily's always been close to you. You should tell her of the serious consequences of not guarding her tongue.'

'No, I won't go and see her; it's not something I feel I can do,' Adam said after a lengthy pause. 'But I know who can help her. He's the best one to care for her now. In time I think she'll realise that.'

'Can he be trusted with something like this?' Ben asked, frowning anxiously.

Adam considered that. 'I think I'd trust him with my life,' he said.

Chapter Twenty-Six

'How did you know I'd be here?'

'Just did. I had a clue,' he owned up. 'Smudger's mum has seen you walking up the lane a few times.'

'Something terrible's happened, guv'nor,' Lily whispered.

'Yeah, I know. Adam Reeve came to see me about an hour ago. He was in a bit of a state but I got the gist of it.'

'You know it was my fault then.'

'Wasn't your fault, Lily.'

'It was . . . I started it all off by hitting her. I couldn't stop meself 'cos she's a cruel, wicked woman.'

Lily hadn't lifted her cheek from her knees while talking. She'd heard someone come into the basement and, without taking her eyes off the black window, had sensed his presence.

She was sitting on her mattress, knees drawn up and hands clasped around them. A single candle stump was burning, tracing their two misshapen shadows on to the wall.

'I'll get the blame. I don't care. She said she wished my baby sister had died . . . she said she would've killed her by leaving her by an open window to freeze to death. She called my mum a slut ... ' Lily's voice tailed off into a suffocated sob. She looked up at last and asked the question she was dreading hearing the answer to. 'Miss Fox is dead, isn't she? I'm not sorry. I'm glad.'

Greg sat down beside her, his back against the sooty wall, and put both arms around her.

Lily immediately took his comfort, turning her face against his jacket. 'I missed Davy ... I was too late to tell him Mum's baby hadn't died after all.' She covered her face with her hands. 'When I got to Charing Cross, the guard said the train had gone. He said one of the lads in uniform had been walking up and down asking if anyone had seen his sister.' A sob burst from her throat and she burrowed her face deeper into his shoulder. 'Can't believe Davy's gone and I didn't kiss him goodbye. Can't believe any of it's really happened.'

He moved her tangled hair off her wet cheeks and soothed her with a gentle stroke. 'You'll get over this in time. I know it seems like the end of the world, but it isn't, Lily. Trust me ... it isn't ... '

'Miss Fox is dead, isn't she?'

'Yeah ... and it's her own fault. Adam told me she went for you, then tried to stab the master's son and he defended himself. There's no need to worry. The Old Bill think it's an open-and-shut case of her keeling over, pissed as a newt. Which is pretty much what happened as far as I can make out. She sank half a bottle of Scotch; the coppers know she wouldn't have been able to stand straight.'

Lily jerked up her head to blink at him in amazement. 'The police have been to the workhouse already?'

Greg nodded. 'Adam and Ben Stone have dealt with that end of it.' He planted a kiss on her tangled hair. 'So, all you need to do is think of a way to break the news about your sister to Davy. Be over the moon, won't he?'

Lily shook her head. 'He won't ... not when he knows we might never trace her. That horrible cow's the only one who knew where the baby ended up.' Lily groaned in despair. 'I was so close to my sister ... I could have snatched her away that night if I'd known.' She gazed at Greg through swimming eyes. 'I was right by her on the day she was born. It was the evening I climbed over the wall to see Davy. Miss Fox was out on the street too. I thought she was running away from the fire, but she must have been smuggling the baby away. Harriet was all hunched up in her cloak, as though she were hiding something under it.' Even *had* she known at the time what the officer was doing, Lily realised she couldn't have saved her sister from her certain fate. She had been too young and too powerless to rescue herself from the workhouse back then. 'I don't even know the baby's name. She won't be a Larkin if she's been adopted. All I know is she'd be four now and that she has fair hair.'

'Adam overheard the master saying she's got a patch of freckled skin on her chest, like her father.' Greg tilted up Lily's chin, encouraging her with a smile. 'Little girl with a birthmark like that ... an orphanage will have a record of it. Just need to find the right place that took her.'

'Thanks ... that *is* something to go on, at least.' Lily gripped his fingers, spontaneously kissed them in gratitude. 'I'll go and get Davy,' she burst out. 'He'll want to come back and help me search. I know he will.' She felt animated, ready to jump up, but Greg held her still.

'I'll help you search, Lily. Davy's got to wait for leave or his discharge. Could be he'll be back for good in a few months.' Greg knew that was unlikely. The battles were far from done and the casualties mounting.

Lily shook her head. 'I have to tell Davy *now*. If something happened to him, he'd never know the truth. There's three of us ... Maude Larkin's kids.' Her eyes gleamed with the wonder of it. 'Last year I thought it was just me left. Davy would never have gone if he'd known this. Why's fate so unkind?'

'Give Davy a little bit of time to settle in then write and break the news,' Greg suggested.

Again Lily shook her head. 'I wouldn't know how to write something like this in a letter. Anyway, it would come as a terrible shock. If he doesn't concentrate on what he's doing, he *will* end up catching a bullet.' She closed her eyes as dread curdled her belly. 'He shouldn't have gone. He's far too young. He's *got* to come home now.'

'He can't Lily, you know that. If he tries to come back without permission, he'll be in big trouble, sixteen or not.' Greg held her close to him until she stopped fidgeting and seemed ready to listen to reason. 'I'll help you find her. We can start going round the orphanages and what about the Dr Barnardo's home.'

'Adam might know where newborns end up if there's no room for them in the workhouse nursery. Fanny used to fret they'd run out of cradles and give her boy to a foster mother. I'll go and ask him tomorrow morning.'

'He's leaving tonight for Dover, and taking an earlier passage to France than he planned to. He's dead keen to get away. Can't say I blame him.' Greg paused. 'I know you'll miss him. He said to tell you he'll write.'

'Adam's gone as well?' Lily sounded forlorn. 'He said he had a new job, that's all I knew.'

'Probably didn't want to worry you.'

'I will miss him. Without him helping me and Margie in that hateful place ... ' Lily sighed and hung her head, thinking everybody she loved was leaving her.

'You over him now?' Greg asked.

Lily gave a nod. 'Miss Fox told me I wasn't his type, but I think I already knew he just liked me as a friend. She called him a nancy boy.' Lily frowned.

'Did she now ... ' he eventually said, when it became clear Lily expected him to enlighten her. 'Well ... there's worse things she could have come out with. Just means he prefers the company of men to women. He's got a bloke he lives with. I met him. Seems nice.' Greg found his cigarettes.

'Hope they're happy then.' Lily had considered his answer and got the bones of it. She didn't mind that she'd been infatuated with a man who'd no interest in her as a woman. She didn't even feel foolish; Adam Reeve was worthy of any person's adoration, man or woman. 'Love's love, I suppose,' she murmured. 'When you throw your heart up, you don't know where or when it'll land.'

Greg took a drag of his cigarette and exhaled smoke. 'Yeah ... it turns up just like that and kicks you in the teeth.'

'You talking about Jane?'

'Nope.'

'*Not* Sally Diamond.' Lily clucked her tongue in disgust.

'Nope.'

'If Adam's going to France, I'll go and join him. He's bound to want a clerk over there with all the patients' records needing to be kept up to date. While I'm there I'll find Davy, and tell him about our sister, face to face.'

'You're not going.'

'I am … if Adam will employ me. I'll write to him tomorrow.'

'You're not going, you're too young.'

'You can't stop me,' she challenged.

'You don't need to go. I will. I'll find Davy and I'll tell him about your sister, and together we'll do whatever we can to find her.'

'You don't need to humour me. I'm not hysterical.' She jerked herself into a different position, sitting back on her heels, facing him. 'I know you wouldn't go, you've got a business to run. You told me that.'

'Yeah … well, things happen and things change. You're up to running a costermonger business. Probably do as good a job of it as me, too, after a while. Smudger can help. You'll keep it ticking over till I get back, won't you?'

She gazed at him for a long time, searching his soul for deceit, but he didn't flinch.

'Why're you doing this for us?'

'I'm doing it for you, Lily, as you well know.' He took another drag on his cigarette. 'Why didn't you ask me where my heart had landed?'

He smiled as she dropped her eyes bashfully from his. He traced her cheek with a finger. 'It's all right, you don't have to say it back. I'll still go and find the sod.'

'I might want to say it back, Gregory,' she said softly. 'Just not sure yet.' She gazed at him.

He leaned forward and touched his lips to hers. 'Right, well, that might help you decide. Then, when you are ready, you let me know.'

She nodded and returned him a kiss, just as softly, feeling shy and excited and comfortable all rolled into one.

But there was something else, a tenderness ... the sort of ache she used to have for her mum and Davy, and even for her father when he looked so tired and so sad. 'Can I have a cigarette?'

'You want one?' He sounded genuinely, comically shocked.

'Why not? I'm sixteen and I feel more grown up. Might as well find out if I like them.'

'Might as well,' he echoed, and lit her one. 'What d'you reckon?' he asked solemnly after she'd choked and coughed a few times. 'Acquired taste?'

'Mmm ...'

'You hungry?'

She shook her head.

'You tired?'

She nodded. She felt drained ... but at peace. She gave up with the cigarette and handed the glowing stub to him. 'Had enough for now. Try again tomorrow.'

He stubbed out their cigarettes on the brick floor, then drew her down to lie beside him, turning her to face away so they fitted together like spoons. Then he pulled her moth-eaten old blanket up over them.

'You never told me who I remind you of, or what happened to you,' she said as she snuggled into him and put her hands over his on her belly.

'My cousin ... you remind me of her. And the scars on my back were got 'cos I never stopped running away from the industrial school to see her after I found out she was ill. And that's enough about it for now,' he finished huskily.

'I'm sorry ...' Lily whispered, tightening her hands on his in comfort.

'Let's go to sleep, Lily.'

She was quiet waiting for sleep to claim her, but her mind was busy. She'd met many people and much had happened since she'd walked out of South Grove in her workhouse uniform. She'd felt different emotions, some brutal and some exquisitely sweet. And the first time she'd felt that way had been when Gregory Wilding dropped a pound note on the master's desk and bought her back her dignity, and her freedom.

'You asleep?' she whispered after about five minutes, smiling into the darkness.

'Nope . . .'

'I am sure now . . . I know where my heart's landed . . . '

Epilogue

Christmas Eve 1914

By the time Lily reached the warehouse, she was breathless. She'd run all the way from home, with something to say to Gregory burning into her mind with such urgency that even the stitch in her side couldn't slow her down. Neither could the icy pavement covered with a smattering of settling snow. Christmas Eve had dawned and the misty atmosphere of yesterday had dispersed to leave air that was as sharp and bright as sparkling wine. She pushed open the door and sped inside, uncaring of finding a hostile Sally Diamond within.

He was on his own, stocktaking, pencil and notebook in hand, an image of him she'd seen before, on her first day as his clerk. He'd been inspecting the line of carts, noting their defects. She'd been feeling rotten because of her brother's behaviour. After years of separation, Davy had preferred to go off with his pals than spend time with her in a precious reunion. But Gregory Wilding, a man she barely knew, had been kind to her. In his gruff way he'd tried to make things better.

He turned fully towards her, frowning. 'What's up?'

The phrase was another reminder of that first day when she'd walked to freedom with him in her workhouse uniform, boots digging blisters into her heels. She'd chased after him, yanked on his arm, frightened of losing sight of him in the market crowds. Back then she'd liked him, not loved him. She loved him now, and again was frightened of him disappearing. 'Why d'you leave without saying goodbye? You should have woken me.'

He put the pencil behind an ear and the notebook in his pocket and came over to her. 'You were fast-o. Didn't want to disturb you.' His smile transformed into a throaty chuckle. 'Missing me that much, eh?' He rubbed his knuckles on her cheek. 'That's good.'

She hugged him fiercely. 'I thought you might have gone to the recruiting office.'

'No . . . not yet.'

'I don't want you to go,' Lily blurted. 'I was in shock yesterday, I know that now. I was talking rubbish about anybody going to France to find Davy.' She took a deep breath. 'I've calmed down. I was scared you might have already signed the papers. I'll wait till Davy comes home on leave, then tell him about our sister.' She cupped Gregory's face, kissed his cheek, sighing in relief. 'It'd be wonderful if we've found her by the time he gets home.'

'Come and sit down, Lily . . . I'll put the kettle on.' Greg could feel her trembling in his arms and urged her towards the chair.

Lily sank into it, as she had so many times before, swaying the seat on its pedestal. Her chair. Her desk. She ran possessive fingers over the battered old wood of its littered top, watching him and reflecting on things.

'Where's your secretary?'

'Right where she should be ... sitting at her desk.'

'You know what I mean,' Lily said darkly.

'Yeah I know what you mean. Sally found another job.'

Lily considered that, feeling glad the blonde had gone, yet hoping he'd not sacked her. She wouldn't wish that on anybody. A livelihood was precious, and Lily had discovered that a job at Wilding's was worth holding on to. 'Did you fire her?'

'It was her decision to go.' He handed Lily her tea.

Lily clasped her fingers around the hot mug, warming them. 'You told her about me?'

'Yeah ...' Greg sat down on an upturned crate and took a gulp of tea.

Lily imagined there had been no amicable parting between them, but didn't ask any more. He had never pried too deeply, even though he'd known about her infatuation for Adam Reeve. Other loves were in the past.

'You're feeling better this morning then?' Greg said, as though knowing to change the subject while she was feeling philosophical about his past girlfriends.

She nodded, though frowning. 'I wish I'd kept my mouth shut. You won't go, will you? Please promise you won't join up.'

He shoved a hand through his hair and sighed. 'You haven't pushed me into this, honest. I've been thinking about enlisting for a while. I have to do my duty, Lily. Same as every able-bodied man should. This war isn't going to go away, much as I wish it would.'

'You've got a business to run,' she shrilly reminded him.

'Yeah, and I've got a woman to love and a home to buy for us and, God willing, in time, some children to feed.'

He put down his tea and stood up, pulling her to her feet to face him. 'I want all those things . . . with you. But until we get this war won, none of us know what might happen or what we might have in the future. Nothing's certain, and I don't like that. I want to help put things right for this country and can't do that here, selling fruit and veg. If things go bad for us in this war, and bombs keep dropping, I might not have a warehouse or a business to run. While I'm away, I know you'll be keeping the home fires burning. I trust you and you have to trust me. You keep your end of the bargain and I'll keep mine. Then, with any luck, we'll have that house and those kids. Drive us round the bend, I expect, won't they?' He kissed her, rested his cheek against hers. 'Let me go . . . I won't if you say no . . . but . . . '

Lily wiped her teary eyes on the rough wool of his donkey jacket. She knew if she denied him, he'd lose his self-respect and then he'd resent her. There would be nothing left. 'Love you,' she said huskily.

'And I love you. Anyhow, waiting for that future will give me time to do me courting,' he said, smiling against her lips.

Lily thought about what had happened last night. When she'd told him she loved him, she'd received her first proper kiss, long and slow and burning with desire and tenderness. When finally it was over, he'd lifted her up and carried her into the big bedroom and they'd slept on a comfortable mattress with a fluffy eiderdown pulled up over them. But they'd not undressed, and she'd fallen asleep in his arms, her head on his chest.

Lily wanted more of that, more of him, and felt as though it might all be denied to her if he went away. Yet every word he'd said was true, and thousands of other women throughout the land had heard similar arguments from their sons and their husbands as they prepared to go to war. Men and women, all battling against fears of what the future would bring.

'I'll get undressed tonight at bedtime.' It was intuitive, spoken without a conscious decision to coax in an age-old way.

'No ... it's not how gentlemen do their courting,' he said softly. 'I'll take you out for a nice dinner. We could go to the flicks if you like. Then I'll take you home and give you a goodnight kiss.'

'I know there's more to it than that. Johnnies are involved,' she said waspishly.

'I know you know there's more to it than that. You're friends with Fanny Miller ... ' he observed ruefully.

'Yes, I am,' Lily pertly agreed. 'So don't treat me like a kid.'

'I'm not. But you're sixteen, Lily, and you've led the worst sort of sheltered life in that dump in Whitechapel. You're still young, and so far you've not seen much of what goes on in the world. You might change your mind about what you want.'

'You think I'll not want you 'cos I'm too daft to know about real love?' She sounded shocked and indignant.

'No ... I know you're not daft. I love you and know it's true.' He stared at her with solemn tenderness. 'But we need to wait for a while, until you know it's true for you.'

'It is.' She smiled. 'Did we start courting last night?'

'Yeah ... '

'I suppose I could put up with that a while longer ... ' she said flirtatiously.

'Me too ... ' He grabbed her and kissed her. 'Right, a courtship until I get demobbed is long enough. When I come back it'll be with a wedding ring.'

'Is that your idea of a proposal, Gregory Wilding?' She tutted and rolled her deep blue eyes. 'And you with all that experience with girls.'

'Yeah ... but you're the only one I ever loved or wanted to marry.'

'You're the only one I ever loved, though I'll always adore Adam. I used to dream we'd be married and he'd take me away from the workhouse. Then you came along and rescued me. This is a better dream.' She turned her back to him, pulled his arms about her middle, remembering how he'd held her last night. 'It's snowing outside.' She led him to the door and for a moment they gazed at the grimy Poplar street speckled with snow before stepping outside to feel the icy flakes stinging their faces. 'Let's make tomorrow wonderful; a Christmas to remember. Though I'll miss Davy. Hope he gets something nice to eat.'

'Might not get turkey but he'll have his rum ration to tuck into.' Greg chuckled. 'Later today we can go shopping for our first Christmas dinner. In the morning we'll cook a feast round at mine. If you're good, might even buy you a present.'

'Can't buy you one back; I've spent all my savings,' she sighed.

He lifted her up against him, spun them, laughing, round and round beneath falling snowflakes, in the place where she'd re-found happiness. 'When I come home on me first leave I'll want your answer about being my wife. If you say yes, it'll be the best present of all.' He let her feet touch the ground. 'Let's go inside before we freeze.'

Lily took his hand, walking daintily to watch her step. He went inside but she hung back for a moment more, staring into the quiet whiteness that had already started to veil their footprints. 'Haven't forgotten about you. I will find you, even if it's just to bring you flowers . . . ' she promised her sister.

Keep reading from an excerpt of the next book in the Workhouse to War series, *Stray Angel* . . .

STRAY ANGEL

Kay Brellend

Prologue

Late August 1910

'Is she as scrawny as a newborn should be? The major mustn't suspect a thing or I'll be out on my ear. I'm not stumping up cash for her if she won't pass muster.'

'She's very small and appears to be only hours old, m'm.' The elder of the two women had pulled back an edge of grubby wool to gaze at a tiny crinkled face still smeared with vernix. The infant was so pale and still that she could have been a corpse, but the baby pedlar who'd brought her into the house had assured them she wasn't. Vera Priest stroked a minuscule cold hand. She gave a satisfied nod as the scrap of humanity responded to her touch by curling some fragile fingers.

'I'd better have a look at my daughter then.' The younger woman had been carrying on this conversation while styling her long auburn hair at the mirror. She discarded the brush on the mantelpiece and came to inspect her purchase. Having gazed with faint distaste at the swaddled infant, she drew a finger through its downy hair, then wiped the digit on her skirt. 'Well she is fair like him, so that's something. She'll have to do. If you deliver a letter to his club, the major will be by tomorrow for a look at his daughter. He won't part with another penny until he's seen the evidence his bastard's arrived. It's not a boy, so he'll be disappointed. But there we are.' She shrugged her silk-clad shoulders.

Vera suspected the major would be disappointed thinking his by-blow had drawn breath, but she kept that to herself. The distinguished fellow had not been happy when his mistress had told him she was pregnant. She'd subsequently miscarried, but he'd never been advised of it. By then he'd found himself a new fancy piece. His cast-off had been determined to get what she saw as her due. A meal ticket for the foreseeable future was in the offing for as long as he believed he'd fathered a child with her.

He was an honourable man and shouldered his responsibilities, however unwelcome, so Major Beresford had assured his ex-paramour through gritted teeth. His hoity-toity wife might contest his good opinion of himself, though, should she discover a regular stop-off point on his way home from chairing the Board of Guardians meetings. He made out that he went to his club in St James's for a nightcap; Cheapside was where he actually headed, because that was where he housed his lady friends.

'Is Mrs Jolley still here?' A noise from beyond the door had drawn their attention from the motionless bundle.

'She is, m'm.' Vera knew why Jolley had reminded them of her presence by banging the hall chair against the wainscot. 'She insists on being paid before she leaves. I did ask her to meet me tomorrow, somewhere away from here, to quickly get rid of her. She wouldn't have it, though, and said she'd wait.'

'I'd rather get the dratted woman settled up now. Her sort can make a nuisance of themselves. I shan't give her an excuse to come back again.'

While her employer went into the hallway, Vera was left holding the baby. She tiptoed closer to the door to peep through an aperture and watch the transaction. Twelve pounds was counted out in one-pound notes and handed over. Then there was a brief conversation between the two. Vera was about to turn away when she heard Mrs Jolley mention the name of the child's mother. Vera pressed closer to the door, her jaw dropping and her eyes growing round as she listened. Mrs Larkin had been a respectable widow, fallen on hard times, who'd passed away in childbirth in the Whitechapel workhouse infirmary. Mrs Jolley had decided to stress her credentials and assure her customer she'd only sell a baby of good blood. Not that she needed to go to the trouble. Betsy Finch would've taken a piglet in a blanket if she knew she could pass it off as her lover's illegitimate offspring and maintain her nice lifestyle.

Mrs Jolley said her fulsome thanks and a goodbye. A moment later Betsy came back into the room. 'You will find a wet nurse for the creature, won't you, Vera?'

'I will, m'm,' Vera said, licking her parched lips. 'Did Mrs Jolley say the mother's name was Larkin?'

'I think that was the name she mentioned ... poor old stick pegged out having this one.' Betsy shuddered. 'Glad I didn't have to go through it. Buying a kid is so much easier.' She giggled, starting to brush her hair again, then pinning it up into an elegant bun. 'I'll be bloody glad when I can stop hiding away and go out again now the deed's done.'

'Did Mrs Jolley say if it was *Maude* Larkin in the workhouse?'

'Don't think I heard more than Larkin mentioned.' Betsy turned around, frowning. 'Why, you don't know the poor cow, do you?'

'Just a name from the past,' Vera said. 'It jogged my memory. All forgotten now.' In fact Vera had never met Maude, but a while ago she'd been acquainted with the woman's husband. She'd overheard Charles Larkin speak affectionately about his wife. Vera had felt sorry for Charlie when his world fell apart because he fell prey to a vixen, masquerading as a respectable lady. At least Betsy Finch was honest about who she was, even if she did intend pulling the wool over the major's eyes about this pathetic orphan.

'Well, what are we going to call this little perisher?' Betsy sighed, sending the baby an aggravated stare.

Vera uncovered the mite's face again, seeing that her eyes were open, staring at her. She searched the baby's features for a likeness and persuaded herself she'd found it. 'How about Charlotte?' Vera said. 'I think that name would suit.'

January 1915

'Fine sodding New Year this is going to be!'

'What is it, m'm?' Vera called out, having heard her increasingly foul-mouthed mistress ranting in the front parlour. Since she'd been abandoned by her high-born lover, Betsy had let her standards slip.

Not long ago the letterbox had chimed as the postman

used it. Usually Vera would collect the letters from the mat, but Charlotte had been coughing and she'd been rubbing the little girl's back. Vera took her hand to lead her down the stairs. 'Come and say good morning to your mama, my dear.'

They entered the parlour to find Betsy Finch with a piece of paper shaking in her rigid fingers. 'The bleeding bastard's only gawn and died on me!'

'Mind your tongue! I'll take Charlotte back to her room, then we can talk.' Vera had rebuked her employer before about the language she used in front of the child. At one time Betsy would've slapped her servant down. Now, she couldn't be bothered, having either been at the rum, or be feeling the effects of it. Her first boyfriend had been a sailor and she'd developed a taste for his tipple.

When Vera returned, having settled the little girl on her bed with some toys, she found Betsy sitting in an armchair with her elbows dug into her lap and her head in her hands.

Vera retrieved the paper that had been screwed up and hurled to the floor. She already had an idea of the bad news the letter might contain. Having flattened it enough to read it, she felt her heart sink on being proved right. The major had been killed in action in France. At Ypres. Vera was thankful that at least his commanding officer had responded to their enquiry. Perhaps he'd had other such letters from desperate females petitioning for news of their 'dear close acquaintance Major Beresford' as he'd not been in touch for a long while.

Her mistress could feel satisfied that the unpaid allowance, the long silence, hadn't been an intentional snub as she had suspected. Vera knew men better than the

younger woman did, though she'd only had a close relationship with her late husband. Betsy had never sought
intimacy with a fellow's mind ... just another part of his
anatomy and his wallet. Vera had tried to persuade her
mistress that the major was a creature of habit and something other than spite had caused his regular payments
to suddenly stop.

'Well, you know what this means, don't you?' Betsy
scrubbed her eyes with a hanky and pursed her lips.
'We're both out on our arses, and the kid too.'

Vera could get another live-in position as a general
domestic. But her mistress had only one quality, and it
wasn't as attractive as once it had been. When Vera had
started working for Betsy Finch five years ago, the girl had
been a vivacious good-looker of twenty-four. It had been
easy to see how she'd caught the major's eye. Now she
was embittered and appeared older than her years due to
heavy drinking and keeping bad company. Betsy had been
supplementing her allowance from the major by 'seeing
gentlemen', although to give her her due she hadn't started
doing that until he had put her off. When too pie-eyed to
know what she was doing she sometimes brought one of
the punters home with her. Thankfully it had been a rare
occurrence. But Betsy wasn't as discreet as she needed to
be – hence her suspecting the major had sussed her out
and cut off his funding.

Over the years he had turned up a handful of times to
see his 'daughter'. The first time had been just after the
child arrived, to satisfy himself there indeed was one.
His last visit had been several months ago, when he'd
appeared on the doorstep looking smart in his army
uniform. He'd patted Charlotte on the head, asked if

she could write her name and read some words – both of which she could, courtesy of Vera having spent time teaching the four year old her numbers and letters. Betsy had received scant attention during his brief stay, and she'd brooded on it afterwards. She'd not boasted since that she could lure him back if she really wanted to. He'd always turned up unannounced, convincing his ex-lover that it was a strategy to catch her out in wrongdoing so he could cut ties with her and remove the child to a foster mother.

'What will you do now, m'm?' Vera asked. Once Betsy had attracted high rollers; now it was spivs on the make. Two had attempted to take her 'under their wings'. She had resisted allowing a ponce to handle her earnings. In return she had received several right-handers. The last had left her with a faint scar across her top lip.

Despite her mistress's deplorable ways, Vera had some loyalty and affection for Betsy. Not as much as she had for Charlotte, though. To all intents and purposes, the child was Betsy's daughter, and Vera feared for the little girl's future now this had happened. Having received no reply to her question, she repeated it.

'Dunno ... thinking ... ' Betsy snapped.

'A proper job, perhaps in a dress shop might suit you, being as you're so stylish.' Vera tried flattery. 'You've some lovely outfits to wear to interviews.'

'Ain't considering *that* sort of job.' Betsy snorted. 'I'll barely make rent. I'll have to go and see Mikey.'

'Why? Do you want another punch in the face?' Vera asked dryly.

'Don't need no lectures off you.' Betsy pointed a finger. 'I can't pay you wages now the money's run out, so you might as well start packing. The bailiffs will be on their way soon enough. Rent's due again.'

Vera knew that was true; she'd fielded the tallyman when he'd turned up at the door last week. 'I'll pack Charlotte's things in with yours.' Vera turned to go but hesitated in leaving the room. She hated the idea of the child being stuck with a woman who showed her neither care nor attention. In four years, Betsy had barely acknowledged the small person she'd to thank for keeping a roof over her head. She'd only put some effort into the sham of being a mother when the major showed his face. Other than that, Betsy left her servant to attend to Charlotte's needs. Vera had never been able to persuade her mistress to read the little girl a story, or tuck her in at night.

'Once I find myself a position, I'll pay a visit and look after her as often as I can to give you a break.' Vera yearned to offer to keep Charlotte, but couldn't. A female domestic with a child in tow was unemployable.

'I won't need a break from her.' Betsy got up from her chair with an air of finality. 'She won't be coming with me. It's the kiss of death being saddled with a brat in my line of work. If you can't have her, she'll have to go back where she came from.' Betsy snatched the letter from Vera's hands with a curse and threw it on to the fire. 'That's the end of him, and it's the end of us, Vera. We've been a good team, but it's time to go our separate ways.' She went to the sideboard and emptied the depleted bottle of rum into a tumbler. 'I have got one last job for you, though. Pack up the kid's things then take her back to Mrs Jolley. She'll have to find someone else to take the girl. Somebody'll bite at a pretty little stray with fair hair.' Betsy dispatched the rum in two fast swallows, smacking her lips and slamming down the empty glass. 'Whatever you do, though, don't bring her back here, because I'll be gone.'

Chapter One

September 1915

'I can't talk business with a woman, ducks!' Rory Scully emphasised the idea was absurd by whacking his flat cap against his thigh and exploding in laughter. 'Especially not one as young as you. Where's your boss? I'll deal with Mr Wilding.'

Scully crossed his arms over his broad chest, eyeing the girl up and down. She looked about seventeen and had a tumble of chestnut-brown waves framing her lovely face, but his gaze soon shifted to her figure. She might be young but she was luscious, and he could understand what that randy hound saw in her. She was no shy pushover, though, and was regarding him now with a challenging glint in a pair of gloriously blue eyes.

'Is the gaffer due back soon?' Scully tucked his cap beneath an arm. He'd removed it on entering Wilding's costermonger premises. It was only a token civility; he'd nothing nice in mind.

'In about three weeks' time, with any luck. You'd better take a seat if you're intending to wait for him.'

Lily Larkin's tone was ironic, but she gave the fellow a smile. He wasn't the first man to swagger in to the warehouse and treat her as the hired help. Not so long ago she had been a costermonger's apprentice clerk, taking orders. But not now. Since the man she loved had gone to France to fight, she was running his market business with the help of her friends and colleagues.

Scully turning up and demanding to see Gregory had brought him to the forefront of her mind . . . not that Lily needed much of a reminder. He was constantly in her thoughts, despite the problems piling up. Scully wanted to see Gregory Wilding, did he? Well, not as much as she did!

'Where is the skiver then . . . off on his holidays?' Scully put on a good show of seeming surprised. 'Getting idle in his old age, is he?'

'What do you want, Mr Scully?' Something about him jarred on Lily; and it wasn't just his assumption that she was too young and dumb to discuss business with him. She sensed he wasn't all he was making out to be. Most people who knew Gregory Wilding were aware by now that he'd enlisted and gone overseas.

'I want to make your boss an offer he can't refuse.' Scully perched on the edge of Lily's desk, forcing her to sit back in the chair to keep at a decent distance. 'And I'd like to make you one at the same time, but reckon I might get my face slapped if I did.'

'You'll get more than that when the guv'nor gets back and finds out you've been trying it on with his gel.' Bobby Smith had just come into the warehouse, unseen.

Lily stood up, signalling that she was fine, but it didn't stop her workmate eyeing the visitor with hard suspicion. Bobby knew his sort: all big mouth and big ideas and not much to back it up. He looked the part of a successful coster, though: sturdy rig-out and healthy tan from having been outdoors in summer sun. He was mid-twenties, Bobby guessed, of medium height and muscular. His biceps bulged beneath his shirt, as he crossed his arms then cocked his head in a mocking sort of way. Bobby would have liked to bash the smirk off his chops.

'You've got a sidekick helping you, have you, love?' Scully's calculated condescension turned Bobby red.

'Smudger's my right-hand man.' Lily introduced Bobby Smith by the nickname everybody used. 'Now, we've got stocktaking to do, so if you've said all you want to . . .'

'Oh, I haven't even started, ducks.' Scully's tone had changed. He wasn't playing now. 'I'm looking to buy a premises to expand my market business.' He leisurely budged off the desk. 'At present I've got a nice concern going over the other side of the water, but I want to come this way and build my little empire.'

'This place isn't for sale.' Lily cut to the chase to get rid of him.

'Everything's for sale, love.' He gave her a lewd look. 'If the price is right. Your guv'nor understands that. When you're older and more clued up, you will too.' He nodded at the Primus stove on the shelf with some cups set neatly close by. 'Now, how about you make us a nice cup of tea and we can have a chat about things.'

Lily knew he was out to rile her, so she simply put her hands on her hips and gave him an old-fashioned look.

Scully chuckled at her defiance. Wilding certainly knew how to attract talent. His preference had been for blondes, so perhaps this one was just an employee. The chivalrous pal might be trying to protect her by calling her the boss's girl. Wilding was known for wiping up waifs and strays, and it'd paid off; the astute sod had prospered through it. Scully had heard he'd taken on a clerk and had assumed it to be another grateful youth who'd toe the line. Wilding must have lost his wits to volunteer, leaving ragamuffins running his depot ... or so Scully had thought, and he hadn't been alone. But now he'd met them he'd changed his tune. These two weren't timid little wretches. They were strong and confident.

'Person could die o' thirst in here,' Scully mournfully said. 'Come on, rattle them cups 'n' saucers and tell me yer name.'

Smudger took a threatening step forward, getting het up that the fellow wouldn't leave. Lily defused the situation, saying lightly, 'I'm Lily Larkin but, like I said, nothing here is for sale. I'm old enough to know that.' She extended a hand for Scully to shake. She might not like him, but it was in her nature to be polite, even to patronising Jack-the-lads. She jerked her fingers from his grip. 'Sorry, not making tea 'cos we're too busy to stop. I'll let Mr Wilding know you called when he's back on furlough.'

The planked door of the warehouse swung open and a fair-haired young woman walked in, swinging a shopping bag. 'Got the stuff for tea; they had a few custard creams left ... ' Margie Blake fell quiet on noticing the visitor.

'Good ... we'll have those when we get home,' Lily said smoothly before Scully again invited himself to join the party.

'Custard creams, eh? My favourite.' Scully insolently doffed his cap to her before flipping it on to his head. 'Blimey ... there's quite a contingent keeping Wilding's open for business then.' He looked Margie over, aware she had shoved a crippled hand out of sight behind her back when he paid attention to her. Apart from that blemish, she was another nice-looking lass.

'Unless I can sell you some fruit and veg or rent you a barrow, I'll say good day.' Lily wasn't giving him tea and biscuits, though she was gasping for a cuppa herself.

Scully sauntered to the door then turned about to assess the trio. Smudger looked the eldest, but Lily Larkin was the one with the savvy and would be the nut to crack. The fair-haired girl he dismissed as no trouble whatsoever. Scully gave the warehouse another glance. A place like this in a prime spot in Poplar was just what he wanted, and he wouldn't get a better chance of a crafty strike while Wilding was off the scene. He stopped his eyes roaming over the stacked equipment with an acquisitive glint. They were all watching him, but the smart girl got his foxy smile. The little cow was reading his thoughts about taking it all, lock, stock and barrel . . . including having her into the bargain. 'You remind me to your guv'nor, won't you, now? And let him know I'll be back for that chat.' He sniffed, rubbing a finger beneath his nose. ''Course . . . if he's unlucky and don't come back, then it'll be me 'n' you having that talk, Lily Larkin. You'll wish you'd offered me that cup o' tea then, love, eh?'

'Oh, he'll be back, and I'll tell him what you said, don't you worry about that,' Lily replied through gritted teeth, hating Scully for playing on her fears for Greg's safety. She wanted to slap him down for being too familiar and using her name, but bit her tongue. He was itching for her to backchat him. It would give him a reason to hang around, so she turned her back on him.

Bobby put a boot against the swinging door, slamming

it into the frame to let Scully know he was glad to be shot of him.

'He's full of himself. Didn't like him one little bit. Do you know Rory Scully, Smudger?'

'Never heard the name, but he does put me in mind of somebody; can't think who at the moment. Guv'nor probably knows him. Ain't many people in this game who've escaped his notice.'

'Said the wrong thing, did I?' Margie started unpacking the shopping bag with her left hand. Her right had deformed fingers that made her clumsy.

''Course not . . . ' Lily lit the Primus and put the kettle on. 'He was just having a nose around and thought he could wangle a cup of tea while he did so.'

Margie Blake was Lily's best friend . . . a friendship that had been forged when they'd both been inmates of South Grove workhouse in Whitechapel. Margie had started working at Wilding's a few months ago and kept the accounts books up to date. She could write nicely with her left hand and had received a good schooling in English and arithmetic, as had Lily.

Previously Lily had been the clerk, but now she and Smudger shared the management of the place. They were responsible for the buying of stock at Spitalfields and Billingsgate and operated a market stall, selling produce six days a week. The workforce at Wilding's had halved since the war started. To make up numbers, a neighbour's school-leaver son had been roped in to take out a barrow on street rounds. Joey Robley was a strapping lad for thirteen and had no trouble pushing a loaded barrow. But he was green when it came to dealing with shrewd housewives wanting something for nothing, or when fending off rivals poaching on his patch. Joey did his best, but the business could do with a mature recruit who'd take no nonsense. And Lily reckoned she knew just the person ... if Fanny Miller was willing to give street trading another go.

The previous year, Lily, Margie and Fanny had been partners in a small business selling household goods door to door. Though they'd enthusiastically thrown themselves into it, it had foundered due to their inexperience and lack of cash to invest. They were all older and wiser now, and Wilding's was showing a healthy profit, though not as much as when Gregory had been running the show. Lily didn't want to let him down and was determined to improve the takings.

'I parked our van up round the corner.' Bobby had gone to the door to watch their unwanted visitor departing on a horse and cart. 'You all right, Lil?' She was frowning and nibbling at her thumbnail. 'Ain't worried about that prat, are you?' He approached the desk and dropped some purchase invoices on to its top, then put a comforting arm about her shoulders. 'All gob that one. S'pose you could write and tell the guv'nor, though, just in case his leave gets cancelled like it did last time. Guv'nor'll let us know how he wants us to play it if Scully shows his face again.'

Bobby Smith had an unrequited yen for Lily. He'd liked her from the moment the guv'nor had turned up with his new clerk. Though looking thin and bedraggled and younger than her years in her workhouse uniform, Lily Larkin had soon shown she possessed the spirit of a lioness. In Bobby's eyes, her only fault was her tendency to mother her twin brother and tolerate his mistakes – and there had been many. But Davy Larkin was now a boy soldier on the Western Front and, though Bobby reckoned

Davy mad to have gone, he also privately thought the separation of brother and sister would do them both good.

'I'm not worried about Scully ... he's just blowing hot air.' Lily was still brooding over his spiteful remark. She prayed every night that her boyfriend and her brother were keeping safe. That was why she wouldn't write and distract Gregory with news of Scully's visit when he needed to concentrate on doing his job. Please God, he'd soon be home on leave and they could talk. 'Let's have that tea. Then Marge and me will have a tot-up of the takings when Joey gets back with the barrow. Hope he's sold out and not had any trouble today.'

Joey had come back a few weeks ago with a black eye, when the Burdett Road boys tried to muscle in on his round. Bobby had had to work the patch with him for a while to show the interlopers that Wilding's wasn't giving ground. Lily had run the market stall with just one-handed Margie's help, and they'd all pitched in doing the accounts in the evening. 'It's high time I caught up with Fanny Miller; she's just the person Joey needs to help him out. Wonder if she'll take the job?' Fanny wouldn't take any nonsense off lairy lads.

'She will if she's still stuck in that bloody rag shop; you know she hates it,' Margie piped up. 'I'll come on a visit to Fanny with you.' Margie upended the boiling kettle, pouring steaming water into the teapot. 'I'd love to see little Ronny again. Wonder how he is?'

'Not so little, I reckon.' Lily smiled, remembering Fanny's sturdy son. The boy had accompanied them on their street round when no childminder could be found to care for him during the day. Lily and Margie had become like surrogate mums to Ronny, taking turns to pacify him

396

or change his nappy if Fanny was busy with customers. 'I expect he's up on his feet and might even be talking by now. Can't wait to see him.'

They gathered round the desk and tucked into their tea and biscuits. Lily had almost forgotten about Scully as she dwelled on a much-anticipated chat with Fanny. But not quite . . . his leering face was still hovering at the back of her mind.

'How about we go this Sunday to see Fanny?' Margie suggested.

'Can't do it this weekend . . . already got something planned,' Lily said.

The other two looked expectantly at her.

'There's a place in Bloomsbury that I've not visited yet. It might have a record of my sister.' Lily sounded excited and showed them two sets of crossed fingers before sipping at her tea.

Bobby and Margie gave her sympathetic smiles, then turned their attention to the plate of biscuits, saying no more on the subject. At intervals they glanced at Lily, lost now in thoughts of family, not friends.

Both of these friends, in their hearts, believed that Lily should give up chasing a lost cause. Every time she came back from an orphanage none the wiser, she would be down in the dumps for days. But Bobby and Margie adored her too much to make her sad by telling her she was wasting her time and prolonging her own agony, looking for a child that had probably died long ago.

Chapter Two

Bloomsbury, London

'Your half-sister will be fortunate to have survived such early disadvantages, Miss Larkin.' The matron of the Foundling Hospital gazed at her visitor over her clasped, capable-looking hands.

'I imagine so ... but why did you mention it?' On the opposite side of the desk, Lily sat forward in her chair. The matron had sounded sympathetic, rather too sympathetic. 'Have you seen something worrying in that book? Has my sister died in this place?' Lily's voice had sharpened in anxiety. She cocked her head trying to read the writing on the page of the open ledger.

'Please don't upset yourself, Miss Larkin. I have searched entries for the date you gave but not come across a likely girl, living or deceased.' The matron closed the book. 'I'm simply bringing to your attention that infants who have suffered a poor start in life are more susceptible to nasty childhood diseases.'

'Oh ... of course ... I understand.' Lily relaxed slightly, removing her white-knuckled fingers from the edge of the desk. She couldn't deny that this particular infant had suffered bad luck from her first breath. She'd been premature and her mother had passed away giving birth to her, but Lily refused to believe her half-sister was doomed. She was determined to find out what had happened to the little girl, though she had nothing to go on other than a description of her as fair-haired and feeble. Be that as it may, having won the struggle to exist, Lily believed the baby would have battled on, and thrived. They were cut from the same tough cloth, Lily was certain, and the love she felt for the sibling she'd never met was overwhelming. Sometimes she would talk to the child in her head, beg her to hold on because her big sister was coming to take her home.

Lily and her twin brother had been inmates of the Whitechapel workhouse when their widowed mother gave birth. The newborn had been spirited away from the infirmary, to be dumped like rubbish so as to avert a scandal. Since leaving that dismal place, Lily had learned more about their mother's harrowing final hours in labour. Lily had begun her search months ago at a small local orphanage. No match for her sister had been found, leaving Lily feeling both disappointed and relieved.

On exiting that institution along an echoing corridor, she'd passed half-glazed double doors leading to a classroom. Within she'd glimpsed rows of blank-faced tots seated silently at desks. Only one boy had glanced over at her; a thwack of a cane on a blackboard had soon put a stop to his interest in the visitor. Lily prayed her sister hadn't spent her infancy in an atmosphere as miserable as that. Lily and her brother had at least been blessed with some happy memories of normal family life. They'd entered the workhouse with their mother when they were ten years old, and their father's death rendered them destitute. Lily had been optimistic that things would be pleasanter at the Foundling Hospital. On walking up the drive earlier, she had stopped to watch children playing chase on a field. Inside it was larger and airier than the grim orphanage, and the atmosphere smelled less sour.

This matron seemed a kindly soul; Lily hadn't been made to feel that her presence or her questions were a nuisance. She fidgeted on her chair, reluctant to get up and go. 'Would you have another look in the book, please ma'am?' The request was accompanied by an appealing smile. 'My sister might not be registered under the name of Larkin but Stone.' It was a long shot. The workhouse officer who had smuggled the baby away was unlikely to have allowed another woman's child to bear the name of her lover.

'My sister has a freckled birthmark on her chest and has fair hair and would be five years old now.' Lily had already supplied this information, but she repeated it with emphasis before adding something she'd so far kept back. 'A Miss Fox would have brought the baby here from the Whitechapel workhouse. She might have pretended to be the baby's mother so you'd take her.' From their conversation so far, Lily had picked up that strict rules applied to admissions. Mothers had to have been of good character before the father of the child abandoned them. Most importantly, a mother had to make a personal application, an impossibility in this case. The moment the matron comprehended that the child wouldn't have qualified for admission she had closed the ledger, obviously believing a further search would be a waste of time.

Lily itched to unclasp her hands and reach across the

desk to snatch the book. She wanted to read it herself to make sure there weren't any clues to her sister's whereabouts concealed within.

'This Miss Fox is surely the best person to approach to trace your sister's whereabouts,' Matron pointed out.

'That's not possible ... she's dead now, you see. An accident.' Lily always got goosebumps when that violent incident crossed her mind. 'Unfortunately Miss Fox didn't tell anybody where she'd taken the baby.'

'Oh ... I see ... ' the matron said in a considering way.

The older woman had cottoned on to there being nothing straightforward about this missing orphan's story. God only knew she was right to think there was more to it. Lily hoped she wouldn't ask why the baby hadn't been put in the Whitechapel workhouse's nursery with similar unfortunates. Jittery about having revealed too much, she shot to her feet. 'Thank you for your time then, ma'am. I'll try elsewhere.'

'Just before you go, Miss Larkin ... ' Matron also stood up. 'Please don't get your hopes up, but no harm in taking a look in another journal. You have jogged my memory of something that was mentioned by a colleague many months ago.' She opened a filing cabinet and selected a book, flicking back through the leaves. 'Somebody else did enquire about a female child with fair hair and a birthmark having been admitted.' She frowned at the entry. 'I didn't immediately think of it as my deputy conducted that interview. Oh, I am mistaken in any case. This enquiry was for a four-year-old girl, only recently made homeless.' She shook her head. 'We wouldn't have taken a child of four. Only infants below the age of their first birthday are considered. Not everybody is aware of that, or if they are, they believe we might make exceptions. But we cannot, I'm afraid. Those are the rules.' She began to close the book with an apologetic smile.

Lily's heart had started to race. Had her sister's father had a change of heart and decided to look for his child after all? He had been lied to, as Lily had, and been led to believe that Maude Larkin's baby had been stillborn. But unlike Lily, Ben Stone had decided to leave well alone where his illegitimate daughter was concerned. Lily didn't hate him for his view; in fact she herself had also wondered whether to accept that her sister might be settled with a new family ... if she'd survived the trauma of her first days.

'Was the visitor's name Mr Stone?' Her excitement caused her question to emerge in a squeak.

'Oh, it wasn't a gentleman.' The matron found her place in the book again and this time read more of what was logged. 'A woman came looking for the girl. A Mrs Priest, an acquaintance of the mother.' Matron reached the bottom of the page. Suddenly her expression tightened. Mrs Priest had originally turned the child over to an individual called Mrs Jolley on the instruction of her employer, the girl's mother. The child's father had perished in the war and his widow was no longer in a position to support her daughter or her housekeeper. The servant now regretted what she'd done and wanted to trace the child to care for her herself. Despite Mrs Priest's efforts to locate the woman, she'd been unable to. Mrs Jolley had vanished.

And well Mrs Priest might rue what she'd done! Mrs Jolley, or whatever other name she went by, was an unscrupulous character. Many innocents handed over to her had disappeared without trace. It wasn't the first time the baby pedlar's name had been brought up in Matron's office by mothers searching for children handed over to her. Jolley lured her customers in with lies about foster parents who would provide a fresh start in healthy countryside homes. Poor women, abandoned by feckless men and unable to provide for their children, would beg or borrow money to give to Mrs Jolley in return for her worthless promises. Matron feared that for some of those poor children, Jolley had been a go-between from mothers to graves, rather than to a better life.

In this case the girl's mother was reportedly alive, so that was a glimmer of light that the tot put in Jolley's clutches was not related to Miss Larkin.

'What is it?' Lily demanded. She'd witnessed the change in the matron's expression and it greatly disturbed her.

'This child isn't an orphan. Her mother is now an impoverished war widow and unable to care for her daughter. It isn't a match.' Matron returned the book to the cabinet. Without convincing proof of a connection, she believed it better to keep quiet than alarm her visitor with details of Jolley's involvement.

'Have you at least their names and an address? The mother might have adopted her daughter and it is a start . . .'

'There's no mention of an adoption, so it seems unlikely that's the case,' Matron interrupted, clearing her throat.

'Please give me the names,' Lily insisted. 'I need something to go on, 'cos I won't ever stop looking until I find out what happened to her.'

Matron relented a little bit. 'Mrs Priest is seeking Charlotte Finch. The family lived in Cheapside but have now all moved away. Mrs Priest hasn't given us her new address. My colleague no doubt made it clear to her that we've had no dealings with the child so wouldn't be getting in touch.'

'Thank you for telling me that and for seeing me today.' Lily suspected Matron might be keeping something confidential back ... but so was she. A secret surrounded this search for her sister that even her brother knew nothing about.

'You could always try the Barnardo's home,' Matron suggested. 'The girls' shelter is by all accounts a pleasant place. Perhaps your Miss Fox might have taken the child there. Here ... I have the details.' Matron picked up a card with the address pre-printed. 'We keep these to hand out to people like you, searching for family members.'

'Thank you ... ' Lily beamed at the woman and offered her hand to be shaken. She'd learned more today than she had in many months. Charlotte Finch was a four year old with fair hair and a birthmark ... her sister would have still been four earlier in the year. Lily felt a surge of joyous hope. If it *were* her sister, the brave little thing had outrun her bad luck. She had battled through her infancy and the perils it had held. Now she would be five. Starting school. A child, not a baby.

Having said her farewells to the matron, Lily walked briskly down the drive, unaware that the older woman was observing her departure from her office window. Lily looked at the address on the card and some of her optimism wilted. The Barnardo's home was a long way away. Harriet Fox would never have bothered taking the baby that far. She would have offloaded the newborn quickly, somewhere conveniently local. Lily refused to feel too dejected. Her sister might have been transferred from a

City shelter to the Barnardo's home, then adopted from there and brought back to London by her new parents. Lily knew she could tramp the streets around Cheapside, knocking on doors and making enquiries, but hitting on the right street, or on neighbours who might recall Mrs Finch who'd moved away, would be like finding a needle in a haystack. She realised her best chance was to concentrate on finding the housekeeper. Already Lily liked Mrs Priest. The woman had been a servant, yet had been fond enough of little Charlotte Finch to check on her welfare and her whereabouts. The housekeeper wouldn't have given up; she would have continued in her quest, just as Lily was carrying on with her search. At some point their paths might cross, and then Lily would discover whether they were both hunting for the same child.

Miss Larkin had stopped to watch the boys playing cricket on the green before passing out of the open gate. Even though the young woman was now gone from sight, Matron continued to gaze into the distance, lost in disturbing memories.

She had been a probationer nurse in 1896 when a carpet bag pulled from the River Thames was found to contain a baby's corpse. More babies had been found to have died similar disgusting deaths at the hands of an evil, avaricious woman. Amelia Dyer had long since gone to the gallows for her heinous crimes. But there had been other baby farmers hanged since, for taking cash for foster care before disposing of a child they'd had no intention of keeping. Matron sorrowfully shook her head. For as long as desperate women needed homes for children, villains would prey on them for easy money. Ten pounds to foster a child until it was of an age to care for itself. Most of them would have been lucky to attain another birthday once their mothers parted with them.

'Good luck in your search, Lily Larkin,' Matron murmured in a heartfelt way before turning away from the window.

Acknowledgements

Many thanks to Anna Boatman and the editorial team at Piatkus Books for their enthusiasm and support for the Workhouse to War series.

Thanks also to my agent, Juliet Burton.